✦ A STORY BY ✦

JONATHAN AUXIER

AMULET BOOKS

NEW YORK

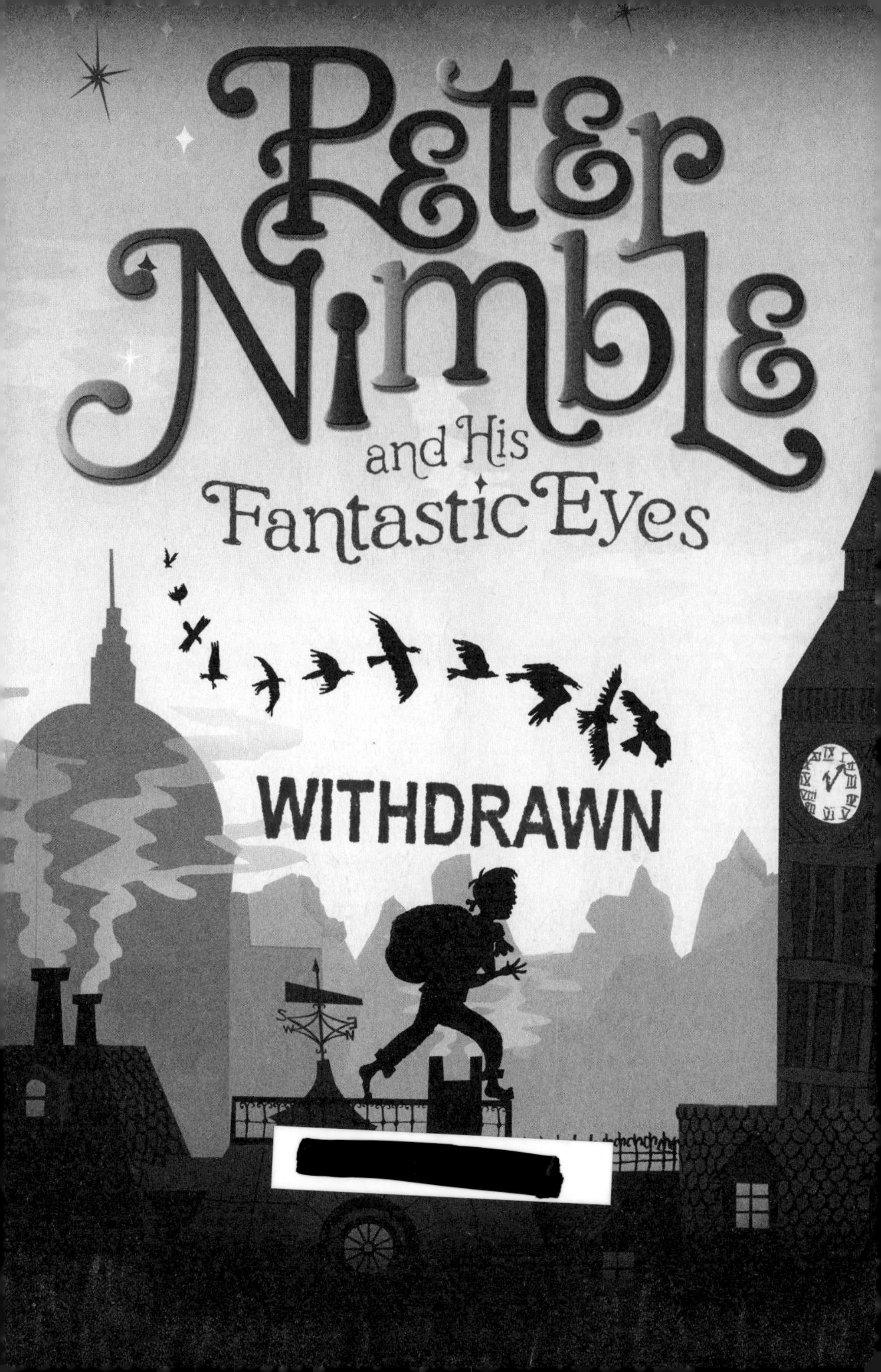
Peter Nimble
and His
Fantastic Eyes

For Mary

Fools as we were in motley,
all jangling and absurd,
When all church bells were silent
our cap and bells were heard.

The Library of Congress has catalogued the hardcover edition of this book as follows:

Auxier, Jonathan.
Peter Nimble and his fantastic eyes : a story / by Jonathan Auxier.
p. cm.
Summary: Raised to be a thief, blind orphan Peter Nimble, age ten, steals from a mysterious stranger three pairs of magical eyes that lead him to a hidden island where he must decide to become a hero or resume his life of crime.
ISBN 978-1-4197-0025-5 (alk. paper)
[1. Magic—Fiction. 2. Eyes—Fiction. 3. Robbers and outlaws—Fiction. 4. Blind—Fiction. 5. Orphans—Fiction.] I. Title.
PZ7.A9314Pet 2011
[Fic]—dc22
2010048692

Paperback ISBN: 978-1-4197-0421-5

Text and chapter illustrations copyright © 2011 Jonathan Auxier
Title page illustrations copyright © 2011 Gilbert Ford
Book design by Chad W. Beckerman

Printed and bound in U.S.A.
15 14 13 12 11 10 9

Amulet Books are available at special discounts when purchased in quantity for premiums and promotions as well as fundraising or educational use. Special editions can also be created to specification. For details, contact specialsales@abramsbooks.com or the address below.

ABRAMS The Art of Books
195 Broadway, New York, NY 10007
abramsbooks.com

Contents

PART TWO
ONYX

PART ONE

GOLD

CHAPTER ONE

PETER NIMBLE'S FIRST TEN YEARS

Now, for those of you who know anything about blind children, you are aware that they make the very best thieves. As you can well imagine, blind children have incredible senses of smell, and they can tell what lies behind a locked door—be it fine cloth, gold, or peanut brittle—at fifty paces. Moreover, their fingers are small enough to slip right through keyholes, and their ears keen enough to detect the faintest clicks and clacks of every moving part inside even the most complicated lock. Of course, the age of *great* thievery has long since passed; today there are few child-thieves left, blind or otherwise. At one time, however, the world was simply thick with them. This is the story of the greatest thief who ever lived. His name, as you've probably guessed, is Peter Nimble.

As with most infants, Peter came into this world with no name at all. One morning, a group of drunken but good-hearted sailors spotted him bobbing in a basket alongside their ship. Perched on the boy's head was a large raven, which had, presumably, pecked out his eyes. Disgusted, the sailors killed the bird and delivered the child to the authorities of a nearby port town.

Though the magistrates had no use for a blind infant, a local bylaw required them to at least give the boy a name. By silent show of hands, they christened him Peter Nimble, after a misremembered nursery rhyme. With this name and nothing else, he was sent off to make his way in the world.

For the first while, he was nursed on the milk of a wounded mother-cat, whom he met after crawling beneath the local alehouse. The cat permitted baby Peter to live with her in exchange for his picking the lice and ticks from her fur—until one tragic day some months later when the alehouse manager discovered them huddled beneath his porch. Furious at finding vermin in his establishment, the man shoved the whole family into a bag and tossed them into the bay.

Using his skillful fingers to untie the knot on that bag marked the beginning of Peter's career. Being furless and naturally buoyant, he managed to make it back to shore without too much trouble. (The cats, on the other hand, did not fare so well.)

✦ ✦ ✦

Until this point, you have been witness to Peter's rather typical infancy—probably not unlike your own. But it was only a matter of time before he distinguished himself from the teething masses. The first hints of this appeared in Peter's uncanny gift for survival. Since he had no parents to purchase clothes and food for him, he found it necessary to take matters into his own hands.

There is an old saying about how easy it is to "take candy from a baby." This saying is utterly false; anyone who has tried to take *anything* from a baby knows well what sort of crying, kicking, and general commotion will ensue. It is very easy, however, for babies to take things from *us*. Despite being blind, young Peter had no trouble sniffing out fruit stands and vegetable carts to steal from. He would toddle wherever his nose led him and innocently cut his teeth on whatever food he wanted. He soon began to pinch other necessities, such as clothes, bedding, and a bandage for his eyes. He tried stealing shoes, but found that he preferred going barefoot. By his third birthday, he was an expert in petty theft and a known menace to the vendors. More than once he had been caught in the act, only to slip away before the constable could be alerted.

One problem with a life of crime is that it lowers your chances of social advancement. Law-abiding citizens take one look at children like Peter and turn the other way—never to offer sweets, toys, or hope of adoption. In providing for himself, our boy had all but guaranteed that he would grow up parentless and alone.

All that changed, however, when he met an enterprising fellow named Mr. Seamus.

Mr. Seamus was a tall, wiry man with meaty hands and an

enormous head. Because of his clumsy touch, he had been unable to live out his dream of becoming a cat burglar. Instead, Mr. Seamus had taken a career as a beggarmonger. A beggarmonger, as you might imagine, is someone who deals in beggars. The man had built up a business of adopting orphans, maiming them good and proper, and then sending them out into the streets to beg for coins. Any child who dared come home empty-handed was throttled and sold to the workhouse. All told, Mr. Seamus had probably gone through about thirty orphans in his career.

Peter was five years old when the beggarmonger first spied him beside a fruit stand in the market. "Hullo, boy!" Mr. Seamus said upon his approach. "What's your name?"

"They call me Blind Pete, sir," the small boy said, still too young to know not to talk to strangers.

Mr. Seamus leaned closer for a better look at him. It was his experience that blind children made especially successful beggars. "And where are your parents?" he asked.

"I don't have parents," the boy answered. By now Peter's hunger was getting the best of him, and so he quickly reached a hand behind his back and stole an apple from the fruit cart.

Mr. Seamus glimpsed this action out of the corner of one eye, and it nearly took his breath away. The boy had stolen the apple not from the top of the stack, but from somewhere deep in the *middle*, leaving the outside completely untouched. For an ordinary person, such a feat would be impossible, but for this filthy child it was second nature. Mr. Seamus knew at once that he was standing before a very gifted thief.

The man leaned closer, eyeing the boy's delicate fingers. "Well, Pete," he said in his sweetest voice. "My name's Mr. Seamus, and I'm ruddy glad we met. You see, I'm a great, important businessman, but I've got no son to share my riches with." Mr. Seamus took the apple from Peter's small hands, biting into it as he spoke. "How would you like," he bit again, "to become my business partner? You could live with me in my mansion, eat my food, and play with my dog, Killer."

"What kind of dog is it?" Peter asked, hoping very much it was big enough for him to ride.

"It's a . . . *Siamese*," Mr. Seamus said, after thinking a moment.

"Are Siamese big?"

"The biggest. I suppose he could swallow you whole if he wanted." Mr. Seamus tossed the apple core into his mouth and swallowed it whole. "Now, what do you say, boy?"

✦　✦　✦

There was no mansion. There were no riches, servants, or feasts. Killer was real enough, but he was missing a leg and quite old—and like most old things, he hated children. Instead of giving Peter rides, he spent most of his time limping, growling, and lapping the drip off his disgusting snout.

Mr. Seamus gave up beggarmongering and never looked back. He sold off his other orphans and devoted himself entirely to Peter's education in thievery. For the first year, he locked all the boy's meals inside an old sea chest. If Peter wanted to eat, he had to pick the lock with his bare fingers. This not only taught him valuable burgling skills but also saved Mr. Seamus a great deal in expenses. The boy went hungry for over two weeks before getting a first meal in his new home. When he did finally manage to unlock the chest (by stumbling across the "McNeery Twist" maneuver), the scraps were long spoiled. But eventually he grew more adept at picking locks, until at last he had gone through every one in his master's collection.

Mr. Seamus also trained Peter in the fine art of sneakery—how to creep over floorboards, rooftops, and even gravel so as not to make a single sound. The boy proved a fast learner and soon mastered the gamut of thieving crafts, from window-cutting to advanced rope-work. By the age of ten, Peter Nimble had become the greatest thief the town had ever seen. But of course no one actually *saw* him: they only saw the open safes and empty jewelry boxes that he left behind.

Every night Mr. Seamus sent Peter into the town to steal. And every sunrise Peter returned to Mr. Seamus with a burgle-sack full of loot. "Worm!"—which is what the man had taken to calling him— "you done ruddy well. Now get out of my sight!" With that, he would lock the boy inside the cellar, leaving Killer to stand guard.

Peter didn't actually mind the cellar all that much. Being blind, he didn't care about the lack of light, and sitting down there was far better than looting honest people's houses. Whatever wrongs he may have committed (and stealing things *is* wrong), Peter was still a good child who wanted nothing to do with burgling. Every morning as he curled up to sleep on the damp cellar floor, he would pretend that he could sneak past Killer, break into Mr. Seamus's great treasure room, and return all of the stolen goods to their rightful owners. He would imagine thankful townsfolk rescuing him from cruel Mr. Seamus and inviting him to live forever in a big, warm house full of food and singing and other joyous children. In short, he would dream of being happy. But this was only a dream, and every sunset he would wake once again to the shouts of Mr. Seamus and be kicked back outside for another evening of pilfering the possessions of honest citizens.

And so it went for Peter Nimble. He was miserable, mistreated, and forced to commit misdemeanors—day after day, season after season, year after year—until one very special, very rainy afternoon, when he met a stranger who would change his life forever.

CHAPTER TWO

THE HABERDASHER'S MYSTERIOUS BOX

On top of his nightly thievery, Peter also had household chores. Every second-Tuesday, he was sent out by Mr. Seamus to fetch (steal) food from the market. This particular second-Tuesday was no exception. "Get up, worm!" Mr. Seamus hollered as he clumped down the cellar stairs shortly after dawn. "It's grocery day. I don't feed you just to loll around here all morning."

Peter had spent the night burgling and had just gotten to bed an hour before. "You don't feed me anyway," he muttered in what can only be called an act of sleepy stupidity.

The next moment he felt a big, meaty fist grab hold of his hair and yank him to his feet. "Don't forget who you're talkin' to, worm!" Mr. Seamus said, dragging Peter's scrawny frame upstairs and through the main house. "Just for that, it's a double-shift. You'll bring me food *and* money . . . and a chew toy for Killer!" The dog licked his chops appreciatively as they passed.

"Yes, sir! Forgive me," Peter said with genuine remorse. He knew better than to talk back, but words, as you know, sometimes have a way of slipping out.

"Save your 'sorries' for the hangman." Mr. Seamus shoved the boy into the street and threw his burgle-sack after him. "That had better be full when I see you again! Or else!" he said, slamming the door.

Peter picked himself up and slung his bag over one shoulder. Hearing fat raindrops percolating in the clouds high above, he sighed.

Rain presents a unique problem for those in Peter's line of work. You see, when it rains, rich people seldom come out for fear of melting. If they do venture out of doors, they are usually accompanied by umbrella-bearing servants who keep a close watch for pickpockets. There is nothing a town loves to do more than hang pickpockets, and any criminal hoping to steal a wallet under such circumstances is putting himself at great risk. It was for this reason that Peter had hardly managed to nick a single thing over the course of this unpleasant, rainy afternoon.

He was rounding a corner with his shirt full of broccoli and kippers, thinking about how much trouble he would be in if he didn't bring any money back for Mr. Seamus, when he happened upon a crowd of people gathered by the dock. This was a great stroke of luck; as a rule, pickpockets thrive on tightly packed crowds. Even better, all of the umbrella-bearing servants were just as distracted as their masters. The boy ditched his groceries and set to work at once. He carefully picked his way through the crush, lifting billfolds from eager onlookers and trying to figure out what was causing such a commotion.

"Do you tire of looking like a friar?" a voice boomed from somewhere beyond the crowd. "Is your scalp as bare as an Alp? Not anymore! This fine turban—made of bearskin from the dark South Seas—will restore your luscious locks overnight!" The voice belonged to a man standing somewhere to Peter's left. "Hats for every head! Whatever your need, look no further!" His voice was confident and smooth, his words like a spell holding the crowd captive.

It might be wise to pause a moment and explain the many details of this scene that were lost to Peter Nimble. He was unable to see the leaning tower of hats perched atop the man's head. He was also unable to study the speaker's sharp jaw, crooked red nose, and long, owlish eyebrows. The only thing Peter knew was that this man had provided a perfect opportunity for a young pickpocket to practice his art on a hapless crowd.

Peter continued "wallet shopping," slipping his fingers into pockets and purses with ease. He had to suppress a grin—the people were so focused on the Haberdasher's patter that none of them felt a thing. The man was presently sharing an account of where he found his wondrous wares. He claimed he had journeyed beyond the borders of the map to the great uncharted waters of the world. There he discovered hats made from tapestries, toadstools, and dragon scales, "All of which I offer today at a special discount!" he exclaimed.

Peter considered the man's words as he loaded his burgle-sack. The boy found himself half wishing such magical places really did exist—they would certainly be more appealing than his port town. But of course they weren't real, he reminded himself; it was all just fairy-tale nonsense.

"Nonsense, you say?" the Haberdasher's voice broke in. "Perhaps I can convince you otherwise?"

Peter stopped mid-nick. It almost sounded as though the man had just addressed him directly. "But of course, lad!" the voice said.

The boy slid his fingers out of the constable's back pocket as he felt the eyes of the crowd turn on him. "M-m-me, sir?" he said, pulling the flap over the mouth of his burgle-sack.

"Who else? I wonder if I might *steal* you away for a moment?"

Peter did not move.

The Haberdasher changed his tack, addressing the man beside Peter. "Oh, constable?" he said. "Would you clear a path so the lad can *pick* his way through?"

Peter's throat went dry. He listened as the burly lawman waddled past him, nudging people aside with his baton. "You heard the fellow," he said in a commanding voice. "Let the boy pass." Everyone waited for Peter to step forward.

"Don't be shy, lad!" the Haberdasher chuckled. "It would be *criminal* to leave us all *hanging.*" The man obviously knew what Peter had been up to and was threatening to expose him for his crimes. Peter had no choice: taking care to look harmless and clumsy, he groped his way to the front of the crowd.

The Haberdasher grabbed his hand, enthusiastically shaking it. "Nice to have you on board!" He turned back to the audience. "And now I have a special demonstration for you lucky folk!"

Peter tried to get a sense of his surroundings. To his right was the Haberdasher, who smelled of wet wool mixed with a tinge of regret. Immediately behind him was the man's carriage, pulled by a pair of . . . no, not horses. Peter had robbed a sea circus when he was seven, and since then had retained an excellent nose for exotic animals. *But what were these strange creatures?*

"Keep clear of the zebras, lad. They kick!" The crowd laughed at the good-hearted warning.

Peter, however, was far from laughing. It was almost as if this man could read his mind. *But that was impossible.*

"Hardly," the man whispered, leaning close. "It only takes a bit of practice."

Peter backed away from the stranger, bumping straight into his wooden carriage. As he steadied himself, his fingers landed on something cold, metal, and familiar.

A lock.

Peter's pulse quickened. If there was one thing he loved most about his job, it was picking locks. He considered every lock to be a personal challenge. By definition, locks are designed to tell you what you can't do. You *can't* have the food inside this trunk. You *can't* escape this cellar. You *can't* learn what's inside this carriage. Each lock jailed a treasure that demanded to be liberated, and Peter was always happy to oblige.

The boy ran his fingers over the dead bolt, which was slick with rain. It was tempered steel, the sort of material used for guarding only the most valuable secrets. He slid his hands farther along the door, feeling for the hinge, but instead he came across a thick hasp that connected to another lock. And another. And another. The entire carriage was covered with locks of every shape and size. He smiled to himself—this was suddenly getting much more interesting.

While Peter cased the carriage, the Haberdasher spoke to the crowd. "The time has finally come for me to reveal a hat more amazing than all my others combined! One made especially for you!" The people leaned forward in eager anticipation. "Now, we all know the chief problem of living in a port town—the smell! How can one hope to maintain dignity in a place that forever reeks of fish?" There was a general murmur of agreement from the people as they sniffed the air in disdain.

"Well, reek no more!" The Haberdasher produced a stack of flimsy leather skullcaps. "These caps, tanned and stretched in the purest air of the Cloudlands, are *guaranteed* to remove all unsavory scents from their wearers." The crowd broke out in astonishment.

"Impossible, you say? To prove my claim, I present to you an expert judge . . . one who lives by his nose alone."

Peter, who had been secretly studying the carriage locks with his fingers, lowered his hands as he once again felt the crowd's attention fall on him. The Haberdasher took the boy's shoulder. "Everybody knows that blind people have a keen olfactory sense, able to detect even the faintest of odors. That is precisely why I have called this young urchin to assist in my next demonstration." He gently guided Peter back into the crowd. "If you would, lad, I'll ask you to smell the constable here."

Peter stood motionless in front of the lawman, who shifted his weight awkwardly from foot to foot. "Go ahead, have a good sniff," the Haberdasher said to the boy. "What does he smell like?"

Peter could tell that the man was looking for an honest report, and the truth was none too pleasant. "He smells like fish, sir?"

The Haberdasher gasped, clearly pleased. "Fish, you say?! What else?"

Peter sniffed again. "And stale beer?"

"And?"

Peter could not resist. "And . . . belly wind!" The crowd burst into laughter at the red-faced constable.

"A toxic blend, indeed!" the Haberdasher said.

"Now, see here!" the lawman blustered. "Keep on like that, and I'll arrest you both!" Before he could object further, the Haberdasher offered the constable a leather cap.

"Would you be so kind as to place one of these miraculous hats on your head?"

The officer, still blushing, removed his helmet and set the cap on his bald crown. He offered the crowd an embarrassed smile.

The Haberdasher turned back to Peter. "And what about now, lad?"

Peter hesitated, his nose inches away from the constable's sweating belly. The man smelled exactly the same. But being a clever boy, Peter understood at once what the Haberdasher wanted him to say. He didn't trust the man, but something deep inside him— his burglar's instinct—told him to play along.

"And what does he smell like now?" the Haberdasher repeated, his voice slightly more urgent.

Peter sniffed loudly and gasped. "Where'd he go?!" He stumbled forward, groping the air in mock confusion. "The constable was here a moment ago . . . but now his smell has *completely vanished!*"

The onlookers cheered with delight. "There you have it!" the Haberdasher said, bowing. "What more proof do you need?" Hands from the crowd hurled coins at the man in order to get one of his marvelous caps.

As the people pushed close, shoving and shouting, Peter felt torn. He could easily sneak away right now with what he'd already stolen. It would be more than enough to appease Mr. Seamus. On the other hand, he was also keen to find out what secret treasure lay inside that carriage. While it was true that Peter did not exactly relish stealing from ordinary people, the prospect of stealing from the Haberdasher seemed entirely acceptable. After all, wouldn't he be helping a scoundrel get his just desserts? Peter decided it might be worth his while to linger a bit longer. "Need any help, sir?" he said to the man.

"How very thoughtful!" The Haberdasher thrust an empty purse into the boy's hands. The bag was not canvas but thick velvet; its drawstring was laced with fine thread and tiny jewels. "Help me collect money from these fine customers. And while you're at it," he leaned close, tapping the burgle-sack at Peter's side, "kindly return your pickings to the pockets they came from. A boy could get hanged for such things." He pushed Peter into the group. "I'll make sure it's worth your while!"

Peter wandered through the crowd, collecting coins from eager customers. Every time he passed someone whose wallet he'd stolen, the boy replaced it before the victim could notice anything was amiss. He continued in this manner until his burgle-sack was empty and the Haberdasher's purse was full. The smell was intoxicating, almost too much to bear, but he knew better than to touch even a single coin. If this strange Haberdasher could truly read thoughts, he'd catch the boy in a second. Peter would just have to be patient until an opportunity presented itself.

When the townspeople finally dispersed—all of them wearing cheap leather caps and sniffing themselves—the Haberdasher returned to Peter's side. "That was some fine acting earlier. We made out like bandits, you and I. What is your name?"

"Alistair," answered Peter, who had learned by now never to trust strangers.

"Is it?" The man took the purse from Peter's hands. "Well, *Alistair*, I couldn't help but notice your interest in my fine carriage. A pity you can't see it, hmm?"

"It seems a fine carriage indeed," Peter said, trying to sound as pathetic and blind as possible. "I can smell the fresh paint."

"Smell anything else?"

"No, sir."

The Haberdasher lifted one coattail and removed a large brass key ring from his belt. He began opening the dozen padlocks securing his carriage door. "One never can be too careful. The riches in this carriage could change a fellow's lot for good. Still, I've yet to meet a thief who could best these bolts." Peter smiled to himself as he listened to the *click, click* of latches springing loose. His favorite sound.

When the Haberdasher finished the last lock, he opened his carriage and leaned inside. The moment the door swung past Peter's nose, his pulse quickened. He had spent ten years learning the scents of silver, ivory, and gems—but none of those smelled half so valuable as whatever was inside that carriage. While the man stashed his takings, Peter put his senses to work, absorbing every detail he could about the carriage: how large the cabin, how firm the floor, how great the plunder.

Once finished, the Haberdasher closed the carriage door and refastened all of the locks. "Safe and sound," he said, dusting his hands. "And don't think I forgot about you! Here's something for your trouble."

He tossed out a small coin, which Peter caught midair. The man gave an impressed whistle. "Those are some reflexes you have there. With a touch like that, who needs eyes?"

Peter turned the coin over in his fingers. It was made of heavy metal and had a hole cut into its center. "I'd give my hands up in a heartbeat, if it meant I could see," he said.

"Yes, I'm sure you would," the Haberdasher murmured softly. For a moment, Peter heard something tighten in the man's throat before he coughed and clapped his palms together. "Listen, Alistair, I'm dying for a drink. Would you mind watching my carriage whilst I slake my thirst in the tavern? The contents are very special, and I wouldn't want the wrong person to get his hands on them."

Peter could not believe it was going to be this easy. "Well, I *suppose* I could . . ."

"Splendid! I knew I could trust you!" he called, already on his way.

When the Haberdasher reached the porch of the alehouse, he turned back, regarding the boy from a distance. "It was an honor to work with you, *Peter Nimble*. I pray we meet again soon!" And so saying, he tipped his cap(s) and disappeared through the door.

✦   ✦   ✦

It took the better part of an hour for Peter to pick the locks on the Haberdasher's carriage. When he did finally manage to break inside, he found the purse just as the Haberdasher had left it. It was spilling over with coins—enough money to satisfy Mr. Seamus for a month.

But then something else caught his attention. As he reached for the jewel-encrusted bag, his arm brushed against a plain, wooden box, no bigger than a loaf of bread. There was no filigree or ornament adorning the lid, only a small brass lock. Peter touched the keyhole, and a quiver shot through his whole body. He knew that this was the thing he had smelled before, something more rare than all the riches that surrounded it. Unlike the cheap hats, this box really did seem to have come from another world—someplace beyond the borders of the map.

Peter hesitated. He only had room in his burgle-sack for one thing, which meant he would have to choose. A purse full of riches or a box full of . . . mystery. Before he could be detected, Peter took the box and slipped back into the rain.

Ten minutes later, the boy had snuck past a sleeping Killer and was tiptoeing down the cellar stairs as fast as he could. It was almost sunset now, and he didn't have much time before Mr. Seamus would send him back out to work the houses. He was exhausted, but exhilarated, too. Peter knelt in a corner of the basement and removed the wooden box from his bag. He smiled, breathing in the rich, musty odor. It was a sweet, intoxicating smell, like nothing he had ever encountered before. With every step on his journey home, the scent had grown more overwhelming. Now he could hardly bear it.

Peter cast an ear to the stairs, making sure he was alone. If he was lucky, he might be able to pocket some of the contents before turning the rest over to Mr. Seamus. He flexed his index finger and slid the tip into the keyhole. *Click.* The lock opened. He raised the lid and felt inside.

The box contained six eggs.

Peter frowned, confused, and again ran his hands over the smooth shells. The treasure was nowhere to be found, only these ordinary hen's eggs. He scratched his neck. After opening the lid, the peculiar smell had only become stronger; the treasure had to be in there somewhere. He felt around the box, searching for a seam or signs of a false bottom.

Peter took one of the eggs between his fingers and brought it to his nose. It smelled valuable—even more valuable than gold. *But how could that be?* He rubbed the smooth shell against his cheek. "What are you hiding in there?" he whispered.

"Worm!" Mr. Seamus appeared at the door. He lumbered down the stairs with Killer at his side. "Them vegetables you swiped is soggy!" he said, spitting. He was clutching half a squash in his hand; the other half dangled from his disgusting mouth.

"It was raining!" Peter said as he closed the box and rose to his feet. "Everything gets soggy in the rain!"

"That's no excuse!" Mr. Seamus flung the squash at Peter's head.

The boy could easily have dodged the attack, but he had learned long ago that self-defense only made Mr. Seamus angrier. It struck his ear with a soppy splat.

"That's not why I came down here." Mr. Seamus clopped down the stairs, sucking his fingers clean. "I heard there was a good crowd out by port today—I want my pickings."

"There were too many servants. All I could get was this," the boy said, offering up the coin with the hole in the center.

You must remember that Peter was standing in the dankest corner of a very dark cellar, and it was for that reason that Mr. Seamus was unable to see the Haberdasher's box with its six special eggs. Killer, however—whose sense of smell was almost as good as Peter's—caught on at once. He leapt forward and snapped at the boy's feet.

"Sounds like Killer disagrees," Mr. Seamus said, stepping closer. "What's that you're hiding?"

"Nothing, it's—"

But it was too late; the dog had got hold of the wooden box and dragged it to his master's feet. Mr. Seamus squatted down to inspect the goods. "That's a good boy," he said, letting Killer lick the leftovers from his chin. "Holding out on me, eh, worm? Let's have a look." He opened the lid and greedily dug through the box, searching for whatever treasure was inside.

"Is that it?" he said in disgust. "Just a bunch of ruddy eggs?"

"Forgive me! I thought it was filled with valuables, but I didn't open it till I got home."

"Why on earth not, you stupid brat?" Mr. Seamus tossed one egg high into the air and caught it again. "At least they'll make me a better supper than those vegetables. Come on, Killer."

Peter listened as Mr. Seamus started back up the stairs with the box of eggs under one arm. "Wait!" he cried desperately. "They're ... rotten! All of them!" He didn't quite understand how or why, but he knew he could not lose that box.

The man stopped and sniffed the contents. "You sure? Smell fine to me."

"You know my nose. I can smell riches; I can smell lies; I can smell a person's age. Those eggs are rotten straight through." Peter made a gagging sound, pretending to sound ill. "Even from here, I can barely breathe!" His heart was pounding—*he could not lose that box*. "Please forgive me. I promise I'll bring something better next time."

"Right you will," Mr. Seamus said. "And as punishment, you'll have to smell 'em a bit longer!" He tossed the box to the cellar floor. "And I expect you to steal extra tonight to make up for wasting my time. Otherwise, it'll be a lot more than eggs that I break!"

"Yes, sir! Thank you for your kindness!"

Mr. Seamus grunted, slamming the dead bolts into place as he and Killer shuffled back into the kitchen. When Peter was certain he was alone again, he steadied his nerves and crawled to the box. He lifted up the lid, afraid of the yolky mess that might be waiting for him—but the six eggs were unharmed. He took one in his fingers and gently shook it next to his ear. The yolk swished around inside the shell. He wondered if something would be hatching from them— perhaps a rare bird? Or perhaps it was the richest yolk in the world, fit for a king's omelet?

Thinking about omelets made Peter hungry. Little boys, as you know, eat more than ordinary people—or at least they are *supposed* to. Peter, however, was kept on a strict diet of fish heads and onion peels by Mr. Seamus, who claimed that hunger built character. The boy shook the egg a little harder. *Fit for a king?* Licking his lips, he cracked the egg open and let the yolk slide down his throat.

Peter gagged on the firm, round object. Something was wrong. He coughed and spit it back into the broken eggshell. This was no ordinary egg yolk. Peter touched its surface, and as he did, a great warmth came over his whole person. He felt the overwhelming urge to learn if the same strange thing was inside all the eggs. Carefully taking each egg in his fingers, he cracked them into perfect halves. He poured each yolk into its bottom shell and set it back into the cushioned floor of the box. Peter held his head over them, waiting for a miracle.

Now at this point, it would be wonderful if Peter knew what he was looking at. While certain things in life may seem obvious to seeing people like you and me, this was not so for Peter. Books, for example, with all their adventure and wonder, were completely lost on him. Though he could tell you how many pages a volume had just by holding it, or how old it was just by smelling it, or who had read it before just by ruffling the pages, he had no way of telling what the title was (unless, of course, it was gilded on the spine). But these six yolks had neither spine, nor gilding, nor anything else that would help Peter identify them.

"What are you?" he asked, taking the open box in his hands. Had Peter been able to see, his heart would have stopped. A smile would have crept across his face, and his dry throat would have let loose its first real laugh in ten miserable years. Because Peter Nimble had stumbled across something too wonderful even to imagine— something that could only be described as *fantastic*.

⌾ CHAPTER THREE ⌾

PETER *versus the* MUMBLETY-PEG GANG

The rain had stopped by nightfall. Peter left the house for work just as the courthouse clock struck ten. He had wasted his precious napping hours poring over the Haberdasher's box, so he was exhausted before even setting foot outside. He winced at the thought of how difficult the night ahead of him would be; Mr. Seamus never made idle threats, and unless Peter wanted to get a beating, he needed to steal a great deal of loot before sunrise.

Peter figured the best place to start would be with the Haberdasher. He knew firsthand that the man had a purse overflowing with coins, and that velvet bag alone would be enough to satisfy Mr. Seamus. While the boy told himself that this was the reason he was searching for the Haberdasher, the real reason was something different altogether. The truth was, Peter had a burning desire to learn more about the strange little eggs in the strange little box. Every drop of his burgling sense told him that these six yolks were worth far more than his entire life-stealings put together.

Sneaking past Uncle Knick-Knack's Pawn Shop (where he often did business) and the shuttered stands along Market Row (where he also did "business"), Peter finally reached the place where the Haberdasher had been stationed. He sniffed the cold air for any signs of the man's trail. Nothing. He dropped to the ground and felt for wheel tracks in the puddles. Nothing. He swept the streets, haunted the inns, and scoured the docks, but he found not a single clue. It was as though the man had never been there. The only proof of his existence was the box tucked under Peter's arm and the great mystery that came with it.

✦   ✦   ✦

Peter was growing frustrated. He had spent hours trying to find the elusive Haberdasher and still had two nights' worth of burgling ahead of him. "If only I had someone to tell me what these eggs really are," he muttered as he slid out of the upstairs window with four candlesticks, two cuckoo clocks, and a cheap leather skullcap. His thoughts were interrupted by a sudden scream.

Screams, as you know, are dreadful, shrill noises that tiresome people make when they want attention. They are rarely effective, as most hearers simply plug their ears and go on about their business. But there is another kind of scream that cannot be ignored so easily: the cry of a creature facing death—a primal, desperate gasp that speaks not to the ears, but to the very quick of our beings. Peter had heard that sound only once before, when freeing himself from a bag of drowning kittens. He was now hearing that terrible scream again, and it was very close.

Peter stood stock-still on the roof's edge. One of the most important skills that any burglar must master is remaining still. Though less glamorous than safe-cracking and wall-scaling, it is just as useful. After Mr. Seamus's training, the boy had even learned how to stop his heart from beating so that guard dogs would ignore him in the darkness. (This trick had thus far failed to work on Killer.) Peter listened to the cold night air. The first scream had been so short that he had missed its exact location.

A few moments later, he heard the cry again. It was one of the animals by the town stables. Peter weighed the half-empty bag around his shoulder. He had a lot of burgling to do and couldn't afford another distraction. The screaming continued until he could bear it no longer. He stowed his loot and went to investigate.

Peter raced through the town until he came to a small alley that ran behind the stables. He could hear what sounded like a horse neighing. He heard other sounds, too—jeering voices and the occasional clatter of metal against cobblestone. The alley made a sharp turn, and Peter's foot caught against an old jug. He stumbled, almost dropping his precious box of eggs. Regaining his balance, he poked his head around the moonlit corner to listen.

"What a shot!" someone cheered. "Right on the stripe!"

"That's a fault! Blade's gotta turn *twice!*" another whined.

"Shut up an' throw already!"

Peter inched closer, trying to assess the situation. The animal smelled like a nag or mule—he couldn't be certain so close to the stables. Whatever the breed, it was putting up quite a struggle. Just then a deep voice spoke, silencing the others. "Step aside, you babies. Lemme show you how it's done." The words sent a chill down Peter's spine. He recognized that voice. It belonged to Pencil Cookson.

Pencil Cookson was the meanest, nastiest, most dangerous boy in the port. He was several years older than Peter and twice his size. Pencil was also an orphan, but for different reasons altogether. It was said that when he turned eight, his father—a drunkard facing debtor's prison—had sold his son as a cabin boy to a local ship's captain. Pencil was deathly afraid of the water, and he refused to go. When his parents tried forcing him, he overpowered them both, mother and father, and dispatched them with a pencil he had been using to complete a grammar lesson. (That was how he had gotten his name.) Shortly after orphaning himself, Pencil assembled a crew of the vilest, most heartless boys in town. They called themselves the Mumblety-Peg Gang.

For those of you who have never played it, mumblety-peg is a rousing game for rough boys consisting of tossing a knife and trying to make it stick into the dirt. It is a relatively harmless pastime—unless, of course, it is being played by Pencil Cookson and his Mumblety-Peg Gang. It was a known fact that these boys were so tough that instead of aiming at the ground, they aimed at each other's feet . . . or even worse, at the feet of whatever unlucky victim they managed to corner.

Peter sorted through the shouts, cries, and clanging from the alley. It sounded like there were five boys out tonight. Plus one victim. From the scuffling of their steps, Peter concluded that the gang must have pinned the animal to the ground and was trying to get the knife to land in its backside. Peter pressed himself against the wall, glad he was safely hidden.

Or at least he *thought* he was hidden; the very next moment, the game was interrupted by a shout. "Oi! Who goes?!" one of them hollered in Peter's direction. "Thought I seen somethin' move by the street there." The rest of the gang turned and stepped closer.

Peter remained completely still. He could tell by the coolness of his skin that he was standing in shadow, away from the moonlight. Just to be safe, he stopped his heart from beating.

"I don't see nothing," Pencil said after a moment. "Just some old barrels."

There came a *thud!* and some frantic neighing.

"Hey! The clopper's tryin' to get away!"

"We ain't done playin'!"

"Keep her down!"

Apparently, the animal had tried using the distraction to escape from its persecutors. Peter relaxed a bit as the gang's attention fell back to the game.

Now, the first thing that a boy—or anyone, for that matter—should do in a dire situation is ask himself the Rascal's Questions. Peter, being a master thief, knew the questions by heart.

Where was he?

Behind the town jail, just before midnight.

Were there friends nearby?

Peter had no friends. Besides, being a thief, he didn't want to be spotted out at night.

Were there weapons nearby?

Peter thought for a moment and smiled. Perhaps he had something even better.

He slipped out of the alley and ran to the local jail. One dead bolt later, he was through the door, surrounded by dozing prisoners. Peter tiptoed through an empty cell block and gently removed a long chain and several sets of shackles from the wall. For an ordinary person, moving chains quietly is an impossible task: no sooner do you lift one end than the other drops, or goes *chink, chink* against your arm. Not so for Peter Nimble. In no time he had returned to the alley and was silently fixing the shackles around each of the bullies' ankles.

Peter's expert fingers latched the clamps shut without a single member of the gang noticing. He threaded one end of the chain through the bullies' fetters and led the other around the corner, across Town Square, and to the roof of the courthouse.

Any respectable town has at least one tall building in it, and atop this building there usually sits a big, important clock. Peter's town was no exception. The courthouse belfry had recently been gutted to make way for an enormous mechanical clock—a bold first step into a more modern world. Every hour, a mechanical pelican sprang out like a cuckoo to squawk the time and put on a little show, flapping its wings and spinning in a circle. Peter could hear that the hands of the clock were approaching midnight. He hoped that the gears controlling them were strong enough for his purposes.

Taking the chain in his mouth, he unlocked a maintenance panel and slipped inside the tower. Every inch was filled with slowly turning clockwork. Peter found the mechanical pelican sitting dormant between two giant cogs, waiting for its next performance. He knelt down and looped the chain around the creature's brass feet. While securing the links, the master thief could feel faint vibrations of the Mumblety-Peg Gang stomping and cheering at the far end of the square. Peter's plan was set; all he had to do now was keep the gang from killing their victim before midnight.

Peter returned to the street and followed the chain back to the stables. At the mouth of the alley, he remembered the empty ale jug he had tripped on before—a perfect distraction. He picked up the jug and took aim at the meanest, nastiest, most dangerous voice of the bunch.

Crack! The jug smashed square against the back of Pencil's head, shattering into a hundred pieces. "*Arghhh!*" he shouted, massaging his bruised crown. "Who's there?!"

It was too late now for retreat. Peter stepped into the moonlight. "Behind you," he said, trying his best to sound brave. "And there's another one coming if you don't leave off." This was actually a lie; Peter hadn't been able to find a second ale jug anywhere.

"Well, looky-look," Pencil said, stepping closer. "Seems we got ourselves a do-gooder."

"I—I'm warning you," Peter's voice faltered. "You leave that horse alone."

"Horse?" one of the other boys said, snorting. "What are you, *blind?*" This last remark, even though it was true, was still a mean thing to say.

"Hey, I seen you before," another boy said. "You're that mincy little kid Seamus keeps 'round—the *worm!*"

"We'll see who's mincy," Peter said by way of comeback. "You've got ten seconds." The gang laughed, circling closer, flipping their blades in their hands. Peter remained where he stood, only moving to dodge the occasional swipe of a knife. "Five more seconds!" he said.

"Then I better move fast," Pencil said. Quick as death, he snatched Peter's throat and lifted him clear off the ground.

The boy gagged, struggling to pry the choking fingers from his neck. "Almost . . . time . . . ," he gasped.

"Right you are!" Pencil tightened his grip. "Almost time you join us for a game of mumbl—"

You may well have guessed that Pencil Cookson was about to say "mumblety-peg," and you would be right. But his words were cut off by the sound of the great clock striking midnight. The mechanical pelican sprang from its perch and began to spin and squawk, winding the chain around its body like thread on a spool. The bullies' shackles pulled tight. Pencil, in his shock, let go of Peter. Before any of them knew what was happening, the five boys of the Mumblety-Peg Gang were whipped off their feet, dragged through town, and lifted halfway up the clock tower, where they dangled by their ankles like a bunch of nasty, cursing grapes.

✦   ✦   ✦

While Pencil and his gang took in the view from the courthouse, Peter climbed to his feet and dusted himself off. He could hear uneven snorting at the end of the alley and knew that the animal had not fled. He could smell blood on the stones from where it had been cut. "Are you all right?" he said, moving nearer.

As he approached, a pungent musk filled his nose. It was a smell he had learned just that afternoon—the smell of zebra. "You belong to the Haberdasher," he said, reaching out a hand. Instead of recoiling, the beast inched closer and pressed its nose against his palm.

Peter knelt down and took the zebra's head in his thin arms. "What have they done to you?" he said, gingerly stroking its nape. The animal shivered under his gentle touch. Peter pressed a hand against its ribs, feeling the faint pulse. As he soothed the creature, its heartbeat slowly strengthened, finally returning to normal.

"I suppose your master left you behind," he said, helping the zebra to its feet. "If only *you* could tell me about those eggs." At the mention of eggs, the beast whinnied softly in his ear. If he didn't know better, Peter would have guessed that it had understood him. But that was impossible . . . animals couldn't understand speech any more than they could talk themselves.

As if in reply, the zebra limped to the end of the alley where the Haberdasher's box was lying. It took the box in its bruised jaw and brought it to Peter's feet.

The boy was uncertain what to do. "You want me to open it?" Peter asked. The zebra whinnied again, nudging his hand toward the box. Peter crouched down and slipped his finger into the battered lock. *Click!* The lid popped open.

"Now what?"

He heard the creature lower its head and sniff at the contents inside. It took one yolk, then another, in its teeth and dropped them carefully into Peter's open palm. Then the animal stepped behind him and tugged the bandage away from his eyes.

"I—I'm sorry," he said. "I still can't tell what you want."

He reached a hand out beside him, hoping the zebra might instruct him further, but the beast had inexplicably vanished. "Hello?" he said, turning around. He strained to hear hoofbeats or snorting, but there was nothing—only the two mysterious yolks in his palm. He rolled the round balls between his fingers; something about their size and texture was hauntingly familiar. He pressed his nose against their warm skins. "I know that smell from somewhere," he murmured to himself. "But where?"

It was in this moment that Peter had what doctors call a "flashback." This is a fancy medical term that means to remember things from one's past. Peter gasped as his entire being was overcome with smells and sounds from long ago. He remembered shouts and roars. He remembered being stuffed into a basket. He remembered owning his very own pair of yolks just like these, until they were viciously pecked from his sockets.

"It's a pair of *eyes*," he said. He sat back in a daze. Could it be true? It was all too perfect for a blind boy to end up stealing a box full of eyes. Three pairs, just waiting to be found. He studied each pair, now able to detect slight differences in their weights and sizes. The first pair was molded from the finest gold dust. The second had been carved from slick, black onyx. And the final pair was made of two uncut emeralds—the purest jewels he had ever touched.

Peter took up the golden eyes in his hand and felt his pulse quicken. This was the pair that the zebra had selected for him. The animal was telling Peter what to do.

The boy released a deep breath and steadied his hands. Ever so gently, he slipped the two eyes into his sockets.

He blinked.

And just like that, Peter Nimble vanished into thin air.

The next moment, Peter found himself underwater. This change of environment caught him so off guard that he wasn't even able to take a breath, instead catching a lungful of stinging brine. He flailed his legs, kicking in a direction he desperately hoped was up. When his head finally broke the surface, he heard two sounds: the first was the thunderous roar of falling water, the second was a great symphony of *tinking* glass. He spun around, blindly searching for anything that might help him keep afloat. One of his hands knocked against something small and hard. An ordinary glass bottle. He swept both arms wide, feeling bottles of various shapes and sizes floating all around him. Where was he? Currents churned around his thin legs, towing him back into their depths. He sputtered as he struggled to keep his head above water. "Help!" he cried out, coughing. "Someone help me!"

As you may have guessed, Peter could not swim very well. His few encounters with water had taught him to keep a healthy distance from the stuff. He tried to recall what led him to this dreadful predicament. That last thing he remembered was slipping a pair of golden eyes into his sockets. Then—*poof!*—suddenly he was in deep water, surrounded by hundreds of *tink-tinking* bottles.

And now he was about to die.

For a thief, death is something of an occupational hazard. Peter had more than once contemplated the possibility of his end, whether by gallows or guard dog. But the thought of drowning now filled him with sadness. He had discovered the box of eyes only to lose it a moment later—he didn't even have a chance to try the other two pairs.

His body was overcome with an icy chill. Peter sank deeper and deeper below the surface, his mind growing murky. The last bubbles of air slipped from his mouth and nose, and he realized he would never again feel the warm sun or smell the sweet breeze or hear the patter of rainfall. But then, a faint voice sounded in his ears.

"Taaaallyyyy-hooooo!!!"

It was coming from somewhere high above. The cry grew louder and louder until it plunged into the water beside him. The next thing Peter knew, the voice—now a terrified, bubbling scream—was beside him. The stranger kicked against his head, frantically trying to swim free.

Whoever this new person was, he had iron shoes, and the jolt to Peter's crown was enough to knock the fight back into him. Sensing someone so near struggling for life somehow gave Peter the overwhelming desire to live himself. He strove with every last whit of his strength to reach the air above. Grabbing hold of the stranger's fur coat, the boy managed to climb his way back to the surface of the water.

"Release me, you brute!" the stranger snarled, kicking Peter's ribs. "I didn't come this far only to drown at your vile hands!"

Now, for those of you who have ever tried drowning another person, you will know it is far more difficult than books and ballads let on. No sooner does your victim's head disappear underwater than he turns into a ferocious animal, scratching and biting to survive. This was the position Peter found himself in as he and the stranger both sputtered and spun across the *tink-tinking* surface of the water.

The boy could feel his strength flagging, and so he opted for diplomacy. "Wait," he said, wriggling free from a headlock. "Fighting like this will drown us both—we've got to work together!"

The thin arm around Peter's neck loosened its grip slightly. "And what, exactly, do you suggest?" the stranger said.

Peter kicked his legs, trying his best to keep both their heads above water. His companion was small, but unusually heavy. "First get rid of those shoes and that fur coat."

"Ho! Very funny!" the voice spat back. "Any other dazzling ideas?"

"Just stay calm, and let me think," Peter said, spitting out saltwater. He knew he had to act fast—he was still cold, his legs were getting tired, and he wouldn't be able to keep afloat for much longer. Plus he was finding it rather hard to concentrate with the incessant *tink-tinking* of bottles everywhere. And that's when the idea struck him. "The bottles!" he said. "Get as many as you can!"

Peter opened his burgle-sack, which was still slung around one shoulder, and shoved a bottle inside. He swept his arms across the surface of the water, grabbing hold of every bottle he could find and stuffing it into his sack. If he and the stranger gathered enough bottles together, they might be able to keep themselves afloat.

"By Jove, it's working!" the stranger exclaimed, finally apprehending the plan. "What a brilliant—*Ooh!* There's one to your right! Get it!" Peter couldn't help but notice that most of the work was being left to him, but before long, he had completely filled the sack with bottles of all shapes and sizes. Their task completed, the two of them clung desperately to the makeshift buoy. "Righto," the stranger said. "Now what?"

"Now we get out of here. Do you see any land nearby?"

"Of course I do . . . rather too much of it, I might add."

Peter sighed. "You're going to have to be a little clearer with me. I'm blind."

"Oh, forgive me!" the stranger stammered. "I hadn't realized . . . terribly sorry to hear it." The stranger painted a picture of their surroundings. "It seems we're in a basin of some sort at the bottom of a hollow. The walls are maybe thirty hands high. That deafening noise is the giant waterfalls pouring in from every direction."

Waterfalls. So that was the sound he'd been hearing. Peter could now discern the individual rivers thundering down into the pool. Each seemed to rumble and churn with its own specific song. "Do you see an easy way up?" he asked.

"None, I'm afraid. There are some exposed roots ahead of us, but I don't think I'll be able to—" Before the stranger could finish, Peter began kicking them toward the edge, arms wrapped tightly around his float. He swam about twenty yards before his hand struck a rocky wall, veined with roots. The boy took hold and hoisted himself out of the water.

"Wait!" The stranger clung tightly to Peter's pant leg. "Please don't leave me . . . I'm afraid I'm not much of a climber."

The boy sighed. Whoever this fellow was, he sure seemed helpless. "I need my hands to climb, so just hang on to my leg there," he said, hoisting his bag over one shoulder. "And try not to fidget."

✦   ✦   ✦

Peter managed to scale to the top of the basin without too much trouble. The lattice of gnarled roots gave him good purchase, and the stranger—once out of the water—proved far lighter than he expected. In no time they both found themselves standing before a lush meadow that smelled faintly of cinnamon.

"What is this place?" Peter marveled, breathing the sweet air. The stranger had let go of him and was now crouched low to the ground, shivering. Peter reached down, offering to help him to his feet. "Sorry I tried to drown you," he said.

"That's quite all right." The stranger backed away. "I appreciate the lift. That was some shrewd thinking with the bottles, there."

Peter shrugged, emptying the sack at his feet. "I'm just glad it worked." He was having a difficult time placing the stranger's voice. It carried the bravado of a soldier, but was pitched in the high tenor of a maiden. "My name's Peter. What's yours?"

"You may call me . . . ," the stranger enjoyed a dramatic pause, "Sir Tode."

Peter tried to make sense of the information. "You said 'Sir' . . . but that would mean you're a *knight?*"

"Of course I'm a knight," Sir Tode shot back. "We're not all steeds and flashing armor, you know . . . not anymore, at least."

It is a fact that knights are notorious quarrelers, angered by even the slightest criticism. Peter knew this, and thought it best to keep clear of his wrath. "Oh, I meant no insult, sir!" he apologized. "It's just, I've never met a real knight before." The only knights Peter knew of were wealthy, fat men who ran trade routes and sat in governments. But Sir Tode sounded more heroic, like something from a fairy tale or nursery rhyme. Peter reached out his hand. "May I feel your face? Being blind, it's the only way I can—"

"I'd rather you didn't come any closer!" the knight growled. "I admire your inquisitive spirit, but I'm in no mood for petting."

Petting? This stranger was definitely hiding something. And come to think of it, why would a knight need rescue from drowning? "Pardon me, Sir Tode . . . but aren't knights trained to swim across moats and such things?"

"Indeed we are. However, I'm afraid I, er, can't paddle very well at the moment. You see, I'm also sort of a . . . *kitten*."

"You're a talking cat?!" the boy exclaimed. Though he lived in a world with many strange things, talking animals were not among them. Peter, like all children, had always loved stories about cuddly, talking creatures. He also loved stories about knights. The idea that he was speaking to a cuddly, talking, *knighted* creature was almost too much to bear.

"I am a human knight," Sir Tode corrected, "who has been trapped inside the body of a cat . . . and a horse."

As uncanny as it may sound, this description was completely accurate. Once upon a time, Sir Tode had been a normal knight, frittering his life away with duels and damsels. One unfortunate evening, however, he and his noble steed made the mistake of quarreling with a stray kitten outside the window of a sleeping hag. Hags tend to be rude on the best of days, and their disposition is only worsened by lack of sleep. Without a moment's consideration, the cranky old witch waved a dishrag out her window and said a magic word, turning Sir Tode, his horse, and the kitten into a single, ridiculous creature.

While there was indeed something *kittenish* about him in size, Sir Tode's delicate frame was encumbered by twitchy horse ears, a wispy tail, and a set of clumsy hooves. His face, which was also catlike, had been blessed with two scruffy eyebrows and a bushy gentleman's mustache—a painful reminder of his lost distinction.

Peter struggled to comprehend what he'd just been told. "I guess that explains why you're so small. And why you complained when I said to take off your coat and shoes."

Sir Tode gave an irritated growl; Peter wasn't the first person to find amusement in the diminutive knight's affliction. "I'll have you know, it's only temporary. As soon as I track down the hag that hexed me, all shall be righted."

"How long have you been searching for her?"

The knight gave a bitter sigh. "A lifetime," he said. If Peter didn't know better, he would have thought he heard a slight tremor in Sir Tode's voice. But that was ridiculous—everyone knows knights are forbidden from crying.

Sir Tode had, in fact, been searching for *several* lifetimes. An unfortunate feature of his curse was that he could not age until the hex was lifted. With every year that he searched, the world grew up around him. Hags eventually became extinct, and Sir Tode was left to wander, alone and without hope. That is, until very recently, when hope came to him in the form of a chatty taverner who claimed to know of a cure. "Aye, cat!" the red-nosed, owly browed man had whispered. "Get ye to the isle that sits atop the world! It's there ye'll find just what you need . . . and what needs you!"

Ever since, Sir Tode had been sailing day and night in the hope of discovering this miraculous island. After a month at sea, his vessel reached the dread Ice Barrens, where it was seized by the most horrible storm he'd ever seen. He was tossed overboard and left clinging to a tiny plank of wood for his very life. The raging currents carried him farther and farther until finally they sent him right over the edge of a waterfall and onto Peter's head.

Remembering all this put Sir Tode back in mind of his mission. He had been warned by the Taverner not to tarry, dawdle, or lollygag—and talking to inquisitive blind boys skirted dangerously close to all three. "If you'll excuse me, I have much ground to cover before daybreak."

"Wait!" Peter called after him. "I don't even know where we are."

"Nor I," Sir Tode said over his shoulder. "Thanks again for the help back there. Good luck with . . . being blind."

Peter was not so easily discouraged. He ran to catch up to the small knight. "Maybe we could walk together? It might be safer?"

Sir Tode gave an exaggerated sigh. "I don't mean to sound ungrateful, but I was given strict instructions to travel alone. And that is exactly what I intend to do."

"But where are you traveling?" Peter asked.

"I'm not entirely sure. That Taverner told me to follow the Lode Star." He squinted up at the constellations overhead. "But frankly, I don't recognize this sky at all."

While Sir Tode busied himself trying to get his bearings, Peter got an idea. "Sir Tode," he said in his most ingratiating voice, "if you are truly a knight, then you must know all about the Knight's Accord?"

There was a pause. "Of—of—of course I know about it!" Sir Tode blurted. "Why . . . I helped *write* the Knight's Accordion!"

Peter smiled to himself. There was, of course, no such thing as a Knight's Accord, because knights, being proud, rarely agreed on anything. If this Sir Tode *was* a knight, he certainly didn't know the rules very well. Peter continued. "Then of course you're aware that by the rules of the accord, if someone—a blind boy, for example— saves your life, you are required to grant him a single request?"

Sir Tode's eyes narrowed. "You're not going to make me be your pet, are you?"

"Of course not! Just, you know . . . a friend?"

At these words, the old knight's mustache twitched ever so slightly. "Your *friend?*" The truth was, it had been many years since Sir Tode had known anyone who might consider him a friend. It was also true, now that he thought of it, that it was his sworn duty to protect the meek—and blind children were nothing if not meek. "Very well, little blind boy—"

"Peter," he corrected. "Peter Nimble."

"Very well, *Peter Nimble*. You saved my life earlier, and for that I am bound to grant you this single boon. I shall be your friend for the rest of the night, during which time you shall be permitted to travel alongside me until we reach either lodging or certain death.

As my ward, you fall under my protection. Should we encounter any brigands or marauders or—"

His words were cut off by voices from behind the hill. "Hide!" Sir Tode said with a start. He bit down on Peter's pant leg and dragged him to the ground.

The two of them lay flat in the dark grass, listening as the shouts came closer and closer.

"Make haste, Mr. Pound!" one of the voices called. "We mustn't keep them waiting!"

Peter could tell there were two people—both sounded like men. One of them was young and strong; the other seemed much, much older.

"Is anyone there?!" the younger voice called out. "Hul-looooooo?!"

Peter hesitated. "Wait a minute, I think I recognize that voice . . ."

"*Shhh!*" Sir Tode hissed. "Do you want us to get marauded?!"

"They're by the lake, Professor!" the voice spoke again. "I heard the lad just now!"

At these words, Sir Tode looked up. "Goodness, you're right. He *does* sound familiar. If I didn't know better, I'd say it was . . ."

Sir Tode saw a man appear over the meadow, holding a firefly-lantern. The light shone soft against his countenance, revealing a crooked red nose and pair of owlish eyebrows. "Ah! There you are!" the man said with a hearty laugh.

"The Haberdasher!" Peter gasped.

"The Taverner!" Sir Tode gogged.

Indeed they were both right, for Peter's Haberdasher and Sir Tode's Taverner were one and the same. The man's marvelous hats were nowhere to be seen, and his flashy coat and tails had been replaced with a habit and cowl. "Well done, *Alistair,*" he said, offering a hand to the boy. "You certainly didn't waste any time in getting here."

Peter scrambled away from him. "Who are you really? And where have you brought us?" His fists were balled, ready to fight.

The man remained still, unmoved by the threat. "My name is Mr. Pound. As for bringing you here, I can hardly take credit for that. It was all the professor's doing!"

"The what?" Peter said.

A second man hobbled through the meadow to join them. "Don't listen to a word he says, Peter." His voice had a cobwebby quality, and he smelled of stale gingerbread. "Mr. Pound is too modest for his own good. It wasn't *all* my doing . . . only mostly."

"Who are you?" Peter demanded. "And how do you know my name?"

The old man chuckled. "I am Professor Cake. This is my island. And I know quite a bit more than just your name, Peter Nimble."

CHAPTER FIVE
THE TROUBLESOME LAKE
of PROFESSOR CAKE

Peter woke to the whistling of a kettle. He was lying in a grassy hammock that was rocking gently in the breeze. He was dry and clean. Someone had removed the golden eyes from his sockets and put a fresh bandage around his head. Likewise, his tattered clothes had been replaced with new ones—cut just like his old rags, but made from sturdy cloth with fine stitching. Peter swung his leg off the hammock and carefully reached for the floor. He got up and felt his way around the room, taking in the surroundings. He was standing on an open deck that seemed to be supported by two giant tree branches. The kettle that had woken him was boiling on a cast-iron stove, which groaned gently in the corner. Peter couldn't tell how long he'd slept; the air smelled like night, yet his skin felt a great radiance prickling against it.

"That's the moon," Professor Cake explained, shuffling down a wooden staircase. "She hangs a bit lower in these parts of the world."

Peter turned his face to the heavens. He had always been able to feel moonlight, but never this strongly. He could almost taste it shining down through the canopy of leaves. The old man hushed the kettle and set to making tea. "You certainly were tired. Slept clear through the day."

Peter felt the stiffness in his joints that comes from a long, restorative slumber—a rare sensation for him. "I didn't mean to be a bother," he said.

The old man clucked, waving off the apology. "I can't say I blame you, child. With the skies so close, the sun can become quite overwhelming. I much prefer nights myself—the world takes on greater dimensions when obscured by shadow." Peter had never seen a shadow, but thought he understood the professor's meaning; he had more than once reflected on the secret pleasure of being awake while the town lay sleeping.

The professor led Peter to a dusty wingback chair and handed him a mug of mulled tea. The boy sat and took in what details he could about his host. Professor Cake was a hunched old man with a voice as knotted as his knuckles. His shuffling steps were punctuated by the *tap* of his cane, which was made from ostrich spine. His musty suit was muffled by several layers of long coats, and the boy could hear a small pocket watch ticking somewhere inside the folds of his vest. The man's scent reminded Peter of the eyes, and he wondered what had become of them.

"They're on the floor, beside your feet," the professor said, settling into a chair. "I had Mr. Pound fish the box out from the lake this morning. The hinges squeak a bit now, but nothing to bleat about."

Peter reached down to find the box waiting for him. He marveled at how this strange man seemed able to hear his very thoughts, just like the Haberdasher.

"I should hope so," the professor said with a chuckle. "I am, after all, the one who taught him how. Mr. Pound is my apprentice. It was his job to deliver the eyes to you. My apologies for the whole traveling-salesman charade, but I had to make certain you were the boy I had in mind."

"Like some kind of test?" Peter said.

"The word 'test' makes me think of school." The professor shuddered slightly. "But suffice to say, you passed with flying colors. I should note that we put some very thorny locks on that carriage, ones that have baffled scholars for centuries. I am pleased to see they were no match for your talents."

Peter was confused. "You *wanted* me to steal the eyes?"

"Of course, my child! I made them just for you . . . and let me say it was no small effort."

Just for him. Peter took the box into his lap and opened it. He ran his fingers over the contents.

"Three sets of eyes: gold, onyx, and emerald." There was a hint of pride in the old man's voice. "Hope you don't mind, I took the liberty of removing the gold pair from your sockets while you were asleep—couldn't run the risk of you disappearing on us, could we?"

Peter still didn't understand. "Professor, I don't think the eyes work. When I put the gold ones in, I couldn't see a thing." He touched the bandage around his head, imagining what it would be like to never need it again.

"They worked fine, thank you very much. I daresay they're the reason you're sitting here right now." He read confusion on the boy's face. "Peter, these are no ordinary eyes. These are *Fantastic* Eyes."

The words sent a tremor along Peter's spine. "What does that mean?" he said.

"It means they do fantastic things, of course! Those gold ones, for example, instantly transported you to the last place they beheld: my island. That was my rather clever way of getting you here."

"What if I put them back in again?"

The professor considered this, stroking his beard. "Well, the last place you had them out was in this very room, so I suppose they'd take you here. I should warn you, though. This particular pair can get you in a lot of trouble if you're not careful—so don't go putting them in unless you really mean it."

Peter was having trouble keeping up. Every answer the old man gave only made him want to ask another question. "So, you're telling me it was the *eyes* that made me appear in the water?"

"The Troublesome Lake," the professor corrected. "I couldn't think of a softer place for you to land. I assumed you could swim, seeing as how you grew up in a port town. Evidently I was mistaken. Sorry about that—I hadn't expected the Troublesome Lake to be quite so . . . troublesome." Professor Cake, like most brilliant men, couldn't resist a good play on words from time to time.

Peter's next question—one of dozens—was interrupted by a shout from outside. "Gentlemen, your supper is getting cold!" It was Mr. Pound, leaning from a rope-bridge, wearing a smoldered apron. "I should add that if you don't join us immediately, Sir Tode has threatened to eat your portions!"

"I said no such thing," the knight protested, licking what smelled like pancake batter from his mustache.

Peter jumped to his feet. "Sir Tode!" All this talk about Fantastic Eyes had made him completely forget about his fellow traveler. "I'm surprised you didn't get *marauded* without me," he said, smiling.

"Very funny! If I recall, *you* were the one afraid of being left alone out there. It would have been cruel of me to abandon a helpless blind boy."

"The same helpless blind boy who saved you from drowning?"

Sir Tode gave a low growl. "Perhaps I should have stuffed *you* into that sack?"

"You'd have to catch me first!" Peter was not expecting his challenge to be taken up literally, but no sooner had he spoken than the knight pounced from the rope-bridge and knocked him to the floor. Mulled tea splashed all over the tree house, and within seconds the two of them were wrestling across the deck, trading insults, jabs, and gibes.

Mr. Pound joined Professor Cake, who was watching the fight with keen interest. "You probably hoped they might be getting on a bit better, eh, sir?" he said.

The old man chuckled. "Heavens no, Mr. Pound. This is far preferable. I don't think I could have planned it better myself."

Being wise, Professor Cake knew that any relationship not beginning with a punch or two would most assuredly fade over time: it is a well-known fact that brawling begets friendship. Already Peter and Sir Tode were planting seeds of mutual respect that might one day blossom into something far greater—a friendship to rival the stuff of legends.

✦   ✦   ✦

The evenings on that island were happy ones for Peter, perhaps the first in his life. He was clothed, fed, and cared for in a way he had never before known. He kept the box of Fantastic Eyes with him at all times. The boy was tempted more than once to try them on, but he resisted for fear that they might spirit him away from this blissful place.

Most nights, Mr. Pound tended to dinner and the garden while the professor whittled the hours away in his workshop, a rickety turret stacked to the eaves with books and empty glass bottles. Meanwhile, Peter and Sir Tode were given free rein to explore every last inch of the grounds. The pair spent countless hours catching insects and digging in the mushroom orchard—all the while becoming more and more dependent on each other. Each time Peter encountered something that smelled, sounded, or tasted strange, he would ask Sir Tode to describe it.

"It appears to be a large painting draped over some poles like a tent," the knight remarked upon finding one such artifact just off the path.

"A painting of what?" Peter asked.

"Stars and planets, mostly. With little lines and numerals going back and forth across the whole thing. Hello, I think there's something *moving* underneath . . ." The knight pushed his snout between the cobalt folds.

"Ah! I see you've found my Gazing Mat!" Professor Cake looked up from the nearby stable, where he was feeding tomato soup to his zebras. "A wonderful trinket. It helps me keep an eye on things. Be careful poking around there—you might never get back out."

Sir Tode scoffed. "Nonsense. It's just a harmless—*Ahhh!*" He suddenly leapt away from the mat, tripping backward and tumbling into a shallow stream. "I—I thought I saw . . . something," he muttered, shaking himself dry.

The professor approached and offered him a towel. "I don't doubt it. There are all sorts of 'somethings' in that canvas. And if I look close enough," he said, turning to Peter, "I can even see the port town where you grew up. The shops you burgled. The basement you slept in."

It took a moment for Peter to understand the meaning of the man's words. "You've been watching me?" he said.

"You and many others," the professor said, moving past the stables. "Walk with me, child. It is time we speak of why I brought you here."

Professor Cake led Peter down a path that followed the shoreline. Gentle waves lapped against the boy's bare feet, mixing salt into the cinnamon air. "These waters, they don't smell like the ocean back home," he said.

The old man smiled to himself, clearly impressed by the observation. "That's because it *isn't* the ocean back home." He steered Peter in the direction of a small inlet. "Your port waters are up ahead there, just a few yards past the pear brambles." Peter concentrated, and he could indeed detect a change in the breeze—something about it really did smell familiar. "The fact is, at this isle meet all the waters of the world, many of them from seas far beyond the reach of your ships," the professor explained.

Peter wondered if these distant seas led to the magical lands that the Haberdasher had described in his patter.

"The world is filled with uncharted waters," the professor said, perceiving the question. "And the farther out you sail, the deeper and more enchanted they become."

"Enchanted waters? Is that where Sir Tode comes from?" Peter asked. He could hear the knight off in the meadow, battling a swarm of fireflies. ("Give up now, you infernal sprites!")

Professor Cake listened with him and chuckled. "I understand why you'd think that. But no, Sir Tode is from your world . . . only not as it stands today. He was born back when your shores were riddled with possibilities—dragons, hags, whatnot. That was before reason took hold." His voice became sadder. "Now Sir Tode is all that remains. A relic of a bygone age."

The old man turned from the shore and led Peter inland. They walked along a stream that—like countless others—flowed toward the center of the island. "No matter its birthplace, every sea in the world eventually dies here: at the Troublesome Lake."

The two of them were now standing at the grassy edge of the basin. Over the rush of water Peter could hear the gentle *tink-tinking* of innumerable bottles. The sound filled the air with a soft, almost mournful song. "Professor?" he said after a moment. "Why do you call it the Troublesome Lake?"

"Because every one of those bottles is filled with troubles. When people need rescue—be it from starvation or madness or heartbreak—they often seal a note in a bottle and cast it out to sea in the hope that someone will find it and help them."

"Does it work?"

"Rarely, I'm afraid. Usually the bottles float for years, arriving here long after they can do any good." The professor took a long butterfly net propped against a nearby tree and reached down into the basin. He fished out a bottle from the water and read the message inside:

Shipwrecked. Dying of thirst.
Please send water at once.

The old man sighed, removing his spectacles. "Poor fellow. He's probably a pile of dust by now." He observed a moment of silence for the thirsty man.

"That must be hard," Peter said. "Hearing all those troubles and not being able to help."

"It is. But every person, both great and small, is asked to do difficult things—and this is the difficult thing that I must do." He dabbed his wizened eyes with a handkerchief and replaced his spectacles. "Yet occasionally I come across a message where there's still time. When that happens, I do my best to help. That's why I called you here, Peter Nimble."

The boy feared that Professor Cake had him confused with someone else. "But I didn't write a note," he said. "I don't even know *how* to write."

The old man reached into his vest pocket and removed a small green bottle. Inside was a tiny scrap of paper. "A while back, I came across a very special message, written by someone in great need."

"Can you help whoever wrote it?" Peter said.

The professor leaned down and pressed the bottle into Peter's hand. "I just did."

Mr. Pound hummed over the stove, mulling a fresh pot of sweet tea. Peter sat at the table behind him, deep in thought. He had encountered so much in recent days—magical eyes, enchanted knights, and now this. The boy didn't yet trust Professor Cake, but this was one of the only times in his life that an adult had treated him with true kindness, and that alone was enough to make him listen. Still, he was afraid of what might be waiting inside the tiny bottle.

"Oh, uncork the thing, already!" Sir Tode, who sat beside him, took the bottle in his teeth. With some struggling, he removed the stopper and shook the message free. "It appears to be a riddle of some sort," he said, smoothing out the paper with two hooves.

"Can you read it to me?" Peter asked.

Sir Tode squinted at the faded scrawl:

Kings aplenty, princes few,
The ravens scattered and seas withdrew.
Only a stranger may bring relief,
But darkness will reign, unless he's—

"Oh, blast," he said. "The last bit's smudged. I can't make it out."

Mr. Pound appeared behind them to refill their mugs. "The notes we get usually don't rhyme so well. This one must have been written by a poet, or a troubadour. When the professor found it, he thought of you immediately, Peter."

"Whatever it is, it sounds terribly exciting," the knight said.

"And terribly confusing," the boy added.

"Right on both counts!" Professor Cake creaked down the workshop stairs. He pulled an armchair next to Peter and joined them at the table. "The second line of that note leads me to believe that this bottle came from the Vanished Kingdom."

"The what?" Peter said.

Professor Cake leaned back in his chair and lit the bowl of his briar pipe. "Many years ago, there was a land surrounded by ancient seas. The soil was dry and unforgiving, but also full of magic. It is said that the people there lived in harmony with the beasts, who could think and speak like men. Together they constructed a spectacular palace—a walled paradise of unparalleled beauty. It took them years to build. And then, on the eve of its completion, the whole place . . . vanished. Disappeared completely." He leaned back, tamping the ash in his pipe.

Peter and Sir Tode waited for more information, but none came. "That's it?" the knight said, somewhat frustrated. "That's the whole story?"

"It's as much as I know," Professor Cake answered. "Of course, disappearing lands aren't all *that* uncommon—my own island, for example, is fairly well hidden—but the real question is *why* did the kingdom vanish, and what's happened to it since?"

Peter was confused at hearing two adults discuss impossible things as though they were everyday occurrences. "Don't you think there's a simpler explanation?" he said, thinking of a rule he had once overheard about how the easiest explanation was usually the right one. "Maybe the sailors just got turned around? Or someone marked the kingdom down wrong on the map?"

"Do not confuse simple with simpleminded," the professor said. "A boy your age should know better than to consider anything impossible." He rose from his seat and went to the cupboard. Inside he found a long roll of paper, which he brought back to the table and unrolled for Peter. "I had Mr. Pound purchase this map while visiting your hometown," he said, placing a mug on each corner to keep it from curling up. "It contains every speck of land your mapmakers have ever seen."

Peter lowered his head over the parchment, taking in its musty odor. "I know this map," he said with a trace of a grin. "I stole it from the town museum last month, and Mr. Seamus sold it to Uncle Knick-Knack's Pawn Shop." He placed his fingers on the map, feeling where the ink had formed tiny ridges on its surface. Peter could trace the various seas and rivers that divided the land. Having the whole world reduced to a few squiggly lines made him sad, somehow. He stopped at a speck of ink near the middle of the page. "That's my port, isn't it?" he said softly.

"It is," the professor answered. "Only made smaller in every way. Maps have a way of doing that." He took the boy's hands in his own and moved them to the far edge of the paper. "What do you feel now?"

Peter ran his fingers over the smooth surface. "I don't feel anything," he said. "It's blank."

"Not blank. *Undiscovered.* Out there lie wonders beyond anything your merchants and sailors have ever dreamed of. Impossible worlds waiting to be explored."

These words filled Peter with a sharp longing, like the feeling that came over him every time he found a lock. The map was telling him where he *couldn't* go—and Peter wanted to prove it wrong. "So you think the message came from somewhere out there?" he said. "Is that where the Vanished Kingdom is?"

"There's only one way to know for sure," Professor Cake said.

Peter took the note from inside, turning it over in his fingers. "What about the rest of the riddle? All that stuff about kings, and darkness, and . . . *ravens*?"

The old man lowered his pipe, releasing its smoke in a perfect globe. "Those things are for you to discover. All I know is that the author of this message needs someone to seek them out and save them. I think that person is you."

"A real, live quest," Sir Tode said, his voice full of yearning. "Just like the old days."

Much as Peter wanted to share the knight's enthusiasm, he couldn't. "Why would they need me?" he said to the professor. "Shouldn't you go help them? Or Mr. Pound?"

"Mr. Pound will be detained on other business. As for myself, I'm not much for travel. I'm afraid it has to be you, Peter."

"But I'm just a kid," he insisted. "I'm small. And I'm *blind*—"

Professor Cake cut him off. "Not anymore you aren't." He reached over and scratched Sir Tode behind his horsy ears. "Sir Tode will be your eyes. That is, of course, if he's willing to join you on your quest?"

The knight nearly fell from his stool. "Me?" he said, hardly daring to believe it. "Well . . . if you *need* someone, I suppose I might be persuaded."

"Then we're settled," the professor said.

Peter stood up from the table. "Nothing's settled!" he said with surprising force. He could feel a kind of anger building within him—the kind born from shame. The old man remained still and waited for him to finish. "You said it yourself, Professor, the person who wrote that note needs a hero—someone noble and *good*." He slumped back into his seat. "I'm just a criminal."

"So what if you are?" the professor replied flatly. "How many well-behaved boys would have made it this far? Would they have broken into that carriage? Would they have battled that gang of bullies? Yes, you've broken a few laws, but there's one law to which you've always remained true." Peter heard this and somehow knew exactly what the man was talking about—it was that stirring inside him that had made him help the zebra. Professor Cake went on, "In my experience, heroes are no more *good* than you or I. And though occasionally noble, they are just as often cunning, resourceful, and a little brash. Who better fits that description than the great Peter Nimble?"

Now, just because you and I are well aware that Peter Nimble was a great thief does not mean that Peter himself knew. Being raised by someone as nasty as Mr. Seamus, he had never actually received a compliment in his lifetime—unless you count being called a "great nuisance" or "the world's biggest maggot" as compliments. For Peter, being told he was anything more than nothing was something of a shock.

"Plus, you have these." The professor pushed the box of Fantastic Eyes toward him. "From here on out, they belong to you."

Peter tried to imagine how the eyes might be of use on such a journey. He had already worn the golden eyes, which made him vanish to the last place they beheld, but what about the other pairs? The black ones and the green ones?

Sensing the boy's thoughts, the professor spoke again. "Telling you what the eyes do would be akin to telling you what *to do*. Trust me, Peter"—and here he placed a hand on the boy's arm—"when the time comes, they'll be just what you need."

Peter traced a finger along the corner of the box, feeling a mixture of longing and dread. To think he had once hoped it contained only money. Instead, he found a treasure beyond his imagining—one that could lead him to great adventure . . . and even greater danger. Yet he wasn't sure the eyes were worth the price the old man was asking. "I suppose I have to give them back if I don't go?" he said.

"Not at all. The eyes are yours to keep. I'm sure your Mr. Seamus could make a tidy profit on them."

Peter groaned. He had almost forgotten about Mr. Seamus.

"Listen, my child. Your life up to this point has been an unpleasant one. Hard. Painful. Empty." He took Peter's hand in his gnarled fingers. "But all of those trials have prepared you to do something selfless and great. Some people search their whole lives for such a calling. Few are lucky enough to have it delivered in a bottle."

Peter tried his best not to scoff. "I wouldn't exactly call myself 'lucky,'" he said.

"Perhaps you will change your opinion. Someone in that kingdom is in peril. They need a hero. They need Peter Nimble and his Fantastic Eyes."

Sir Tode stepped close and rested a hoof on the boy's shoulder. "Think of it, Peter, a *real adventure*."

Peter tried, but all he could hear was the voice of Mr. Seamus

calling him "worthless," "filthy," and "worm." And with each remembered insult, his faith in himself grew less and less. "I'm sorry," he said
after a moment. "I'm not sure I'm the boy you're looking for."

Professor Cake rose from his chair. "Important decisions are
seldom easy. It is your destiny, and the choice is yours alone." He
removed the golden eyes from the box and pressed them into Peter's
palm. "I've arranged it so that these eyes will transport you back to
your home, back to the life you know. There you can safely resume
your career of eating scraps and stealing baubles from hardworking
people. If you choose to help, however, I can promise you nothing
more than risk, sacrifice, and perhaps death. All to aid a stranger in
need." He shuffled across the deck, pausing at the open doorway. "I
wish your options were more comforting," he said, and climbed up
the stairs.

Sir Tode lingered behind for a moment. "Peter? If you and I did
go—"

"I'm sorry to ruin your adventure," the boy muttered.

"Of course. It's only . . ." He cleared his throat. "I should have
liked . . . having a friend." So saying, the knight clopped down from
the table and out of the room, leaving Peter alone with his thoughts.

✦ ✦ ✦

Professor Cake had been right about daytimes on the island. The
morning hours were nothing like the dewy dawn of Peter's port
home. Instead, a broiling sun loomed over the whole horizon like a
giant, fiery compass.

"Well, it's about bloody time!" Sir Tode said as Peter shuffled into the kitchen for breakfast.

The boy met the rebuke with a great stretchy yawn. He had been awake the entire night, considering the professor's offer, trying to decide what he should do. It was a choice between comfortable misery and terrifying uncertainty. More than any argument or reasoning, the thing that persuaded Peter to stay was this: Professor Cake had given him a *choice*—a gift that no one had ever offered him before.

"You've made a brave decision, my child." The old man led him to a chair at the breakfast table. "Wiser still, you elected to stick around for Mr. Pound's farewell-fritters!"

Peter took his seat before a mountain of rum-filled pastries and sizzling butter sausages. "You had better eat up," Mr. Pound said, bringing him a warm plate from the stove. "This may be your last hot meal for a long time."

"Before this place," Peter said, gulping down a steamed pickle heart, "I'd never even *had* a hot meal."

"Then finish that serving already so we can get you seconds!" Peter didn't need to be told twice. He was already through half the sausages and a loaf of bog toast. Mr. Pound whistled. "You've quite the appetite, lad! I'll be sure to pack a bit more food in the *Scop* before you leave."

"Shrolff?" said the boy, his mouth stuffed full.

"Why, that's the name of your ship, Captain Peter!"

After breakfast, the two men led them to a small dock where the *Scop* was waiting. Peter climbed on board and started exploring. This did not take long, as the craft was little bigger than a bed. There was a thin mast with a single-sheet sail. The stern was piled high with food and supplies for the journey. The only things missing were a map and compass. "If the kingdom has vanished," Peter asked. "How will we know the way there?"

"How indeed?" the professor smiled. He took the green bottle from Peter's bag, handing him the note from inside. He then knelt down and secured the empty bottle to the prow with a bit of string. The moment the bottle was in place, Peter heard a faint whistling, created by the breeze moving over its open mouth. "That song will tell the wind where it came from," Professor Cake said, rising with the help of his cane. "It should get you close enough."

"Our very own vessel, Peter! Isn't she grand?!" Sir Tode skittered up the mast to practice his lookout. "Adventure-ho!" he bellowed, peering off into the distance.

Peter listened to the endless waves rolling into the shore. The *Scop* rose with them, knocking against the edge of the dock. "Is she seaworthy?" he asked.

"Worthy and then some," Professor Cake said. "Mr. Pound built the *Scop* himself."

Mr. Pound, who was busy with the sail, proudly patted the ship's mast. "A lot of my heart went into her planks. If you trust her, she'll take you wherever the wind leads." Peter did not find this particularly comforting, as the wind could easily lead them straight off the edge of the world. Still, he was committed now, whatever the course.

The professor faced the sea and took a long breath the way adults do when they have important advice to impart. "My child, there are some things I should tell you before you leave. First, Sir Tode is your companion on this journey, and whatever happens, the two of you must always stay together; he may be the only friend you encounter— and trust me, you will need a friend. Second, the Fantastic Eyes are very precious. They took me a great deal of time and love to create; don't let anyone you meet learn of them or their power. And whatever you do," his voice suddenly became grave, "do not try the remaining pairs until the moment is right—you will know when that is. And last, Peter Nimble, I have called you forth not because of what you may become, but because of what you already are. If ever you find yourself in serious trouble, remember your nature above all things."

Peter did not know how to respond to this; he only nodded his head and hoped that the old man was right.

"If you don't mind," Sir Tode shouted from his perch, "I'd like to get *some* adventure in before nightfall!"

Mr. Pound had finished packing the remaining supplies on the *Scop* and was now loosing her moorings. A sharp gust of wind snapped the sail tight, nearly dragging him into the water. "Better hop aboard," he hollered. "The wind's getting antsy!"

Before he even knew what he was doing, Peter seized the professor in a fierce hug. "Thank you . . . for everything."

The old man's jaw tensed. "All right, then; don't dawdle." He helped Peter aboard, tucking the box of Fantastic Eyes safely under a pile of dried beef leather. "Remember my words, Peter. And let us hope that we will one day meet each other again!"

As they all shouted their final farewells, the boy waved a hand over his head. Clutched in it was a message he could not read, describing a place he could not fathom. A gentle wind brushed across the water, pushing their vessel away from shore and into the horizon.

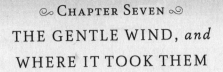

CHAPTER SEVEN

THE GENTLE WIND, *and* WHERE IT TOOK THEM

The start of any journey—whether pilgrimage or promenade— is one of life's true joys. Every moment is charged with an excitement about things to come. Obstacles and complications are seen not as discouragement, but as seasoning that only improves the flavor of one's adventure. Such was the case for Peter and Sir Tode as they embarked on their sea voyage. The gentle wind that had called the *Scop* away from Professor Cake's island pushed them farther and farther into the great blue, charting a course by the bottle's lilting song.

The food that Mr. Pound had packed for them was delicious. There was, however, the question of how long it would last. Peter had learned to master his hunger through a lifetime of wrestling scraps from Killer. Sir Tode, on the other hand, had to juggle the combined appetites of a man, a horse, and a cat. More than once the knight found himself cursing Professor Cake for not packing a horn of plenty among their rations, "or at least a good ham!" Eventually, the two of them discovered a fishing trick that brought them the food they needed: Sir Tode would lean out over the water, watching for any fish that swam close to the surface; when he spotted one, Peter would dive after it, grab hold of the passing mackerel or sea-hen, and then use the golden eyes to whisk himself—and the very confused fish— back aboard the *Scop*. However unappetizing raw fish for breakfast, lunch, and dinner might sound, it went down nicely with a few sips of fresh rainwater.

As you probably know, salty water is not good for people to drink, and finding good drinking water in the middle of a vast ocean can be quite a chore. Luckily, Professor Cake had had the good idea of trapping a small bit of storm cloud in a wineskin. Every so often, the wineskin would rumble and—when opened—reveal itself to be full of fresh rainwater. Between this, Peter's fishnapping, and the gentle wind, the two travelers were well cared for on their journey.

Every so often, Peter would ask Sir Tode to read the riddle again for him, noting that it was important for them to keep their mission in mind.

"If it's so important," Sir Tode would grumble, "why don't you memorize the blasted thing already?"

Kings aplenty, princes few,
The ravens scattered and seas withdrew.

Only a stranger may bring relief,
But darkness will reign, unless he's—

Every time he read it, they were stumped anew by the missing final words. "What do you think the rest of it means?" Peter asked one afternoon. "What's that stuff about kings and princes?"

"And why on earth would they bother themselves with birds?" Sir Tode said with a note of feline contempt.

"Perhaps it's saying that ravens scattered the kings and princes? Maybe they've taken over the whole kingdom?"

"But that's impossible. How can *ravens* overthrow a kingdom?"

"You would be surprised what evil things ravens can do," Peter said. (If you recall, it was a raven that had pecked out his eyes as a baby.) "Yes, I'm sure that's it. The note talks about 'darkness' conquering—ravens are as dark as night." While Peter didn't actually know what "dark" was, he had often heard ravens described in such a manner.

"So once we find this Vanished Kingdom, we're supposed to save it from a bunch of evil birds?" Sir Tode shuddered. "I wonder how many of them there are!"

Peter shrugged. "Millions, probably. I only wish we knew how the riddle ended. I'm sure that last part would help everything make sense." And with that, the two travelers fell into silence as they imagined what might await them on the other end of their voyage.

There is something wonderful that happens between true friends when they find themselves no longer wasting time with meaningless chatter. Instead, they become content just to share each other's company. It is the opinion of some that this sort of friendship is the only kind worth having. While jokes and anecdotes are nice, they do not compare with the beauty of shared solitude. It was a fact that as the days drew on, Peter and Sir Tode were spending less time talking and more time simply sitting side by side, listening to the sea.

Sometimes, however, while drifting under the glittering night firmament, Peter craved conversation, and he would make Sir Tode describe what he saw in the moonlit water below. Fish much prefer the witching hours, and with the dark came thousands of sea travelers, swishing and splashing alongside their boat. Being an enchanted cat-horse-man creature, Sir Tode took little interest in traditional animal varieties, and he usually tried to maneuver the conversation toward a subject he knew better. "They say," he would intone in his most ominous voice, "that the deeper you dive, the bigger they are. Why, some of them are so gigantic, their fins can move the very tides of time."

"Sea monsters?"

"Indeed!" Sir Tode would answer. "Some are called mer-lions, or krakens, or what have you . . . others are too horrible and ancient even to be named. I happen to be something of an expert on monsters, having encountered a few in my former life. Land dragons mostly— which are *much* more fierce." And here Sir Tode would segue into his best version of how he came to be knighted, which involved slashing his way out from the belly of a fiery, three-headed swamp dragon.

(I say "version," because the knight's biography seemed to take on larger and larger dimensions whenever he told it, which was often.)

Sir Tode had, in fact, made something of a career out of this story. In the months after his knighting, he had roamed the countryside on horseback, enjoying a sort of celebrity at the various taverns and inns he passed. He would tell the locals all about his daring exploits, leveraging his status into free room and board whenever possible. Such was his happy life, until his unfortunate encounter with the sleeping hag. "I do wish that I had taken my knight-errancy a bit more seriously," he confessed one evening, after treating Peter to a particularly harrowing version of his tale. "I never once had the chance to rescue a damsel and always thought that the other knights secretly held that against me."

"Maybe there will be a damsel where we're headed?" Peter offered. "Or, better yet, a magician who can remove the curse?"

"Not likely, I'm afraid. When I was younger, you couldn't kick a stump without turning up a spot of magic. But those days are long past. Hags have all disappeared . . . along with everything else worth the telling." The old knight blinked up at the sky, thankful Peter couldn't see the tears in his feline eyes.

Peter also recounted his own misfortunes, telling the story of how he was discovered floating in the bay, his first year with the mother-cat, and his miserable years as the "business partner" of Mr. Seamus.

"Thank heavens you will never have to worry about that nasty fellow again," Sir Tode said. "Ah, dear boy, I only wish that I had been there to adopt you myself. You could have been my page, or my stable boy. What fun we would have had then!"

Peter was touched by the remark, but knew it was just flattery. "I do not think a blind page would have been of much use to you."

"Nonsense!" Sir Tode leapt down from his post. "Why, you've the makings of a great warrior in you!" And saying this, the knight took a stale baguette in his mouth and swiped it through the air. "*En garde*, young swain! It's time you learned to fight!"

"But I already know how to fight," Peter said. "I can bind a man's ankles from thirty paces, or stay his tongue with just a needle and thread."

"Sneaky, dirty tricks—rubbish! What you need to learn is good, proper *hero's* fighting. Take your sword." He dropped the baguette at Peter's feet and grabbed another for himself. Peter took the loaf in his hand and jabbed it a few times in the air above Sir Tode's head.

"Heavens, you're hopeless," the knight said with a groan. "It's a *sword*, not a cattle prod. You think I could have slain an entire nest of dragons by *poking* them to death?! You must swipe! Swipe with all your might!"

And thus Sir Tode began training Peter in the art of dueling. It was not entirely a successful endeavor. The knight was so small that he could not attack above the knees. Things were not made easier by the fact that they were confined to the deck of a tiny boat, which was pitched in all directions by the rolling sea. As you already know, both boy and knight were none too skilled at swimming, so they had to take special care not to swashbuckle themselves overboard. Worst of all, Peter's blindness meant he had trouble orienting himself amidst the loud huffing and puffing of swordplay. More often than not he would trip over his own weapon and crash into the mast.

"If that baguette were sharpened, you'd be in thirty pieces by now!" Sir Tode would scold. "Elbows up! Knees bent! And never forget to watch the other chap's *feet*."

"But I can't *see* your feet!" Peter would complain. "And I can't hear a thing because I'm too busy trying not to get my head hacked off—it's useless!" And with that, he would throw down his bread, wallowing in self-pity. Emotions can run high when two people live in such very close quarters for an extended period of time. And though incredibly talented, Peter was as impatient as any other boy. He didn't like the idea that this hero thing might take some time to master. Slowly, though, over the many days of the voyage, the knight's lessons began to sink in, and Peter found himself able to thrust, parry, and foin his loaf with the best of them.

✦   ✦   ✦

Over time the luster of new beginnings wore off, and things that at first were exciting became maddeningly dull. Peter and Sir Tode's life became a seemingly endless cycle of raw fish and bad weather. The only thing worse than a perilous adventure is a boring one, and the limits of the duo's patience were tried more than once as they slalomed between squalls, broke through blizzards, and drifted across doldrums.

But however slow their progress, progress it remained. The tiny green bottle never stopped its song, and the steady wind guided them ever forward, past the fringes of the known world to the great, unmapped waters of possibility. The change of setting was subtle, and they did not fully notice it until a certain dark night when they were paid a visit by a dogfish named Frederick.

The two travelers were sleeping soundly beneath the starry sky when a fishy voice whispered from the water.

"Hey! Psst!" it said, nudging the boat.

Peter leapt up, grabbing his baguette. "Who goes?!"

"Sorry to wake you, mate. I was hoping you could spare a tick to help out a fish in need?"

"A what?" Peter could have sworn the voice said *fish*.

"Down here, in the water. The name's Frederick. Frederick the Dogfish."

"Fish don't talk," Peter insisted, still too groggy to realize he was no longer in charted seas.

"Well, I'm talkin', ain't I?" The dogfish chortled. "Me and pretty much everything else that swims 'round these parts . . . except maybe the krill. Dumb as dinghies, they are."

This gave Peter pause. He had encountered so many impossible things since his journey began that he couldn't rule out a talking fish, no matter how absurd it seemed. "Where are we?" he asked.

"Edge of the world, mate. Deepest waters there is."

"The edge of the world," Peter murmured, recalling the inkless void on the professor's map. He sniffed the night air, catching a faint mustiness, like the waft of yellowed pages. Maybe the fish was right? Maybe this place *was* different?

Frederick continued, somewhat impatient. "Look, I need your help with something real quick, then I promise to leave you be." Peter listened as the dogfish sloshed to one side. Then he heard a loud *clank* against the edge of the boat. "I got this hook in my cheek and I can't seem to shake it," he said.

Peter reached out his hand to discover a long metal barb. "It's awful big," he said.

"An' that's just the tip! See, I was out swimming near some murky port and I spot this big old cow just floating in the water, right? Well, of course I take me a little nibble, and next thing I know—*whammo!*—I got this whopper of a hook in my mouth. Ruddy thing's stuck clean through my cheek."

A *cow?* Peter wondered just how big this fish was. Still, his instincts were pushing him toward compassion. "So you want help pulling it out?" he said, inching closer.

The action was interrupted by a sudden scream. "*Ahhh!*" Sir Tode cried, dragging Peter back from the boat's edge. "Shoo, beast! You'll find no midnight snack here!"

The knight had woken only the moment before to see Peter reaching into the mouth of the most enormous dogfish imaginable.

Frederick was the size of three elephants, maybe four. Each of his bulging fish eyes was bigger than a meat pie, and just one of his great floppy ears could have covered their tiny boat like a blanket. Poking out from his scaly cheek was a huge silver fishhook longer than a man's arm. "He'll swallow the boat whole!" Sir Tode exclaimed as he shinnied up the mast. "Begone, vile monster!"

"Aw, calm down, mate. I weren't gonna eat no one. I was just hopin' to . . ." and here Frederick's words trailed off. "Just forget about it. Sorry for waking you." He hung his giant head (if fish can indeed hang their heads) and swished back out into the darkness.

Peter leapt to his feet. "Frederick, wait!" he called.

"*Shhh!*" the knight hissed. "He's almost gone!"

Peter quite literally put his foot down. "Sir Tode, I'm captain of this ship, and I say we help him. You of all people should know what it feels like to be judged by appearances." There was a long silence between the two of them. Despite his lack of eyes, Peter was staring the poor knight down. Finally, Sir Tode relented, grumbling something about waste of time and respecting one's elders.

The boy hailed Frederick, who swam back, tail swashing behind him. All told, it took them nearly an hour to remove the jagged hook from the fish's enormous mouth. "*Bloody gill!*" Frederick cursed when they finished. "Feels good to get that out—thing tasted somethin' awful! I tell you, that's the last time I go swishin' around them giants' ports."

"Giants' ports?" Sir Tode said, glancing out over the dark waves.

"No worries, furball. Those waters is nowhere you can get to. And it's a good thing, too—they don't take kind to littles floating about. No, seas 'round here is more full of leviathans, turtles, blood eels . . . and now one grateful dogfish."

"All those things live here?" Peter said, straining to hear giant fins moving in the water below. He reasoned that any place with talking dogfish might also contain other wonders. "You don't happen to know if there used to be a kingdom in these waters?" he asked. "It had a big, fancy palace that vanished."

"Don't know about a kingdom, mate, but there's definitely some good coral a few dives thataway . . . or was it *this*away?" He swished in a circle, nearly capsizing the boat.

Peter steadied himself on the rocking deck. "That's all right," he said, reasoning that any fish careless enough to get stuck with a hook was probably not too good with directions. "I just thought I'd ask."

"Don't mention it, mate," Frederick said. "You pair ever need a favor, I'd be glad to lend a fin."

"Oh, splendid!" Sir Tode muttered. "I don't suppose you have a mailing address?"

"Nah, just ask around for Good Ol' Frederick. You do that, I'll find you all right. Thanks again!" And with that, Frederick the enormous dogfish turned around and disappeared beneath the surface.

Peter and Sir Tode sat in silence, contemplating what had just transpired. "Well, Peter," the knight said at last. "It seems I owe you an apology."

The boy shrugged, wiping his hands dry. "Sometimes it's best not to judge people for being different."

Sir Tode gave an exasperated groan. "I *meant* about it being a waste of time." He tapped the fishhook lying on the deck. "It appears that you just won yourself a sword."

Peter picked up the hook, noting its balance. He gripped the eye loop in one hand and ran his other across the curved barb, which tapered into a perfect point. He swiped the blade in the air—it responded with a pure ringing sound that sent a prickle along his arm. "It appears so," he said, suppressing a smile.

And that is how Peter Nimble acquired the silver fishhook from the land of Gog and Magog, where no man has—or ever will—set foot.

✦　✦　✦

As it happened, Frederick the Dogfish had been right about Peter and Sir Tode being close to dry land.

Very dry land.

Sir Tode was the first to make the discovery. He had just awoken from a fitful night's sleep—the result of some particularly strong winds. Morning had since broken, and the knight was enjoying a good stretch when he noticed something strange: the *Scop* was not moving. In fact, no matter how he wriggled his body, the dripping vessel remained completely still. He rolled over, shook himself dry, and climbed the mast for a better view at his surroundings. What he saw made him gasp aloud.

"Peter?" he said hoarsely. "I—I think you should wake up now."

The boy, who had slept horribly during the previous night's storm, was not pleased at the suggestion. "Get up yourself," he muttered, pulling a blanket over his ears.

Sir Tode gave him a hoof to the rib. "Peter!" he repeated. "It's *gone*."

"What's gone?"

"The sea . . . It's totally disappeared."

By this point, Peter had noticed that the ship wasn't rocking like usual. Also missing was the familiar sound of waves lapping against the prow. He reached a hand over the edge of the boat and found not water but dry, hot sand. "Last night's storm must have washed us ashore," he said.

"I don't think you're listening," Sir Tode insisted. "We couldn't have been washed ashore because *there is no shore*. There's just sand—miles and miles of it." However unlikely this sounded, his description was accurate. The *Scop* was surrounded by dunes that stretched out in every direction without interruption. The knight swallowed hoarsely. "Why, it's almost as though—"

"The seas withdrew." Peter said these words with him. This was, of course, a line from the riddle and possible evidence that they had at last reached their destination.

"The Vanished Kingdom!" Peter shouted, clambering overboard.

"The Vanished Kingdom!" Sir Tode called, leaping after him.

The two ran circles around the boat, heaving armfuls of sand in the air like hot, granulated confetti. "We made it!" they cheered. "The Vanished Kingdom!"

This celebration, however, was cut short by a new voice. "All right, you lot!" it barked. "On your feet!" Peter couldn't see that the voice belonged to a great, burly man wearing a ragged military uniform. Upon his head sat a gray moth-eaten barrister's wig. He was marching straight for them. "Line up, nice and orderly! Let's see them hands!"

"Sir Tode, be my eyes," Peter whispered.

"It's a man, a big man . . . and he has an even bigger axe." The knight was not exaggerating. Strapped across the fellow's back was an enormous, rusted battle-axe.

The man lumbered closer, reaching for his weapon. "I know you heard me say 'on your feet,'" he repeated, "so's I won't bother repeating myself."

Given the size of his weapon and relative proximity, Peter and Sir Tode thought it best to oblige. They scrambled to their feet, awaiting further orders. "Right," the man said with a sniff. "Gather your things from the vessel—*quickly* now." Peter found his burgle-sack in the bow and slung it over one shoulder.

"Step aside, please." Peter and Sir Tode did as they were told. The moment they were clear, the man swung his axe and chopped the *Scop* clean in half.

Sir Tode gawked at their now-shipwrecked ship. "I say! You'd better have a bloody good explanation for that!"

The man grinned at them. "Can't have you lot tryin' to escape, can we?"

"Escape?" Peter protested. "I don't understand."

He gave a cruel snort. "Why, boy, you've landed yourselves in the Just Deserts. And you're gonna be here for a long, long time."

CHAPTER EIGHT

TRAPPED *in the* JUST DESERTS

Peter swallowed hard. "The what?" he said.

"The Just Deserts," the man repeated smugly. "S'where rotten thieves and troublemakers get *just* what they *desert*." Both Peter and Sir Tode knew he probably meant to say "deserve," but thought better of correcting a stranger wielding an axe bigger than both of them put together. The man leaned close, inspecting Peter. His putrid breath nearly made the boy gag. "You're a bit rosy-cheeked for a Missin' One, so I'd wager you was a thief of some kind, right?"

"I—yes," Peter answered, too taken aback to think up a good fib.

"S'what I thought." He hocked up a bit of phlegm and spit it to the ground. "Now the king's banished you here. That way you can't muck up his kingdom, right?"

"Kingdom?" Sir Tode said, glancing around. "You don't mean the *Vanished* Kingdom, by any chance?"

"I mean the king's kingdom." The man holstered his axe. "My name's Officer Trolley. I'm *royal* warden of this here prison. S'my job to welcome newcomers and guard the coast, such as it is." He led them over the next dune and stretched out his arm with pride.

"Goodness, Peter," Sir Tode said, knowing his friend could not fully appreciate the view. "It appears we're not the first ship he's grounded." Every few yards there lay the splintered remains of different boats. The wreckage was scattered across the desert as far as the eye could see.

"'Course you ain't," Officer Trolley said proudly. "I see to each 'n' every vessel that comes in here. Otherwise, you lot might try to sneak off on us." Through with small talk, Officer Trolley decided to move on with the proceedings. "All right, let's get you processed. Hands out, please!"

He took a T-shaped branding iron from his belt and plunged the end into a miniature cauldron, which hung from one shoulder like a ladies' handbag. "Tell you honest, s'been a while since I had the pleasure." He grabbed hold of Sir Tode's hoof and read him his rights:

"*UnderAuthorityOfHisTrueMajestyLordIncarnadineThis HumbleServantHerebyPronouncesYouTraitorsToTheTrueCrown*

BanishingYouToTheJustDesertsForTheFullDurationShortOrLong
OfYourWorthlessLivesBarringAnyHopeOfReliefOrParoleAmen."

All of this was uttered in a single, impossible breath that left the listeners more than a little terrified.

Officer Trolley pulled his iron out from the cauldron. Peter could feel the heat radiating from the red-hot tip. He listened as the warden brought the brand toward Sir Tode's foreleg. "I—I think there's been some confusion, Officer Trollop!" the knight said, squirming. "You see, we're on a quest! My friend here has been given six magical—"

Peter reached down and clapped Sir Tode's mouth shut before he could say anything more. But it was too late. Officer Trolley released the knight and swung his iron beneath Peter's nose. "Magical what?" he said with keen interest.

"Carpets!" Peter said, fibbing good and proper this time. "We were caught selling them on the streets." He remembered Professor Cake's warning about keeping the Fantastic Eyes a secret at all costs.

"Carpets, eh?" The officer rubbed his stubbly chin. "No wonder you lot been exiled—old magic's banned all through the kingdom . . . along with most everything else." He dropped the branding iron in the sand—it seemed a new idea was forming in his bewigged brain. He licked his lips and spoke in a sweeter voice. "You didn't perchance try and smuggle any of them carpets out with you? Let's have a look in that little bag of yours."

Peter snatched his sack away before Trolley could take it. The burly man unholstered his axe once more. "Come on, hand it over. I'm only doin' my *official* job." In truth, Officer Trolley—being a selfish, underpaid employee of the king—could not care less whether or not the two had smuggled in magical artifacts. His real intent was getting his hands on a flying carpet and using it to escape back to the kingdom himself. You see, though Officer Trolley represented the law in the Just Deserts, he too was trapped: the place proved such an effective prison that not a single man, woman, or creature on either side of the law had ever managed to find a way out. And while it was true that he enjoyed his job well enough, there was only so much pleasure a man could derive from smashing newcomers' boats and branding their hands. After nearly ten years, the novelty had worn off. "Now, show me them goods before I lose my patience," he demanded, taking a step closer.

Peter and Sir Tode were backed up against an old skiff named *Zelda* and were fast running out of options. "What should we do?" Sir Tode asked through clenched teeth.

Peter at once recalled the professor's admonition to trust his own instincts. What were his instincts telling him now? In this particular case, his instincts were telling him to run like blazes. And that is exactly what he decided to do. "Run!" he screamed. "Run like blazes!" They dived between Officer Trolley's legs and sprinted as fast as their feet would carry them.

"Hey! That's bad form!" the man shouted, stumbling after them.

"Running's against the rules!" As it turned out, Peter's instincts were spot-on: Officer Trolley was a useless runner on account of his two wooden peg legs. How Sir Tode had failed to notice this before was a wonder, but it was a happy discovery for both of them as they fled over the hot dunes and out of sight. The brutish warden staggered, tripped, and cursed his way after them, falling hopelessly behind. Within a few minutes, they had run so far that the man's angry complaints of "Bad form!" had completely faded away.

+ + +

Even though Officer Trolley had said that no one could escape the Just Deserts, Peter and Sir Tode were determined to try—for the sake of their mission, if not their own lives. If any of you have ever tried trekking through a sandy wasteland, you are well aware of how difficult it can be. Sand has a genuine knack for working its way in between the cracks of one's toes and other sundry parts. This is all the more unpleasant when those bits of sand are hot to the touch, as was the case in the Just Deserts. The sun overhead seemed reluctant to move past noon, which left Peter and Sir Tode with little sense of their bearings. More than once they found themselves in a heated debate over whether they had already passed a particular weed or piece of wreckage.

"We can't just walk in circles forever," Peter said, kicking the sand in frustration. What few provisions he had salvaged from the *Scop* had long since been eaten, and were now replaced with a gnawing pain in his stomach. "If we don't find food and shelter soon, we'll die out here." He rubbed his sunburned neck, which was already beginning to blister.

Hearing the distress in his companion's voice, Sir Tode thought this might be a good time to broach a somewhat ticklish subject. "Peter?" he said, choosing his words carefully. "I'm all for slogging through this barren death trap on hoof, but have you considered that there might be a *simpler way?* Something to help us along?"

"You're talking about the Fantastic Eyes." Peter sighed. This wasn't the first time his companion had brought them up; in fact, Sir Tode had spent much of their sea voyage dropping little hints about how much easier things might be were they to *employ* the gift Professor Cake had so kindly given them ("If you ask me, it's downright ungrateful not to give the other pairs at least a test-blink!"). As you have undoubtedly noticed in your own life, unsolicited advice amounts to little more than criticism, and Peter had grown increasingly weary of these "suggestions." He answered the same way he always did. "The professor said we shouldn't try the other pairs until the moment was right. He told me—"

"Yes, yes, caution and all that," Sir Tode cut him off. "We knights have many virtues, but patience is not one of them. We're in the middle of a desert with no supplies, no map, and no clue where we're headed—sounds like the exact right moment to me!" He took a gentler, more persuasive tone. "And admit it, aren't you *the least bit* curious about what those other two pairs can do?"

The truth was, Peter hadn't stopped wondering about that since the morning they weighed anchor. He had already used the golden eyes—but what of the black and green pairs? He reached into his sack and removed the wooden box. "Maybe you're right," he said, running his fingers over the lid. "I mean, we'd only be using them to help someone."

"That's more like it!" Sir Tode clopped up next to him. "Now which pair are you thinking?"

Peter knelt down and unfastened the lock. He smiled, remembering how his entire body had thrilled when he first touched those golden eyes that night in the alley. He ran his hands over the other pairs, hoping to feel a trill or flicker—some clue telling him what to do. But he felt nothing. The eyes might as well have been made of stone.

Peter sat back, slightly frustrated. His instincts, which had so often guided him through dangerous spots, remained in this moment maddeningly silent. He reached into the box and scooped up the shiny black eyes. "How about these?" he said, feeling their slick, grainless texture.

Sir Tode watched with eager anticipation. He braced himself as Peter untied the bandage around his head and brought the eyes closer. It was at about this time that a sense of foreboding began to creep into the knight's consciousness. He thought back on Professor Cake's words. There was no question that the wise old man meant Peter well; would he trouble himself with a warning unless there was good cause? What if, like the golden pair, these eyes whisked his friend to some other distant place? What if he vanished completely, leaving Sir Tode to fend for himself?

"Hold up, Peter," the knight started. "Perhaps I was a bit rash just then . . ."

"Don't try and stop me now," the boy cut him off. "And you might want to stand back." Before his friend could object further, Peter slipped the cold, black eyes into his sockets and blinked twice.

All at once, he felt water rushing through his head. The sound swelled to a deafening roar, drowning out his every thought. Peter clapped both hands against his ears, trying to contain the churning and splashing inside his skull. He collapsed to the ground, but the grains of sand felt red-hot against his skin. The boy opened his mouth to scream, but all the air had been sucked from his lungs, leaving only a suffocating vacuum. Over the din, he could hear Sir Tode calling out. The boy convulsed mutely on the sand, unable to reply, unable to stand. He had no idea what was happening—but he was certain it was about to kill him.

The next moment, Peter felt a sharp *crack!* against the back of his crown. The blow was so hard it seemed to jar the air back into his lungs, and a few seconds later he was on his hands and knees, gasping, but still alive.

"Wha . . . what happened?"

"I knocked those blasted things right out of your skull is what happened." Sir Tode glared at the two black eyes lying on the sand. "They started changing you, Peter. Your entire body went all green and slimy, and your hands . . . I've never seen anything like it . . . and hope never to again."

Peter massaged his swollen fingers back to life; they had gone completely numb the moment he had put in the eyes. His skin was clammy, and his spit had a brackish taint. He retied the bandage around his head and tottered to his feet. "Whatever was happening, it almost killed me." He took a deep breath, tasting the warm desert air as it swelled into his lungs. Already he was beginning to feel more like his old self. He scooped up the two eyes from the sand, wiped them off, and placed them with the others.

Sir Tode watched him relock the box and tuck it back into his bag. "Peter, you don't suppose the professor *meant* them to hurt—?"

"Of course not." There was genuine shame in Peter's voice. "The professor meant for me to use them wisely. He gave me strict instructions, and I ignored them." The boy still had no idea what the remaining Fantastic Eyes were meant to do, but he knew he wouldn't dare try them again until the time was right.

✦   ✦   ✦

If possible, the hours following the encounter with the black eyes were even bleaker for Peter and Sir Tode. The sun only burned hotter. Their hunger only grew worse. Were it not for the professor's wineskin, the weary travelers would have succumbed to the elements a dozen times over. Still, they forged on, moving in what they agreed was a generally eastward direction.

While traveling, the pair tried to piece together what they could about the Just Deserts. Other than wrecked boats and the occasional bird dropping, the landscape seemed to be completely empty. "If this is really a prison," Sir Tode said, stopping for a rest, "then where are all the other people?"

"Dead, I suppose." Peter uncapped the wineskin and poured a few drops on his neck and arms before offering the rest to his friend. "I've been thinking about something Officer Trolley said before. He mentioned a king . . . do you think that's the 'kings aplenty' in the rhyme?"

"I don't see why we can't assume that," Sir Tode said, settling into what little shade Peter's thin frame provided. "But then I'm confused—if the king is in power, shouldn't everyone be happy?"

"So maybe he's an evil king? Or a monster king?" Here the boy shuddered. "Or a raven king?"

Sir Tode could sense the boy was growing uncomfortable with all this talk of monsters and ravens and decided to change the subject. "Fair enough, but the real mystery is who wrote the confounded thing."

"It must be a poet or a great philosopher. Whoever he is, he can answer all of our questions when we find him." Peter stood, wiping his sweat-covered brow. "Assuming we can make it that far." He adjusted his burgle-sack around one shoulder and continued walking.

✦ ✦ ✦

Night eventually fell in the Just Deserts. The sun tucked itself below the horizon, and the day's heat was replaced by chilling cold. Peter and Sir Tode agreed they should seek shelter under one of the many boats beached along the endless shore. The knight picked a ship with the letters "BS' JOY" scrawled across what remained of her stern, the rest no doubt lost in an encounter with Officer Trolley's axe.

Once settled, the pair set to building a fire. Sir Tode went off to scrounge for scrap wood while Peter busied himself with lighting a punk. This was a relatively simple job, for Peter, being a smart thief, always kept a kit of thieving essentials in his bag— including a small piece of flint. In case you have never needed to build a fire in the middle of a desert, flint is a magical black stone that creates sparks when struck against something hard. A punk is any object that is used to hold a red ember for the purpose of lighting firecrackers or pipes. In this instance, Peter was using a dried locust husk that he had found in the sand. Sir Tode returned, dragging a netful of wood scraps by his teeth. Within half an hour they had a crackling bonfire.

"Well, that was a miserable day," the knight said, limping to Peter's side. "And we're no closer to getting out of here than when we started." He yawned and curled himself into a little ball against the boy's feet, a habit he had acquired during their sea voyage.

Peter lay in silence, listening to the fire and trying not to think about food. For a moment, he thought he heard sounds in the distance—footsteps and whispers. He sat up to listen more closely, but he heard only the wind.

"You don't suppose there's something out there?" Sir Tode said, reading his friend's alarm. "Some terrible fiend stalking the sands?"

"Who knows?" Peter said, settling back in. "There's no use worrying about it. We're alone for now, and we need all the rest we can get if we plan to survive that sun tomorrow." And with that, he extinguished the fire and went to sleep.

Sadly, Peter could not have been more misguided. For crouched not ten feet away from them was just such a fiend.

∽ CHAPTER NINE ∽
POOR OLD SCABBS

Peter woke in the middle of the night to the sound of someone rustling through his bag—which he happened to be using as a pillow. In half a heartbeat, the great thief was on his feet. "Don't move!" he said, drawing his fishhook.

"Please, no!" a voice whimpered. "Don't hurt Poor Old Scabbs!" The prowler had good reason for alarm: Peter's blade was resting on his throat.

"I could kill you if I wanted," Peter said, pushing the point into the prowler's skin.

"No! Poor Old Scabbs is harmless, he is!" By now the man (whose name was, in fact, Old Scabbs) had dropped to his knees and was trying his best to grovel at Peter's feet—a difficult thing to do with something sharp against your throat. "It was terrible wrong of Poor Old Scabbs sneaking about so! He meant no harm but to sit at the warm bonnie-fire. Pecked to pieces, if he's lying!"

Peter turned over the man's palm, feeling the red *T* branded into his flesh. It was the same mark that Officer Trolley had planned to burn into his own hand. "You think I can't tell a thief when I meet one?" he said.

The old man snatched his arm back. "*T* for thief, says you? . . . *T* for *tricked,* says I!" He clutched his hand close to his chest.

Peter listened to the man's sniveling and decided he posed no immediate threat. "Get up," he said, lowering his weapon.

Bowing and thank-you-ing, the stranger staggered to his feet. "Sweet, trustful LittleBoy," he said. "Poor Old Scabbs'll just go on his way now—"

"Not quite yet." Peter nudged Sir Tode with his foot. "Wake up. We have a prowler."

"A prowler?!" The knight jolted awake, half yawning, half snarling. It took him a moment before he could fully comprehend Peter's meaning, but when he laid eyes on Old Scabbs, the situation became clear. "Coward! Thought you could get the jump on us? Attack us in our sleep? Well, think again!" He gave a few sharp snaps at the man's feet to prove his mettle. "Admit it! You were trying to steal the Fantastic Ey—"

"Quiet!" Peter interrupted. "Just check my bag and make sure the box is safe."

Sir Tode dug his snout through the sack. "Everything seems in order—but what's this?" He emerged holding a round stone in his teeth.

Peter took the rock, hefting it in his palm. He recognized it instantly as a crude decoy. "He must have slipped it in my bag so I wouldn't notice something had gone missing." But what had Old Scabbs swapped it for? Instead of sorting through all his supplies, Peter thought it might be faster just to search the prowler's person. He tossed the rock aside and pulled the old man closer to inspect him with both hands.

Old Scabbs was, by anyone's standards, one of the most miserable fellows who had ever lived. A ridiculously curved spine left him just a hair short of four feet tall. His knees, arms, toes, fingers, and hair were all knotted and gnarled. After so many years in the Just Deserts, most of his regular clothes had long rotted away. Patches of matted body hair sprouted in all directions from his malnourished frame. His toenails and fingernails were thick and curled, not having been clipped in years. His skin felt clammy up to the neck—only his leathery, sunburned face betrayed the fact that he had been living in a desert.

When Peter's fingers reached Old Scabbs's mouth, they found it tightly shut. "Open," Peter commanded in his sternest voice.

"No, no, no," the man muttered, his jaw clenched tight. "It's all Poor Old Scabbs is got. LittleBoy's not takin' it from him."

Being a master thief, the boy was well aware of all the best places to hide stolen goods. "He's got something in his mouth, I can smell it."

Sir Tode gave a menacing growl. "So cut it open."

"No!" the old man pleaded through pursed lips. "KittyPet must believe Old Scabbs! He don't got nothing stolen in his mouth! He swears it!"

"Then prove it!" Peter said, kicking him in the shin for emphasis. He did not like bullying old men, but he couldn't be too careful—for all he knew, there were a hundred more thieves lurking in the darkness, and if he and Sir Tode failed to look mean enough, they were as good as dead.

"Owww!" Old Scabbs howled, clutching his leg.

"Answer honestly if you don't want another one," Peter said. "What did you take?"

The old man finally gave up. "Forgive Poor Old Scabbs! He *was* looking to burgle the bag, it's true, and he's terrible sorry. But he was only wanting a little nibble." He dug into his matted beard, fishing out a single lemon.

Peter and Sir Tode inspected the stolen article. They had both assumed he was after treasure, or weapons, or wine. "He risked his life . . . for a *lemon?*" Sir Tode said, puzzled.

Peter took the fruit from the man's open palm. "He's clearly mad."

Old Scabbs collapsed at Peter's feet. "Oh, LittleBoy have mercy on Poor Old Scabbs! Just let him have one wee bite . . . for his lucky tooth!" And with this he stretched his mouth wide for them to see. The man had been telling the truth; his mouth was completely empty save a single brown tooth in the front row. "It's the only one he's got left, and he needs to keep it good 'n' healthy!" He clutched Peter's leg. "Please, LittleBoy!" He was barely intelligible through his sobs. "All he asks is one bitty drop!"

"I'm not sure I follow." Sir Tode wrinkled his snout. "What good would a drop of lemon do your tooth?"

Those of you who are asking the very same question have clearly never been pirates or buccaneers. If you had been, then you would know that lemons and other citrus fruits are used to defend against a nasty disease called "scurvy." Scurvy comes from a lack of a magical vitamin that prevents one's teeth from rotting away during ocean voyages, which is why they call it "Vitamin Sea." Sailors are prone to this disease because, as you may know, lemons and oranges do not grow in the ocean. For this reason, citrus fruits are a precious commodity aboard boats, worth even more than gold.

Though the Just Deserts were not on the ocean, they too were rather isolated and thus devoid of Vitamin Sea, so most all of the prisoners had indeed lost their teeth to scurvy. Poor Old Scabbs had been fortunate enough to kill a man for a jug of orange juice several years before, and by rationing it carefully, he had been able to keep his one remaining tooth alive. This tooth conferred a great deal of status upon Old Scabbs and made many of the other prisoners quite jealous.

But like so many things in life, orange juice fades, and eventually Poor Old Scabbs's tooth started acting up again. The man was so terrified of losing his last denticle that he had tried sewing it into place with a needle and thread. That, however, only made things worse, leaving the tooth enmeshed in a knot of decaying black twine.

Now, Peter—having been raised in a port town—knew all about how important Vitamin Sea was. Because of this, he had taken care to pack a lemon or two before sailing off on his quest and wasn't eager to give them up, no matter how much the miserable man groveled.

"Have mercy!" the miserable man groveled. "Poor Old Scabbs'll do anything LittleBoy asks!"

Peter paused for a moment. This old thief was the only other person they had met since fleeing Officer Trolley, and there was no question they could use an ally in these treacherous sands. Perhaps the boy could turn this encounter to his advantage? "All right," he said. "We'll share some of our lemon with you. But you'll have to give us something in exchange."

"What can Old Scabbs give, says you? Why, he's got nothing *to* give."

"We only want your help. How long have you lived in this place?" Peter asked.

"Can't hardly call it living. Poor Old Scabbs was sent to the Just Deserts ten years ago. Punished for what terrible wrong he done to them little ones." And here his face fell with shame. "Poor Old Scabbs is bad, bad, bad . . ."

"What in heaven's name did you do?" Sir Tode pressed.

But Old Scabbs would share no details; he just repeated, "Terrible wrong . . . terrible, terrible wrong . . ."

Peter didn't want the old man to lose focus. "And you've been wandering here all those years since? You must know these deserts well."

"Why, Old Scabbs knows them like the warts on his head!" he said, eager to please. "There's not a grain of sand that's not a friend to him." Saying this, he took up a handful of sand and started petting it.

"Good," Peter said, putting away his fishhook. "Then you shall be our guide. And if you help us, I'll give you the whole lemon."

At these words, the old man's eyes welled up with tears. "Yes, yes! LittleBoy won't be sorry, says I! Old Scabbs'll be a guide straight and true—he'll take right proper care of LittleBoy and his KittyPet!"

"I am no man's pet," Sir Tode warned, but Old Scabbs was too busy trying to kiss Peter's feet to heed him.

"Then we have a contract," Peter said, holding out the lemon. "If you break your end of the bargain, I'll call the Blight on your head. Do you understand?" Old Scabbs nodded furiously, snatching the fruit with both hands.

Peter figured that since they were already awake, they might as well get started. "Which way takes us out of the desert?"

"'Out of the desert,' says you?" their gnarled companion chuckled, as though this were a particularly witty joke. "And thieves say Old Scabbs is mad! Why, there ain't no 'out' for such as us—

unless LittleBoy counts the grave!" He burst into laughter. "Old Scabbs can guide him *there* no trouble!" He slid a finger across his neck to illustrate his meaning.

Sir Tode eyed the man with growing concern. "Peter, I'm beginning to have second thoughts about our guide."

Peter reassured him, "He's only kidding about that last part. Escape might be too hard for an old man like him, but I've never met a gate I couldn't unlock. And if all else fails, we can just scale the wall." He turned back to Old Scabbs. "Can you at least take us as far as the border?"

The man sniffled, wiping his tears. "The border, says you? A terrible dangerous place, says I. Still, Old Scabbs made a contract, so the border he'll go!" He shook Peter's hand, then pulled him close. When he spoke again, it was with chilling clarity. "But be warned, LittleBoy. You best put dreams of escape right out of your mind." He cast a wild eye to the skies around him. "*No one* quits the Just Deserts . . . not even *Them!*"

Without another word, he released Peter's hand and led the way into the night.

✦　✦　✦

As it turned out, Old Scabbs was a fine guide. He truly did know the place like his own warts, and demonstrated this fact by calling "hello" to all the wrecked boats they passed. Eager to please his new benefactors, the man was happy to answer any question they had about the Just Deserts.

"How do we find food here?" Peter asked after his stomach loosed a particularly loud rumble.

"Hungry, says you?" Old Scabbs gave a low cackle. "The eatings here might not be what LittleBoy's accustomed to." He knelt down and stuck his arm into the sand. After a brief struggle, he pulled out a long, fat centipede. He broke the squirming critter into two pieces and popped them both into his mouth. "Mmm, tasty!" he said, merrily chomping away. "If he's lucky, LittleBoy'll find a good, plump fire ant! Why, last year Old Scabbs caught one big as his fist, he did!"

"Ugh," Sir Tode said queasily. "I don't even want to imagine what you must drink."

"D-d-drink, says you?" The old man's jaw went slack, letting sandy bits of centipede fall. "Oh, if only he could . . ." He retreated into his own thoughts, smacking his mouth and muttering nonsense. "Cup o' tea from the kettle for Poor Old Scabbs?" he said to no one in particular. "Nay, just swallow your spits."

The question of what Old Scabbs drank (if anything) was but one of many questions their guide could not answer. They were not, for example, able to determine how all of these boats got here from the shore—or whether the Just Deserts even had a shore, for that matter. Neither were they able to learn anything more about what Old Scabbs and the others had done to get banished. "You mentioned there were other prisoners," Peter finally said. "But we've been walking for hours and haven't met a single soul."

The old man whirled around, offended. "Not a soul, says you? And what of Poor Old Scabbs? Ain't he a soul?"

"He means other people *besides* us three, you old lump." Sir Tode was growing more than a little weary of their guide. It was a fact that most people who encountered Sir Tode were so startled to hear him speak that they treated him with respect, if not fear. Old Scabbs, however, proved stubbornly uninterested in anything he had to contribute—which went a long way toward explaining the knight's rather truculent mood.

"Why does LittleBoy let his pet talk so terrible cruel?" he said to Peter. "Maybe he should eat KittyPet for punishment! Maybe share a nibble with Poor Old Scabbs, too, mmm?"

"How can I be his pet when I *speak?!*"

"Of course KittyPet speaks. Old Scabbs never seen a pet that didn't."

Peter pulled the fishhook from his bag, drawing the man's full attention. "Sir Tode is not my pet. He is a brave knight, *and* my friend. You will treat him as you treat me: with respect. Do you understand?"

Old Scabbs responded with a frantic "Yes! Yes!" directed less at Peter than at the point of his gleaming blade.

From then on, the travelers continued in relative silence, broken only when Old Scabbs had to secure safe passage through enemy camps. Each time he would scramble ahead and shout into the darkness:

Blinded and binded in whitest yarn,
Here comes Old Scabbs, who means no harm!

A moment later, a voice would call back, "Pass, thief!" Old Scabbs would then march on, leading Peter and Sir Tode through a cluster of wrecked ships. The first time they went through a hollow like this, Peter noticed the faint sound of heartbeats all around them. When he asked about it, Old Scabbs only shook his head. "Some thieves is not to be trusted! Terrible wicked, says I."

As the night wore on, the moon began to dip closer and closer to the horizon, and Peter could smell the dew percolating up from the ground. In the last hours, he had had time to mull over all the things they had learned about the Just Deserts. He knew there were other prisoners and that the warden had destroyed all their ships. Still, there was one thing Officer Trolley had said right before trying to brand them that didn't quite fit. "How often do new prisoners arrive?" Peter asked, catching up to his guide.

"Newcomers? Why, Old Scabbs ain't *never* seen newcomers to the Just Deserts, excepting LittleBoy and KittyPet." He paused a moment, considering this fact. "Hmm . . . mighty peculiar, that is."

Peter jumped in, not wanting the old man to think too hard about their mysterious arrival. "So if there are never any newcomers, then that means you were all sentenced here at the same time?"

"Sentenced, says you? We thieves was *tricked* here, says I!"

"Hold on," Sir Tode said, joining the conversation. "Are you saying that every prisoner here is a thief?"

"Every last one." Old Scabbs marched ahead to catch a beetle of some kind.

The knight shivered. "An entire prison full of thieves? No offense, Peter, but I can think of few things more dreadful."

No sooner had he said this than a cry rang out from somewhere ahead. "Thieves take cover!" it said.

Old Scabbs stopped at once, listening. Another voice—this one closer—repeated the cry: "Thieves take cover!"

Peter could almost hear the blood drain from Old Scabbs's face. "Not good! Not good, says I!" The old man fell to his knees and started frantically digging a hole, tossing handfuls of sand over his head. "Old Scabbs must hurry! *They* are a-coming!"

The cry sounded again and again, each time closer than the last. "Thieves take cover! . . . Thieves take cover!"

"What's all this now?" Sir Tode said, growling. "Take cover from what?"

"Hurry, KittyPet!" The old man was now trembling all over. He scooped sand around his pasty body, burying himself. "Light-o-day's nearly come! Old Scabbs must hurry and hide hisself—or else *They* might catch him!" All through the night, he had been dropping occasional hints regarding some mysterious "They," but whenever asked about it directly, he would be overcome with fits of terror.

"*They* who?!" Peter tried for the hundredth time.

"Old Scabbs is warning LittleBoy and KittyPet to hide, and hide quickly!" He bellowed, "THIEVES TAKE COVER!" and plunged his face into the sand, leaving only the top of his head exposed.

"Er, Peter?" Sir Tode said, growing nervous. "Perhaps we should listen to him, just this once?"

Old Scabbs reached out from the sand and pulled them both to the ground. He lifted his face, which was pale with panic. "They're here!" he whispered, cupping his filthy fingers over their mouths. The two lay motionless on the sand, waiting.

And then *They* came.

At first Peter heard a faint rustling, like a mast-jack flapping in the wind. Then the sound grew louder, filling out into a chorus of hundreds, then thousands—all pounding furiously against the air. Dread washed over the boy as he felt the tumult in the skies above. The noise thundered past them, eclipsing the moon and cloaking the desert in icy shadow.

Finally, after what seemed like ages, the storm passed, and Peter felt the safety of moonlight once more. He remained still, waiting until the sounds completely disappeared, leaving empty silence. "What was that?" he asked, afraid to hear the answer.

Old Scabbs leaned close, wild terror in his voice. "That, LittleBoy . . . were the *ravens!*"

Peter couldn't sleep. There were several good reasons for this.
First, it was almost noon, and the sun was already blisteringly
hot. Second, he was buried up to his neck in itchy, bug-ridden sand.
And finally, just a few hours earlier, a monstrous flock of ravens had
flown right over his head. No matter how Peter reassured himself
that his current hiding place was as safe as any, his survival instinct
was telling him to keep moving. He listened to the gentle snoring of
Sir Tode and Old Scabbs, buried on either side of him.

"Sir Tode," he whispered.

The knight's mustache twitched. "Land ho," he murmured
dreamily, then jolted upright, remembering the previous night's
events. "Wait, what?! Are *They* back?"

"No, but I want to explore a bit while Old Scabbs is sleeping."

Peter quietly pulled himself out of the sand. "Come on," he said, helping his friend free.

Sir Tode yawned and shook a tick from his ear. "Are you certain we should go traipsing about like this? The old coot warned us it wasn't safe to travel in daylight. Just this once I'm inclined to believe him."

"We'll be fine." Peter emptied the sand from his sack and slung it over one shoulder. "We walked all yesterday without running into trouble."

The knight groaned. "No, no trouble at all . . . unless you count heatstroke, blisters, and axe-wielding wardens."

After some debate, Peter convinced Sir Tode that the best course of action would be to explore farther east before returning to Old Scabbs in the late afternoon. "That would still leave us a few hours to rest before heading back out again," he persuaded his friend. Sir Tode agreed to the plan, but only on the condition that he be allowed to ride in Peter's bag.

The two set off in the direction they had been following the previous night, searching for signs of life. In the daylight, they did not have to search very long. "I say, Peter, there are men sleeping all over this place," Sir Tode said from his new perch. It was true; hidden in the shadows of every wrecked boat was the snoring head of a prisoner, which stuck out from the sand like some sort of unsightly weed. "It's a wonder I didn't spot them before."

"It seems like all of the prisoners treat their wrecked boats like houses," Peter said. "I bet when Old Scabbs was calling out boat names, he was actually saying hello to other thieves." The boy's deduction was spot-on. On the whole, the prisoners of the Just Deserts were extremely territorial. When they first arrived, each man claimed the wreckage of the vessel that brought him. Every day when they slept, the prisoners would bury themselves in the shade of the shattered hull. In fact, the reason that Old Scabbs discovered Peter and Sir Tode in the first place was because they had inadvertently squatted beside his home, *Scabbs' Joy*.

"What do you think their crime was?" Sir Tode asked.

"I'm not sure. But it must have been something awful to deserve this fate." The most common punishment in Peter's hometown had been hanging. The thought of public execution had always terrified him, but perhaps life in this place was worse than death? "They all sound so miserable. Not to mention the way they smell."

"They don't look much better, I assure you," Sir Tode observed.

The idea that he might possibly end up like one of these prisoners made Peter ill. "That's all the more reason for us to find a way out of here and help whoever wrote that message."

The two travelers kept on exploring until just before noon, when they decided to stop and find something to eat. Though Peter had no interest in swallowing bugs, he knew how important it was to keep strong. Sir Tode, on the other hand, had gotten over his initial queasiness and was now having a delightful time discovering all sorts of savory new insects. "Not half-bad!" he said, chomping merrily on a spotted sand-weevil. "So long as you keep away from those stingers."

Peter was not listening. A breeze had just rolled over the crest of the next sand dune, and with it came a sweet, new fragrance. He raised his nose, taking in the cooler air. "There's water over that way. I'm sure of it," he said.

Sir Tode, who was still growing accustomed to his companion's extraordinary senses, balked. "You can *smell* water?" he said.

Peter ignored the comment. "It's maybe half a league away," he said. "If we can find a water source, we might be able to fish for some real food." He started off in a new direction. Sir Tode spit out his mouthful of bugs and followed after him.

Within a few minutes, they had reached the top of a large hill. "Good heavens," Sir Tode said. "Remind me never to doubt your nose."

The boy grinned. "I thought you might say that." He could now hear a faint trickling sound ahead. "It must be a spring of some kind. Do you think there might be any fish in it?"

Sir Tode gave a wry chuckle. "Boiled, maybe. It looks like a giant rock, and it's shaped exactly like . . . a *teakettle*." The knight stared at the bizarre landmark, trying to decide whether or not it might be a mirage. "It's got a handle and spout and everything."

Looming in the distance was indeed a large boulder shaped like a kettle. It was roughly the size of a house and had been hollowed out and filled with water. "I can feel a current moving underground,"

Peter said when they came closer. "It must flow up through the bottom, like a well." The pair managed to scale the handle without too much trouble. There were no signs of fish in the water, but it was at least potable. "Who do you think put it here?" Peter mused, dipping his blistered feet into the pool.

"Someone strong . . . or at least very determined." Sir Tode examined the chisel marks on its surface. From this height, he could see nearly all of the Just Deserts, and he took the opportunity to scout their surroundings. "I think I see the border in the distance. The horizon ends with a long stripe of *black* that stretches out in both directions—some kind of wall or fence, maybe? And right in the middle, there's a spire poking into the sky."

"That must be the prison gates. Do you think we can make it by nightfall?"

"Perhaps." Sir Tode squinted. "It's hard to tell from here."

"Well, at least we know we're headed in the right direction. And in the meantime, we can rest a moment before walking again." While the professor's wineskin did an adequate job of keeping them alive, it was far from ideal. Trekking through the desert had left both of them extremely dusty and not a little chapped. Moreover, the last bath taken by either of them had been in the Troublesome Lake some time ago. Though boys generally make a point of hating baths, Peter Nimble was willing to make an exception just this once.

The cool water instantly revived the two travelers. After some experimentation, they figured out a way to use the spout as a sort of shower tap: whenever one of them jumped into the well, it would raise the water level and spray out a refreshing stream.

The kettle also proved a perfect spot for Peter and Sir Tode to improve their swimming skills. Because of the rock's curved walls, they were able to support themselves while they practiced breathing, kicking, and diving. By the end of an hour, they were both able to keep themselves somewhat afloat.

Once the travelers were thoroughly clean, they stretched out on the rim of the rock and dried themselves under the desert sun. "What do you think lies on the other side of that wall?" Sir Tode asked.

Peter shrugged. "The Vanished Kingdom, I hope. Whatever we find, I'm sure it will answer at least some of our . . ."

Sir Tode turned and regarded his silent friend. "Some of our what?" he said.

But the boy had become still. For in that moment, a great shadow slid over his body, blotting out the sun. Peter clasped Sir Tode's mouth shut. He lay rigid, listening in terror as a noise overhead grew louder and louder.

It was the sound of wings.

And it was headed straight for them.

CHAPTER ELEVEN

THE RAVENS *of* KETTLE ROCK

Peter lay completely still as the giant flock wheeled overhead. "How many are there?" he whispered to Sir Tode.

The knight stared at the storm of black wings thundering across the sky. "Thousands," he said, swallowing hard. "P-p-perhaps they'll pass without seeing us?"

"Keep calm, whatever you do." The boy knew his friend was prone to panic. In truth, he was just as frightened as Sir Tode. Peter could almost feel their eyes scanning the sand as the birds flew a circle around the rock. He tensed at the sound of razor-sharp talons braking against the wind. "They're coming to land," he said. "Our only chance is to hide in the water before they reach the rock."

"*In* the water? Forgive me, but I seem to have misplaced my gills!"

The boy put a reassuring hand on his friend's foreleg. "When I say so, we'll both dive below the surface and swim up inside the spout. If we can make it to the top, we'll be able to breathe without being seen." It was a feeble plan, but he could think of nothing better.

Peter listened carefully to the ravens' movement. Sunlight slid back over his skin as birds swooped southward, dipping briefly behind a dune. "Now!" he said. The two rolled themselves into the water seconds before the mighty ravens touched down all around them.

For Peter, being submerged was like being in a nightmare. While his expert ears could still pick out echoes, it was near impossible to identify where they were coming from. He couldn't smell without inhaling water, of course, and his hands and feet were too busy kicking to be of any real use. Peter could hear the tiny splashing of beaks snapping at the water's surface. *Could ravens swim?* No, they were only drinking at the top of the well. The splashing sounds grew more and more faint as he and Sir Tode kicked deeper toward the bottom of the kettle. He knew the spout must connect down there somewhere. At last his hands found an opening in the rock. He pushed Sir Tode up into the spout's entrance and wiggled in after him. Peter remembered the last time he and the knight had been underwater like this; they had been fighting *against* each other. Now the two of them were working together.

Peter was about halfway up the spout when his lungs began to give out. The narrow walls were closing around him; his veins felt like they were going to explode. Sir Tode's hoof connected with his nose, and he tasted his own blood spreading in the water. The boy struggled on, cutting his feet and arms against the wall of rock. He could think of nothing but air, of nothing but the surface. His heart was pounding so loudly he was sure the birds could hear it. He didn't care; he had to breathe again.

Peter finally broke through the water's surface. He was wedged next to Sir Tode, inches away from the lip of the spout. Cold water lapped around his chin. The master thief panted heavily, trying to hear what was happening outside. Had the birds seen them dive into the well? There was squawking all around the rock. It sounded like talking, but it was difficult for Peter to make out any words. Pausing for a moment, he took control of his heartbeat—slow, slower, stopped. Calming his hands, his nose, his ears, he concentrated on the scene outside. There were definitely voices mixed in with the squawking. It sounded like arguing, but that may just have been the way birds talked.

The flock grew quiet as an incoming bird landed among them. "Captain Amos, we found the vessel!" it shouted.

"And what of the warden, Eli?" another raven responded. This one sounded much more confident than the first bird. Its voice reminded Peter of the admirals he had heard marching about his port town. "Did Trolley know why they had come?"

"The warden knew nothing, sir. He claimed they flew eastward. He believed they had magic carpets with them."

"Rubbish. Carpets don't fly, not even magic ones. Still, we should patrol the border in case they plan to cross." The second bird—the one they had called Captain Amos—went on. "Titus, I am holding you responsible for finding these strangers. Take an unkindness of fifty back to the Nest and keep lookout for two travelers—a boy and a cat!"

"You heard him!" Titus squawked. "Flap!"

A group of ravens leapt into the air, proclaiming, "Long live the True King!"

The rest of the flock responded as one. "And long live his Line!" The birds cawed and flapped, cheering the small troop as it disappeared into the skies.

Peter was confused by what he was hearing. The ravens sounded like an army of some kind. They had clearly been alerted to his and Sir Tode's arrival. They also made reference to some "unkindness" they were plotting, which confused him even more. Were these ravens planning to hurt someone? Perhaps the king? No, they had said, "Long live the True King." Whatever was going on, Peter knew he and Sir Tode weren't safe where they were; it would only take one bird to glance casually into the kettle's spout and they would be discovered.

No sooner had this thought crossed his mind than he heard a scratching by his ear—a pair of talons had settled onto the lip of the rocky spout. Peter grabbed Sir Tode, who was still breathing heavily, and pinched his mouth shut. The knight struggled in protest, but

Peter expertly began stroking his throat, keeping a firm grip on a special pressure point behind the ears—an old trick he had learned from Mr. Seamus for sedating ornery house cats. *Thank you, Mr. Seamus*, the boy thought to himself for the first time in his life as Sir Tode became still.

The scraping noise became louder as the raven poked its bill into the spout. "The water is foul this day," it said, inching closer to Peter's head. "It smells tainted, as though someone—" His investigation was interrupted by a cry.

"Look here!" a voice called from the base of the rock. "I've found signs of a traitor!" The raven at the spout jumped away to join Captain Amos and a few others on the ground.

"I noticed a lump in the sand when I landed," the first raven went on. "It looks like there's a weapon inside."

Peter knew at once that they had discovered his burgle-sack, which he had hidden—apparently not well enough—before climbing the rock. "This blade is not from the armory," Captain Amos said. Peter listened as the bird pecked at the metal. "It must have come with the strangers."

These words caught the attention of the rest of the flock, many of whom flew closer to see. "We should patrol the immediate grounds," Captain Amos continued. "Asher, Jude, search the area for tracks. If they have been here recently, we may be able to follow them."

Two ravens squawked, "Yes, sir!" and took to the air.

The other ravens set to inspecting the rest of the objects inside the bag. Peter listened to the sound of beaks removing its contents one at a time: his burgle-kit . . . the box of eyes . . . the wineskin . . . the riddle . . .

"Let me see that scroll," Captain Amos ordered, taking the piece of paper in his talons. After a moment, he turned to the flock. "You should all hear this," he said, reading the words aloud:

> *Kings aplenty, princes few,*
> *The ravens scattered and seas withdrew.*
> *Only a stranger may bring relief,*
> *But darkness will reign, unless he's—*

The birds absorbed these words in silence. "A *traitor?*" one bird whispered. "Who would dare summon a traitor?"

"Someone who is either very foolish or very desperate," Captain Amos replied coldly. "Whoever wrote this petition, it is clear they do not know of us."

A grumbling rose up from the flock. "Ten years we have waited for word from the other side," a voice called out. "And *this* is what we get?"

"How much longer will Justice ignore us?" another cried, to which several more ravens squawked in agreement.

"Peace, brothers!" Captain Amos called out in a reproving tone. The birds fell silent to let their leader speak. "I hear your concern, but we must remember to keep faith." Peter sensed that the bird was fighting to suppress his own disappointment. "It is clear that these strangers are somehow connected to our tale—but whether for good or ill remains to be seen. Perhaps this box will hold the answers we seek?"

Peter cringed as he heard the sound of a beak pecking against the keyhole. He silently prayed that ravens—even murderous talking ones—could not open locks . . .

Click.

The boy listened, horrified, as the birds lifted the lid and peered inside. "Sweet Justice," Captain Amos said after a moment.

The ravens crowded closer and began to whisper amongst themselves. "What magic is this . . . But Simon, Mordecai . . . *Could it be* . . . ?" Soon every voice in the group was chanting the same thing: "The Line! The Line! The Line!"

Peter did not understand what any of this meant. All he knew was that these ravens had discovered the Fantastic Eyes and were somehow alarmed by what they saw. He could hear their hundreds of hearts beating faster and faster. "The Line! The Line! The Line!" The chanting continued until it was interrupted by the return of Asher and Jude.

"Traitor approaching!" they squawked. "Port side!"

The flock fell silent and immediately leapt to action. Every bird that was perched upon the rock hopped clear and glided to the sand. Peter could tell they were waiting for something, but what?

A new voice answered his question. "Keep away, LittleBoy!"

it cried, approaching with frantic footsteps. "Keep far away from Kettle Rock, says I!"

Peter realized at once who it was. Old Scabbs must have woken up and followed their tracks to this spot. He clenched his jaw and silently begged for the man to turn back. As little as he liked the crazy old felon, he liked the ravens even less.

But Old Scabbs kept on. "LittleBoy and KittyPet must heed what Old Scabbs says. Get out of daylight, before—!" His voice left him as he topped the ridge to find a thousand ravens waiting for him. The old thief fell to his knees, choking with terror.

Captain Amos hopped forward. "Traitor, you have been shown mercy on the condition that we never see your miserable pink carcass again."

"O-O-Old Scabbs knows it, he does!"

"You have returned our consideration by flaunting your accursed face during daylight. Even more, you have trespassed upon our sacred rock."

"Old Scabbs is sorry, he is! Terrible sorry! Please, don't peck him to pieces! The ravens is kind and merciful! They forgave him once before—Old Scabbs remembers it!"

"Once, and never again. That was our promise."

"Promise, says you?" A bitterness crept into the man's voice. "Don't tell Old Scabbs of promises! By promises, he should be a rich man!" The outburst was met by cold silence, and Old Scabbs instantly realized that he had made a grave error.

"I see our mercy was wasted on you," the raven said. "We shall waste it no longer."

"W–w–wait!" The miserable old man scrambled to his feet, getting an idea. "The ravens never asked *why* Old Scabbs come by their rock. He was coming to bring the ravens a *gift!* Two juicy little strangers, mmm! Leading them straight to the Nest, Old Scabbs was!"

Peter heard these words, but could not believe them. *Was Old Scabbs really planning to betray them?* The old man gave a devilish cackle. "It's true! A plump kitty cat and fresh little blind boy! Just for your—"

His words were cut off by a storm of flapping and squawking. "*Nooo!*" he howled as the birds attacked.

By now Peter had given up stilling his heartbeat. He had also forgotten all about stroking Sir Tode's neck. The two were shaking with terrible fear; Old Scabbs was being pecked to pieces not twenty paces from where they hid. Peter's lips trembled as he held his friend close. He could taste Sir Tode's salty tears, which were streaming down his snout and into the water. They huddled together, listening to the final cries of their former guide.

There was a solemn hush in the moment after the execution. Captain Amos spoke again, this time more softly. "Traitor, we shall bury you in one piece. That is more than you deserve. May the worms of the earth show you similar kindness." He raised his voice to the flock. "In Justice we say . . ."

"Long live the True King!" the others cawed back. The ravens somberly went about digging a shallow hole in the sand for Old Scabbs's remains. Peter listened intently to every sound, and as he did, he wondered about the man's dying words. Would he really have delivered Peter and Sir Tode to these wicked creatures?

Peter's mouth had gone completely dry; he sipped some of the water around his neck but found himself too nauseated to swallow. "P-P-Peter?" Sir Tode whispered as quietly as he could. "Are we going to die?"

To this question, the master thief had no answer. Outside, the birds had completed their task and moved on to other matters. "Eli," Captain Amos commanded. "Take the weapon and this box to the Nest. Real or not, we cannot risk letting them fall into our enemy's hands."

"Yes, sir!" the raven named Eli responded. He snatched the objects in his claws and started for the horizon.

Captain Amos turned back to the flock. "Brothers, it is a great riddle indeed that brings blind strangers and rhyming-scrolls to our deserts. Whether or not the Line has returned remains to be seen. As always, we steel our beaks, sharpen our claws, and wait for Justice." Peter detected a new urgency in the captain's voice. "We can only assume that our enemy has learned of the strangers as well. I have no doubt he will try to strike. And if he does, *we shall not fail a second time!*" He beat his great wings against the air, soaring high as he squawked, "LONG LIVE THE TRUE KING!"

There was a mighty roar as a thousand birds flapped after him. "AND LONG LIVE HIS LINE!!!"

✦   ✦   ✦

Peter and Sir Tode waited until nightfall before wriggling back down the rocky spout. This was even more difficult than swimming up, and by the time they worked their way to the base of the kettle, they barely had strength to kick to the surface.

They came up to cool moonlight. Peter rolled himself onto the top of the rock and listened to the desert air. Far, far away, he could hear footsteps. Maybe more prisoners? He listened again for the sound of wings or talons or caws. Nothing. He helped Sir Tode onto his back and climbed down to the sand below.

The ground around the kettle was still heavy with the stench of violence. "Do you see him?" he asked, shivering a bit.

"To your left, about thirty paces." Sir Tode led him to a small mound in the sand. They stood in silence over Poor Old Scabbs's grave.

"No one deserves that." The boy's voice was tense with rage. Peter was no stranger to violence or even death, but nothing had prepared him for this. Old Scabbs had been *murdered* in cold blood. Peter could not say how, exactly, but he knew that this event had profoundly changed both him and his journey. He returned to the base of the rock and began collecting his scattered possessions. The ravens had left everything but his fishhook and the box of Fantastic Eyes. Among the items, he found Old Scabbs's precious lemon.

Peter carried it to the grave. "Sleep well, old thief," he said, crushing the fruit in his hand. The cuts on his arm stung as the juice ran down his wrist and dribbled over the sand.

Sir Tode stepped to his side, blinking across the endless desert. "It sounded like those birds understood our riddle."

"Of course they did," Peter said bitterly. "It's about them. Whoever wrote it needs us to stop the ravens."

Sir Tode suppressed a shudder. "I hope you're wrong. They've got us beat in numbers and strength. Even with the Fantastic Eyes, it would be suicide."

These words filled Peter with fury and shame. The professor had specifically warned him against letting others learn of the Fantastic Eyes. And now, thanks to the ravens, he had failed. "Our first step is to steal the eyes back. Then we'll worry about fighting." He hefted his bag over one shoulder and started off in the direction of the great spire, the spot the birds had referred to as the Nest.

Sir Tode shook his head, walking alongside him. "I agree with the basic principle, Peter, but *how* are we going to pull it off?"

"Simple." The boy gestured toward the rolling dunes, dotted with wrecked ships. "We're getting help."

Peter and Sir Tode continued eastward under the giant moon, trying their best to forget the mortal screams of Old Scabbs. The faint breeze, which had long since dried their clothes, pushed softly against their faces. The terrain of the Just Deserts was growing hillier, making it more difficult to maintain a straight line. Being from a port town, Peter knew how to navigate by the stars—the only problem was that he could not see them. More than once Sir Tode had steered them off course by misunderstanding the boy's directions.

"No," Peter said, realizing they had veered south once again. "The Pole Star is the *big one*."

"Well, they all look bloody small, if you ask me! How am I supposed to tell the one from the other?"

The two argued about this and many other things, until they finally agreed to put their navigating frustrations aside and do some thinking about the riddle. "Let's assume that the ravens are working for the king," said Peter, who had since memorized the words.

"So that's settled, then? The king is evil?"

The boy nodded. "If the ravens work for him, then he's definitely evil. Also, Captain Amos called Old Scabbs a traitor—we have to figure out why."

"Perhaps he and the other prisoners tried to stop the evil king?"

"But how? What was their crime?"

Sir Tode considered this question. "The note mentions 'kings aplenty.' You don't think there could be more than one? Perhaps a good king and a bad king are at war?"

"It could be . . . and maybe it's the good king who's written this note and needs us to rescue him?"

"Or perhaps the bad king wrote it?" Sir Tode said. "Or someone else altogether?"

"It's all so confusing!" Peter grumbled. "If only we knew how the stupid riddle *ended*. I'm sure that last bit is the key to this whole puzzle."

By this point you have probably guessed, like the ravens, what the last words of the note were. For anyone familiar with rhyming verse, figuring that out would be a simple matter of compiling a list of potential rhymes with "relief" and trying out all the words to see what makes the most sense. Sadly, because Peter was too busy being a thief instead of a schoolboy, he was still having trouble figuring out this vital clue.

"Whatever the answer, I'm sure it's right under our noses," Sir Tode said. "But between my whiskers and your blindness, we'll have a rough time spotting it!"

Peter didn't share Sir Tode's amusement. "At least I have an excuse," he muttered. Ever since their ordeal at Kettle Rock, he had found himself growing more and more irritated by the knight's constant foolery. They had witnessed a grisly murder, and yet Sir Tode continued to treat everything like some kind of game.

They continued in silence until reaching a series of escalating ridges, at which point Peter stopped. "There's a campfire down there, behind that second hill," he said, sensing the change in temperature. "Someone's just put it out."

Sir Tode had learned better than to argue with his friend's uncanny senses. He stared into the darkness, wondering what awaited them. "Peter," he said nervously, "you know we don't have to do this."

"Yes, I do," the boy replied, wishing he still had his fishhook. "Stay close."

A few minutes later, they were standing over a wrecked boat named the *Snark Hunter*. Beside it were the remnants of a bonfire, where someone had been roasting centipedes. "It looks like a campsite," Sir Tode whispered. "Only it's deserted."

Or rather, it *looked* deserted. Peter listened to the cool air—there were definitely heartbeats nearby. The boy raised his open hands and cleared his throat:

Blinded and binded in whitest yarn,
Here comes Peter Nimble, who means no harm!

There was a brief pause, then came the sound of several men pulling themselves out of the sand where they had been hiding. Peter heard five in all. Each smelled quite a bit like Old Scabbs and probably looked no better.

"We thought you was marauders," one of them explained, embarrassed.

"Or Officer Trolley," another said.

"Or ravens," spoke a third. And at this final thought, each of them shuddered.

"We're fellow prisoners," Peter said. "And we're looking to get to the ravens' nest."

The old men responded with concerned chuckles. "I'm afraid you've got it backward, sonny," a stout one named Patch said. "You're trying to keep *away* from the Nest. Far as possible, in fact. Here, sit down and have yourself some dust maggot; maybe that'll clear your head." The old men all shuffled closer, urging Peter and Sir Tode to join them around the fire, which they relit. The two newcomers sat down, realizing just how hungry the previous day had left them.

Over dinner, the prisoners introduced themselves as Patch, Clipper, Cough, Bogie, and Twiddlesticks.

"Those are all burgle trades," Peter said upon hearing their names. "Just like Old Scabbs." Scabbing, if you are not aware, is the art of swapping goods. For example, if you were interested in stealing a ruby ring off of someone's finger, you would take the ring and leave a bit of twine tied 'round a pebble so that the victim wouldn't notice that their precious jewelry had gone missing until they actually *looked* at their finger. This is exactly what Poor Old Scabbs had tried doing when he replaced the lemon from Peter's bag with a rock.

"Of course, chum!" the one named Twiddlesticks said. "We're all called after our thieving specialties—just like you, Peter *Nimble*."

"Who says I'm a thief?" the boy protested.

The one named Bogie leaned close. "Why, when you been at it as long as us, you gets a feel for it, hmm?"

"And from what I spy, I'd say you was among the very best," Clipper added. The other men muttered in agreement, saying things like, "Those fingers!" and "Slinks like a shadow!"

Peter blushed, remembering what Professor Cake had said at the beginning of their journey about him being a great thief. "Thanks, I guess."

While enjoying their grub(s), Peter and Sir Tode listened to the old men share stories about life in the Just Deserts. The men explained how the ravens slept heavy at night and let the prisoners roam free—provided they remained completely hidden during the day. Sir Tode treated them to a harrowing retelling of what had happened to Poor Old Scabbs, and how he was now buried at the foot of Kettle Rock.

"That's a shame," Clipper tsked. "He had a right nice tooth, he did. I've half a mind to visit the grave—only it's too dangerous, seeing as how the ravens is always flapping about there."

"So you won't go near Kettle Rock?" Peter said. "Even at night?"

"Not a chance," the thief named Bogie said. "I ain't ventured by there in eight years, not since my first run-in with a pair of guard birds." He raised his hand, showing off his three missing fingers. "Only reason Scabbs went anywheres near that place is on account of him being touched in the head."

"If you don't go to Kettle Rock, how do you find water?"

The old men all smacked their mouths in wistful silence. "Oh, you gets used to it," Cough said, wheezing.

This was just the opportunity Peter had hoped for. "Maybe I can help with that?" he said to the men. "My friend and I have come here because we need your help. We have to get something back that the ravens stole from us."

Patch spat bitterly into the sand. "'Course they stole from you, sonny. That's what they do is steals from us till we gots nothing left. Why, everything we ever had in the world is locked up in that Nest of theirs."

The tallest of the group, Twiddlesticks, slid close to Peter. He placed a long, spindly arm on the boy's shoulder. "Don't mean to let you down, chum. But it's not likely we're going to cross those birdies again. We're lucky they let us live at all."

"If there's one law in the Just Deserts," Clipper added, "it's that you be good and grateful that the ravens is so soft on us. They have good cause to wants us dead!" A few of the others groaned at this sentiment.

"But what did you *do* to make them hate you all so much?" Sir Tode said. "I'm sure it's a story worth hearing."

The men lowered their heads, hemming awkwardly. Only Clipper answered, muttering something about how "awful bad" they had behaved. "Why, the sound of those cries shivers me right to this day," he said.

Peter felt a flash of annoyance at Sir Tode's changing the topic of conversation. Who cared what these old men had done? What mattered was the mission. He rose, returning to his subject. "My companion and I are going with or without you. However, if you agree to help us, I can give you something in return." He pulled the rumbling wineskin out of his bag. "Clear, fresh rainwater." He uncorked the end and began to pour the bottle's contents out onto the sand. Seeing this, the prisoners dropped to the ground, took handfuls of mud into their mouths, and sucked the grains dry, moaning with relief.

Peter replaced the cork, cutting off their supply. "This skin contains a bit of magic inside that can give you enough water for ten lifetimes. If you help us, it's yours."

The prisoners looked to one another, their mouths still full of sand. Peter dangled the prize before them, letting them hear the rumbling rain cloud trapped inside. The five men watched the wondrous wineskin, their bodies swaying back and forth ever so slightly.

Twiddlesticks spat the sand from his mouth and stood up. "Right, chum. What'd you have in mind?"

+ + +

Peter knew that the key to succeeding with a major burglary was preparation. If they were to have any hope of getting the Fantastic Eyes back, he would need as much information as possible. "First I need to know about this Nest," he said to them.

"It's like this," Twiddlesticks explained. "The Nest is big . . . real big. It sticks out of the sand like a giant's thimble. Guard birds are everywhere—especially in daytime, when they're all flapping about."

Peter nodded. "So we need to hit them before sunrise, while they're still asleep. That way we will only have to deal with a few guards and not a whole army." He turned to the old man named Patch. "I'm going to need a diversion. What materials have you got with you?"

"Nothing much. Maybe a few scraps o' sail and whatnot."

Peter scowled, thinking. "You'll have to pull more things together for this job. Can you fashion an axe?"

The thief responded with a delighted cackle. "I think I sees what you're up to, sonny. I'll get right on it!"

"Twiddlesticks, you'll do locks with me."

"Of course, chum," he said, cracking his knuckles.

"Bogie, we're going to need you to go in there and learn the layout first. Just find out where the locks are and how many guards are stationed at what posts."

The thief named Bogie sighed. "I was afraid of that . . . it's only, I'm out of practice something awful."

"I'm sure it's been a long time," Peter said. "But some things you never forget. Meet us back here in an hour."

"Right, right." Bogie picked himself up and marched toward the horizon.

Sir Tode almost swallowed his tongue as he watched the prisoner walk away. With each step, Bogie's figure blended into the surroundings until there was nothing left. "Why, he's disappeared completely!" Only when the knight squinted his eyes and looked in the *exact* right place could he make out footprints forming in the sand. "Is that a thieving magic?"

"No, just a knack," Peter said. Unable to see for himself, the boy was glad to hear that Bogie was so good at his trade. It seemed every thief here possessed skills beyond anything he had encountered back home—skills that nearly rivaled his own. He just hoped that it would be enough. "Cough," he said, returning to the plan. "I'll need you to distract the guards when we get there. Think you can pull them away?"

"Easy-peasy," Cough said, already collecting a supply of good pebbles for his pouch.

Peter moved to the last of them. "And that brings us to you, Clipper. I need you waiting at the cough to jump out and—"

"N-n-no, sir!" the thief interrupted. "I know what you're gonna ask of me, and I won't do it!"

"We need you," Peter persisted. "Without you to clip, the guards will be able to alert the whole flock, and then we're good as dead. You can use my bag."

"I said no! I'm not doin' it again!" By now the old man was choking back dry sobs. "I agreed to help nick the joint, but I *won't* clip nobody—it's too much!" He backed away from the group.

"Be reasonable, chum," Twiddlesticks said, a note of menace in his voice. "You know the boy's plan won't bloody work without a clipper. Besides, it's not like you haven't done it before."

Peter folded his arms. "I need a clipper. And if I don't get one, the deal is off. No wineskin."

"Wineskin, pshh!" Clipper kicked the sand. "This whole business stinks something awful! I don't want no part in it! Never again—I swore it!" He stepped close to Peter, whispering, "You watch yourself, little one. *There ain't no shelter in a den o' thieves!*" This was a well-known thieving proverb, but the boy hadn't the slightest idea how it applied to his situation. Before he could respond, the old man turned heel and ran for the hills. Peter listened to him stagger over the dunes, moaning, "Never again!"

"What was that about?" the boy said, turning back to the rest of the group.

"Ignore him," Twiddlesticks said. "He's a coward with a conscience." At this, the other men chuckled. "You still got us. Bogie can clip well enough. He's not as fast, but he can tie a knot with the best of 'em."

Peter sighed. It wasn't ideal, but it would work. "So it's settled. We meet back here in an hour and head for the Nest."

"Right!" The men sprang from their seats and started off in different directions.

Peter and Sir Tode now sat alone before the warm fire. "I hope this works," the boy said, showing uncertainty for the first time. "These men are great thieves. But I'm not sure they can be trusted." He patted the rumbling wineskin in his bag, just to double-check that it was still there.

"Peter?" Sir Tode cleared his throat. "Have you got any job for me?"

The boy had been afraid the knight would ask this. "Not tonight. I'm going to need you to just stay close."

"But—"

"These men are experts. You're going to have to trust me." He offered a halfhearted smile. "Don't worry, though—I'm sure your gifts will be of use soon enough."

✦ ✦ ✦

The thieves returned within the hour, each one practically giddy with anticipation. Twiddlesticks had rubbed his finger joints with some sort of foul-smelling worm extract that left them shining and slick. He was now talking sweetly to each of his long fingers, calling them his "lovelies." Bogie had come back early and was already drawing a map of the Nest's layout in the sand for the others. Cough had his pouch crammed full of smooth, round pebbles, perfect for throwing.

When Patch came around, the group nearly had a heart attack. He was wearing what (from a distance) looked exactly like a ragged military uniform. "The warden!" Sir Tode gasped as the axe-wielding figure lumbered over the hill.

The prisoners instantly jumped to their feet and ran for the dunes. Peter waved his arms, calling them back. "It's just Patch! I can smell him."

The others hesitated for a moment. They looked behind them to see the "warden" on the sand, doubled over with laughter. "I got you sorry lot!" He shook so hard his wig slipped off, revealing Patch's ruddy face. "Got you good, I did!" The thieves tiptoed closer until they were all huddled around him. The man had somehow dyed his rags to look the spit-and-image of Officer Trolley. The axe they had been so afraid of was just a few scraps of splintered wood.

"Well, I'll be snickered," Twiddlesticks said. "It's really you."

"Told you I was good!" Patch twirled his wig on one finger. "None of you lot believed me before when I says I was the best patch there ever was! Shoulda seen your ruddy faces when I come over that hill, though! Showed you good, I did!" He launched into new fits of laughter.

"Excellent," Peter said, nodding. "If he fooled all of you, he'll definitely fool the ravens."

The group took off for the eastern horizon shortly after midnight. In order to keep pace, Peter suggested that Sir Tode ride in his bag. "This might be a good place for you to stay during the mission," he said in an effort to spare the knight's feelings. "If I'm in trouble, you can spring out and surprise whoever's attacking."

Sir Tode was beginning to feel left out. "The professor gave me one job, Peter—to be your eyes. How can I do that from the bottom of a bag?"

Peter ignored the question and kept walking with the thieves.

The moon lit their way as they dashed over cool, sandy hills. Peter heard muffled heartbeats, but they encountered no one. "Where are all the other prisoners?" he finally asked Twiddlesticks.

The old thief hemmed. "Oh, they're around, chum. Just shy is all."

The group reached the Nest about an hour before dawn. Peter ducked behind the closest hill and let Sir Tode out of his bag for a breath of fresh air. "What's it look like?" he asked his companion.

Sir Tode peeked over the crest. "Good heavens . . . it's *gigantic*." For once, he was not exaggerating. The Nest that stood before them was at least a hundred feet high. The entire thing was made from scraps of wrecked boats. It was indeed shaped a bit like a massive thimble, only more narrow. Rising up from its base were four turrets, each guarded by ravens flying night watch.

Sir Tode huddled close to his friend. "Peter, are you sure about this plan? We don't know the whole story behind this place." He cast a nervous glance at the four prisoners creeping over the dunes. "And these men—"

"—are the only chance we have," Peter said. "Besides, without them, I can't get back the Fantastic Eyes and finish my mission."

Sir Tode fell silent for a moment. "I thought it was *our* mission . . . ," he murmured softly.

Peter and the thieves assembled behind a dune facing the rear wall. Bogie filled them in with a few more details. "Now, I seen three guard birds at each side, that's six in all. There's a couple more flappers at each high turret and maybe the odd patrol bird inside. The main barracks is where the birds is sleeping—you *don't* want to linger there. You should find a staircase that'll take you straight to the toppermost level. That's where they hides their treasure. Now, there's locks plenty on that door, so Twiddlesticks and sonny gots their work cut out for 'em."

"Think you can handle it, chum?" Twiddlesticks asked, nudging Peter.

The boy grinned, cracking his knuckles. "Just try and keep up." Despite the unpleasant company, he was beginning to enjoy being in his element—here was a whole band of adults that admired and respected his abilities. He helped Sir Tode into his satchel and slung it over one shoulder. "Are we ready?"

"Of course," the others replied.

By now you have witnessed how truly gifted Peter Nimble is, despite his handicap. You have heard him referred to as a master thief by multiple authorities, and you have seen him work his way out of numerous dangerous situations. You may be thinking that his blindness is no handicap at all, and that it somehow gives him an advantage over the average seeing person. Some of you may even be thinking to yourselves, "Boy! I wish *I* were blind like the great Peter Nimble!" If you are thinking that, stop right now. Because whatever benefits you may believe that blindness carries with it, you must understand that there are just as many disadvantages.

For example, if you were to give an order to a bunch of thieving prisoners, and they answered "of course" while smiling to one another and rubbing their hands, you would see this and know that they were planning something terrible—which was exactly the case here. Peter Nimble, however, could *not* see this, and therefore was not alerted to any immediate danger. Normally, Sir Tode would spot this sort of thing, but since he was confined to the bag, the shifting eyes, rubbing hands, and nasty smiles went undetected.

"Good," the boy said, totally oblivious. "Let's get to it." And with that, Peter, Sir Tode, and four untrustworthy thieves crept toward the Nest.

eter's plan had several parts. The first was to get past the perimeter guards; the next was to take care of the ravens on the turrets. Luckily, he had an expert patch, a brilliant cougher, and a serviceable clipper.

Peter and the others hung back while Patch—still dressed exactly like Officer Trolley—went out to meet the guards. If you haven't guessed, a "patch" is someone who disguises himself, usually in fine clothes, in order to get close to a target. Patches generally operate near or within gaming rooms, wedding chapels, and other spots filled with well-dressed, stupid people. Peter knew from the conversation at Kettle Rock that the ravens were on speaking terms with the warden; he only hoped that the guard birds wouldn't see through the makeshift disguise too quickly.

"Hey, you lot!" he heard Patch call in his best Officer Trolley imitation. "How goes the night?"

"It goes as it should, warden," one of the ravens replied. "We fly vigil, protecting our sleeping brothers. Why are you so far from your post? You know you are not welcome here."

"Ease off. I was only in the area and thought I'd say hello."

"Which you have done. Now, go before we lose patience with you," the bird said.

It sounded to Peter like Officer Trolley and the ravens were not on the best terms. Still, they weren't attacking him . . . yet.

While Patch tried his best to keep the conversation going, Cough crept past the guards and around the side of the structure. His body was buried under the sand with only his eyes and nose poking out for air, like some kind of bearded crocodile. When he was within throwing distance of the Nest, he lifted his arm from the sand and tested the wind.

A "cough" is a burgling trick where you create a distraction by making a noise. The most common cough is when an amateur thief hurls a rock through a nearby window, hoping to draw a dim-witted watchman away from his post. Cough, however, was no amateur, and when he set to throwing rocks, the effect was nothing short of magical. Taking several pebbles from his pouch, he tossed them one at a time into the darkness. With each flick of his wrist, another stone fell, sounding exactly like a footfall in the sand. To enhance the deception, he tossed his voice in the same direction, making it sound as though two people were whispering as they ran past.

"Silence, Trolley!" a guard bird snapped, interrupting Patch in the middle of a knock-knock joke. The bird hopped around and peered into the darkness. "Who goes?" he cawed.

Cough tossed another handful of stones around the corner.

The raven heard the sounds again and turned back to his brethren. "There's definitely someone out there. It could be the strangers."

"Could be!" the "warden" said in agreement. "You lot better have yourselves a look. I'll watch things here."

"Not likely," the first bird snapped. "Aaron, stay behind and keep an eye on this one."

"Yes, sir!" the young raven named Aaron responded. The other guards flew around the corner to inspect the noise.

Peter listened to the action from his hiding place. The way was almost clear. Right now, Bogie was waiting just around the corner with an empty sack, ready to clip the approaching guard birds. "Clipping" is a thieving term for kidnapping, usually performed on young heirs in hopes of winning a ransom. Though Bogie was strong, Peter knew that what they needed was an expert—someone fast and steady who wouldn't become confused by struggling victims. He found himself wondering why Clipper had abandoned the group.

The guards touched down right beside Bogie, who had completely melted into the shadows. He may not have been an expert clip,
but he had his own knack that assured him the element of surprise.
Within a few short seconds all three birds were trapped in his bag,
flapping and crowing like mad. To muffle the sound, Bogie buried
his victims in the sand, stomping down on the mound. "That ought
to keep you flappers quiet," he said, grinning.

The noise of the clipping had not gone unnoticed. Aaron, the
remaining guard, looked toward the sounds. "G-g-good Justice!"
he said to the man he thought was Officer Trolley. "Did you hear
that?! Maybe we should call someone?"

Patch raised his wooden axe. "You ask me, that sounds like a
bloody awful idea." Before Aaron could make a noise, the thief swung
his weapon down.

Thwump!

Peter winced as he heard the blade strike the bird's body. The
boy took a deep breath, reminding himself that the ravens were evil.
He heard Patch give a low whistle, signaling that the way was secure.
Peter and Twiddlesticks lifted themselves out from the sand and
crept toward the Nest.

Since ravens could fly, they had no need for a front door; instead,
they came and went through holes in the plank walls. The birds had
taken care to ensure that these gaps were too narrow for a full-
grown adult to pass through. But not a boy of ten. "All right, chum,"
Twiddlesticks said, giving Peter a boost. "Easy on the landing."

Peter wriggled between the broken mastheads and shattered oars (earning himself and Sir Tode more than a few splinters in the process). He reached the other side and dropped to the ground without a sound. "I'm in," he whispered back through the wall.

"Stairs is to your left," he heard Twiddlesticks say. "I'll be waiting at the drop."

Peter kept a hand against the wall as he crept through the fortress. Bogie's description had not done the place justice. While he did mention a barracks full of sleeping ravens, he failed to explain that the barracks took up the *entire* Nest. Peter stilled his nerves as he listened to the thousands of tiny heartbeats—each one a different deadly bird, asleep on its perch. He felt Sir Tode trembling through his bag. The boy reached inside and gently massaged the knight's ears. "Calm down," he whispered to his friend. "I've got everything under control."

Peter's foot came to a rickety staircase. He knelt down and put his ear to the first step, testing for creaky spots with his fingers. Only then did he dare place his weight upon the plank. He did this with each and every step, climbing higher and higher above the sleeping birds.

Halfway up the tower he came to an opening in the wall. He could hear Twiddlesticks pacing back and forth in the sand below. Behind him were Patch, Cough, and Bogie, stuffing the last of the guards into sacks. Peter took a length of rope, which had been painstakingly woven from assorted body hair, and tossed an end down. Twiddlesticks grabbed hold of the cord and was soon standing with Peter inside the Nest. Without a word, the two thieves continued up the stairs.

They arrived at the topmost deck to find a long balcony running along the back walls. Scattered everywhere were piles of nautical equipment—fishing nets, compasses, sextants, and sails. Just as Bogie had said, a locked door stood in the back corner. Peter couldn't smell any treasure, but the scent of the Fantastic Eyes was strong enough. "This is the spot," he said.

Twiddlesticks cracked his knuckles. "All right, my lovelies. Time to shine." It had already been decided that he would take the outer padlocks while Peter would manage the dead bolt in the center. To be assigned the more difficult lock was a great honor, and Peter couldn't help but feel proud as he slipped his finger into the narrow keyhole and set to work on the tumbler.

They finished the job in less than ten minutes. "That dead bolt was a chore and a half," Twiddlesticks said, pushing the door open. "Couldn't a done it without you, chum."

"Let's just find my box and get out of here." At this point, Peter thought it might be safe to let the knight out of the bag. He pulled the flap back so Sir Tode could look about. "Not a word," he whispered. "I can't let you walk about—your hooves make too much noise."

Sir Tode peered around the moonlit chamber, letting his eyes adjust. The treasure room had very little treasure to speak of, and he couldn't help but think that it looked more like an armory than anything else. There were no jewels, no paintings, no fine cutlery—only stacks and stacks of knives, harpoons, and sharpened oars. He looked up at Peter, but the boy was too focused on finding his box to note the irregularity. Nor did he seem to notice when Bogie, Patch, and Cough snuck into the room after Twiddlesticks. Now they were all four of them silently hurling armloads of weapons out the window and onto the sand below.

"Um, Peter . . ." Sir Tode whispered.

"*Shhh!*" the boy hissed. "You don't know how to burgle-whisper. If you wake the ravens, we're all dead." Peter set back to feeling his way across the room. His nimble hands were still groping about for the box when he came across a sharp blade. "*Ow!*" he cried, sucking the blood from his cut palm. "What's a spear doing in a treasure room?"

The other thieves were too busy with their own work to pay any heed to his question.

Sir Tode tried again. "Peter, I *really think* you should—"

"Found it!" Peter exclaimed. And indeed he had: on a small table in the middle of the room sat the Haberdasher's box; beside it lay the fishhook. Peter took back his weapon and then opened the box, checking to make sure all six eyes were still inside. "Now let's get out of here," he said quietly.

"Not so fast, chum," a voice spoke behind him. Before the boy could move, a set of long, well-oiled fingers snatched him by the throat. "It was real swell of you to come up with a plan for sneaking into the roost like this, but I think I'll take the helm from here out."

Peter struggled against the grip. "Twiddlesticks?"

"Feels good to have a blade in my hand again." The thief pressed a rusted dagger against Peter's throat. "This job just got a lot bigger than your little nick. Now, why don't you give us whatever's in that pretty little box of yours? You do that and I might even let you fight on our side."

"Your *side?*" Peter was about to say something naive, like "I'm confused, what side?" when he was interrupted by a shout from outside.

"Ambushhh!!!"

The four thieves darted to the window and looked below. "It's Clipper!" Bogie said. "That backstabbin' rat!"

The old thief was tearing over the dunes, waving his arms and screaming with all his might. "Ambush!" Clipper wailed. "They're coming to kill you, birdies! Wake up! Wake—!" Peter heard someone grab hold of the shouting man. There were sounds of a struggle, and then nothing.

"Looks like ol' Cross-Stitch got him!" Bogie said, delighted. But it was too late—Clipper's cries had already awoken the ravens.

The thieves listened to confused squawks in the barracks below. "Titus? Aaron?!" Captain Amos shouted, sounding the alarm. "Come alive, brothers! We're under attack!" The fortress shook as every bird inside leapt from its perch and flapped into formation.

"You heard the cap'n," Twiddlesticks said to Patch, who was clutching a rusted foghorn. "Rally the rogues!" Patch put the horn to his lips and let out a loud, long blast.

Far below, hundreds of wild, roaring, hairy men leapt from hiding spots in the sand. They scrambled across the dunes, grabbing whatever weapon they could find. Waving their knives, spears, and harpoons in the air, the prisoners of the Just Deserts stormed the Nest.

The moonlit sands, which had been quiet only the moment before, were instantly transformed into a bloody battlefield. Cries echoed across the dunes as blade struck beak. With the help of their newly returned weapons, the prisoners were easily able to hack a hole into the base of the Nest. Now the thieves were stomping their way through the darkness, murdering anything that moved. The ravens were great warriors, but confined by the walls, they had neither the range for attack nor the height for retreat.

"Long live the True King!" Captain Amos shouted above the tumult.

"And long live his Line!" his troops echoed as they flapped and pecked at their attackers.

Peter and Sir Tode had by now fled to the open balcony and

were trying to find the stairway. "Good heavens," the knight said, watching the carnage through gaps in the floor. "It's a massacre."

Peter didn't need to be told this—he could hear the squawks of dying ravens everywhere. He gripped the deck and tried to calm himself. This is what he wanted, wasn't it? The ravens were evil, and he was supposed to stop them. No matter how much the boy repeated this to himself, he couldn't shake the feeling that he had just let something terrible happen.

"Peter!" Sir Tode snapped him back to attention. "We've got to get out of here! The birds are coming our way!"

Sure enough, a troop of ravens burst through the deck, showering them in splinters. "By the lookout!" one of them squawked. "They've got the strangers surrounded!"

"Kill the traitors!" another cawed.

Twiddlesticks and the other thieves formed a tight circle to protect themselves from attack. Peter, who was caught in the middle of this formation, crawled through the men's legs and headed for the stairs. He was so overwhelmed by the frenzy of the fighting that he didn't realize he was moving in the wrong direction—straight for the edge of the balcony.

Sir Tode, who was still riding on Peter's back, looked up just in time. "Peter, stop!" he cried.

The boy froze, heart pounding. "What is it? What do you see?"

"There's a sheer drop right in front of you. And it's over-looking a great chasm!"

Peter inched back from the ledge—he had nearly just crawled them straight to their deaths. "Can we jump across it?" he asked.

"Goodness, no!" Words could not capture the enormousness of the thing yawning before them. It was miles long and miles deep. *This* was the large black stripe that Sir Tode had seen on the eastern horizon. "I can't even see the other side," he said. Peter understood for the first time since landing in the Just Deserts how truly inescapable this prison was.

The combat was raging all around them. It sounded as though the ravens were starting to keep up their end of the fight. The battle had smashed several holes into the Nest wall, which afforded them the maneuverability necessary for battle. They dove toward the thieves, unleashing wave after wave of attack. Captain Amos, who had flapped his way to the balcony, was striking fiercely at Twiddlesticks, shouting, "Die, traitor!!!" with every snap of his beak.

Birds were flying all around Peter and Sir Tode, nearly pushing them over the edge of the balcony. "Back, villains!" the knight shouted, swatting his forehooves to keep the attackers at bay.

Peter was overwhelmed by the chaos. His keen senses faltered in the midst of the gruesome noises, foul smells, and jarring movements all around him. He drew his fishhook from his bag and weakly swiped at empty air. He began to fear they would be pecked to pieces or knocked into the precipice. He covered his ears, trying to drown out the noise, but it was useless. "I don't know what to do!" he said, choking back a sob. "I can't sort out anything I'm hearing."

"We'll have none of that!" Sir Tode said, pulling Peter's hands away from his ears. "We broke into this place to get those Fantastic Eyes—I say we put them to use!"

The thought of using the eyes frightened Peter. The last time he had tried a pair at Sir Tode's behest, it had nearly killed him. But what other option did they have? He pulled the box from his bag, opened the lid, and reached inside. When he touched the eyes, however, he found his hands were shaking too hard to tell different pairs apart. "Help me!" he called. "I don't know which pair to use!"

The knight dropped to his hooves and galloped to Peter's side. "Just stay calm and let me think." He looked at each of the three pairs. The black eyes were out of the question, and for all he knew the green ones were just as bad. "We had better stick to the pair we know," he said. Sir Tode was using the word "we" when he really meant "you." He had already decided that his only concern was getting Peter away safely—even if that meant being left behind himself. He took the golden eyes in his teeth and tried to think of a way the boy might use them to get clear of the ravens and prisoners. But from where he stood, all he could see was endless desert and bottomless pit. Then he caught a glint of something metal behind him. It was an old spyglass, salvaged from one of the wrecked boats.

Sir Tode dropped the two eyes into Peter's shaking palm. "I want you to concentrate on my voice," he instructed. "I'm going to get you out of here, but first I need you to follow me *very closely*." Peter nodded dumbly and placed his hand on Sir Tode's back. He followed the knight into the fray.

The spyglass was mounted to the end of a long plank that jutted out over the chasm like a diving board. Sir Tode hoped the rotting wood was strong enough to support their weight. Steeling his nerves, he placed a hoof on its surface and inched out over the chasm. "You're lucky you can't see this," he said, eyeing the darkness below. At last they reached the spyglass, which was pointed toward the horizon. The knight couldn't tell what was out there, but *just maybe* this device could. He rose to his hind legs and squinted through the eyepiece: in the distance, he could make out the faint silhouette of a tower against the predawn light.

Sir Tode dropped down. "Listen carefully, Peter. I need you to place the gold eyes so they're peering into this spyglass— steady hands now, we can't afford to misfire."

Before Peter could say a word of disagreement, Sir Tode

clambered atop his shoulders, allowing him access to the spyglass. The boy reached out and pressed the first golden eye against the eyepiece. He could feel the plank sagging under their combined weight. "Get the stranger!" he heard a voice crow. "He's on the lookout!" Birds swooped above and below them. Talons rained down like black hail, clawing at his arms, his clothes.

Twiddlesticks rolled across the deck and staked his blade through a fallen bird's chest. "It's the boy they're after—clip 'im!" A surge of prisoners followed his command, charging toward Peter. A thief in front crept onto the plank—knife in his teeth, open bag in his hands. The wood groaned under the added weight, and Peter thought he heard a rusted nail snap.

"Once and never again!" Captain Amos squawked, swooping down and knocking the man right over the edge. The thief's scream continued down and down until it faded into nothing. Peter felt the ravens form a tight circle around him and Sir Tode. The maneuver confused Peter; it seemed like the ravens were trying to *protect* him—but that made no sense. "Sir Tode, what's happening?!" he shouted.

"I think they're trying to knock us into the chasm!" The knight grunted as he batted his hooves in the air. "Hurry up with those bloody eyes already!"

Peter held the second eye up to the spyglass, letting it see into the distant horizon. "All done," he said.

Captain Amos flapped down toward Peter's arm. "Wait,

stranger!" he squawked over the noise. "There is something you must know! Justice has brought you to—"

"Now!" Sir Tode leapt from Peter's shoulders, knocking the bird away. "Put the eyes in *now!*"

On this command, Peter slipped the two golden eyes into his sockets. He blinked, and the sounds of battle instantly vanished. Peter felt himself falling through the open air until he landed headfirst against a flat rock, and the world went silent.

PART TWO

ONYX

CHAPTER FOURTEEN

THE PERFECT PALACE

Peter woke to find himself lying in a soft bed. The bed was so soft, in fact, that for a brief moment he thought himself floating in the Troublesome Lake again. The box of Fantastic Eyes was clenched safely in his arms. His muscles were sore and he could feel a dent in his chest where the hinges had dug into his breastbone. He slowly pried his fingers away from the wood and massaged his stiff arms back to life. How long had he been holding the box like that? Just to be safe, he opened the lid and checked to make sure the eyes were still there. The black and green pairs sat in their individual eggshells, just like always. For a moment he panicked—where were the golden eyes?—but then he touched his swollen eyelids and realized they were safely within his sockets. He slipped them out and placed them with the others inside the box.

Drawing back his dense comforter, Peter tried to get a fix on his surroundings. The entire room reeked of some sickly perfume, no doubt named after a flower. So far as he could smell, there was no one nearby. He propped himself up and instantly grew dizzy. Feeling his head, he discovered that it was heavily bandaged. Was he injured? How badly? The bandaging was no expert job. It seemed that someone—a child, most likely—had taken a giant ball of rags and clumsily tied them around his head. He pried back the dressing and found a deep, rather severe gash in his crown. The boy winced as his fingers probed the wound. The blood was several days old. He wondered how long he had been in this strange place.

"H-h-hello?" he said, falling back onto his great, fluffy pillow. There was no reply. "Can anyone hear me?" Still no reply. The last thing Peter could remember was being in the Just Deserts. *What had happened?* He faintly recalled something about ravens, and thieves, and—

"Sir Tode?" he called weakly. He could neither hear nor smell his friend nearby. They had been poised together over some great chasm. They had tried using the golden eyes to escape together, but now Peter was completely alone. The boy's head began to throb, and he set out a hand to steady himself. He remembered some kind of battle at the Nest. There was chaos and screaming all around them. He faintly recalled the birds swooping to his defense and their leader, Captain Amos, trying to tell him something . . .

There were definitely some pieces missing to this puzzle.

Thinking of puzzles, Peter remembered the rhyme. He took a breath and concentrated on coaxing the words from his fuzzy mind:

Kings aplenty, princes few,
The ravens scattered and seas withdrew.
Only a stranger may bring relief,
But darkness will reign, unless he's—

"Good grief!" a voice cried behind him. "You can't be up—you're *ill!*"

Peter yelped in surprise. He hadn't realized someone was nearby. "Who are you?" he said, spinning around.

A sweet voice chuckled. "Oh ho, sir! I should think the more appropriate question is: Who are *you?*" Hearing her speak, Peter could tell she meant him no harm. But where did she come from? And why did she call him "sir"?

"Me?" he said, stammering. "My name's . . . *Justice.* Um, Justice Trousers." (You must remember that Peter, who was not a skilled fibber on the best of days, was suffering from an impressive head injury, which prevented him from coming up with anything more believable.)

"Justice?" The woman pondered this for a moment. "I don't think I've heard that name before. What does it mean?"

"It's just a name," Peter fibbed again. The truth was, it was the last thing he remembered hearing before escaping from the Nest.

"Well, it's a pleasure to meet you, Mr. Trousers! My name is Mrs.

Molasses. It's an old word that means happiness and kindness." Peter knew full well that "molasses" meant no such thing and was actually a word for a sort of sticky sweet stuff used in hourglasses and candy, but he thought it rude to contradict her. The woman continued. "Sir, you are more than welcome in my home, but I insist you lie back down. I simply can't have you bleeding all over my nice clean floor." With that, she grabbed his shoulders and forced him back onto the pillow. "You really did give me a fright," she went on, puffing slightly. "What, with that icky blood everywhere, it's a wonder I got it cleaned up before the stains could set!"

Peter felt the giant mess of rags wrapped around his crown and silently agreed with her. While Mrs. Molasses tucked him back into bed, the boy put his senses to work as best as his condition would allow. From her voice he could tell Mrs. Molasses was definitely a grown-up. She reeked of the same sickly perfume as the rest of the room. Her hands were plump and soft, and she betrayed a shortness of breath when pulling up Peter's covers. By all indications, Mrs. Molasses seemed to be the sort of person usually referred to as "jolly."

"What were those words you were saying when I walked in?" she asked, fluffing a pillow. "They sounded so pretty, so *odd*."

"What were they?" The pain in his head was a dull throb now, and with each passing minute he was growing more and more obtuse. "Just a . . . nursery rhyme," he said through a yawn.

"Nursery?" She considered this. "I don't think I've heard of that word, but I do like rhymes a great deal. Why don't you get some rest, and then we can *nursery rhyme* together in the morning?" And with that, Mrs. Molasses pulled the covers tight around Peter and left him alone to fall asleep, which he did almost immediately.

✦ ✦ ✦

When Peter woke again, it was in a panic. "The eyes!" he cried out, jolting up from his pillow. His entire body was drenched in sweat, and his arms were empty. The last he could remember, the box had been tight against his chest. He faintly recalled a strange woman who had come and tucked him in (something no one had ever done before). And now the box was gone. It had all been a trick, and he had fallen for it. Peter scrambled to his feet and searched the room. He rifled through empty dressers and frisked the immaculate floor, but could find no sign of the eyes. "How could I be so stupid?" he said, slamming a drawer. "That woman's probably miles away by now."

"Yoo-hoo!" came a cheery voice directly behind him. Peter gave a start and stumbled forward. This was the second time the Molasses woman had been able to sneak up on him. He suspected it was due to the fact that she and the room were both doused in the same awful perfume—the stuff seemed to be working as a sort of camouflage, which, along with her surprisingly light step, made the woman difficult to track. "I was just off in my cleaning nook," she said, taking the box from under one arm and returning it to Peter. "It was so dirty, I thought I'd just give it a teensy little spiffing-up. Good as new!"

He checked the lock for scratches. "You didn't open it, did you?"

The woman chuckled, wagging a finger. "Oh ho! Very funny, sir.

It has a *lock* on the front—no one can open those things! I honestly don't see why you keep a box like that at all, seeing as how getting inside is quite impossible."

Peter didn't quite understand what she meant, but thought it best not to argue. "I've got a key," he explained.

"Key?" She plucked some errant leaves from a fig tree planted in the corner. "Another one of your silly words? You certainly must come from a strange place, Mr. Justice Trousers."

Talking with this woman made Peter's head hurt, but he decided to persevere, hoping to learn something about his current predicament. "Where are we? What is this place?"

"Not place, my good sir, *palace.*" She sighed. "The most perfect palace in the world!"

"How long have I been here? In this palace?"

"Well, when I found you, you were lying in the middle of my courtyard, bleeding like a fountain," she chirped. "I took you home with me, dressed your wounds, and set you to sleep right in this very bed. Three days later you woke up and introduced yourself. Do you recall that? After that, you slept another two days, and—*ta-da!*—here we are!"

"I've been here for five days?" he said, struggling to do the math.

"No, *three days* and then *two days*. Five is something else altogether . . . I think."

"And you're certain I was alone?" Peter was growing anxious to learn what had become of Sir Tode.

"Lone as a lemon drop," she said.

The boy bowed his head. His friend had not made it across the chasm. For all he knew, Sir Tode was still fighting in that awful battle—and it was all his fault. The thought filled him with pain, the twin aches of loneliness and guilt. "Speaking of lemon drops," Mrs. Molasses continued cheerily. "Are you hungry?"

While Peter felt too distraught to eat, his body disagreed. It responded to the question with a long, loud grumble. "Sounds like I am," he said, embarrassed.

Mrs. Molasses clapped. "Oh, splendid! Then come along, Mr. Trousers. Do I have a treat for you!"

✦   ✦   ✦

Peter and Mrs. Molasses bustled down long corridors and staircases, all of which smelled like fresh soap. Doors lined every hall, marking a separate home for each citizen. "Notice how perfectly clean these vestibules are!" she would say, extending arms to her left and right as they went. "The king himself sees that they are scrubbed each and every night!" Peter had since removed the rags from his head and was wearing his usual bandage around his empty sockets. If Mrs. Molasses noticed the change, she chose not to mention it. Peter darted from side to side as they walked, trying to take in every detail he could. There were lots of people about. They all smelled sweet and sounded happy. Every few feet, Mrs. Molasses would stop to introduce her guest to another neighbor. "Yoo-hoo! Mr. Bonnet! This is my new friend Mr. Trousers . . . I found him dying in my courtyard!"

"Pleased to meet you, sir!" the person would exclaim, shaking Peter's hand vigorously. "We're always happy to have visitors here in the palace!" There would follow an inevitable pause, and then: "Actually, we've never *had* any visitors before . . . but we're certainly happy to have you!"

They worked their way to a vaulted path that Peter thought might be a bridge. Sir Tode would have told him exactly what he was seeing, but he was gone now. The boy realized with shame how much he had taken his friend for granted in the desert. Sir Tode had tried to warn him against trusting the thieves, but Peter wouldn't listen. He had treated the knight as little more than a hindrance—stuffing him away in the bottom of his bag. Despite everything, Sir Tode sacrificed himself so that Peter could complete their quest. The boy swore to himself that he would do just that. "No matter the cost," he whispered.

His first step would be to verify that this was, in fact, the Vanished Kingdom. From what he could tell, the palace resembled Professor Cake's description. There was a vine-covered wall lining the outside. Balconies, bridges, and stairways ran in all different directions. Every inch of the place was carved from solid rock and furnished with lovely gardens. "It must have taken a long time to build this palace," he said to Mrs. Molasses.

"Oh, years and years!" she replied. "Our king made the entire thing with his *bare hands*. Imagine that, Mr. Trousers!"

"Why do you call me mister?" Peter said. This particular question had been bothering him for some time.

"Because you, Mr. Trousers, are a *man*," she explained. "Granted, a rather short one. But still, in our kingdom, we call all men 'mister' so-and-so, and all women 'missus' so-and-so. Now, I don't know how it works where you're from—" She gasped, touching his arm. "Heavens! I do hope it's not the other way around. That would be most embarrassing!"

"No. It's like that where I'm from, too. Everyone calls me mister." Peter didn't want to pursue the point further. Still, it was strange for this woman to be talking to him like he was a grown-up. "Mrs. Molasses, how old are you?" he asked, not understanding that such questions were never to be asked of jolly women.

"Old?" she asked.

"When was your birthday?"

"Birthday? I'm not sure I understand you. That word sounds *sort of* familiar, though . . . birthday . . . birthday . . ."

"Forget it," Peter said. He wasn't sure he knew how to explain what a birthday was to someone who didn't already know.

"Oh!" Mrs. Molasses snapped her fingers. "I bet you meant to say *bathroom!* You wanted to know where our *bathroom* was. Is that correct?"

"Er, yes . . . I never forget to wash my hands before eating," the boy said, offering his least convincing lie to date.

Mrs. Molasses led Peter to a bathroom along one corridor. Even the toilets, he noted, smelled clean and fresh. He washed his right palm, which had been cut rather badly during the fight at the Nest. The pain took him back to those final, terrifying moments on the balcony. Perched above the yawning chasm. Talons clawing at his clothes. He remembered Sir Tode's voice in his ear. The weight of his friend's hooves as the knight jumped from his shoulders. "Put the eyes in now!" he had cried as the plank snapped beneath them . . .

"Yoo-hoo, Mr. Trousers!" Mrs. Molasses's voice rang from the outside corridor. "We shouldn't want to miss our supper!"

Peter forced himself back to the present. He stepped outside, drying his hands on the tail of his shirt (as little boys do), and followed Mrs. Molasses into the Eating Hall.

The Eating Hall was a great open courtyard surrounded by stone pillars. Peter could hear water pouring down from spigots high above. The water flowed into a shallow stream that ran under footbridges and planters around the perimeter. The center floor was occupied by an enormous table, big enough for hundreds. Unlike everything else in the palace, this table was made of wood. Cut into its surface was a shallow moat filled with water. Large serving platters drifted along the surface, piled high with every type of food imaginable. People laughed and chatted, taking their seats around the table.

Peter could hear a dozen birds singing from their pedestals. These birds were not singing in the whistle-way that he was accustomed to—instead, they were actually *singing*. Their little voices rang out in perfect harmony:

> *A perfect end to a perfect day.*
> *We love our king—hip-hip hooray!*

Peter listened as they took a short breath and sang the rhyme again. And again. And again. He noticed that they seemed to mumble the line about the king every time. *These birds know about rhyming,* he thought to himself. *Maybe they could help me figure out how my riddle ends?* Each warbling voice was accompanied by a faint jingling sound that the master thief's ears couldn't quite identify. He decided to investigate the sound after dinner. In the meantime, he could smell the feast floating before him, and his stomach was demanding its due.

Peter took his seat and started to fill his plate with food. But before he was able to take a bite, Mrs. Molasses and a woman named Mrs. Sunshine each seized one of his hands. The entire table raised their arms, saying "Long live the king!" in unison. The birds joined them with somewhat less enthusiasm.

Long live the king. Peter mulled the words over in his mind. There was something familiar about that phrase. Wasn't that the rallying cry of the ravens in the Just Deserts? But somehow it sounded different the way Mrs. Molasses and her friends said it.

The food smelled just as Mrs. Molasses had described it: absolutely perfect. The honey crepes were thick and tender. The oak loin was ripe and juicy. For drinking, everyone had goblets of whole cream. It was a feast beyond Peter's wildest imaginings. But every time he took a bite, his taste buds caught a faint, earthy bitterness beneath the surface. And no matter how much he drank, he could never completely wash down the bad flavor. Still, it was food, and his stomach appreciated the attention.

Peter helped himself to plate after plate, all the while eaves-dropping on the conversations around him. From what he could tell, the whole palace gathered for a feast like this every night. "Without a feast to cap it off, the day simply wouldn't be perfect, now, would it?" Mrs. Molasses said, dabbing her lips with a serviette.

Peter was starting to agree with her about this place being perfect. Everyone was polite, happy, and well fed. He was even getting used to being called sir. He thought how much nicer his life would have been if someone like Mrs. Molasses had adopted him instead of nasty Mr. Seamus. This entire palace seemed as though it had been plucked straight from his own dreams . . . only, *not quite*. Like the food, there was something behind the clean floors and cheery voices that made him uneasy.

Just then, the air was split by a deafening sound—*Clanggg!* It echoed across the courtyard, shaking the foundation. "Bedtime! Bedtime!" the people screamed, throwing goblets and forks from their hands and instantly leaping to their feet. Every one of their voices was tinged with the unmistakable sound of terror.

Clanggg! The noise came again; this time Peter recognized it as the bell of a giant clock—but much larger than the one he grew up with. He thought it strange that he hadn't heard the hands moving during supper. The clock chimed again and again, shaking the plates and cutlery. "What's happening?" he said as Mrs. Molasses dragged him from his seat at the table. "What about the mess? What about *dessert?*"

"No time for questions!" She was pushing him through the crowd. "We must get home for tuck-in!"

Despite her size, the woman was surprisingly fast, and it was all Peter could do to keep up. He tried to get her to slow down, but it was no use. With each chime of the clock, she and the others grew more and more terrified. As they frantically raced up bridges and stairways, the perfect palace was transformed into sheer pandemonium.

Mrs. Molasses rounded a corner and thrust Peter into her home. "Safe!" She dove in after him and slammed the door, still panting, still trembling. "One mustn't *ever* drag his heels at tuck-in, or else . . ." and here her words trailed off as some unspeakable fear caught her throat.

"Or else what?" he asked gently.

Mrs. Molasses swallowed, pushing the fear back down. "Or else you won't get enough sleep, Mr. Trousers!" She smoothed her apron and re-pinned her hair. "Off to bed now!"

Peter knew she wasn't telling the truth. Like all adults, Mrs. Molasses made the mistake of thinking that people simply believed what they were told. But Peter, even more than most, had a knack for picking out false notes—and in this moment, Mrs. Molasses's cheery tone sounded nothing if not false.

He followed his host into the spare bedroom. The great bell was still chiming. "Gosh," he said in his most innocent voice, "that giant clock sure is fancy."

"Clock?" she said, confused. "Oh! You mean the *Bedtime Bell*. Never you mind that. It's just a bit of the king's magic to help tuck us in." The boy was confused by her explanation—he had never heard anyone refer to a clock as "magic" before. The woman helped him into bed, changing the subject. "I am stuffed! Wasn't that a simply *perfect* supper?"

The Bedtime Bell struck its final chime, and then Peter heard a deep, clockwork rumble that *ticked* and *whirred* all around them—behind the walls, underneath the floor, above the ceiling. It was as though the very stones were alive. Mrs. Molasses happily went on with her work, paying no notice to the trembling houseplants and furniture.

The rumbling stopped as abruptly as it had begun, ending with a *Skhhrrr—THUD!* The sound was familiar to Peter's ears: A dead bolt had slid tight across Mrs. Molasses's front door. He could hear the *thud!* of dozens of other dead bolts doing the same all down the corridor. Somehow, the clockwork was locking every door in the palace.

At last, there was silence once more. Mrs. Molasses put the finishing touches on Peter's bed, softly humming the bird-song from supper:

A perfect end to a perfect day
We love our king—hip-hip hooray!

"There, all snug!" she said, patting Peter's bandaged head. "And just think, we get to do it all again tomorrow!" She blew out the candle and shuffled off to her own perfect bedroom.

A CHAT *with* PICKLE

Not ten minutes after Mrs. Molasses had extinguished the lights and glided off to her bedroom, Peter discovered for himself what had so frightened all the people at supper.

There was a monster in the palace.

He could hear it in the corridors outside. It moved with a terrible *scraping, clinking, shuffling* sound that seemed to echo on forever. Its voice was even worse—a hollow, miserable wail that curdled Peter's stomach and turned his arms to gooseflesh. He listened, pulling the covers tight around his body. Was this what he'd come to save them from?

If there was one thing Peter found even more disturbing than the awful noises outside, it was the fact that Mrs. Molasses was sound asleep in the next room. There was no way she couldn't hear the horrible monster just outside her door. And yet she was peacefully dreaming the night away in her perfectly made bed. The boy supposed that after enough time, a person could grow accustomed to anything—no matter how loud it growled and moaned and rattled and roared. Peter, however, had far too many questions to even think about sleeping. He decided it would be best to go investigate. From the king's extreme security precautions, it was clear that the monster was very, very dangerous—otherwise those giant dead bolts wouldn't be necessary. "If only I had my fishhook," he thought for the hundredth time that night. He had already checked his bedroom for something that might make a weapon, but the best he could do was a throw pillow.

Peter tucked the box of Fantastic Eyes under one arm and crept into the foyer. When he reached the front door, he knelt down and placed his ear against its surface. Through the metal he could hear a hundred shuffling footsteps. Was it a giant centipede? No, Peter could now make out that what he had thought to be one horrible voice was actually a chorus of dozens—all grunting, moaning, and wheezing. The boy waited patiently until the monster, or monsters, had disappeared around the corner, and then he set to work.

For Peter, as we know, the average dead bolt, though tricky, was hardly insurmountable. But the lock on Mrs. Molasses's front door was far from average. The mechanism was made of thrice-tempered steel and reinforced by gears in the door frame. "Who would make a door that locks on both sides?" he wondered quietly.

Since waking up in the palace, the boy had been spending more and more time talking out loud to himself like this. While for some people that may be a sign of madness, for Peter it was more a sign of loneliness.

The boy knew that without the proper tools, he couldn't open the door—which meant he would have to find another way out of the house. He could find no windows along the front wall, but he did notice a faint breeze flowing out from beneath Mrs. Molasses's bedroom door. He turned the handle and slipped inside.

Mrs. Molasses was asleep in her bed. Peter could hear the woman tossing her head, caught up in some kind of nightmare. "N–n–no," she moaned. "Give him back . . . Give him back!" The master thief moved to the far wall of the room and searched for the source of the draft. The air was coming through a screen door that opened onto a small courtyard. He stepped outside, taking extra care not to disturb Mrs. Molasses as he passed.

The temperature in the courtyard was mild—perfect, really. Peter paused, enjoying the moonlight against his skin. "This must be the yard where Mrs. Molasses found me," he said to himself. Getting out of the perfumed house meant that he could finally use his nose again. He took a long, deep breath . . .

He could smell Sir Tode!

Peter raced to the center of the yard and pressed his nose against the cold stones. There was a bit of dried blood in the mortar cracks. Some of it belonged to Peter; some of it belonged to Sir Tode. "We both made it across," he whispered, almost afraid to speak his hope aloud. "But how did we get separated?"

He studied the ground for more clues. He could feel chips in the stone where they had both landed—there were a few scattered raven feathers that must have come over with them when they transported. Then, farther along, he could smell a third person: someone had snuck up on them. This person smelled filthy, even worse than the prisoners of the Just Deserts. Peter followed the trail to reconstruct what had happened. The stranger had tried to take Peter's burgle-sack, but there had been a struggle, because Sir Tode must have been inside it. The stranger was too fast, though, and managed to restrain the knight, running off to . . . where? Peter followed the scent, but couldn't tell where the kidnapper had gone. It was as though Sir Tode and the stranger had simply disappeared.

Somewhere in the distance, a vicious snarl shook the air. The sound filled Peter with new dread. For all he knew, one of those monsters had captured his friend. If so, he only hoped that the creature was keeping Sir Tode alive for the time being—then, at least, there was a chance Peter could save him.

He ran to the low wall surrounding the courtyard. From the howling wind below, he could tell the other side was a steep drop. He tossed a pebble over the edge and listened as it fell, and fell, and fell. "This palace must overlook the same chasm as the Just Deserts," he said. "Only on the other side."

"'Course it does," a tiny voice replied.

Peter spun around, balling his fists. The voice was so faint that even Peter's incredible ears had trouble making out the source. "Who are you?" he asked.

"I'll give you three guesses! Now, move your bloomin' foot so I can get on with me doodling." Peter crouched down and felt along the base of the wall. "Hey! Hands off, you big bully!" the voice shouted.

Peter scooped up a tiny beetle hiding in a crack of the mortar. "It's you that's talking, isn't it? You're a talking beetle!"

"Oh, well done," the beetle clicked. "What tipped you off?"

Peter was still too young to understand that the beetle—who was rather irritated at being snatched up—was making fun of him by employing a bit of sarcasm. "I just listened to where your voice was coming from," the boy explained. "I have very sensitive ears."

"Well, ain't you special? Supposin' you want a prize now? Listen, I don't go snatching you up in me pincers all willy-nilly, so howsabout you do the same and *put me back down?!*"

"I'm sorry. It's just that I'm a little lost. I'm new here and I need to find a friend of mine. I think he was kidnapped by a monster."

"Sure, I seen him," the beetle said. "Big ugly bloke in a bag, snatched up by some other big ugly blokes. A real brawl that was. Hissing and flapping and such—thought they was gonna up and squash me, I did."

Peter's stomach lurched as his worst fears about Sir Tode were confirmed. "Then what happened?" he begged. "Where did they go?"

"Honestly, I don't pay mind to you bigs all that much. Soon as I was clear of stomping distance, I just went back to me work—speaking of . . . *Ta!*" And with that, the grumpy beetle hopped from Peter's palm and scuttled away.

Peter stood back up. "Well, that was a perfectly useless conversation," he said with a sigh. Now, there is a wonderful thing in this world called "foresight." It is a gift treasured above all others because it allows one to know what the future holds. Most people with foresight end up wielding immense power in life, often becoming great rulers or librarians. Sadly, Peter (being a ten-year-old boy) was built without any capacity for foresight. And so he continued walking, unaware of how his chance encounter with a grumpy insect would prove to be nothing short of *transformational.*

Though unimpressed by the beetle, Peter wondered whether it might be worth seeking out some friendlier, more observant animal to question. He remembered the little birds singing in the Eating Hall during supper. Maybe they could tell him about the monsters, or even Sir Tode? He took up the box of Fantastic Eyes and started for the main corridor.

Mrs. Molasses's courtyard was cut off from the main palace, but Peter had little trouble scaling the ivy-covered walls. Soon he was standing on an open bridge that, if he recalled correctly, would lead him straight to the center of the palace. He retraced his route from earlier in the day, taking care to stay clear of the monsters pacing the hallways. Every so often, he would hear them moving nearby—there would be a sharp cracking sound, followed by a hundred horrid moans as the creatures slinked down this or that corridor. It sounded to Peter like they were also working their way toward the Eating Hall. "Then I'd better hurry," he murmured, redoubling his speed.

Peter reached the broad passage that connected to the Eating Hall. He sprinted ahead, but halfway down its length he ran smack into a series of flat iron bars. The boy fell backward, dropping his box of Fantastic Eyes, which clattered noisily against the stones. He climbed to his feet and reached forward. The obstruction, which had not been there during the day, was part of a gate that cut off the Eating Hall from the rest of the palace. He ran his fingers along the edge, deducing that the gate was controlled by the same clockwork that locked Mrs. Molasses's front door.

Though Peter was an accomplished contortionist, he could tell straightaway that the gaps were too narrow for him to pass through. The situation was infuriating—he could literally *smell* his destination just a few paces ahead. The boy considered finding an alternate entrance, but he deemed it too risky with so many monsters about. He picked up the box of eyes and thought about how they might be able to help him. Perhaps he could use the golden eyes to transport himself to the other side? He opened the lid, and as he did, his hand was drawn toward a pair in back. Peter began to scoop them up, but when his fingertips met their surface, he gasped and pulled away.

Those were not the golden eyes.

Peter swallowed and reached into the box once more. Again, as if by magnetic force, his hand pulled toward the same pair. He ran his fingertips over their slick, grainless texture and shivered with dread. There was no question: he was supposed to use the black eyes.

If you recall, Peter's last experience with this particular set of enchanted eyes had left a salty taste in his mouth. Had it not been for Sir Tode's judicious knock upside the head, Peter would most certainly have suffocated right there in the desert. But this time seemed to be different. This time the eyes were calling to him. Terrified as he was, Peter knew, deep down, that he must answer.

He lifted the black pair from their eggshells and closed the lid. "All right, you two," he said. "I'll give you another chance—but you'd better promise not to kill me." The eyes maintained a worrisome silence. Peter slid the box behind a nearby plinth and faced the gate. He untied his bandage and took a deep breath. He slipped the eyes into his sockets and blinked.

This time Peter did *not* stop breathing. Nor did he hear the sound of water. Instead, as he opened his lids, he felt his feet and hands grow rigid. The ground beneath him began to transform, expanding into a great rocky canyon. "What's happening to me?!" he shouted, but his voice came out small and weak. Peter still couldn't see a thing—he was blind as ever—but his whole body felt different, somehow. His fingers were useless; he couldn't even tell what they were touching. Moreover, he had an awful taste in his mouth. What *was* that? Was he *licking* the ground? Wait, it wasn't his mouth at all—it was his feet! *He could taste the floor with his feet!*

Peter skittered about, trying to gain his bearings, but the corridor had grown enormous. No matter how far he ran, the huge wall never seemed to get any closer. "What did these eyes do to me?" he clicked, extending his antennae. "*Ahhh!*" Peter screamed, realizing that he did, in fact, have antennae. For the great thief had just been transformed into a shiny black beetle.

Being a beetle took some getting used to. Peter was not accustomed to running so much just to cover a small distance. On top of that, his blindness was even more difficult to manage: he suddenly had to get used to a whole new set of senses—different taste, different touch, different hearing—and he had no sense of smell whatsoever. Soon, however, he had figured out how to feel his way around with his feet, and to understand what his antennae were telling him.

Given his change in size, the gate no longer posed a problem. Peter crawled right beneath the iron bars and was soon on the other side. He scuttled into a shadow, and plucked out the Fantastic Eyes with his forelegs.

Within seconds, Peter Nimble was a little boy once again. He tied the bandage around his head and tucked the black eyes safely into his trousers pocket, contemplating what had just occurred. The golden pair made him trans*port;* this pair made him trans*form.* But why a beetle? Why on earth would Professor Cake give Peter such a strange ability? He thought back to when he tried the eyes in the Just Deserts. Sir Tode had said Peter's body was transforming then, too, but in a different way: his skin had gone all clammy and he couldn't breathe. Whatever the answer, the boy knew there was more to this pair than met the eye(s).

Peter entered the Eating Hall and discovered that it, too, had been transformed. The place was an utter disaster. Food and dishes were scattered everywhere. Gravy boats and crocks of pork pudding had already gone bad. The boy wrinkled his nose as he stepped between congealing cream balls and pools of cheddar-brine. The bitterness he noticed while eating had become stronger—he could now smell it wafting up from every overturned plate. "Who could have made this mess?" he breathed to himself. Then he remembered the state of panic that had overcome all the people when the great bell struck. He cast an ear upward, listening for the movement of the clock's hands, but he heard only a steady grinding.

The master thief picked his way across the floor until he came to a tiny bird nestled atop a stone pedestal, sleeping soundly. If the monster carried Sir Tode past this hall, then perhaps these birds could tell him where they went. He remembered hearing a faint jingling sound accompanying the birds during supper. Exploring with his fingers, he discovered that the creature's ankle was fixed with a tiny gold shackle and chain. Were the birds being held prisoner?

"Pardon me?" he whispered. "I need your help."

The bird jolted awake, flapping and shouting:

The perfect morn has come at last.

Peter pinched its tiny beak shut before it could wake the others. Still, the creature muffled its way through the second line:

Let's praise our king and break the fast!

The bird was clearly terrified and struggled with all its might to break free from his grip. Peter could feel the animal's little-bird heartbeat racing impossibly fast as it flapped in his hand.

"I'm not going to hurt you," he said. He tried running a finger along the bird's nape. He wasn't sure whether birds even had napes, but the trick seemed to help. Slowly, the creature calmed itself.

"W-w-why is it dark?" it finally spoke. Peter could now tell by the voice—and the short feathers—that this bird was a girl.

"Because morning hasn't come yet," he said. "I'm here for information."

The little bird started to shake. *"I haven't seen a thing! Long live our—!"* Peter pinched her beak shut again. He was afraid all this singing would wake the other birds or—worse—draw the attention of whatever monsters were wandering the halls.

"I'm not with the king," he said. "I'm here to set you and your friends free. But I need you to be quiet, otherwise we might both get caught."

The bird stopped protesting. "I—I saw you at supper. You're the visitor, Mr. Trousers."

"I am." Peter wriggled his fingernail into the tiny lock, popping it open. "But my real name is Peter Nimble."

"Pickle Sparrow, sir." She curtsied, stretching her newly freed leg.

"Pleased to meet you, Pickle. I was hoping you could answer some questions for me about this place."

The bird considered this for a moment. "First set my sisters free," she said firmly.

Peter snuck around to all of the other birds and unfastened the latches around their ankles. There were twelve sparrows in all. Roused from slumber, each bird instantly began to sing, just as Pickle had done. She did her best to quiet them and explain the situation. When they learned that the stranger had opened their shackles, they stopped singing and looked at Peter with great awe. With a neat curtsy—for they were all girl birds—each sparrow chirped her thanks and fluttered off into the night.

Once her sisters were safely away, Pickle hopped back onto Peter's palm. "We don't have much time till the Night Patrol arrives," she said. "What would you like to know?"

Peter had learned from his time with Old Scabbs that the best way to interrogate someone was to make every question about that individual: there is nothing people like to do more than talk about themselves. "I want to know why you're chained up like this," he said.

The bird stretched her wings. "We're chained up here because the king doesn't want us to escape."

While that was the usual reason for locking someone up, Peter couldn't imagine how it was worth the trouble. What possible threat could these little sparrows pose to a king? "Why doesn't he want you to escape? Is he afraid of you?"

"Oh yes!" She leaned close. "He thinks we might fly off and fetch help . . . and we will, too!" she said, pluming herself proudly. "Even if the journey kills us!"

Peter marveled at this little bird's courage. "When I was at supper last night, the big clock went off and everyone started running about. Why was that?"

"I do not know what a clock is, sir. But every night and every morning the king works a great magic bell. It's for their own safety— the people have to clear the corridors before the Night Patrol comes." As she finished speaking, Peter heard a roar echo from a nearby terrace. The bird loosed a terrified chirp, nestling herself deep into the boy's palm. "That's them now!"

The Night Patrol. Those must be the monsters he had heard earlier. Peter could tell they were working their way toward the Eating Hall—there wasn't much time left. "What exactly is the Night Patrol?" he asked.

"Oh, they're horrible, sir! They could gobble you up, feathers and all! That's why the people's doors get locked at night—so the Night Patrol won't get them. Anyone wandering the halls after curfew is fair game. If the Night Patrol sees you flapping about, the most you can pray for is that they'll make it swift."

Peter thought that this Night Patrol sounded rather similar to Pencil Cookson and his Mumblety-Peg Gang. Only much, much worse. "You're saying the Night Patrol works for the king?"

"Of course they do. They're the king's personal army . . . only he's no king, he's a tyrant! He keeps all his subjects under lock and latch, and makes us say we love him. And if anyone disagrees, he sends the Night Patrol to their door. And worst of all," her voice fell to a peep, "he's made them all forget!"

Peter was running out of time. He could now make out the sounds of *scraping, clinking* footsteps approaching from the hall. "I need you to be very clear with me, Pickle. *What* has he made them forget?"

"Not what . . . *who!*" she said. "The locks on the doors aren't just there to keep people safe. It's to keep people from getting out and seeing the *Missing Ones.*"

It was just as Peter had suspected. If the locks had been only for protection, then it would have been possible to open them from the inside. The king was hiding something, something he didn't want them to see. "These Missing Ones? Who are they?"

"Well, what's the one thing missing in this whole palace? The one thing that every kingdom needs?"

"I don't know . . . *dirt?*" he stammered. "Why don't you just tell me?"

Pickle shook her tiny head and hopped back. "He was afraid they'd outwit him. He knows how clever they can be. So instead, he locked up every last one of—" and before she could finish, she gave a shriek. The little bird leapt from Peter's hand and fluttered into the air.

"Locked up all the *what?*" Peter called after her. But it was too late. Pickle had disappeared.

"Hoy!" A voice roared directly behind him. "Who goes there?!"

∽ CHAPTER SIXTEEN ∽
THE NIGHT PATROL

Peter froze. He listened as a pair of razor-sharp claws *scraped*
against the courtyard floor. The master thief had been so
focused on getting answers from Pickle Sparrow that he hadn't
noticed that the groaning pack of monsters had finally worked its
way to the center of the kingdom. Everywhere Peter turned, his ears
were met with the miserable *clink-clink* of dragging chains.

The Night Patrol had found him.

"Hey, LongClaw!" the voice roared again. "You'd better get over
here!"

Peter heard another creature stomp in from the opposite side.
"What now?" it growled.

"I was bringin' the chiddlers by just now when I heard voices
inside. Definitely sounded human."

"Human, eh? Must have got trampled at tuck-in, poor things," the second said, snapping what Peter could now tell was some kind of whip against the floor.

"What do you say, boss? Think we should tell the king?"

"No need for that, Maul. I say we just keep the fun between ourselves."

Peter slunk deeper into the shadows, trying to grasp his situation. He could tell they were huge by the way the floor winced with each step. Their whips sounded like they had bits of glass braided into the ends. It also sounded like each of them was carrying some kind of long chain in their free hand. Their voices were deep and fierce—especially that of the bigger one, LongClaw. Peter could hear little splashes of drool falling onto the ground at their feet.

"Whoever's in there," LongClaw snarled, "you're in violation of the king's Royal Curfew—the punishment is death!"

"Yeah! If you beg real pathetic-like, we *might* make it quick."

"But if you try and escape, we make it real slow . . . and *real fun.*" They broke into wild fits of laughter, snorting and wheezing. The awful sound sent chills along Peter's arms. He couldn't imagine what kind of horrible monsters he was up against, but he was pretty sure they were serious about killing him. He slowed his racing heart as the creatures lumbered through the wrecked Eating Hall.

"Come on, now. We ain't got all night!" LongClaw swept a pedestal aside with his mighty arm. The stone pillar smashed against the far wall, exploding into a hundred pieces. Peter swallowed—if that creature could shatter rock, who knew what it could do to bone? Suddenly, he caught a whiff of musk in the darkness, and his whole body went cold.

They were apes.

For those of you who have only seen domestic apes, you might not realize how truly horrifying these creatures can be. While they vary slightly from species to species, most wild apes have two terrible, cracked horns sprouting from their brow, which join in a giant tusk right where the nose should be. Their mouths are wide and drooling, filled with ivory fangs that stick out in all directions. Many years before, Peter had happened upon one such monstrosity while robbing the hold of a sea circus. The encounter—which nearly resulted in Peter getting his arm bitten off—still haunted him to this day.

Peter crouched in the shadows, listening as the Night Patrol came closer. He reminded himself that animals in the Vanished Kingdom were different from those back home—and in the case of these apes that might mean even more deadly.

"Look at this bloody mess!" LongClaw kicked over a platter of liver biscuits. "Place reeks like a hog-sty."

"That's humans for you," Maul said, scraping leftover pudding-wurst off his heel. "Bunch of disgustin' creatures."

"Watch your gob!" LongClaw swiped at his head. "The king's a human, you know. If it weren't for him teaching us to speak with all his books and charts, we'd all be in a jungle somewheres, flinging dung and sucking ticks off our ruddy humps!" He raised the chain in his free paw. "But now we got slaves to do that for us, don't we?" He gave a sharp yank to the chain. From somewhere around the corner came a hundred miserable groans and sobs.

"*Slaves,*" Peter thought to himself. "They must be fettered to the other end of those chains." But as pitiful as their cries were, the boy knew he was no good to anyone if those apes got hold of him. His first concern had to be with his own survival. The Night Patrol was blocking the exits, so running wasn't an option. He could try scaling the wall, but it would be just as dangerous—apes have predator's eyes and would spot his movements in a second. No, the only thing to do was keep very still and hope they lost interest.

"Hold up," LongClaw said, taking a step in Peter's direction. "I think I whiffed somethin' by the back wall."

"Human, right? Like I said!"

LongClaw raised his scourge. "Flank the perimeter! I'll check them shadows!"

The apes split up and started working along opposite walls of the hall. Peter pressed his body against the pedestal, trying desperately to come up with a plan before they reached him. He felt the black pair of Fantastic Eyes in his pocket. He didn't much savor turning into a tiny, squishable insect right now, but he was running out of options. If he was lucky, maybe he could crawl away before they spotted him.

"Hoy! There it is!" Maul said, spotting Peter's elbow in the shadows. "Somethin' moved over there."

They charged ahead, knocking planters and pews out of their path. Peter didn't have a moment to spare. He ripped his bandage off and pressed the two black eyes into his sockets. The next moment, he felt his whole body changing once again. The ground beneath him expanded as he shrank down and down. But something was wrong—his hands weren't just shrinking, they were sprouting *feathers!* Peter opened his mouth to yell, but all that came out was a high-pitched "chirp!"

The apes kicked Peter's pedestal aside. They stared down at the floor. "You dumb lout," LongClaw said, clobbering Maul upside the head. "It was just one of them twittin' birds." The ape was speaking the truth, for hopping on the ground before them was a tiny, terrified sparrow.

A bird! Peter thought to himself, flapping his wings. *But how?* The how didn't matter at the moment—he had to get out of there. He quickly learned that being a bird was not nearly so easy as being a beetle: he had no arms or hands, his feet were awkward and long, and his face was covered with feathers. Even worse, Peter couldn't quite seem to manage flapping both wings at the same time. That—combined with the usual blindness—made it pretty much impossible for him to fly more than a few inches . . . if you could even call it flying.

"Hold up. What's she doin' on the ground like that?" Maul said, watching as the flapping bird crashed into a table leg for the third time. "Ain't all sparrows supposed to be chained up, king's orders?"

LongClaw peered at the other pedestals, noticing for the first time that they were each *unbirded*. "Someone's sprung every last one of 'em!" He squatted down in front of Peter. "Maybe this little flapper can tell us what happened. And if she don't, then we'll just have ourselves a midnight snack." He snatched Peter by the tail feathers, dangling him over his mouth. Peter-the-bird's little heart was beating faster than he thought possible. "Hello, morsel," the ape said with a grin. "Care to tell us what transpired here tonight?"

Peter wilted under the beast's hot, putrid breath. The last time he had been this close to an ape, he had nearly lost a limb; now he was facing the possibility of losing a lot more. Unless he wanted to get eaten, he had to think of an answer fast. Peter knew the best lies were mostly truth—that way you can look as honest as possible when telling them. He began to cry. "Don't eat me, sir! I just want to be put back on my pedestal!" All true: Peter didn't want to be eaten, and he very much wanted to be put down.

"Hogwash," LongClaw said. "You tweeters been dreamin' of freedom for years. You peck at them pretty little ankle-chains so much we gotta bloody replace 'em every half-moon. Now, who helped you lovelies escape?"

"It was a . . . a *stranger!*" Peter said, again thinking the truth would be most convincing. "I'd never seen him before!" Also true. "He shouted something about 'down with the king!' and then popped our chains off like magic! My sisters flew away, but I couldn't, on account of . . . of a broken wing!" He thrust out a crooked arm as proof. "I saw the stranger run off, though. He went that way!" Peter pointed in a direction leading *away* from Mrs. Molasses's house.

"A lock-pick?!" LongClaw put his paw straight through the wall. "King'll have our hides if he hears of this!" He threw the bird to Maul. "Your chores can wait. Shackle this one and assemble the horde! I want all apes on the lookout for that stranger!" He stormed off.

Maul carried Peter to an empty (and still upright) pedestal. He took a tiny gold shackle between the tips of his claws and struggled to latch it around Peter's tiny bird leg. At last he succeeded. "Scrawny rat," the ape muttered. "Hardly worth the meat." He took up his whip and lumbered into the corridor.

You may remember that both of the apes had entered the Eating Hall clutching a long chain. As Maul stomped across the floor, his chain pulled tight, dragging a hundred slaves with it. The captives stumbled and rattled and moaned their way right past Peter's nose. *Who are these wretched souls?* he wondered to himself. They were obviously prisoners of some sort. But if that was so, why didn't the king just ship them off to the Just Deserts? Having only a beak, Peter couldn't smell quite as well as usual, but whatever these creatures were, they stank like they hadn't bathed once in their lives. He listened as the miserable procession moved past him. Peter was having trouble sorting out their exact number—sparrows, as a species, are not renowned for their attention spans—but thought he counted at least a hundred heartbeats along the rusted chain.

"Move it, you maggots!" Maul cracked his whip from somewhere down the hall. The mysterious prisoners staggered forward, their groans echoing through the palace.

When the Eating Hall was finally clear of all danger, Peter set to the challenging task of removing the eyes again. While struggling, the great thief wondered about how, exactly, these particular Fantastic Eyes worked. First they changed him into a bug, then a bird—so what was the connection? Peter thought of the brief conversation he'd had with that beetle on Mrs. Molasses's wall. And just before the apes arrived, he had been talking to a sparrow. Maybe these eyes turned him into whatever animal he had last *touched?* If that was so, then meeting that peevish beetle had proved more helpful than he originally realized.

So what had happened the first time he tried these eyes? Peter tried to think back on his journey across the Just Deserts. What animal could he have touched? He assumed that Sir Tode didn't count, so it had to be something else. He remembered how he couldn't breathe and how everything around him (even the air) had burned like fire against his clammy skin—but what sort of animal can't survive its own habitat? "Unless I wasn't in my own habitat," he chirped to himself. "Maybe I was turning into something from the ocean? Something . . . like a *fish*." Peter thought of the shipyard back home, and how the docks were always covered in suffocating fish. That's exactly how he would have died had not Sir Tode been there to save him. He only hoped he'd have a chance to return the favor.

Peter finally managed to remove the black eyes (with the help of both feet and a stray relish spoon) and was soon sitting on the pedestal as a full-size ten-year-old boy once more. The tiny gold chain around his ankle had burst wide open upon his transformation. *I must remember never to handle a snake,* he thought to himself, *or else I'll never get these things out.*

Peter hopped down and raced from the Eating Hall. He had left the box with the other Fantastic Eyes behind a pillar in the corridor; he needed to retrieve them before anyone found them. When he reached the gate, he grew pale. He could smell that someone had been near—someone filthy.

Peter searched the wall for a release mechanism. If these barriers were truly meant to keep people locked *in,* then it followed that there might be some way for the Night Patrol to activate them from the other side. Sure enough, he found a small lever hidden just above his head. Peter pulled it with both hands, and the mighty gate *clanked* up into the ceiling. As soon as there was enough space, he wriggled under the iron bars and ran to the box of Fantastic Eyes.

The remaining pairs were just as he had left them. Whoever had passed must not have noticed them in the shadows. Breathing a sigh, Peter took the black eyes from his pocket and replaced them in their eggshells.

The boy was so focused on the box that he failed to notice *something else* on the floor. Laid out in the middle of the corridor was a large circle of rope, tied off like a lasso. The end trailed down the hallway and disappeared through a crack in the wall through which four pairs of eyes watched.

The spies studied Peter from their hiding place, fidgeting and fussing to get a better view.

"What's he doing?" one of them said.

"Move your fat head, I can't see!" another hissed.

"Both of you, shut up before he hears us!"

Peter snapped the box closed. His ears had just caught whispers at the end of the hall. "I know you're watching me," he called out, rising to his feet.

"Do it!" a voice shouted. Before Peter could react, a snare pulled tight around his legs, whipping him off his feet. His head struck the ground with a deafening crack, and once again his body went limp.

CHAPTER SEVENTEEN

SIMON *and the* MISSING ONES

Peter awoke to the smell of flour. Not the boring perennials that wise men are constantly badgering us to stop and smell, but the white powdery stuff meant for baking and booby traps. Whoever it was that kidnapped him had tied an old flour sack over his head. Peter breathed the dusty air and immediately began sneezing. This led to a gust of flour shooting straight up his nose that made him sneeze all the more. With each sternutation came a sharp pain in back of his head, which was still sore from his ambush outside the Eating Hall. It felt like his fall had reopened the gash in his crown— his temple was pounding something fierce, and he could feel blood trickling down into one ear.

The boy tried moving, only to discover that his entire body had been wrapped from top to bottom in a giant chain. To ensure he didn't wriggle free, a collection of old manacles had been clamped pell-mell to his limbs. From what he could feel, Peter had about ten locks on each arm, fifteen on each leg, and two big ones clenched tightly around his neck. He could tell that the locks were each rusted over, which would not make escaping from them any easier.

Through the flour sack, Peter could hear muffled footsteps and voices approaching. He let his head fall limp—it was probably smart to feign unconsciousness until he could figure out who, exactly, was holding him captive. Silently digging his left pinkie into the keyhole of an ankle bracelet, the master thief did his best to make out what the voices were saying.

"What have you done to him?" a young voice pressed. "We agreed never to use those chains."

"S-s-sorry, Your Majesty! We tried to tie him up like you wanted, but he just kept slipping out of the ropes!" This second voice sounded husky, as if the speaker were fighting back tears. Peter was fairly sure they were both girls.

"Scrape," the first girl chided. "I thought you said he was unconscious when you brought him down?"

"He *was* unconscious!" a boy voice responded. "But every time we cinched a knot, he'd just twitch his arm and the whole thing'd come undone. Like escaping came natural as breathing to him. It was creepy." They had caught Peter performing the Drowsy Dodger. The Drowsy Dodger was an old trick some passing sea-gypsies had taught him years earlier; it involves training your fingers to untie knots in your sleep. Because practicing requires *unconsciousness*, the skill is notoriously difficult to master. Peter grinned underneath his hood—apparently, he was pretty good at it.

The one named Scrape went on. "We finally had to give up and just use our old shackles. I know we weren't supposed to, Your Majesty, but we didn't have nothing else!"

Peter found himself puzzled by the conversation. His captors all sounded very young and a little bit frightened. Stranger still, one of the girls was being called "Your Majesty."

"You gotta believe us, Your Majesty!" the tearful girl said. "We wouldn't of used the chains 'less we really had to. Remember how Pickle said the stranger knew a secret to open all their locks—he must know the king's magic."

Scrape stepped closer. "If he's with the king, then we should kill him now!" Peter took a sharp breath as he heard the sound of a knife being unsheathed. "This is what comes of traitors—"

"Do not harm him, Scrape!" someone commanded, moving between them. Peter hadn't noticed this person before; the voice sounded gritty and old. He relaxed a bit when he heard Scrape's knife slide back into its sheath. The wise voice went on. "I have known a great many traitors in my life, and I do not believe this child is one."

"Simon is right," Your Majesty said. "We should keep him alive at least until we can learn more about why he's come . . . and what he was doing with that note."

The note. That meant that whoever captured Peter also had his burgle-sack. And if they had his burgle-sack . . . then they probably had Sir Tode! The boy's heart swelled as he realized there still might be a chance he could save his lost friend. He unlocked another manacle, redoubling his efforts to break free.

"Justice shall reveal the truth to us soon enough," Simon said. "Have you inspected the box he was carrying?"

"We couldn't open it. There's some kind of lock on the front," one of them answered.

The one called Your Majesty sighed. "Very well. Simon and I will see if we can't swipe a pickaxe from the mines. The rest of you stay with the prisoner. Alert me when he wakes." With that, Your Majesty and Simon left the chamber.

Simon? Peter thought to himself. *Where have I heard that name before?* It sounded familiar, but his head hurt too much to do any quality thinking. The bag was also preventing his ears and nose from working as well as usual. All he could do was continue to pick the locks. If he was lucky, the guards would feel chatty and fill him in on the situation.

"You two heard about Crumpet Sparrow?" one of them asked, feeling chatty. "She never showed up with the others. Her sisters ain't seen so much as a feather since she was freed."

"That poor little bird!" another said. "Y-y-you don't think . . . ?"

"Aw, don't be such a baby. She'll turn up, all right."

It sounded like they were talking about the sparrows Peter

had freed. He remembered one of the voices mentioning Pickle a moment before. What was the connection between those birds and his captors?

"I wonder where the strangers came from," one of the girl-voices spoke again. "Did you learn anything from the other one?"

"Nope. Scrape and me tried everything we could think of to make the stupid thing spill his guts, but all we could get out of him was that we'd never get nothin' out of him."

Could that other stranger possibly be Sir Tode? Peter sure hoped so. His locks were taking a bit longer to open on account of the rust. He had only managed to free one arm so far. Luckily, because of all the chains wrapped around his body, he was able to move that arm without being detected.

"Yeah, that cat's a mean one. I asked him about his friend here and he nearly bit my piggy-toe clean off—"

"Ewww!" the girl-voices shouted. "Don't *show us!*"

It *was* Sir Tode! Peter smiled, imagining the catastrophic interrogation. How could he ever have doubted his friend's ability? Still, it would be best to intervene before they could molest the knight further.

"We gotta find out what these strangers know." Scrape was now pacing in front of Peter. "If they figured out that riddle, we could be in serious danger."

"M-m-maybe he's not a spy?" one of the girls said hopefully. "Maybe it's him that's come to—?"

"Don't even say it!" Scrape cut her off. "We can't afford to get our hopes up like that. Besides, he's just a kid."

The throbbing in Peter's head had finally eased, and he was starting to get used to listening through burlap. He could now clearly count four voices in the room. He knew he could handle a group of this size, but he would definitely need a weapon or distraction of some kind. He could tell from the echoes of their footsteps that they were underground. *There must be tunnels running underneath the palace,* the boy thought to himself. *That's probably how they were able to sneak into Mrs. Molasses's yard and kidnap Sir Tode. But why did they do it? And what was "Your Majesty" planning next?*

Scrape squatted down in front of the prisoner. "Supposin' we get a little rough with Mister Stranger here?" Peter tensed as the boy drew his knife once more. "Maybe then he'll give us some answers?"

Just at that moment, Peter heard what sounded like a small pony gallop in. "You shall do no such thing, little fiends!" Peter almost swallowed his tongue—apparently, Sir Tode had managed a daring escape of his own. "I demand you release my companion at once! And while I'm at it, you brats owe me a personal apology!"

Peter heard shuffling as the four captors scrambled together. "Call Peg!" one of them yelled. "The rest of you—bag him!"

"Once was enough, thank you!" With a fierce growl Sir Tode pounced on his assailants. Peter struggled with his shackles, trying his best to keep an ear on the battle. From what he could make out, it sounded like Sir Tode was managing just fine on his own.

The knight tore through the scrum, battering them with insults and hooves.

"*En garde,* villain!"

"*Owww!*"

"Take that, you ruffian!"

"*Arghhh!*"

"Prepare to—"

"*Gotcha!*" one of them shouted. Peter recognized the voice as the boy named Scrape.

"Drop me this instant, you cowardly tail-grabber!" Peter deduced that Sir Tode had indeed been caught up by his tail. "It's dirty fighting, that's what it is!"

"Oh, I'll show you dirty fighting," Scrape said. "Someone fetch me some rocks and a funnel. We'll see how smart this cat is with a belly full of—"

"TOUCH HIM AND DIE!"

Everyone in the room spun around to find Peter standing behind them, shaking the rusted chains from his body. He had Scrape's dagger, which he had swiped during the distraction. Uncertain how to properly hold the weapon, Peter settled on tossing the blade back and forth between his two hands.

"Peter!" the knight panted, craning his neck. "So glad to see you again!"

The four kidnappers stared at the boy. "Um, you guys?" one of the girls said nervously. "How'd he get out of those chains?"

"And why's he still got the bag on his head?"

Scrape snorted, tossing Sir Tode aside. "He's no killer. He can't even hold a knife right." He rolled up both sleeves and lunged toward Peter.

Scrape was strong and clearly an experienced fighter. But what Peter lacked in strength, he made up in speed. Within seconds, he had bested his opponent and imprisoned the whole group in their own shackles. As it turned out, the guards—Trouble, Scrape, Giggle, and Marbles—were a gang of children not much older than Peter himself.

The great thief pulled the flour sack from his head and paced around his young captives. "Now, we have some questions of our own. And we will do whatever it takes to find the answers." For added effect, he stomped on the foot of the one named Scrape, who had spoken particularly ill of Sir Tode. "If you don't give us answers, my friend and I will slit your throats wide open and . . . and drink your blood!"

Sir Tode wavered on this last threat. "A touch grim, don't you think, Peter?"

It was at this moment that a strange thing happened. One by one, the group began to cry. These were not the sorrowful tears of Professor Cake mourning the dead. Nor were they the pathetic tears of Old Scabbs begging a lemon. No, these were the uncomplicated tears of pure, childlike terror. "P-p-please, mister!" Giggle begged through a bubble of snot in her nose. "Don't drink our blood!"

"We didn't mean it," the boy named Trouble said. "Don't send us to the monsters!" Peter was confused. He was used to dealing with bloodthirsty thieves and nasty beggarmongers, not sniveling children.

Before he could think of what to say, someone else ran into the room. Peter spun around, blade held high. "One more step, and I kill them all!" He only hoped that the threat didn't sound as hollow as it felt.

"Forget about us!" Scrape strained against his binds. "Run away, Your Majesty!"

Peter hesitated. "Your *Majesty?*" he repeated. "Are you with the king?"

"Hardly," Your Majesty said. Peter could now tell for certain that this voice belonged to a girl. She turned to someone standing just behind her. "Simon, disarm him."

Before Peter could respond, Simon swept across the room and grabbed him by the throat. The boy fell to the ground, choking, as eight sharp claws dug into his flesh. "You will kindly put your weapon down," a gravelly voice spoke in his ear. Peter opened his hand and let the dagger fall.

The next moment, Simon was back beside Your Majesty. Peter massaged his throat and rose to his feet. He could tell that Simon was some kind of bird—a very deadly one—but could not quite identify the breed. "What are you?" he asked.

"I am Her Majesty's loyal guard." The creature spoke in a garbled voice. "Your last question leads me to believe you were *not* sent here by the king. Is that correct?"

"I told you we don't know any blasted king!" Sir Tode blustered.

Peter placed a hand on his friend to calm him. Though common sense might say not to trust one's persecutors, the boy felt a small voice inside of him—his thief's voice—telling him to be honest with these strangers. "We've come here to . . . we're looking for someone," he started. "But we're not sure where, or even who they are . . . all we know is they need our help."

Your Majesty pulled a scrap of paper from her pocket. "You're speaking of this note?" she said with amusement.

"It is no laughing matter, I assure you," Sir Tode said. "Whoever wrote that message is in grave danger, and we were on our way to help them—that is, before you so rudely *kidnapped* us."

A great silence came over the room. Though Peter could not see it, all the children's eyes were locked on Your Majesty, waiting for the girl to speak. She unfolded the paper and read aloud:

Only a stranger may bring relief,
But darkness will reign, unless he's . . . a thief.

"A thief!" Sir Tode stomped a hoof. "By golly, Peter, I think the girl's cracked the riddle!"

"Of course I did." She returned the note to her pocket. "After all, I wrote it."

CHAPTER EIGHTEEN

AN UNLIKELY HERO

Peter and Sir Tode sat in a small, musty room deep below the Perfect Palace. They were chewing mushroom stems and sipping from tin cups of stale water. Crouched around them were five children and a bird. A single candle stub flickered on the dirt floor, providing the only light for the entire chamber. The darkness did not much bother Peter, because he was blind. The other children could see well enough, because they had not been in proper daylight for over ten years. Sir Tode, however, was nervous and jumpy. He kept close to Peter, huddling against the boy any time a strange noise echoed through the tunnels.

The leader of the group introduced herself as Princess Peg. She was a tall girl about the same age as Peter. Like the other children, she wore rags and no shoes. Every inch of her body was covered in the same stale grime that masked each of their scents. It was only when she spoke that Peter could catch the faintest indication of her regal lineage. "It seems so long since I sent that message," she said, setting down her cup. "You can understand how I lost hope of it reaching anyone."

Peter couldn't help but feel skeptical. "If you're really a princess, what are you doing here? Shouldn't you be up in a tower somewhere, braiding hair and riding ponies?"

"Maybe," she said with some bitterness. "But instead, I grew up underground, a prisoner of the king."

"That sounds miserable," Peter said. He thought about how even Mr. Seamus let him out once in a while for errands. "But why would your own father keep you prisoner?"

Her Majesty gave the sigh of someone who does not like explaining the obvious. "The king is my *uncle*. He stole the throne from my father after I was born. When he took over, he had me and the others locked up."

"There's loads more than just us," the girl named Giggle said.

"Hundreds!" Marbles added. "The king keeps 'em all chained up for his slaves. He forces them to do chores for the whole kingdom."

"S'why the dumb place is so clean," Trouble said, wiping a finger on his trousers leg. "Every night the monsters drag them through the palace and make them scrub every speck."

Monsters? It sounded to Peter like these children were talking about the apes he had encountered. "You mean the Night Patrol," he said.

The princess shrugged. "You call them the Night Patrol, but for us they are simply monsters. When you have seen enough of your friends eaten whole, you put aside all formalities."

Peter was trying his best to follow their story, but he still couldn't fit all the pieces together. "So there's an impostor king who has taken over the kingdom and forced a bunch of people to be his slaves . . . How did you five escape?"

"Simon saved us," Peg answered. "He was my father's Royal Guard."

"We ravens used to be many," the bird said gravely. "Now I am all that remains."

A raven. Peter's entire body tensed up as he realized the bird not an arm's length away was from the same tribe that had murdered Old Scabbs.

"After the princess was taken underground," Simon continued, "I sought her out and pecked her locks apart. I did the same for the other children, until my beak would peck no more." The old bird knew something of how blind people could "see" with their hands, and so he hopped closer for Peter to touch him. The boy recoiled but then slowly reached out toward him. Where a beak should have been, Peter found only a mangled stump, snapped off at the base. He thought of how difficult it must be for such a proud creature to be so maimed—it would be like losing his fingers. "It's not so bad," Simon said. "I only wish I had been able to free all of the children."

"Wait, all of the prisoners are *children?*" Peter said.

"Every last one," Peg answered. "It's the first thing my uncle did when he took over the kingdom."

The Missing Ones. Everything the sparrow had told Peter in the Eating Hall was starting to make sense. Pickle had asked him what the one thing missing in this palace was. At the time, he hadn't been able to answer, but now he knew. "There were no children anywhere," he said. "That's what was bugging me so much at supper. Everything was so clean and neat and polite—it was all *too* perfect."

"Forgive me for sounding dense," Sir Tode asked, "but why would a king be afraid of little children?"

"That's easy," Scrape said. "It's 'cause we don't like being bossed around none!"

Simon gave an amused cluck. "You are closer to the truth than you realize, Scrape. King Incarnadine recognized at once the threat that you and your kind posed to his plans. While adults can be intimidated and deceived, a child's constitution is made from far stronger stuff. He knew that a kingdom full of children would never accept a fraudulent ruler." The raven could not have been more right. As you know, children (unlike grown-ups) are far too clever to be tricked by impostors—a fact that goes a long way toward explaining their distrust of wicked stepmothers and substitute teachers.

Simon's words put Peter in mind of a story he had once overheard about a child and a naked emperor. He could not remember all the details, but recalled it was quite hilarious, and quite true. Adults can often be fooled where children cannot. Hearing a grown-up, even a feathered one, speak of children with such high regard reminded Peter of Professor Cake. The boy hated to admit it, but deep down his instincts told him that Simon was just as worthy of Peter's trust . . . even if he *was* a raven.

Giggle sighed. "Pretty soon, our parents forgot who we ever was. The king took away everyone's names so they couldn't remember what he done . . . that's the reason us kids are all named after whatever we are."

"Except for the princess," Scrape said with a touch of awe. "She held on to her real name—that's why she's still a princess."

If Peter could see, he would have caught Peg blushing. "I'm a fugitive, just like the rest of you," she said. "After Simon freed us, we started hatching a plan to rescue the rest of the children. Other than the king, we knew of just one kind of person who might be able to open those locks: a thief. It was our only option. I threw the note into the giant pit surrounding the palace, hoping it would find its way to one of the surviving prisoners in the Just Deserts." She hesitated, and here Peter caught a distinct note of disappointment. "But I guess it found you instead."

"About that," Peter said, trying to ignore the slight. "Why send a riddle? You could have saved us a lot of trouble if you'd written something less complicated."

"It wasn't *that* complicated," she muttered.

"Yeah!" Scrape added. "And how was she supposed to know it'd end up in the hands of some blind dummy and his ugly pet?"

Sir Tode, who up to this point had been listening quietly, had evidently had enough. "I've had enough," he said, leaping to his hooves. "I am a *fierce knight,* known the world over for slaying dragons. Who among you can boast such a feat? And this 'blind dummy' just happens to be the legendary Peter Nimble . . . *the greatest thief who ever lived.*"

At these words, Peter felt every person turn toward him. He shifted his weight, grateful for once that he was unable to return their gazes.

"Child, is this true?" Simon said, hopping closer.

Peter did not answer immediately. When he considered the question, all he could think of was how he had made so many mistakes on the journey so far. But with those recollections came the stronger memory of what the professor had told him on the shore of the island. "It's true," he said. "I've met the thieves of the Just Deserts, and I'm better than the whole lot of them put together—they said as much themselves. Sir Tode and I were chosen to rescue you . . . and that's exactly what we're going to do."

"It *kind of* fits." Trouble wiped his nose. "He's a stranger, at least."

"And he did open all them locks," Scrape added.

"Our hero!" Giggle and Marbles said in unison.

Peg, however, remained unconvinced. "We'll see" was all she could muster.

"Honestly, Princess, I don't care what you believe," Peter said, rising with Sir Tode. "Professor Cake trusted us, and that's good enough for me."

"Who is this professor?" Simon asked.

Peter wasn't sure he could answer this question. "He's an old man who looks after everything. He's the one who found your bottle—it floated to him on the sea."

"The sea." The raven shook his head. "Then Justice has delivered us a miracle indeed. These shores have not touched the great waters for many years now. Not since the Cursed Birthday."

"The what?" Peter asked.

"I am sure you two have wondered how this land came to be hidden from the wide world," Simon said. "Perhaps a story is in order?"

You may have observed in your own lives that there is a great power in storytelling. A well-spun tale can transport listeners away from their humdrum lives and return them with an enlarged sense of the world. No sooner had Simon suggested a story than Sir Tode leapt to action. "A story?" He clopped his hoof against the dirt. "Why, that's a splendid idea!" The knight knew the importance of setting the mood, and he refused to let Simon continue until a proper circle had been formed. The bird stood uncomfortably in the middle of the group, his shadow flickering large against the moldy cavern walls.

"Right then," Sir Tode said. "You were saying something about how this kingdom mysteriously vanished? And a birthday?"

The old raven nodded. "Back then, it was called the Isle of HazelPort."

Peter knew that "hazel" was a fancy word for a color found in some people's eyes. "That's kind of a funny name for a desert, isn't it?" he said, hoping it wasn't rude to interrupt.

"These lands were not always so barren. Originally there was no palace or desert. There were only the stones, the sea, and the sky. The entire realm was owned by a Rich Man with two sons. Though they were brothers, the sons could not have been more different. The youngest, Lord Hazelgood, was of noble and generous heart—"

"That was my papa!" Peg said proudly.

"The older brother, Lord Incarnadine, was rapacious and cruel. He never missed an opportunity to abuse the peasants of the land. The Rich Man was greatly troubled by the wickedness he saw in his eldest son's heart, and he feared what might become of the people if ever he ascended to power. And so, upon his death, he bequeathed the whole of the island to his younger son instead."

"I'm sure that went over well," Sir Tode said.

"It was an equal shock to both brothers. Lord Hazelgood was not much older than Her Majesty when he came to power, but he was already wise enough to know that his father must have chosen him for a reason, and he vowed to honor that trust. At this time, the humans of the land were scavengers, forced to scrounge for rainwater and food. But young Hazelgood envisioned a better future. He would build a great palace to shine like a jewel on the sea.

"When the people first heard of his plans, they scoffed. How could he, scarcely more than a child, ever hope to accomplish such a feat? Each brick would have to be chiseled from rock deep underground. The task seemed impossible.

"Lord Hazelgood, however, would not be deterred. If his fellow humans would not help him, then he would turn elsewhere. He looked among the animals on the island and chose the most miserable group he could find: ravens. Back then, we were quarrelsome, petty creatures. Though fierce, we were too busy fighting amongst ourselves to fight our predators. It was said our tough meat was ideal for salting and preserving, and because of this, we were being killed off in droves. When Lord Hazelgood came to us, only one unkindness remained."

Sir Tode's mustache twitched. "One *what?*"

"An unkindness is the word for a group of ravens," he explained.

"Of course. Like a 'school' of fish," Peter said, wishing for the first time that he had himself attended school—it might have saved him some confusion in the Just Deserts.

"Precisely. As I was saying, there were few ravens left when Hazelgood came to us—I was among them. We were suspicious of humans, and unwilling to trust Lord Hazelgood's words. But one night when a tribe of hunters ambushed our nests, he came to our aid and defended us. He was badly injured, but he managed to save every last egg. From that day forward, the ravens swore to protect Lord Hazelgood and his Line with our very lives."

Princess Peg reached over and ran her hand across Simon's dark feathers. "They've done just that."

"Lord Hazelgood taught us how to fight as one. When guided by a single voice, we were able to defend nests on the ground and dodge rocks in the air. And then we set out to build a kingdom together. Our first act was to dig a great well. Though surrounded by oceans, the island was without any fresh water. There were no rivers or streams anywhere to be found; everyone was dependent on the mercy of passing rain clouds. In his wisdom, Lord Hazelgood knew that if he could provide clean water, the people of the land would join him. Using only our talons and beaks, we dug at Hazelgood's side for seven long years, until finally we found a great spring deep in the earth. We hollowed out a rock and set it upon the spot, where it remains to this day."

"Kettle Rock," Peter said. "We came across it in the deserts."

"The rock stands?" Simon said wistfully. "What I would give to see those hallowed grounds once more. It was Kettle Rock that awakened the people of this land. Once they saw its clear springs, they finally believed that Hazelgood's dream was possible. Over the next ten years, men, women, and ravens worked with him to transform the wilds into a great palace. We tapped the headwaters below ground and brought streams into the streets. We built a home for every person and filled the courtyards with gardens. The town was named HazelPort, and the people crowned Lord Hazelgood their king. We ravens were appointed as his Royal Guard. All was at peace, if only for a season."

Sir Tode, who had something of a knack for narrative, groaned. "Cue the scorned older brother."

"Scorned and scornful," Simon said. "During the years of construction, Lord Incarnadine became consumed with jealousy. He had been robbed of his birthright, and he vowed never to forgive the slight. He refused to set foot on the grounds of his brother's palace, remaining on the outskirts with only a few animals and deranged criminals to keep him company. Year after year, King Hazelgood invited his brother to come build at his side, and year after year the offer was rejected.

"As the towers grew, so too did Lord Incarnadine's bitterness. And finally one cold night, he took to the seas. No one knows where he traveled in those years, but it was whispered that he went in search of dark magic unlike anything seen in this land. And during all that time, he never lost sight of his single aim—"

"Revenge!" Sir Tode said with a bit too much enthusiasm.

"Revenge," Simon echoed more sorrowfully. "It fell on the eve of a great celebration. The palace had been completed, and so the people had all begun building families. Chief among them was King Hazelgood, who had fallen in love with a beautiful woman named Lady Magnolia. Together, they were anticipating the birth of twin children: one boy and one girl. In honor of this momentous occasion, the citizens of HazelPort had decided to throw a great feast.

"On the night the prince and princess were to be born, every soul in the kingdom assembled in the courtyard. The people cheered as King Hazelgood and Queen Magnolia presented their heirs. The girl, who was born first, was publicly christened Princess Peg."

"That's me," Peg said, blushing.

"What was the other twin's name?" Peter asked Simon.

"The second child was never given a name. For on that very night, Lord Incarnadine had secretly returned to the kingdom and disguised himself within the crowd. He brought with him an army of monsters, the likes of which no one had ever seen—a horde of savage beasts, apes from another land, armed for war. Where he found the creatures, I do not know, nor can I say how he managed to gain their loyalty. He had smuggled them into the palace through underground sewers, where they awaited his command.

"When King Hazelgood raised the second child before his subjects, Lord Incarnadine loosed a battle cry, and his terrible army attacked. The creatures swept through the crowd, killing and devouring the people." Simon paused for a moment, overtaken by his emotions. "It was a massacre."

Peter winced as he ran his fingers along the scars on his fore-arm—he knew how ruthless apes could be. "Didn't the Royal Guard fight back?" he said.

"Some, yes. But our forces had already been drawn away. Incarnadine had made a deal with the thieves living in the kingdom— for even a happy kingdom has its share of villains. Right before the christening, the Royal Guard discovered that all of the sleeping children had been stolen from their beds."

"They were all clipped," Peter said with wonder. He remembered how the old thief Clipper had refused to help him back in the Just

Deserts. "I'm not doin' it again!" he had shouted before running off into the night.

"They were *betrayed*," Simon said bitterly. "The thieves hid the infants deep underground where no one could hear their cries and then took to the sea with bags full of gold—payment for their treachery. Incarnadine had given the bags knowing that they would be mistaken for the missing children. When some of our guards reported their hasty escape, our captain led the bulk of our flock in pursuit. It was only after the flock left the palace that Incarnadine and his army attacked. The ape creatures were armed with weapons that could breathe fire and cast spears through the air. Those of us remaining were unprepared for such magic. We fought bravely, but were too few."

"What happened to the other ravens?" Sir Tode asked.

"Our captain and his troop caught the thieves and attacked them while they were still trying to sail to safety. When the men realized how they and their bags of gold had been used as bait, they roared so loudly that it shook the stars from their constellations."

A chill prickled up Peter's neck. "The Back-Stabber's Blight," he whispered.

"The what?" Princess Peg asked.

"It's a horrible curse," he explained. "I've only heard rumors of it before. It's said that when a thief is double-crossed by another thief, he can call a horrible curse upon the back-stabber's head."

"What is the punishment?" Simon pressed with new interest.

"They say that every man under the Back-Stabber's Blight ends up dying the same way: like a miserable worm."

"He deserves no less," the old bird said. "Whether or not your Blight comes to be, it is a fact that his plan worked that night. With the ravens divided, Incarnadine and his army stormed the royal chambers. He murdered his brother, the true king, and seized the throne. To answer your question, *this* was the Cursed Birthday."

"Oh," Peter said, half wishing he hadn't asked.

"So the evil brother stole back his inheritance," Sir Tode said, imagining the dramatic scene. "And thus ends the tale of the Cursed Birthday."

"Not entirely," Simon responded. "King Hazelgood knew his brother's lust for power would not be satisfied with this small island and that soon he would grow bored and sail out to terrorize other kingdoms. So in his final breath, he placed a curse over the land. He declared that so long as Incarnadine reigned, HazelPort's shores would never meet the sea. And at those words, the island trembled from pole to pole. The earth split in two and swallowed the ocean whole, leaving only a borderless wasteland."

"The whole kingdom vanished!" Sir Tode stomped a hoof.

"We've been trapped here ever since," the princess said bitterly. "The big pit surrounding the palace is too wide to cross, even for Simon. No one can get in or out."

"No one but us," Peter reminded her. Though he had declared before that he didn't care what the princess thought of him, he found himself seeking her approbation. "If that's not proof we're supposed to be here, what is?"

"He's got a point," Sir Tode said before moving to a more pressing subject. "Now, I see just a few holes in this story, Simon. You explained how the Just Deserts came about, but how did the ravens seize control of the place?"

Simon blinked at Sir Tode. "I do not understand your question. The ravens and the thieves all drowned when the seas withdrew. I have heard rumor of a few survivors, but . . ."

"Not a few," Peter said. "Thousands. They're led by a bird named Captain Amos."

Simon caught his breath and hopped closer. "Captain Amos? He lives? Did he and his brothers help you on your quest?"

"Yes . . . and no," Peter said. "I think the ravens *tried* to help us, but I made the mistake of trusting the prisoners, and they used me to help break into the armory and steal back their weapons." Hearing the old bird's story made Peter realize just how wrong he had been in trusting the thieves. "When we left the Just Deserts, Captain Amos and the others were still fighting for their lives." He hung his head in shame. "I'm sorry."

"There is nothing we can do for them now. My brothers are strong fighters. Justice will deliver them." The old bird remained silent for a long while, contemplating the war raging on the other side of the chasm.

Peg finished the story. "Once my uncle took the throne, he acted like the whole attack had been a bad dream. The adults woke up the next morning to a clean palace and a hot breakfast. He pretended that he had always been their king, and they his loving subjects. The missing children were never mentioned again, and anyone who dared speak of them was made to disappear. The rest of the grown-ups were so afraid that they went along with the whole thing. After a few years, they forgot we ever existed."

"But how can that be?" Sir Tode exclaimed. "How can parents *forget* their own children?"

"That is a question I cannot answer," Simon said. "Somehow, King Incarnadine has lowered a great cloud over the minds of his citizens. They believe his lies and follow his commands without question."

Peter had heard of traveling doctors who could entrance patients by dangling pocket watches in their faces or touching their temples with magnets—but nothing so powerful as what Simon was describing. He thought back on his conversations over supper with Mrs. Molasses and her neighbors. They had all sounded so earnest in their love for the king. "There has to be an explanation," he said aloud.

Peg shrugged. "It's the same way he controls the locks, and the bell tower, and everything else in the palace: he uses magic."

"You call that stuff magic," Peter said, "but it's just clockwork, right?" This had been bothering him ever since arriving; it seemed like people here knew almost nothing about science or logic. Peter was no genius, but he had been able to understand how gears worked since he was very young. Yet Mrs. Molasses, Peg, and even Simon seemed to treat such things like they were powerful enchantments.

"Perhaps these devices are simple to someone from your land," the raven said. "But here, they are mysteries unlike anything we have seen. The king uses a 'clockwork,' as you call it, to keep both adults and children imprisoned."

"I'd trade with the grown-ups any day," Peg said. "They get to sleep in beds and eat as much as they want. Meanwhile, us kids are stuck in the mines. Since we were old enough to stand, he's had us slaving away on a great magic beast—"

"Clockwork!" Giggle and Marbles jumped in, smiling at Peter. Both girls were developing a bit of a crush on the young thief.

Peg rolled her eyes and continued. "We spent our whole lives in the mines, working a *clockwork* beast that eats through the very rock."

"What's he digging for?" Peter asked. "Treasure?"

She shrugged. "Frankly, I don't care. I'm more worried about staying alive. And now that you two showed up, it's getting a lot harder. The king's tightened curfew, and the monsters have begun random inspections of people's houses. Apparently, one of the sparrows told them about a stranger—I thought they knew better than that."

Peter's stomach tightened. "Maybe it was some other bird that told them?"

"There are no other birds," she said.

Much as he hated to come clean, Peter couldn't let an innocent creature take the blame for his blunder. "I told them." He cleared his throat. "I was trying to rescue the sparrows, but the Night Patrol interrupted me. I told them about the stranger to distract them. It was dark, so they probably assumed I was a bird." He hoped they didn't examine this last statement too closely. "I'm sorry," he said for the second time in as many minutes.

"Brilliant." Her Majesty snorted. "Now it's the blind leading the blind."

Simon explained. "Those sparrows were our spies aboveground. Without them we have no way of knowing what Incarnadine is planning. It is also likely that he has apprehended one of them. When you set the sparrows free, they all reported here—all except for one bird named Crumpet. The king is not above torture. He may have taken her to learn of the stranger . . . but he will undoubtedly learn much more."

The thought of that innocent sparrow being tortured was too much for Peter. "We have to rescue her!"

"I think you've 'helped' enough for one day," Peg said, standing with her back to him. "Trouble, Scrape, you two start preparing a new hideout. Giggle and Marbles will keep lookout." Her orders were interrupted by a ringing aboveground. "That's the Breakfast Bell, which means the king will be waking up soon. We should move."

Peter put his hand to the wall and felt a tremor as dead bolts slid open all over the palace. Many hundreds of people filed from their homes, all walking toward the Eating Hall. He could hear something else above the chatter of hungry citizens: the faintest ripple of water. Peter sniffed the air and caught a scent that had not been there the moment before—a smell both disgusting and unmistakable.

"Where do you think you're going?" Peg said when she saw him packing his recently recovered burgle-sack.

"I have to check on something aboveground," he answered.

"What's the point? They're just eating breakfast."

"I'm hungry." Peter didn't want to tell her the real reason just in case he was wrong. "Look at it this way: if I die, I'll be out of your hair for good." He grabbed a stray coil of rope and stuffed it into his bag—in his experience, it never hurt to have a bit of rope on hand.

The princess found herself caught between frustration and curiosity. "Fine, but I'm coming with you. The only safe way is through the sewers, and you'll never get there on your own." She turned to Simon. "Keep watch on the *fierce knight* and see that he stays out of trouble. Everyone reports back here before the high sun."

And with that, the Missing Ones scattered into the darkness.

✦ ✦ ✦

The journey to the surface was a long one. The tunnels were narrow and slippery, made all the more treacherous by Her Majesty's speedy pace. Within a few minutes, Peter's whole person was soaked and sore. But still, he did not slow down—he wanted to prove himself a worthy hero, and that meant keeping up. As he breathed the dank air, Peter considered what it would be like to have grown up in this strange kingdom. It would have meant slavery, true, but he was no stranger to hardship. He couldn't shake the sense that there was something *right* about this place, something that made him feel more at home than he had ever been in his life. Even Her Majesty, who was rude and bossy, felt somehow familiar.

"I couldn't open that box of yours," she called back to him as she hoisted herself up a ladder. "What's inside?"

"Nothing special." Peter was still nervous about showing anyone the Fantastic Eyes. He remembered the professor's warning to keep them a secret. "It's just some old thief tools."

"Really?!" She helped him onto the ledge. "Can I look at them?"

"Trade secrets." He pushed the bag behind him. "A girl wouldn't understand."

"Fine . . . I didn't want to see them anyway!" Her Majesty resumed running at twice the speed.

Though hurt by her dismissive tone, Peter was relieved that the subject had been dropped. "What do you hope to do once we escape with the children?" he called, hoping that conversation might slow her down. "Will you be crowned queen?"

"I'll go find NoName," she said.

"Go find *who*?"

"NoName. My twin brother."

Peter had forgotten all about the second child. "Simon never said what happened to him."

"No one knows. He disappeared. Trouble and Scrape think he's dead, but I won't believe it. I've asked Simon, but he always gives me some nonsense about 'saving the Line' and 'Justice returning to us.'"

Peter wasn't sure it was wise of the bird to give her false hope like that. "For a baby to survive such a battle," he observed carefully, "you have to admit, it does sound a little unlikely."

"He's alive." She pushed open a rusted sewer grate and stepped into the warmth of daylight. "And someday I'm going to find him. You'll see." But of course Peter couldn't *see* anything—not the halls, nor the sky, nor even the way the morning light glinted off Her Majesty's brilliant, emerald-green eyes.

CHAPTER TWENTY

THE KING'S ADDRESS

Peter and Peg made it to the Eating Hall just before the second course. The princess led him to a secret perch inside the mouth of one of the many stone gargoyles spitting water down into the courtyard. Gargoyles, as you may be aware, are so named because of the way they "gargle" water. It is thought by some that these immortal grotesques were once filthy little children, turned to stone as punishment for the nasty habit of spitting in public. This pair of filthy children, however, had bigger things to worry about than social taboos. Peter and Peg leaned over the bottom row of stone teeth, eavesdropping on the citizens below. As with supper the previous night, conversation was pleasant and food was abundant. Peter could hear people talking through stuffed mouths, saying things like "I do *love* a good fig bisque!" and "My, isn't this sparrow-omelet *divine*?"

The hall had been completely cleaned since the boy was last there, and the sparrows' pedestals had been replaced with potted trees. "A group of children comes through here before dawn to clean up," the princess said. "The grown-ups always leave the place in a terrible—"

Peter raised a finger to her lips, signaling for her to be silent. He needed to concentrate on what was happening below. He could hear people chewing. He could hear the clock tower ticking. He could hear the streams flowing around the perimeter. "Princess, do you see something in the water down there?"

Peg peered over the jaw of the gargoyle for a better view. Everything seemed normal to her. "What am I looking for?" she asked.

Peter concentrated. There was definitely something foul in that water. "Is there anything sticking out of the surface? Like long tubes of some kind?"

"I see some reeds. They're spread all around the hall, every ten feet or so."

Peter nodded, inching closer to her. "It's a good thing we came. I'll wager my knack that the king is planning to attend breakfast this morning."

"That's ridiculous," Peg said. "The king never eats breakfast with his subjects. What makes you so sure?"

"Because his guards are stationed in the water. Look where the reeds are. Do you see any large shadows?"

"Yes," she said after a moment. "A-a-are those monsters?"

"There's nothing quite like the smell of wet ape." The boy tried not to sound smug, but had difficulty controlling his grin. "Stay down! Here comes the king!"

As if on cue, a trumpet sounded, and two dozen armed apes rose from the water. Seeing the dread Night Patrol in broad daylight, the people panicked. Several men fainted right there on the spot. Others began choking on their waffles. There was a mad stampede as citizens threw their food down and shoved and pushed to escape the Eating Hall. But when they reached the corridor, the people found that a gate had been lowered, blocking them off from the rest of the palace.

"Stop, citizens!" an ape roared above the din. Peter recognized its voice as that of the one named LongClaw. The beast paused, checking to make sure everyone was listening before he continued. "Your Gracious King has decided to join you for breakfast. Welcome him!"

The crowd instantly erupted into riotous applause the likes of which Peter had never heard in his life. He listened as the men and women stomped and whooped and cheered with all their might. The master thief, however, could sense other things—that their clapping hands smelled sweaty and their cheering throats sounded dry.

The king entered from a small door at the base of the clock tower. Peter could not see him, of course, but he could hear well enough. Every step echoed with a fierce *clank* of spurs. "He's wearing his *clockwork* armor," Peg said. "He never goes anywhere without it."

Peter was at a loss. He was pretty sure she must have meant

something other than "clockwork." But when he listened more closely, his ears caught the faint whir of gears spinning beneath the king's breastplate. The boy studied the sounds, wondering how this strange armor might work.

The applause continued as His Highness stepped to the head of the banquet table. Instead of waving his hand for silence, he simply stood there, nodding.

"What's he waiting for?" Peter whispered to Peg.

"He's waiting to see who stops first," she said.

But no one stopped. The people cheered and cheered and cheered until their hands were red and their voices hoarse. Finally, an old man at the table lost his strength. He collapsed to the ground, his cries giving way to a fit of coughing.

"Enough!" The king called out in a voice both authoritative and indignant. Peter did not think it sounded like the voice of a fierce warrior—there was something almost shrill in his tone. Yet at his command, the crowd fell to instant, terrified silence. The king faced the old man. "Have you no respect for your Great Ruler?"

"P-p-please, Mighty King!" the old man begged. "Have mercy on a loyal subject!"

"Guards!" Fast as a flash, three apes leapt across the courtyard. They pounced on the old man and dragged him by his heels, screaming, down the corridor toward some unseen and no doubt unpleasant fate. When at last his cries had faded away, the king turned back to his subjects. "Please. *Eat,*" he said with a magnanimous smile.

Every person in the hall sat down. They ate in silence, trying to force down perfect mouthfuls of food. This was hard to do, on account of having just seen one of their neighbors "disappear" at the hands of two drooling apes.

High above them, Peter huddled with Peg inside the gargoyle's massive jaw, shivering. He was shivering not because of the cold water rushing past his knees, but because his sensitive ears could still detect the old man's screams echoing somewhere deep underground.

Meanwhile, the adults below chewed, sipped, and swallowed their way through the rest of their meal. Apes circled the perimeter behind them, keeping watch for anyone who might dare offend their king with a slackened appetite. When the people had finally cleared their plates, Incarnadine spoke again. "My dear citizens. You may be wondering why I've graced you with my presence this morning. You see, it has been just over ten years since I completed building this Perfect Palace, brick by brick, with my own hands." He paused for a moment to accept his subjects' enthusiastic applause.

"Thank you, citizens," the king said. "It is so heartwarming to see how you appreciate my leadership, wisdom, and sacrifice."

"We do! We do!" the people shouted.

"And to reward you, I am planning something very big for our kingdom's anniversary."

"All hail anniversary!" the people shouted.

"It will be something that will make my kingdom what it should have been all along! Not only perfect, but *powerful*!"

"Hooray for powerful!" the people shouted.

Peter leaned forward. Whatever the king was planning, it might have something to do with the digging being done underground.

"But before I share that with you, I have something of a more serious nature to discuss."

"Three cheers for serious nature!" the people shouted.

The king scowled at this last declaration. "If I didn't know better, I'd say you were all just repeating whatever comes from my perfect mouth."

"Oh no!" the people shouted, more nervous this time. "We're listening! We love you!"

"That's better," he snapped, somewhat mollified. "As I said before, there is a very grave matter that I must bring to your attention. It seems that a spy has wormed his way into the castle. He is going by the name of Mr. Justice Trousers. And I suspect that he may, in fact, be . . . a *thief!*"

At this, women began hyperventilating while men trembled in their boots. It seemed the mere word had struck terror into the hearts of every subject. "As you know," the king said, "thieves are dark creatures who have evil ways of opening the locks that I have installed to protect you."

The two children listened as the people praised the king and his wonderful "magic" locks. Peter, who had told a lie or two in his day, was not impressed. "He's trying to tell them being locked up is *good?* That's the dumbest thing I've ever heard."

"I know," she said. "But they believe him, all the same."

The king raised his hand, silencing the crowd. "I have been told that this Mr. Trousers has come on a secret mission to assassinate your Worthy King."

A fresh wave of panic rippled through the crowd. "Don't die, Your Highness!" they cried. "We need you!"

"Your concern touches me." He placed a gauntlet over his ticking heart. "However, do not forget that I am the greatest fighter who has ever lived."

Peter snorted at this last statement.

"Don't laugh," Peg warned him. "He may be vain, but my uncle is dangerous. Simon says he can wield not one but *one hundred* swords, and a single sweep of his arm can fell ten men." Her mind flashed to the memory of her dead parents. "Whatever you do, don't underestimate him."

That this man could prove so powerful seemed impossible to Peter, but he trusted Simon to know a good warrior when he met one. Peter had spent his whole life in a town where fights were either drunken and friendly, or silent and petty. True war was foreign to him. He thought of how scared and confused he had been when the battle broke out in the Nest; he was in a different world now.

The boy shook these thoughts from his head and concentrated once more on the king's address. "Loyal subjects! You may be asking yourselves how a spy managed to hide in our midst. I am saddened to inform you that he was smuggled in by one of our own. I present to you all: the traitor!" He banged his armored hands together, and two apes stomped in from the corridor, escorting someone between them.

Peter gasped. He could smell the perfume from all the way up here. "It's Mrs. Molasses!" he whispered.

Peg leaned in close. "Is that the lady who helped you?"

Mrs. Molasses wore shackles around her wrists and ankles. It was clear the woman had no idea what she had missed in the first part of the king's address. She kept pleading, "What have I done? What have I done?"

The princess watched as the apes marched their prisoner to the middle of the hall and hurled her at the king's feet.

Incarnadine resumed his address to the crowd. "Early this morning, my guards apprehended this woman in her home. She was a fine citizen. An earnest admirer of her king and her kingdom. Blessed with a perfect life, she was eager to share her good fortune with strangers." Because nice things were being said about her, Mrs. Molasses began nodding her head, vigorously affirming each word. He continued. "And it is because of this *generosity* that I have called her before you today." The woman gave a brief, bewildered smile— was she being rewarded?

"I have received word that she recently brought a friend to supper. A stranger whom she had been housing for many days. My dear Mrs. Molasses," he said, smiling at her, "would you be so kind as to tell us the name of your esteemed guest?"

The woman beamed, now certain she had been nominated for some sort of hospitality prize. "Your Highness, his name was . . . Justice Trousers!"

At these words, the crowd gave a communal shriek. "Guilty by her own admission!" the king proclaimed. "Citizens, you know this to be the very name of the spy sent to murder me—and this woman is his accomplice!"

Mrs. Molasses gave a faint squeak. "No, Your Highness! Mr. Trousers was a nice man. He was injured! I wanted to help him, to share our perfect palace with him!" She approached on her knees, clutching her manacled hands to her bosom. "He never said anything about being a spy!"

"Of course he didn't *say*, you fool! And you didn't think to ask! Your *kindness*," and he spat out that last word with particular disgust, "has released an enemy into our midst and put my precious life in danger!" He turned back to the people. "Now, what shall we do to her?"

"Punish her!" the people shouted.

"Very well." He marched to the long, wooden table and snatched up a fistful of cutlery, raising it above his head. "Prove your loyalty to me! Take up your arms and *punish the traitor!*"

Princess Peg watched, horrified. "They wouldn't . . ." she whispered. But she was wrong. Without a moment's hesitation, every person in the Eating Hall took up a knife, fork, or serving spoon, chanting, "Kill the traitor! Kill the traitor!" Mrs. Molasses shook in fright as they circled her, screaming and shouting. The apes chuckled, eager to enjoy the show.

"Kill the traitor! Long live the king!!!"

"We have to do something," Peg said, reaching for Peter's hand. But his hand was nowhere to be found. While she had been busy watching the crowd below, the master thief had disappeared.

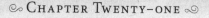

CHAPTER TWENTY-ONE

LILLIAN

Now you, knowing something of Peter Nimble and his Fantastic Eyes, have probably assumed that when Princess Peg discovered her companion had disappeared, it was because he had literally *disappeared*. The truth was far simpler, but no less compelling. The moment the great thief heard Incarnadine's order to kill Mrs. Molasses, he knew he had to do something; if that woman hadn't found him and nursed him back to health, he would be dead. He had been eager for an opportunity to silence Peg's doubts about him once and for all—what better way than with a heroic rescue?

Peter realized there was no chance of him overpowering the mob, never mind the apes. His only hope would be to create some kind of distraction; if he could divert their attention for just a moment, there might be a chance to sneak down there and set Mrs.

Molasses free. But how? He had no coughs or noisemakers large enough to disrupt a roaring mob. He felt around the gargoyle's mouth for something to throw—a loose molar, perhaps. Instead, his fingers came across a rusted hinge that connected the statue's jaw to the wall. Apparently, the gargoyle was acting as a sort of spigot, controlling the flow of water from the sewers.

The boy sprung to his feet and searched the tunnel behind him for some kind of switch to widen the floodgates.

"Peter! What are you doing?" Peg splashed alongside him and snatched at his sleeve. "I thought something had happened to you! You can't just disappear like that!"

"Either help me or get out of my way." He jerked his arm back, forgetting for a moment that she was royalty. "We have to save that woman."

"How? They're about ten seconds from *Long-Live-the-King*ing her to pieces!"

"Then we'd better hurry," he said. "You know these waterways, is there a sort of lever that controls the water flow?"

"A sort of what?" she said, exasperated. "I already told you, the fountains are *magic,* just like the bells, and locks, and everything else."

Peter pushed past her, wading deeper into the tunnel. The princess was clearly going to be of no help. Far below, he could hear Mr. Bonnet take the first swipe at Mrs. Molasses with a mustard fork. The boy winced at the sound of sharp prongs catching against her bustle, shredding the fabric. "I haven't time to explain, Your Majesty," he said. "Please, just go to my sack and grab the rope inside. I need you to anchor it to something secure." The girl chose not to question the command. Without another word she ran to his bag and removed the rope.

"Now, where are you hiding?" Peter murmured, turning back to the sewer wall. The farther he traveled, the deeper the water grew. It was up to his thighs now, dragging against his legs with the force of a thousand gallons. The flow pushed him backward, and he reached out a hand to steady himself. His fingers fell on a small knob connected to some rusted pipes along the ceiling. "Is the rope tied?!" he called back to Peg.

Growing up in underground caves, the princess had learned a thing or two about good climbing knots. The rope was expertly cinched around the gargoyle's outcropped fang. "All secure!" she said.

"Good! Then hold on!" Peter took the knob and wrenched it with all his strength. The pipes groaned as not one but *every* gargoyle above the Eating Hall opened its ugly jaw and loosed a torrential flood onto the people below.

In case you are not familiar with the sensation, a knock about the head is widely regarded as one of life's most unpleasant surprises. Such an assault usually results in the victim spinning around to cry "Who's there?!" at the air behind them. The person might even stupidly pat their head to check for blood. This most often happens to tall people when they walk into lintels or low-hanging branches—a fact that goes a long way toward explaining the perpetual bad mood of giants, Brobdingnagians, and the like.

While the citizens of the kingdom were not remarkably tall, they *were* all receiving knocks to the head from the cascading water. Almost every adult in the Eating Hall whirled around to demand "Who's there?!" while feeling for blood. Because their attacker was no person, but a thundering waterfall, their queries were met with a good soak in the face.

The pandemonium was astounding. There was so much yelling and splashing that it took them several minutes to realize what was happening. All the while, more water rushed down from above, filling the hall to the people's waists and sweeping some of them off their feet.

"The gargoyles are overflowing!" the king bellowed, climbing atop the table, which had itself begun to float. "LongClaw! You're responsible for the waterways!"

"They were fine last night, Sire!" The ape shoved a drowning citizen back into the water. "Someone must have tampered with the controls!"

"That's impossible! No one in the kingdom—" but just as the king was about to say that no one in the kingdom understood basic plumbing, he spotted two young children, both about ten years old, swimming through the chaos—and one of them was his niece!

"The girl is attacking! Capture her!"

"Get the child!" LongClaw snarled, sloshing after Peg.

As you may know, apes are not natural water creatures. They hardly ever drink the stuff in the wild. Every month or so, they might take a long pull from a trough and store the excess liquid in their hump, which lies squarely between their grotesque shoulder blades. Princess Peg, on the other hand, had spent a lifetime wading through sewage and muck. Because of this, the horde of bloodthirsty apes proved none too successful at capturing the fugitive heir. They slogged and splashed through the water, but Peg was too fast.

The girl swam around the perimeter of the Eating Hall, trying her best to draw attention away from Peter. The master thief, meanwhile, had worked his way to the center of the room and gotten hold of Mrs. Molasses. Before the woman knew what was happening, Peter dove below the surface and set to work on her chains. The locks were not difficult, being basically the same mechanism as the ones used on the sparrows. He popped the clasp open and came back up for air. "You're free!" he said, snatching her by the wrist. "Now hold your breath!" He dove below the surface of the water again, this time dragging Mrs. Molasses with him.

Under the water, Peter slowed his heart and concentrated on the splashy confusion. If he focused, he could tell the difference between humans and apes. He felt Mrs. Molasses pulling against his grip as they worked their way to the edge of the hall. They reached Peg's side just in time to help her break through the pile of citizens, who had jammed up the main corridor.

"That gate's blocking the exit," Peter said. "Is there another way out?"

"You might have checked *before* you washed us down here," Peg muttered. "Follow me." She grabbed Mrs. Molasses's other arm and led them through a side corridor. When they came to a small alcove, Peg pulled a stone loose from the wall and shoved them both into a secret passage. She climbed in after them, replacing the stone before anyone could see.

Now, one might think that saving a woman's life would create in her a positive disposition toward her rescuers. You might even think that the saved woman would be thankful and eager to please as she was pushed and squeezed through this or that underground tunnel. This, however, was not the case. After more than ten years of brainwashing, Mrs. Molasses's mind had been thoroughly scrubbed of anything even remotely resembling common sense. Despite evidence to the contrary, she remained entirely convinced that her king was good and that these children were evil. "Let me go!" she shrieked as they carried her deeper underground. "Help! Guards! King! Anyone! The spies have me!"

Peg spun around, exasperated. "Your neighbors were going to murder you—with spoons! You really want to go back up there?!"

"They were only obeying His Highness!" She kicked Her Majesty's shin. "Let me go!"

Peter tried a more diplomatic tone. "Mrs. Molasses, I know you're frightened, but if you keep screaming, those monsters will hear us. Do you really want that?" In answer, he, too, received a kick in the shin.

There is an old phrase that an insecure man once made up to feel superior to his progeny. Sadly, the saying caught on over the years, and now many people believe it to be true: "There's no reasoning with a child." As any levelheaded child can attest, this sentiment is pure nonsense. And while Peg and Peter both rubbed their shins, Her Majesty grasped the truer statement: "There's no reasoning with a grown-up," she sighed, limping ahead. "If she's that stupid, we should just let her die."

"Get back here, Peg!" Peter said with a force that surprised even himself. "This woman may be confused, but she's still one of your subjects. We're taking her with us."

"She'll lead the king and his apes right to our hideout," the girl shot back. "We can't risk that."

Peter considered this for a moment. He knelt down and tore a strip of cloth from his pant leg. With an apologetic smile, he stuffed the fabric into Mrs. Molasses's screaming mouth. "Problem solved," he said. "Now start dragging."

✦   ✦   ✦

The gag worked like a charm, and—kicking and punching aside—Mrs. Molasses was much more agreeable for the remainder of the trip. When the pair finally reached the den, Sir Tode and Simon were waiting.

"Peter!" the knight said, galloping to the boy's feet.

"Your Majesty!" the raven said, swooping to the girl's shoulder.

Peg sighed, dropping her end of the load. "Sorry we were late. Take it up with Peter."

"And so I shall," Simon said and shot him a glare. "We heard commotion aboveground and became worried. I sent the sparrows up to investigate. They said the king has locked everyone in their houses and started door-to-door inspections. Were you seen?"

"You could say that," Peter groaned as he dragged the rest of Mrs. Molasses into the cave.

"Er, who's your friend?" Sir Tode asked, poking her with a hoof.

"Her name is Mrs. Molasses. She's the woman who nursed me back to health. We rescued her from a mob of crazed grown-ups."

"That was foolish," Simon snapped. "We cannot afford to have one of the king's citizens knowing of our location."

"They were going to *kill her*," Peter protested.

"Even so. Her Majesty's safety is more important than any single person. You would be wise to remember that."

About this time, Mrs. Molasses managed to roll herself to an upright position. "Help! I'm in here!" she screamed, ripping out her gag and racing for the tunnels.

Peter lunged across the cavern, tackling the woman. "Hold her down," he grunted. "I'll chain her up."

"No chains," Peg said firmly. "As long as I'm princess, we will never use chains."

"You used them on me," he grumbled.

Simon spoke to Peg in a low tone. "Your Majesty, unless this woman calms down, she puts us all in danger of being discovered. If you refuse to chain her up, then you must get rid of her." He raised a black talon. "I can make it quick."

"I said NO," Peter shouted across the cave. Both princess and raven were evidently surprised he had heard them. "I know it's dangerous, but if you kill her, you're no better than the king."

"The boy has a point," Sir Tode said. "We are not murderers here."

"Speak for yourself," Peg said.

Peter turned back to the struggling woman. He knew there must be some way to cut through the king's lies. "Do you remember me, Mrs. Molasses? I'm the stranger you found in your courtyard."

"Don't be ridiculous!" she spat back. "That man had golden eyes. You have no eyes at all! I never forget a face!"

"I'm not a man, I'm a little boy." He swung his leg around, pinning her in a sort of sleeper hold. "Do you remember what a little boy is?"

The woman looked at him in wild terror. "If it's a sort of torture, it will never work! You can *little boy* me all you want—I'll never give in!" She rolled over, smothering him under her voluminous skirt.

Peter grabbed a fistful of her hair, trying to wriggle free. "Wait a minute," he said, sniffing the perfumed locks. "Where's Trouble?"

"The two boys are scouting the caves," Simon answered.

"Can you bring him here? Please?"

Peg sighed, then nodded to Simon, who quickly flapped out of the cavern. A few minutes later, the raven returned with Trouble in tow. "Did I do something wrong?" he asked, wiping his nose on his sleeve.

Peter, who had since managed to subdue Mrs. Molasses with ropes, rose to meet him. He leaned close, sniffing the boy's hair. "Trouble," he said with a smile. "I want you to say hello to your mother."

There was a long silence.

"My what?" Trouble said, picking a scab on his forearm.

Peter took his hand and led him into the candlelight. "There's nothing to be afraid of. Just let her see your face."

"Don't come any closer!" Mrs. Molasses cowered against the wall, covering her eyes. "Get away from me, you dirty little man!"

Trouble squatted down to get a better look at her. "She's awful fat," he said.

This wasn't working quite as well as Peter had hoped. He knelt beside the woman and gently pulled her hands from her eyes. "Look at him," he said softly. "I know you haven't forgotten."

Mrs. Molasses tried to break away from Trouble's gaze, but she could not. Slowly, as she stared into his pale blue eyes, something changed within her. Peter heard her breath catch and felt the pulse quicken beneath her skin.

"T–T–Timothy?" she whispered.

Mrs. Molasses was now shaking all over. She reached up to touch the boy's face. "I had a baby once . . . he had the most *beautiful* eyes . . . he was . . ." Her great body heaved as she fought back tears. "My baby!" She threw her arms around Trouble, pulling him close against her bosom. "My little Timothy!"

The boy was confused and a bit scared. "Is that really my name?" he asked. "Timothy?"

The woman wept, remembering the horrid day all those years ago when her son was stolen from his crib. "I thought I had lost you forever!" She pulled him closer, and Trouble wept, too—for no child ever truly forgets the love of his mother.

Peg watched all this in silence, thinking of how she had wanted to kill this woman moments before. "What . . . just happened?" she asked.

Peter shrugged. "Underneath all that perfume and grime, something told me they belonged together . . . their smells matched."

"Ha! Their smells matched!" Sir Tode repeated the words like a satisfying punch line. "I told you he was gifted, but you wouldn't listen. What do you have to say *now*?"

Simon hopped down from Her Majesty's shoulder. "Forgive my previous doubts, Peter Nimble. I see now that your arrival is a miracle indeed."

The princess could not go so far as to admit she had been wrong, but she, too, was impressed. "You clearly know your way around a pair of shackles," she said. "Tomorrow we'll go to the mines, and see if you can't help the others." She looked back at Timothy with his mother and could not help but smile. "And thank you."

This approval, however mild, filled Peter with gladness. "Of course, Your Majesty," he said, bowing.

For the next few hours, the cold chamber was filled with more warmth and love than all the hearths of the world combined. Timothy shared with his mother the trials and pains of growing up underground, and each new tale made her weep with renewed gratitude that they were together once again. As the afternoon grew longer, the little boy became tired, and his mother took him in her arms, stroking his matted hair and singing hushed lullabies.

✦   ✦   ✦

It wasn't until evening that the appearance of Mrs. Molasses, whose real name was Lillian, created trouble. It started when the other girls returned from their posts, bone tired. "Who's that?" Marbles asked, glaring suspiciously at the grown-up beside Timothy.

"That's my mum," the boy said proudly. "Peter rescued her."

Marbles gasped, taking hold of Peter's arm. "You found Trouble's mother?"

"I couldn't have done it without Peg's help," he said.

A new thought dawned on the girl. "Well, what about *my* mother? How come Trouble gets one and not me?"

"Yeah," Giggle said, joining her side. "And what about me?"

Princess Peg stepped in and tried to explain the situation. Just when she had calmed them both, Scrape came in from his scout run.

"I heard shouting and came as fast as I could! What's happened?" His fists were balled, ready for a fight.

"Trouble's got a mother," Marbles said. "And he won't share!"

Scrape, who was Trouble's closest mate, looked at his friend with hurt in his eyes. "That's not fair . . . Let us have a turn with her!"

"It's not like that." Timothy shoved them all away. "She's *mine!*"

"Oh yeah?" they yelled, shoving him right back. "Well, what if we *take* her?!"

Peg tried her best to break things up. "All of you, quit fighting!" she shrieked in her bossiest voice. "Or I'll take her right back aboveground where we found her!" But it was no use; bedlam had broken out—complete with crying, spitting, and kicking of dirt.

Lillian could see that stopping the fight would require more than force alone. "Children, *please!*" She thrust herself between them. "I'm all the mother any of you has got right now. I wish it wasn't so, but I will have to suffice for the time being. I'm sure Timothy will be perfectly happy to share me with you. Won't you, darling?"

Timothy looked far from "perfectly happy" about the prospect of sharing his new mother with anyone, let alone several anyones. Instead of answering, he glared at the ground, pushing a mount of dirt around with his toe. "*Timothy,*" Lillian said in a disapproving tone.

"Fine," he muttered. "You can have her some, too."

With that, she encircled all of the children in her great grown-up arms, even pulling Princess Peg into the group. Now, for those of you who have been raised with mothers, the significance of this moment may escape you. However cruel and flawed your own mother may seem, she is certainly better than *no* mother at all. These children had no memories of being held or spanked or fed mush with a spoon. When they were learning to walk or training themselves for the toilet, they had no encouraging voice cheering them on—instead, they had apes ready to eat them alive if they didn't get back to work. Because of this, Lillian's promise to be a mother to every one of them was a bit overwhelming. No sooner had she adopted them than they all burst into tears, clinging to their new guardian.

All, that is, except Peter. The young thief stepped back from the group and joined Sir Tode on the cold, dirt floor.

The knight studied the boy's face in the candlelight. "I'm no mum," he said. "But I am your friend."

Peter rested a hand on his matted nape. "My best friend." And the two of them sat together and listened as Lillian hummed softly to her new family. The Missing Ones had been found at last.

⊱ CHAPTER TWENTY-TWO ⊰
THE CLOCKWORK BEAST

In rescuing Lillian, Peter had definitively answered all outstanding questions regarding his competency. And so the following morning, Peg and the others set out to show him the mines. "I can't wait to see those chains fall off just like magic," Her Majesty exclaimed as she hopped down a rocky stairway. It seemed she had changed her opinion of the young thief overnight. "You should have seen how he popped open Lillian's locks—underwater, even!"

Peter wasn't so confident. Yes, he was a skilled thief, but from the sound of it there were a lot of children who needed saving. He wasn't sure he liked having so many people depending on him. "Let's hope it's that easy," he said under his breath.

Easy, however, it was not. Just getting to the mines proved an ordeal in itself. Peter's adventure in the Eating Hall had clearly rattled the king, who had since posted sentries in all the tunnels underground; it seemed every path was now blocked off by apes. "How many routes are there?" Peter whispered as they waited in a side cavern for some guards to march past.

"Oh, hundreds," Timothy said, holding firmly to Lillian's hand. "We know lots of them, but only the king knows them all."

"The king knows all of the tunnels?" Peter was somewhat surprised; it had been his experience that adults rarely knew about secret passages in their own homes.

"Every last one," Marbles said. "He has this magic piece of parchment that lets him see where they all lead and how they connect to each other."

"You mean a map?" Sir Tode said.

"What's that?" she asked.

Peter and Sir Tode were shocked—these children had never even learned what a map was.

"Map . . ." Lillian repeated the word with a hint of foggy recollection. "Yes, I do believe I remember that one." She lit a candle and brought the children closer. "A *map* is a piece of paper with a picture of the ground on it. Look here: I'm drawing a *map* of this cavern." And with this, she took a piece of coal and began to mark the floor.

"That's just a lumpy circle," Timothy said. "It doesn't look anything like this place."

"True," she said patiently. "But what if Simon was looking at this room while flying overhead? What would it look like then?"

"Dark?" Giggle offered.

"Like a bunch of rocks?" Scrape said, thinking hard. "Because he'd be looking at the rock floor!"

"Very good, Scrape. And what shape would all those rock walls take? Look around a moment, if you have to." The children all craned about, staring at the shadowy chamber.

"A circle?" Timothy finally ventured.

Lillian beamed. "Exactly. So that's what I've drawn on my map. And tunnels would be wiggly lines, like this." The children watched, completely transfixed.

Peg remained with Peter apart from the group. "I learned a little about maps from Simon," she said. "But I don't know enough to explain it to them. They needed a real teacher."

Peter listened to Lillian's lesson, glad that the children were finally learning something. He had never seen a map, of course, but had grown up creating little diagrams in his mind of how rooms were shaped so that he could avoid bumping into things. In his head, these spaces were always alive—shifting and growing as his other senses filled in more details. "If the king has this fancy map, does he know about the cave where you live?" he asked.

"Not yet," Peg answered. "We dug that one ourselves. If he does find out about it, we'll have no place left."

As Lillian and the children continued discussing the mysteries of cartography, Peter turned his attention to the echoing footsteps of the Night Patrol. He could hear them stomping back and forth, grumbling about how much more fun the rest of the apes must be having right now. Mr. Seamus had taught Peter that when guards get bored, they fall into patterns—and it was a thief's job to discover that pattern and exploit its weakness. When the ape sentry marched past for the third time, Peter sensed an opportunity. He turned to Peg. "Your Majesty, I can get us by those apes, but it's too dangerous to move in such a large group. We can't take the others."

The girl rose, dusting off her hands. "Peter and I are continuing on," she said to the children. "I need the rest of you to return to the den and wait for us."

Her friends loosed a communal grumble. "It ain't fair." Scrape jumped to his feet. "How come you and Peter get to do all the fun stuff?"

Before there could be a scene, Lillian intervened. "Because, Scrape, without you, I'll have no one to protect me from those terrible apes. You are such a brave fighter, and I would feel so much better with you at my side." She offered her arm. "Won't you please escort me?"

The boy gave an embarrassed shrug. "I guess," he said and shuffled to her side.

Timothy, not to be outdone, grabbed her other arm. "I'll guard you too, Mum."

"Me, too!" said the girls.

"How chivalrous, all of you!" Lillian led the children off

toward the den. "When we get back, I'll make you some tea and teach you all about *hygiene*. Won't that be fun?"

Peter listened, half wishing he could join her. But he and the princess had more urgent matters to attend to. Peter led the way, with Peg, Simon, and Sir Tode close behind. The small group traveled deeper and deeper underground, stopping to hide whenever they heard the Night Patrol nearby. Eventually they reached a steep tunnel that led toward the mines.

Peter put his hand to the clammy stone. "I can feel something moving down there. Like the whole earth is shaking."

"It's the clockwork beast I was telling you about, the one that eats rocks. We're getting close."

A rough voice echoed up through the dark. "All right!" an ape said. "Fifteen minutes for nap time, then it's back to work! Anyone who grumbles gets fed to the dragons!"

"Dragons?" Sir Tode, who was trying his best to clop quietly, caught up with the others. "The king has *dragons?*"

"I have never heard of such creatures," Simon said, settling down on Her Majesty's shoulder. "It is probably a hollow threat."

Peter sniffed the air for something that might settle the matter— traces of brimstone or venom—but caught only a salty tinge. If he didn't know better, he would have said the odor reminded him of his hometown. But that was absurd: they were miles underground and half a world away.

The tunnel leveled out and opened onto a narrow landing over-looking an enormous cavern. "Welcome to the mines," Peg said.

The rumbling had subsided, better allowing Peter to take in his surroundings. The sheer enormity of the chamber stunned him. He felt heat from torches a hundred feet off. He could hear drips of water falling from stalactites fifty feet above him. And he could smell apes marching back and forth across the wet floor, which seemed to stretch into nothing.

"Careful of that ledge," Peg said, pulling him back. "It's a long way to the bottom." She pointed across the chamber for Sir Tode's benefit. "Over there sleeps the clockwork beast."

The knight squinted through the torchlight and gasped. "Goodness, Peter . . . she wasn't kidding." If the boy were able to see, he would have been greeted with the vision of a nightmarish contraption. The colossal machine was nearly as tall as the cavern itself. The exposed back revealed a tangle of gears, pistons, and springs, all connected to giant circular cages—not unlike the exercise-wheels that scientists use to amuse rodents. Only these particular exercise-wheels were larger, big enough to fit several people inside. The front of the machine looked like a great iron screw that had burrowed deep into the wall.

The drill, which had been responsible for the rumbling, was currently dormant. Its operators—the children—were all resting in the center of the cave. "The slaves are huddled together in the middle of some flat boulder," Sir Tode explained. "There's a moat with dark water surrounding them on all sides."

Peter could hear apes marching around the perimeter, cracking their whips and threatening the children. Each guard held a long chain that ran along the floor and disappeared under the surface of the moat. "That's saltwater," he said, realizing why the smell had seemed familiar to him.

Sir Tode craned his neck and caught a glimpse of a long shadow moving beneath the ripples. "It looks like the apes have something swimming on the other end of those chains." No sooner did the knight utter this than he saw an enormous creature lift its head out of the water. Its slimy body was thick as a pickle barrel and lined with spiny ribbons of fin. The animal writhed and lunged against its leash, which was fastened to a great iron mask that covered all of its head except the mouth. Every snap of its jaws revealed razor-sharp teeth made of glassy bone. It let out a high-pitched scream that sounded as though it could split rock.

"Good heavens . . ." Sir Tode said. "I had thought they were extinct!" He watched in horror as the hideous monster lashed its three-foot tongue through the air, tasting food (children) nearby. It shrieked and snapped, trying desperately to sink its teeth into the soft flesh just out of range.

The slaves all screamed, dropping their food and rushing to the other end of the island. "Look lively, you maggots," one of the apes heckled. A creature on the opposite side of the moat shot its head out of the water, shrieking and snapping as well. The guards fell into wild fits of laughter as they watched the children scurry back and forth between the monsters.

"What are those waterborne fiends?" Simon asked, almost mesmerized.

Sir Tode's mouth had gone dry. "Sea serpents . . . dragons of the deep. They disappeared from our waters a long, long time ago. I remember stories when I was young—it was said that just three of them were responsible for devouring the entire Philosopher's Peninsula."

"And there are at least a dozen down there in that moat," Peter said, counting their shrill voices. This job was getting harder by the minute—no longer just a matter of cracking open some old rusty locks; now there were *sea dragons* to contend with.

"How is it these monsters can breathe underwater?" asked Peg, who, thanks to her father's enchantment, had never seen so much as a lint-mollusk in her lifetime.

Simon tried to answer the question as best he could. "In some faraway places there lives a mighty 'ocean'—water so vast that it can surround entire kingdoms on all sides. It is said that this water circles the world like a scorned lover, forever chasing the moon. Beneath its surface lies a second realm, filled with a magic salt that flows through its currents like the wind through our skies. Myriad strange creatures are born and die within those depths, never to taste the air." The bird shuddered at this horrifying thought.

The girl nodded, only half understanding what Simon's words meant—especially the stuff about scorned love. Before she could ask for further details, a metallic voice echoed through the cavern.

"LONGCLAW!" It was coming from a brass horn mounted to the wall. "I NEED TO SEE YOU IN MY ROYAL STRATEGY ROOM THIS INSTANT. WE HAVE URGENT MATTERS TO DISCUSS. GIVE YOUR SERPENT TO ANOTHER GUARD AND GET IN HERE."

"It's the king," Peter said to the others. Apparently, Incarnadine had rigged a sort of voice pipe that ran from another chamber into the mines. Peter had encountered similar contraptions back home, devised for summoning servants and clerks.

"Aw, I was just startin' to have fun with her," LongClaw protested.

"I SAID *NOW*."

Peter listened as the ape threw his leash down and stomped off into what sounded like a small tunnel. The boy knew that the primary mission was to free those children, but something told him he might want to listen in on whatever "urgent matters" were being discussed. He turned away from the princess and removed the box of Fantastic Eyes from his burgle-sack. He opened the lid and let the golden pair take a good long look at their hiding spot—just in case he needed to make a quick escape. He crouched beside Sir Tode, whispering, "I want to find out what they're planning down there. And I thought maybe . . . if you were willing, that is . . ." He opened the bag, somewhat sheepishly. "I could really use a pair of eyes."

"By all means," the knight said, making himself comfortable inside the sack.

Peter slung the bag over his shoulder. When he approached the edge of the path, Peg grabbed his shirt. "Are you crazy?" she said. "That's a sheer drop!"

"Don't worry about us," he said and pulled himself free. "Just stay out of trouble while we're gone." Peter swung his legs over the ledge and disappeared into the shadows.

For those of you who are not thieves, the art of scaling smooth surfaces (called "cobwebbing") may seem a complete mystery. It is, in fact, one of the most difficult skills for a thief to master, requiring the ability to wedge one's fingers and toes into impossibly small cracks. As you may imagine, such a process is made considerably more tricky by any degree of moisture. The cave walls were slick, and Peter's fingers were stiff from tension. Still, slowly, quietly, he made his way to the base of the cavern, careful to keep clear of the flickering torches.

The mines connected to another chamber that was nearly as large as the first. Peter could smell sulfur and sawdust in the air. All around him he heard the distinctive music of carpentry—hammers pounding, axes cutting, wood snapping. Sir Tode looked out of the bag and described what he saw. "It's a stockpile. They've got cannons, powder casks, harpoons . . . Why, they could take the kingdom ten times over with an arsenal this size." He eyed the huge pile of masts, planks, and oars. "And it looks like they're building a fleet to match . . . but why build boats when there's no ocean to carry them?"

Peter heard LongClaw's voice echoing through a stone archway ahead. He was speaking with Incarnadine. The boy crept through the shadows and slipped inside.

The chamber—which Peter had heard called the royal strategy room—was a small cave lined with torches. LongClaw and the king were huddled around some sort of table in the middle. The lack of echoes made the boy think the walls might be lined with tapestries. Sure enough, he reached out and felt silky fabric hanging beside him. He couldn't see the design, but he suspected it bore a picture of the king. The master thief slipped behind the tapestry, where he and Sir Tode could listen undetected.

"Still no traces of the girl, Sire," LongClaw reported. "But my grunts are scouring the tunnels here, here, and here." He shuffled some papers on the table as he spoke.

"If only you hadn't *crushed* that sparrow," the king said peevishly, "we could have gotten more information out of her. I must find out about this stranger who's helping my niece."

"Given how fast he cracked the fleshy woman's chains, I'd say he's a lock-pick. Maybe even the same one that freed the princess?"

"That's doubtful. It's been years since she broke from her shackles. No, I suspect this is someone new who has come to help rescue her precious subjects. I should like to see him try. No person alive could ever hope to smuggle those brats past my sea serpents."

"A brilliant precaution, Sire," the ape said. "One more thing: we received a post from Officer Trolley this morning."

"Trolley?" Incarnadine chuckled. "What's the old fool got for us? More magic carpets?"

"It seems a war has broken out between the ravens and thieves. Right now the sides are evenly matched."

The king considered this news. "That is excellent for our plan," he said. If ever you have had the chance to spend quality time with a villainous mastermind, you will know that these people are extraordinarily fond of discussing their evil schemes out loud. Much to Peter and Sir Tode's good fortune, it sounded like the king was preparing for just such a monologue. "I want you to send the thieves a barge loaded with weapons," he went on. "If they survive this battle, I may have some use for them once more—it never hurts to have an army of sunburned maniacs at your beck and call."

"You really think they'll trust you again, Sire?"

"Trust me? Of course not. But thieves are cowards, and I am the only one who can rescue them from what's to come . . . which I will happily do in exchange for their services. Besides, it's not like they're swimming in alternatives . . . not yet, at least." At this, the king suppressed a snigger. Peter did not understand the joke, but he suspected that it had something to do with the big anniversary plans the man mentioned in his address to the people.

"Peter, there's a stack of scrolls on that table," Sir Tode said in his quietest voice. "If the king's making boats, then he must have a way of getting them to sea . . . Those papers might show us how."

The boy flexed his fingers. "Leave it to me." He knelt and

collected a handful of coughing pebbles as the king and ape continued their conversation.

"What is the status of the dig, LongClaw?"

"If them squigglers are any sign, we're getting close. There's already cracks around the drill. I say with a little push, we could be soggy by sunrise."

"Then push we shall. Ten long years I've been trapped in this filthy desert!" He raised his armored fist, and Peter caught the whir of clockwork. "It's time at last for my reach to expand. The sooner I sail out, the sooner we can recruit more apes—teach them how to speak and fight like you." The king clapped the creature's shaggy hump. "Imagine that, LongClaw: ten thousand apes under your command . . . and you, of course, under mine." The two shared a conspiratorial chuckle.

Their revelries were cut short by the sound of light footsteps outside the chamber. "What is it now?" the king snapped, not a little irritated at being interrupted in the middle of a good evil laugh.

LongClaw stomped into the tunnel and returned a moment later. "Nobody outside, Sire." He sniffed the air. "But I do smell somethin' about."

"Not likely. These mines are crawling with apes. No one would be that . . ." Here his words trailed off, for as he glanced back toward the table he spied a young boy stuffing maps, blueprints, and ledgers into a cloth bag.

Obviously, Peter hadn't counted on being noticed in the middle of his theft. But life, as you know, often has a way of surprising us at the most inopportune moments. He had been too reckless with his cough, and now he and Sir Tode were trapped.

"If it isn't our little stranger," Incarnadine said with a frown. Despite having the upper hand at the present moment, he wasn't pleased that this intruder had gotten so close.

Peter backed away from the table and slipped a hand into his burgle-sack. "Greetings, Your Highness," he said, rummaging through his bag. "I enjoyed your speech yesterday morn—"

"Shuddup, lock-pick!" The ape grabbed Peter and slammed him against the wall. The boy did not cry out, but instead dug deeper into his bag.

"What'd you have in mind, Sire?" LongClaw ripped a torch from its bracket and brought it close to the boy's face. "Should I gobble him raw, or should I roast him first?" Peter winced as the flames flicked against his cheek.

"Patience, LongClaw. We wouldn't want to kill 'Mr. Trousers' just yet. Not when there's oh so much I have to ask him." Incarnadine stepped closer, and Peter heard the delicate clockwork spinning beneath his armor. There came a *shink!* sound, and then he felt something sharp against his skin. The blade seemed to be spring-loaded, attached to his forearm. "Why don't we start with your real name?" the king said, running his weapon along the boy's jaw.

"M-m-my name is Peter Nimble."

"Peter Nimble?" The king snorted. "Why, that's even worse than Trousers. Tell me, Peter, how did you manage to undo the Molasses woman's shackles?"

"I . . . I have a *key*," he answered weakly. "It's inside my bag."

LongClaw dropped the torch. "Didn't nobody tell you? Keys are strictly outlawed in this here kingdom." He reached into Peter's bag in search of contraband.

The next moment, the bag jerked to one side. "Take that!" a voice cried from within. "And that!"

LongClaw roared, yanking his paw free. Sir Tode came with it—jaws clenched firmly around the beast's shaggy paw. "*Gahhh!* Get it offa me!" the ape snarled and flung Sir Tode across the chamber.

"The cat you can eat," Incarnadine said before returning to his own prey. But when he raised his fist, he saw he was holding not the wrist of a little boy, but an extinguished torch of roughly the same thickness.

Sir Tode's bite had been all Peter needed to slip free and scab the king. The master thief scooped up the scrolls from the ground and dashed to his friend's side. He pulled his bandage away to reveal a pair of shining, golden eyes. "Long live the True King!" he said, and the next instant Peter, Sir Tode, and the scrolls were gone.

CHAPTER TWENTY-THREE

THE MUTT'S NOGGIN

A moment later, Peter and Sir Tode reappeared beside Peg and Simon. They tumbled to the ground, sending scrolls everywhere.

The princess was furious, and not a little startled. "You could have gotten us killed!" She swatted Peter's ear with a map. "I sent Simon down to check on you and he was nearly spotted—and what are these ridiculous papers?"

"We had to find out what they were talking about," the boy said, quickly slipping the box of Fantastic Eyes back into his bag. He retied the bandage over his sockets before the others could notice.

Simon hopped closer. "Your head bleeds, Sir Tode. Are you badly wounded?"

"Only my honor," the knight said weakly. "We fled before I had a proper chance to fight back . . . Why, another minute, and I'd have given that ape a gash to match my own!"

Peg returned to the subject at hand. "That was incredibly stupid—both of you. I knew you weren't ready for this task."

Peter, who had fought so hard to win the princess's trust, resented this. "Sorry if we *inconvenienced* you. I figured we might want to know the king's plans before we rushed into anything." He snatched the scroll from her hand and stuffed it into his bag. "Besides, one of these 'ridiculous papers' might just show us how to break out of this place."

Their argument was cut short when LongClaw stormed into the mines and howled the alarm. Apes scattered in all directions in search of a "brat with golden eyes."

Before Simon or Peg could ask what that meant, Peter started for the tunnels. "Let's go, Sir Tode. Guess we'll just have to risk our necks for *Her Majesty* some other time."

✦   ✦   ✦

As they traveled back to the hideout, the two children maintained a frigid silence. Peg felt bad about the way she had spoken to Peter, but could not come up with any good way of saying "I'm sorry" that didn't also say "I'm wrong." Peter, on the other hand, was too busy compiling a list of all the thankless sacrifices he'd made to even contemplate an apology. Sir Tode and Simon did not speak, but they exchanged occasional looks meant to convey that they, at least, bore no hard feelings.

As with most squabbles, the fight was forgotten when the children encountered a uniting threat. They found one as soon as they reached the hideout: it was empty, their few provisions smashed to bits. There was no sign of Lillian or the children anywhere.

Peter drew his fishhook and sniffed the air. The stench was overpowering. "Apes," he said somberly.

"They must have been waiting here when the others returned." Peg's voice was tremulous. She knelt and picked up a scrap of cloth, torn from Lillian's apron. "If I hadn't sent them back here alone—"

Peter cut her off. "Then we'd be dead, too. You said it yourself: the king was searching the tunnels. This wasn't our fault."

"Not ours . . . mine," she said softly. "They trusted me to lead them." She turned away from the others to hide her tears.

Peter listened to her, and his frustration melted into genuine concern. "We will find them, Your Majesty. You have my word. But right now we have to leave before the creatures come back."

"And go *where?*" She threw down the cloth and stood. "We're trapped! The king knows every tunnel in the kingdom."

Peter couldn't help but share in her despair. Where *could* they go? He shook his head. "There's always the mutt's noggin."

The others were silent.

"It's an old thieves' proverb," he said. "*The safest flea is on the mutt's noggin.* It doesn't matter if our location is secret, or even secure—it just has to be the one place our enemy isn't looking."

Peter slid his fishhook back into his bag. "Your uncle thinks we're underground, so we should go as far from underground as possible . . . and I think I know just the spot."

+ + +

While sneaking through a sleeping palace was simple enough, moving during daylight was another thing altogether. It seemed like everywhere Peter and the others turned, they found apes and citizens on the lookout for the dread Mr. Trousers, *aka* Peter Nimble, *aka* the Golden-Eyed Assassin. It was several hours before they reached the mutt's noggin—also known as the belfry of the clock tower.

"Not like any clock I've ever seen," Sir Tode had observed upon reaching the top of the rickety stairs. "Why, there are no hands at all. Just a blank face, ticking and ticking . . ."

They were on a small wooden platform surrounded by enormous clockworks. Peg touched the cog behind her, which was three times her height. "These same magic wheels live inside the walls," she said. "They make the locks open and close." She pulled her hand back as the cog lurched forward.

Simon was just as mystified as the princess. "And these chimes," he said, hopping toward an iron bell. "They somehow call the sun, commanding its rise and fall." He pecked the rim, which responded with a soft *pinggggg*. He fluttered to a window, checking to see whether it looked any darker outside. "The king alone controls their magic."

Peter attempted—once again—to explain that there was nothing magic about locks or clocks, but Simon and Peg could not be made to understand. "No," she insisted. "It's dark magic my uncle brought back from far-off lands."

Peter was starting to think that the "far-off lands" Incarnadine had visited were no more special than his port town. While no one back there had ever seen talking ravens or enchanted deserts, even the children understood basic scientific principles. He remembered what Professor Cake had said about distant seas being ruled by laws other than reason. He hadn't before considered how that might limit the people living there. "Well, friend," he said to Sir Tode, "it sounds like it will fall on you to decipher these." He took the scrolls from his bag and spread them out on the floor.

When unrolled, the papers were large enough for Sir Tode to stand right on top of them. The knight paced from end to end, keeping his nose close to the markings. "Good heavens . . ." He gave a bitter snort. "The king wasn't kidding."

"What is it?" Peg said, kneeling to examine the strange papers.

Sir Tode pointed a hoof at an image before him. "Your Majesty, this is a picture—a *map*—of the mines. And surrounding them, just beyond the rocks, there's a ring of dark blue."

"Is that the sky?" she asked.

"No, it's water. Lots of it. And that infernal machine is headed straight for the stuff. All those years of digging—your uncle wasn't searching for jewels or ore . . . he was looking for the *ocean*."

"Then he is a fool," Simon said. "Lord Hazelgood ensured that our shores would never again touch the seas."

"But the king's going *beneath* the shores," Peter explained. Even though he couldn't see the map, he had understood the basic principle. "It makes perfect sense. Sir Tode and I overheard him say he was finally going to be free of the curse—this is how he's going to do it."

"But it's an *enchantment*," the princess insisted as if invoking an immutable scientific law. "You can't just *go around* it . . . can you?"

Sir Tode had spent the better part of his life studying enchantments and knew that they were notoriously riddled with loopholes. "I fear he can, Your Majesty. If those sea dragons are any indication, he's already made some cracks in the foundation. It's only a matter of time before he breaks through in earnest."

"Then it is just as Lord Hazelgood feared so long ago," Simon said. "Incarnadine will be free to sail out and besiege other kingdoms."

"Precisely. He's got all the makings of a war fleet down there— just waiting to be assembled." Sir Tode nosed through the pile of scrolls and pulled out another one with his teeth. "Goodness, Peter . . . this is one of *our maps,* like the one Professor Cake showed us. I can see my home valley, and your port town . . . Why, he's moving out in every direction. By the time he's through, half the world will be under his flag."

The princess had never heard of those far-off places, but she imagined the rulers there would fare no better than her father. "How could he take all those lands? Wouldn't he need a bigger army?"

"He's getting one," Peter said darkly. "We heard him bragging about how he planned to gather more apes and train them to fight."

"And don't forget the thieves," Sir Tode added. "They've apparently agreed to help in exchange for their freedom. Apes are smuggling weapons into the Just Deserts as we speak."

"Then my brothers are doomed," Simon said. There was pain in his voice. "Sir Tode, you have seen the places drawn on these parchments. You alone know whether his plan could succeed."

The knight sighed. "I have seen many impossible things in my travels. But before coming here I had never heard of a man who could leash the dragons of the sea, or teach wild beasts to speak like men. Incarnadine carries with him both the magic of your land and the advancements of ours. I fear for us all."

Peter thought about his town: its sailors, markets, and merchants. What if King Incarnadine could really do it? Would

Peter ever be able to go back? The idea of never again smelling the salty port air or treading the puddled alleys filled him with a sadness he could not explain. Like it or not, that place was a part of him. Thinking of his old life reminded Peter of how weak he really was—he couldn't even fight Mr. Seamus, let alone an armored tyrant. He was just as helpless as the slaves. With this came a new, even more disturbing thought. "Sir Tode," he asked, "what happens to the children when the drill breaks through?"

The knight hesitated. "From what I could see, their chains were bolted to that rock in the cavern floor. If they're still down there when that water comes . . . they'll be drowned."

The boy's heart sank; Incarnadine's plan was a death sentence. If Peter failed in his mission, the blood of all those children would be on his hands. "How . . . how many days do we have?" he said numbly.

"None, I'm afraid. If we're to believe that ape fellow, the king's drill should break through by morning. Which means you have to free them tonight."

"All of those locks in one night?" The boy clutched his trembling fingers.

Peg gripped his hands in her own. "It's a good thing we have Peter Nimble—the greatest thief who ever lived."

Peter, however, could not share in her hope. "Princess, there are *hundreds* of children down there. Their shackles are all rusted shut. Even ignoring the apes and sea serpents, a job that size would be . . ." His words fell short. He knew it might take days, even weeks, to get through all those chains. And they had just a few hours. "Not even I can pull that off," he said.

Peter felt her grip loosen slightly. "Don't talk that way," she said. "Of course you can."

The girl's words filled Peter with shame. He could feel the desperation pouring out from her, from Simon, and even from Sir Tode. And he hated himself for not being able to answer it. "There's just not enough time . . . I'm sorry."

Peg let go of his hands. "You came all this way to help us, and now you're telling me *it's too late?*"

"I told you: It can't be done," he said, more insistent. His shame was fast turning into frustration. "Just be thankful we're not locked down there with them." Already the old instinct of self-preservation was kicking in, and the master thief found himself considering his options. "The most I could do is steal a boat—then at least we could escape ourselves."

"That's not good enough." Peg stood up, put her hands on her hips, and spoke with all the authority she could muster. "I *command* you to rescue those children!"

Peter jumped to his feet. "I'm not one of your subjects you can just boss around!" All of a sudden he felt incredibly tired—tired of running, tired of getting kidnapped, tired of feeling hungry and cold. But most of all, he was tired of being responsible for people he barely knew. "Besides, what's the point? Even if I could pick all the locks, what good would it do? We're still trapped here with

apes! Thieves! Sea serpents!" He grabbed a scroll from the floor
and waved it in her face. "Don't you get it, Princess? WE HAVE
NO CHANCE!"

Little girls, especially royal ones, do not enjoy being yelled at. As
much as Peg projected the confidence of a strong leader, she could
still be hurt. Her face was now red, and she was fighting back tears.
"Fine!" she shouted. "Then we'll all just die! You stupid, blind,
selfish . . . *BOY!*" She knocked the parchment from his hands.

"YOU'RE the selfish one!" he spat back. "This isn't about the
kids at all, it's about you getting revenge for your dumb parents."
Peter knew it was an awful thing to say, but he didn't care anymore.
"And by the way, I'm glad I'm blind . . . that way I don't have to look
at your ugly face!"

She lunged at him before he could say another word. Peter had
not been expecting the assault, and he failed to jump clear in time.
Within seconds, both children were on the deck, cursing, kicking,
and scratching with all their might. Peter was a brilliant escape-
artist and hard to pin down, but Peg was far stronger and knew a
thing or two about headlocks. It was an even match. Sir Tode and
Simon looked at each other and sighed. They watched the children
roll across of the floor, trading insults back and forth.

"YOU'RE the ugly one!"

"YOU are!"

"No, YOU are!"

Peter had one leg around Peg's neck and clutched her hair with both hands. The princess was cramming several fingers into his nose and using her free hand to grab whatever she could to batter the boy with: a stray cog . . . a wooden plank . . . Sir Tode . . .

Peter wriggled free, rolled over, and pinned his adversary to the ground. "YOU are!" he said with a triumphant laugh. "Ha! I just beat you *blindfolded!* What do you say to that?!"

In reply, Peg took hold of the box of Fantastic Eyes and brought it down on his head, knocking him out cold.

✦ ✦ ✦

As Peter came to, he expected the others to be crowded around him, asking if he was all right, feeling good and sorry for letting things get so out of hand. Instead, they were huddled in the corner, talking in hushed tones.

"Sweet Justice . . ." Simon murmured. "Is it truly possible?"

Sir Tode gave an amused chuckle. "Well, that certainly would explain the quarreling."

"Are mine that pretty?" the princess asked.

Peter, groggy from the blow, was having difficulty following their conversation. "Wh-wh-what happened?" He propped himself up with his arms. "What are you all talking about?"

Simon ignored the question. "Why didn't you tell us about these earlier, Sir Tode?"

"We were instructed by the professor to keep them secret. Can't believe I didn't make the connection before . . . seems rather obvious now."

Peg ran to Peter and helped him to his feet. "You should have told us," she exclaimed. "You should have told *me.*"

The boy couldn't follow exactly what they were talking about, but he was starting to form an educated guess. "I didn't tell you because it's none of your beeswax," he muttered, rubbing his bruised skull. He pulled away and went to inspect what had caused the stir. It was just as he had feared: the Haberdasher's mysterious box had broken open, and lying on the deck were his six Fantastic Eyes.

"All this time, they were right there in your bag!" Peg tried to touch one, but Peter pushed her hand away.

"They're mine." He fired a scowl in Sir Tode's direction. "And they're *supposed* to be a secret."

"There was no getting around it, Peter. When they saw what was inside, I had to come clean."

Simon shook his head. "The eyes . . . Mordecai . . . It all fits too well . . ."

"What are you squawking about?" Peter replaced the last of the eyes and closed the box.

The raven hopped close and rested a talon on his hand. "I need you to listen to me carefully, my child, because what I am about to say concerns you a great deal."

The boy was curious despite himself. "I'm listening," he said, holding the box to his chest.

"When Lord Incarnadine stole this kingdom so many years

ago, he had only one fear: that someday a *true* heir would grow up to avenge his murdered parents. And so he ordered his apes to hunt down and kill the king's newborn son."

"Why not the daughter, while he was at it?" Peter grumbled. He was still a bit sore at Peg for that knock on the head.

"I cannot say for certain. I suspect that in his arrogance, Incarnadine assumed a girl would be less of a threat to his immense power. And so he instead had her locked away with the other children."

"Why waste a perfectly good slave?" Peg said bitterly.

"Why indeed? I have no doubt Her Majesty's uncle has since revised his opinion." The old raven studied the girl with a touch of pride. He turned back to Peter. "Regarding the second heir, the boy, Incarnadine was unsuccessful. This is because the child's mother, Queen Magnolia, spirited him away before he could be captured. She delivered him into the care of her personal guards—myself and a raven named Mordecai—and gave us our final mission: save her unchristened son."

"Prince NoName," Peter said.

"We knew that Lord Incarnadine would stop at nothing to capture this child. The apes were searching the palace high and low for a male infant with emerald-green eyes, just like his father . . . just like the ones you hold now."

Suddenly, the box in Peter's arms felt like it weighed a thousand pounds. He bit his lip, almost afraid to ask. "What happened to the baby?"

"We had few options. We knew that so long as the child wore those eyes, he would be in grave danger." The raven hesitated, almost unable to speak the words. "And so we *blinded him* to protect his true identity from ever being discovered." The horrid memory sent a shiver through his plumage. "After that, we were able to spirit him away without detection. Mordecai took the screaming baby in a basket and carried him beyond our ken. He was never heard from again."

Peter was having trouble hearing, feeling, smelling, or tasting anything now; his whole being was overwhelmed with memories, long forgotten. "When I was a baby," he whispered, "some sailors found me floating in the water . . . there was a raven perched on my head . . . and my eyes had been pecked out."

"Peter . . ." Peg stepped closer and touched her hand to his face. "*You* are Prince NoName."

PART THREE

EMERALD

CHAPTER TWENTY-FOUR

THE RETURN *of* NONAME

I'm . . . *what?*" Peter took a step backward; his knees had suddenly grown very weak.

"Do you not see, child?" Simon said, momentarily forgetting that Peter, in fact, could *not* see. "You are a true heir of HazelPort."

Tears welled in Peg's emerald-green eyes. "I just knew you would come back!"

Peter had no idea what to say. A minute before, he'd been a common orphan, and suddenly he was a *prince?* He didn't know the first thing about courtly manners, or fancy clothes, or politics—he was a hardened criminal! "I—I'm sorry, Your Majesty," he stammered. "It's some kind of mistake. Those eyes . . . they're not even mine."

Sir Tode scoffed. "Utter nonsense. The professor made those eyes for you alone. Perhaps he knew something you didn't?"

The boy allowed himself to consider the question. Maybe, just maybe, Professor Cake did have a more specific reason for sending Peter to this place? He opened the lid of the wooden box and smelled the sweet odor of the emerald-green eyes—could they really belong to a prince?

Sir Tode chuckled. "Face it, friend. NoName *has* a name."

Peter steadied himself against the iron bell. "I'm sorry. I just need a moment to sort all this out."

Simon alighted beside him. "Your Majesty. It is clear you are startled by this discovery. But I tell you without flattering that it surprises me not a bit. Justice often works in ways beyond our understanding. And when I look at the courage and sacrifice you have already shown on this quest, I see a true prince indeed."

Peg burst into sobs, throwing her arms around Peter. "I knew it! It's really you!" Peter didn't like touching girls all that much, but he thought it might be allowed if they were brother and sister.

"It's all right. I'm here now," he said, patting her on the back. "We're together again." Somehow, speaking it out loud made it more real. Perhaps it *was* possible that he was a lost prince with a twin sister? And that meant the note, the sea voyage, and the deserts weren't all just random occurrences . . . they were his *destiny*. Peter had journeyed across the world—beyond the borders of the map—to free *his* subjects and reclaim *his* crown.

The boy returned his sister's embrace, squeezing her with all his strength. He could feel her heartbeat against his own, and he knew he was finally home.

When all tears were spent, Peter let go of his sister and addressed the group, a new hope in his voice. "However stupidly I might have acted before, I was right about one thing: unlocking the children's shackles leaves them no more free than their parents. They're all still under the king's control. If we're really going to save these people, we have to liberate them once and for all."

Peg took her brother's hand. "How do we do that?"

He loosed a slow breath. "We're going to kill the king."

✦ ✦ ✦

Peter knew they had little time to waste. He could already feel the setting sun dipping below the clock face, which meant suppertime was coming soon—and he did not want to be on this platform when the Bedtime Bell struck. But coming up with a plan for assassinating the king seemed impossible; Incarnadine and his forces were just too powerful. Peter thought more than once about donning the green eyes in hope that they might grant him great speed or strength, but he knew the time was not yet right—he could feel it. Until that feeling changed, he would have to rely on his own wits and abilities.

After yet another heated argument over poisoning the king's wine—Peg refused, knowing he sometimes used children as food—

testers—Peter decided to approach the problem from a different angle. Professor Cake had told him to trust his nature, but Peter wasn't sure *which* nature the man was referring to. Was he a prince or a thief? Having exhausted all princely solutions, the boy decided to imagine their situation as a lock that he had to open. *What type of lock was it?* Well, it was the sort that could kill you, one rigged with all manner of booby traps. There was Incarnadine, protected by his deadly clockwork armor. Supporting him was a horde of vicious apes and at least a dozen horrible sea serpents. Soon, hundreds of thieves would be joining him as well.

If their situation resembled any lock, it would definitely be the Bigelow Brank. The Brank contains a mechanism that, if jarred, releases a thousand spikes from the ceiling down on the perpetrator. The only way to crack the Bigelow Brank is to pick it oh so delicately, and then at the exact moment the latch releases, you have to smash the entire lock with a sledgehammer. When Peter was six, Mr. Seamus had forced him to open one at the local treasury. The boy had no difficulty picking the lock, but was not strong enough with his safe-mallet. The release mechanism went off and great spikes shot down at him. Were it not for his being so thin and frail, he would have been skewered like a *shish kebab*. As it was, the spikes missed his vitals—if only by a hairbreadth.

So, since their mission seemed to be this type of lock, Peter knew that two things would have to happen at the same time: First, he would have to free the captured slaves (this was the lock-picking bit); and second, he would have to smash the king and his army (this was the sledgehammer bit). The boy knew exactly which part would be hardest. "I'm going to need reinforcements," he concluded.

"Well, you've got us three," Sir Tode offered. "But I don't suppose that's what you meant."

"What about the slave children?" Peg said. "If we can arm them, my subjects will fight." She corrected herself. "I mean *our* subjects."

Peter gave his sister a smile. "You're not the only one who will have to get used to saying that. Do you think there's enough of them to overpower the apes?"

"I don't know. But they'll die trying."

"Let's hope it doesn't come to that," Peter said. "Plus, they can't fight until they're free from those chains. There's just no way I can unlock them all in time."

"Maybe you could teach me to do it?" Peg said eagerly.

"Lock-picking takes years to master, and even if you could learn, that's still just two of us. What I really need is an extra hundred pairs of hands."

"If only my brethren were here," Simon said. "Their beaks could finish the job in seconds." The old bird tensed his talons, imagining the conflict raging just across the chasm. He would give anything to be battling alongside Captain Amos and the others. "But alas, there is no way to reach them. The great chasm is too wide. It seems the Just Deserts are a perfect prison indeed."

"But what good is a prison if you can't check up on it?" Peter said, turning to Sir Tode. "The king mentioned communicating with Officer Trolley. And he ordered LongClaw to send weapons . . . he must have a secret tunnel or bridge of some kind."

"And you think we should tag along," Sir Tode said, nodding. "Fair enough . . . but how do we find this LongClaw chap? It's an awfully big palace, and we haven't much time."

Just then, they heard a roar from below. "Oi! Who left this ruddy hatch open?!"

The four were on their feet in a flash. "Apes!" Peter said, stuffing maps into his bag. "We've got to get out of here, quick!"

"Hold on." The princess stopped him and pulled several parchments from his grip. "I think I have a better idea."

✦ ✦ ✦

Jawbone was a simple ape with a simple job: guard the clock tower. His post was a stool set behind the maintenance door; he had to make sure that no one passed without showing papers signed by the king. For ten years he'd performed this rather tedious task without so much as a single incident. It helped that the door was cleverly concealed behind a rosebush; since tramping out-of-bounds was strictly forbidden, it was highly unlikely any human in the palace even knew the door existed—and how could someone walk through a door they didn't know existed? Still, it was Jawbone's sworn duty, day in and day out, to protect the tower with his life. His very, very, very boring life.

All of that changed when the king's address was spoiled by two rotten children and an overflowing sewer system. Immediately after the attack, Jawbone had been called away from his stool to join the rest of the horde for "routine inspections" throughout the palace. The change was as exciting as it was unexpected; Jawbone had gotten to spend nearly two whole days bursting through doors, smashing furniture, shredding sheets, and generally terrifying the hapless citizens. All things considered, it had been the highlight of his military career.

But Jawbone's blissful mood was spoiled when he returned to his usual post to find that someone had propped open the secret door with his stool. The discovery left the ape reeling. What would the king do to him for letting an intruder slip by? "Oi!" he snarled, charging inside the tower. "Who left this ruddy hatch open?!"

The ape did not climb the steps like a human; instead, he swung and bounded up the wooden rail, which groaned under his weight. "Attention, intruder! I know you're up there!" If there *was* an intruder, Jawbone would make certain he or she wouldn't live to expose the breach—but what if it *was* a she? What if he had finally found that meddlesome princess? That would be luck indeed!

He burst onto the platform, swinging his mace over his head. "Come here, you royal snot!" But there was no princess waiting for him. Nothing but grinding gears and a gently rocking bell. "Just my ruddy luck," he said, disappointed at the thought of not getting to eat a princess.

Glancing down at his feet, Jawbone noticed some papers strewn across the deck. The ape took them in his paws and studied the images. He could not read, but the pictures were obvious enough. Someone, whoever it was, was planning a secret attack on the palace—complete with warships and rival apes! A greedy smile played across the beast's swollen lips as he imagined presenting this most important information to his commander. He would be rewarded for sure—perhaps even be put on slave duty, where he'd get to beat children all day long!

"I gotta find LongClaw!" Jawbone dropped his mace and scooped up the scrolls in both arms. He snorted giddily as he stomped down the steps, out of the tower, and into the palace.

✦   ✦   ✦

Peter, Sir Tode, Simon, and Peg all listened from their hiding place inside the giant bell. They could hear the guard shouting below, bursting with excitement: "Hey, BloodHorn! Maul! You two seen LongClaw anywhere? It's really, really, *really* important!"

Peter smirked as he listened. "I never imagined we'd be using the enemy as a guide." He nodded to his sister. "Good thinking, Your Majesty."

"Thank you, Your Majesty," Peg said back. "Now, let's get down there and see if he can't help us find LongClaw."

Following the ape's trail was easy enough (between Peter's keen sense of smell and Jawbone's big mouth, it would have been hard to miss), and the long shadows of the afternoon created plenty of dark places for the four of them to hide as they ran up stairs and across bridges. "That's strange," Peter said as he hoisted Sir Tode onto a ledge. "We seem to be climbing *upward*." He had assumed they were going to be led underground—how else could they cross the great chasm?

As they traveled, the group worked out the remainder of their plan: once they found the king's secret passage, Simon would use it to travel back to the Just Deserts and get the other ravens. "Together, my brethren and I will make short work of those cursed shackles," the old bird said with relish. Then he dropped his head, remembering that his own beak was no more. "Rather, I will have the honor of *watching* them do so."

"He makes a good point," Peg said with concern. "If Simon lost his beak trying to peck open a lock, what's to say that won't happen to the rest of the ravens? We can't afford to disarm our guards like that."

Peter nodded. "Actually, I've been thinking about that same thing. I was able to examine those shackles firsthand when you chained me up in the den." Peg gave an embarrassed groan, no doubt remembering how she had tried kidnapping her own brother. Peter went on. "I noticed that the locks were covered in rust, which meant the mechanism was too clogged to open properly. I'm pretty sure that's the reason Simon's beak snapped. But if we were able to somehow oil the locks beforehand . . ."

"I know just the thing!" Peg grabbed his arm excitedly. "The slave kitchen has barrels and barrels of scouring grease. I can steal some, no problem!" The recent discovery that her long-lost brother was a great thief had produced a rather strange effect on Her Majesty—she was now desperately eager to enter into the profession herself.

"We'll do it together," he said, smiling.

"Brilliant!" Sir Tode clopped his hoof on the stone. "The war's as good as won! We've got an army *and* a way to free the children. The only thing left is to hire a bard who can commemorate our bravery in a song."

"That, and the *sea serpents,*" Simon reminded him.

"Oh, drat." The knight's voice faltered. "I'd forgotten about them."

"We ravens cannot fight in water. Sir Tode, you are the only one among us who has killed a dragon before. We look to you for guidance."

The knight emitted a faint squeak from someplace in the back of his throat. Sensing his friend's discomfort, Peter spoke up. "Sir Tode *is* a brave knight, but defeating all those sea serpents will take a little more than that."

"He is a dragon slayer," Simon said plainly. "What more could we possibly need?"

The boy hesitated. There are times when being a leader is less about having the right answer than about having *an* answer. Peter knew the others were looking to him for a response—his friend most of all. If he didn't say something quick, then their faith in the whole operation might falter. "Just leave it to me," he lied. "I have a plan."

Right about this time, Jawbone found LongClaw at the base of an enormous stone turret. He began boasting to his superior about the tremendous discovery he'd made in the clock tower, even going so far as to suggest a few ideas about how he might be appropriately rewarded.

While LongClaw whipped his subordinate for wrinkling the king's very important documents, Peter and the others crept through the shadows and tried to figure out where exactly they were. The tower before them was by far the tallest structure in the kingdom. An archway at the base revealed the inside to be empty, save a stone stairway that curved around the inside wall. "Those stairs go all the way to the top," the princess whispered. "But I've never seen what's up there—he keeps this place guarded every hour of every day."

Presently, dozens of apes were hauling armaments up the tower stairs. "Hurry it up, you louts!" LongClaw shouted at them. "The king wants these weapons in the desert by sundown!"

"It makes no sense," Peter said. "How can they cross the chasm from all the way up there?"

Sir Tode peered above and gave a report. "It looks like there's a wooden dock sticking out from the turret. There's some kind of largish contraption hanging over the edge. I see flames, ropes, and some sort of canvas *balloon* thing."

"Of course," Peter said. "The king has a dirigible!"

"A dirigi*what?*"

"It's a flying machine," Peter explained. He had never witnessed such a wonder himself, but he had heard talk of them from sailors who had ridden them at carnivals abroad. "That's how he reaches the deserts . . . he just flies there."

Simon squinted up at the barge, trying to make sense of it. "I do not understand this 'flying machine.' Where are its wings?"

Peter ignored the question, knowing it was useless to explain (and also being somewhat uncertain himself). "Sir Tode, if those weapons get across, the ravens will be finished. We have to commandeer that vessel. It's no job for a blind person. Do you think you can pilot it?"

"Me? I wouldn't have the foggiest idea how."

"That balloon you saw is controlled by a furnace and damper. The hotter the fire, the higher the ship will rise." Peter hoped he had it straight. "The rest is just like a regular boat with sails and a rudder." He placed a hand on his friend's shoulder. "You navigated the *Scop* all the way here . . . to a *vanished* island. Sir Tode, I know you can do this."

There was something in Peter's voice that filled the knight with a faith that eclipsed fear. "If you trust me that much, I will try to trust myself . . . but I'm taking Simon with me. If that thing pops, I want someone who can fly back to tell my story."

"I would be honored to fight alongside you," the raven said.

Peg stood up and took her brother's hand. "Then it's time. Peter and I will sneak back to the mines and slime the locks. You and Simon steal that machine, fly across, and fetch the Royal Guard!"

Hearing this summary, Peter realized just how feeble his plan was. His mind flashed through a hundred ways the voyage might go wrong for Sir Tode and Simon. The fire in the furnace could die. The balloon could tear. A storm could blow them off course. Even if they reached the Just Deserts, they would be sailing into the middle of a brutal war. "Sir Tode . . ." Peter started.

The knight silenced him with a tsk and placed a hoof on his arm. "Run along, Your Majesties. You two have a kingdom to save."

CHAPTER TWENTY-FIVE

THE ROOT *of the* PROBLEM

I f Peg and Peter wanted to get the locks greased in time, they knew they would have to reach the slave kitchen before nightfall. The shortest way there was through a hidden passage in the center of the palace. The only problem was that this same route took them right past the Eating Hall . . . and hundreds of watchful citizen eyes. The princess decided they should use the shortcut anyway, hoping that the nightly feast would provide sufficient distraction for her and Peter to sneak by undetected.

As it happened, distractions were unnecessary.

Just as they reached the entrance of the hall, Peter stopped. "No one's eating," he said. Peg strained her ears (which were not nearly so extraordinary as her brother's) and realized that he was right—the glasses were not clinking, the cutlery was not clanking, the people were not chatting. There was just one voice ringing out over the crowd.

"Our waiting has finally come to an end! Soon we rise up in greatness!"

"It's our uncle," Peter whispered. "He's giving another address."

And indeed, he was. The king was telling the people of his plan to take over the world, though in terms that made him sound more hero than tyrant. "Your Brave Ruler will lead you all to victory! We will vanquish the savage fiends of these foreign lands, helping them to love me as you all do!"

"Hooray for victory!" the people shouted, not really knowing what all those other words meant.

"Keep to the shadows," Peter said. "If the king is here, his guards must not be too far off." He could smell nothing, but it didn't hurt to be cautious.

Peg followed her brother, crawling behind a row of potted trees. She peered out over the hall and gasped. "Peter! They're all carrying weapons."

"Who?" He rested a hand on his fishhook. "You see apes?"

She shook her head, horrified. "No . . . the parents . . . they're *armed*." In one hand of each man and woman was a long black spear with a pair of twisted, razor-sharp prongs at the tip; in the other was an enormous shield bearing an imprint of the king's face. Every time the king finished a sentence, the people beat their spears against their shields, stomping and shouting. "This is ridiculous . . . they'll stick themselves if they're not careful," Peg said.

The king's voice rang over the crowd. "The reason I have called this emergency meeting is to update you on the events from this morning. My soldiers and I captured the evil spies, of course. But we have since learned that many more are plotting to besiege this palace. They look just like humans, but smaller, with skinnier arms and legs."

"He's talking about children," Peter said. "He must be afraid they'll try to escape."

"If you see one of these wretched monsters lurking about the palace, kill it without a moment's delay! It is a spy sent to assassinate your king! Don't listen to a thing it says—just attack without thinking!"

"No thinking!" the people shouted.

Peter and Peg sat in the shadows, stunned at what they were hearing. "How can they just *believe* him like that?" she said angrily. Many times since escaping the mines, the princess had wondered whether these lazy, mindless adults even deserved to be rescued— this was one such moment. She reminded herself that underneath each spear-waving maniac was a loving grown-up, just like Lillian. "We have to figure out a way to make them remember who they really are."

Peter nodded, listening to their cries. "If only we knew how the king was controlling them," he said.

Their speculation was interrupted by Incarnadine's voice. "But enough business! We have a great battle ahead of us—and tonight we feast!" He clapped his steel gloves, and giant platters of hot food floated into the hall, releasing delicious, intoxicating smells into the air. Peg watched as Incarnadine took an empty goblet and raised it over his head. "Long live me!"

Every citizen took up a sloshing wineglass and cried "Long live the king!"

As the people drank to their impostor king, the true prince and true princess of HazelPort melted into the shadows and disappeared through a crack in the wall.

✦ ✦ ✦

"Can't you fly a *bit* faster?" Sir Tode said, squirming. "And ease up with that grip, while you're at it!"

"Would you prefer I drop you?" Simon had Sir Tode by the scruff of his neck and was flapping his wings with considerable effort. The pair had decided the safest way to reach the top of the tower was to fly around the outside, where they could ascend undetected. Sir Tode's hooves made him significantly heavier than he appeared, and Simon was forced to make the trip in multiple legs, stopping to rest on whatever outcropped stones he could find.

At last they reached the deck, which extended far over the chasm. Simon flung Sir Tode behind a cask of gunpowder and landed beside him. "Of all the indignities," the knight said, massaging his neck. "Carried about like some kind of bawling infant."

"You make about as much noise as one," Simon muttered under his breath. He marveled at how any self-respecting knight could ever behave so fussily. "We are just lucky that the apes were too busy with their work to overhear us."

"Lucky. Right." Sir Tode eyed the dozens of guards loading pikes and nets into the flying machine's basket. The balloon was fully inflated, and the craft appeared ready to fly. Three guards held on to anchor ropes, pulling with all their might to keep it from floating away.

LongClaw paced among them, shouting orders. "Stoke that furnace! Ape the bellows! Get those nets stowed already!"

"Thought we had slaves for this kind of labor," one ape growled, dumping an armload of shields into the basket.

Another snorted in agreement. "Demeaning! That's what it is!"

LongClaw cracked his whip. "The king needs all the chiddlers for diggin'! Now, stop your whining or I'll *demean* you right off the edge of this deck!"

Sir Tode studied the vessel before them. The flying machine had only two apes aboard, both wearing goggles. The first one was hunched over a great furnace, which fed hot air into the balloon sails; the ape next to him was strapped into some sort of giant bicycle contraption. "I'd bet that's the steering device," he said, studying the brass levers. "If we can get up there, I think I can manage it."

"Excellent." Simon flexed his talons. "I count two dozen guards. How many do you think you can kill?"

"How *many*?" Sir Tode swallowed. "I was, er, sort of hoping you could do the fighting bit."

The raven looked at him, uncertain of whether this was a joke.

"Well, you see . . . I'm afraid I'm not really a big one for bloodshed."

"What of the dragon clan you slew to win your title?" Simon asked, recalling the rather dramatic tale the knight had shared with them back in the den.

"The thing is, my slaying didn't transpire *quite* the way I let on. There was only one dragon, actually, and he sort of . . . well, he did most of the work himself."

This was true. In fact, Sir Tode had been *asleep* for the whole thing. Back then, he had been a simple peasant named Sheepherder Tode. One fateful night, a local dragon—which had been terrorizing the region as of late—swooped down on Tode's unlucky flock, gobbling them up. Like most dragons, the creature had no manners, and taking little time to chew its prey, the monster soon found itself choking to death on a plump ewe. The following morning, when the locals saw the dragon's dead body and Tode sleeping next to it, they proclaimed him a hero and demanded that he be knighted. From that day forward, Sheepherder Tode was called *Sir*.

This had, of course, been a great mark of shame for Sir Tode— one he had been too embarrassed to ever share with another living creature. Until now. "I'm no hero," he said, tears welling in his feline eyes. "I don't deserve your respect, let alone my title. I'm just a shepherd with a fancy name."

Simon studied his companion for a long moment. When he spoke, his voice had lost its harshness. "I, too, know what it means to face terror. I watched the enemy kill my brothers and my king. Once Mordecai escaped with the infant prince, I was completely alone." He paused a moment, unsure of whether he wanted to continue. "You may wonder why it took me so long to work my way underground and free the princess. The reason was simple: I was afraid. I spent years hiding from the apes like a coward. But then one night, from my roost in the rafters, I saw her—my princess—being dragged through the palace halls with the other slaves. It was then that a terrific gust of wind took hold of me and swept me from my perch. In that moment my life of hiding came to an end. Before I knew what I was doing, I found myself flying toward the apes, talons raised for battle." The old raven shook his head. "There are times when Justice demands from us more than we would give. I have no beak, and yet I must fight."

Simon looked to the airship and saw that the apes had finished with their loading and were preparing to launch. He extended his wings. "I am afraid we do not have time to discuss whether you *feel* like a hero—Justice compels us to *act!*" He took hold of the knight and lifted him into the air.

"What in heaven's name are you doing?!" the knight sputtered. "They'll kill us!"

"Not if we kill them first! It's time you earn your title, Sir Tode!"

✦ ✦ ✦

As Peter suspected, the walls of the entire palace had been hollowed out to make way for the locking mechanisms. In this darkness, he was the one to lead. "Keep up!" he urged Peg as he slipped between dormant cogs and wheels. "We've got to get to the slave kitchen before the magic bell starts up."

The princess wriggled beneath a giant wooden gear, imagining what it would do to her skull if it suddenly came to life. Preferring not to dwell on such possibilities, she put her energy into trying to follow Peter, who was several lengths ahead of her.

They dropped down from the gears into a narrow waterway. Unlike the sewers, which smelled filthy, this tunnel carried fresh spring water. Floating along the surface was an endless procession of platters, all piled high with steaming food. "The slave children have to prepare every meal," Peg explained. "They send the platters out to the Eating Hall on these little rivers—that way the grown-ups never have to see who's serving it. If we follow this water upstream, it should lead us straight to where we need to go."

As they traveled, Peter told her all about growing up a thief in a small port town. He talked about Mr. Seamus and his vile dog, Killer. He explained how he stole the Haberdasher's mysterious box and almost drowned with Sir Tode in the Troublesome Lake. He told the story of meeting Good Ol' Frederick and earning his fishhook.

"If only we had a giant dogfish to help us now," Peg said. "I bet he could stop those horrid sea serpents."

THE ROOT *of the* PROBLEM

"It's too late for that. Once we crossed into this kingdom, we lost any way of reaching him. I'm afraid it's up to the four of us . . . and the Fantastic Eyes." Peter patted the box inside his bag.

This led Peg to a question that had been nagging at her for some time. "Why haven't you tried the green pair? They are your birthright, after all."

As desperate as Peter was to don the eyes of Hazelgood, he knew the time had not come. "The professor warned me to wait till the moment was right. That's good enough for me," he said with what could only be described as blind faith.

The princess gave no immediate reply, but Peter heard her mutter something to the effect of "I sure hope he's right."

When Peter and Peg reached the slave kitchen, they found it overrun with apes. It seemed that with all children working in the mines, it fell on the Night Patrol to do the cooking—a task they were enjoying not at all. The air was filled with frustrated snarls and shouts of "Get yer paws offa my soufflé!" and "I'll whisk *you,* if you don't hand over that mixin' bowl!"

With so much ambient chaos, Peter and Peg had little trouble sneaking to the scouring station. Her Majesty dipped a stray goblet inside a large wooden barrel and came up with a cupful of yellowish grease that smelled faintly like earwax. "Slug lard," she said with a smile. "They use it to clean the pans—just the thing for rusted shackles, I'll bet."

She threw her brother the goblet, which he caught and stuffed in his bag. With the help of a rolling dish rack, the two children managed to sneak to the kitchen's service entrance, which led to the mines directly below. But when they reached the small tunnel, Peter stopped.

"There's something wrong," he said, smelling the air. He pointed to a workstation, where completed meals were being placed into the water. A *sous*-ape wearing a leather apron was hunched over the food, applying generous dustings of black powder to all the dishes before sending them off. "What's happening over there?"

Peg, who was nervous about being detected, gave an impatient sigh. "It's just an ape putting a seasoning the king likes on all the food before it's sent out. Come on."

This "seasoning" was the bitter flavor Peter had detected his first night in the palace. "He puts it on *all* the food?" the boy asked, rolling the dish rack closer for a better whiff. There was something familiar about the odor, something he had smelled many times before on the docks in his port town. His face lit up as he realized the secret to his uncle's power. "I know how the king's controlling the adults . . . he's using the Devil's Dram."

"What's that?" Peg asked, alarmed. "It sounds like poison."

Peter shook his head. "It's a special root that you grind up and mix into tea. In the town where I grew up, sailors used to drink it to forget the horrible things they'd seen. It makes your mind weak, sleepy. The effects wear off pretty quickly, which means you have to take it several times a day."

"Like at every meal," she said, suddenly understanding. "Can we stop it?"

"So long as the adults keep eating the stuff, they'll never remember the truth," Peter said. He pushed his bag behind his back and flexed his fingers. "I might be able to swap the powder for something else, but first I would need some kind of distract—"

Before the boy could finish, his sister leapt from behind the rack and jumped onto a counter. "Hey, apes!" she cried, knocking two pots over her head. "Come and get me, you ugly goons!" Apes looked up from their duties to see the girl who had bested them only that morning. They dropped their utensils and charged for her. The princess ran to a stove and kicked over a cauldron of butter soup— scalding hot and very, very slippery. The first ape to hit the puddle slipped and crashed into the floor. The rest of the apes slipped and crashed into him, and pretty soon the entire kitchen was awash with buttery, furious primates.

Peg jumped from counter to counter, hurling insults and pots at the apes, drawing them farther away from the seasoning station. Peter knew better than to waste such a valuable diversion. While the beasts contended with the princess, he ran to the Devil's Dram. Fast as his hands would allow, he emptied the black powder into the trash and refilled the shaker with ordinary pepper. He felt his way to the rear tunnel and hid in the shadows.

A few seconds later, Peg caught up to him. "Good work," she gasped. She took his hand and pulled him down a sludge shoot.

"Now, let's get to the mines—I'll bet Sir Tode and Simon are halfway to the deserts by now."

✦   ✦   ✦

As it happened, Simon and Sir Tode were exactly where we last left them: atop the tower, flying over a horde of deadly apes. Only now the apes were trying to murder them. "It's a ruddy raven!" LongClaw roared upon spotting the intruders. "Slaughter it!" His guards instantly dropped what they were doing and rushed to attack. Simon flew this way and that, trying his best to dodge the assault.

"Higher! Fly HIGHER!" cried Sir Tode, who was dangling from the bird's talons.

"I cannot carry you any longer," Simon squawked. "It is time you fight!" He loosed his grip and sent the knight hurtling into a pile of nets aboard the airship. "You ready the sails, Sir Tode! I'll free the moorings!" The bird flew into the open furnace and emerged a moment later with both talons full of hot coals. The pain was incredible, but Simon did not falter. He circled around the deck, dropping the fire on the three apes holding anchor. Two of the beasts howled, releasing their ropes to swat embers from their eyes. The third ape held his rope fast and slid right off the platform as the flying machine took to the skies.

The ship had been liberated, but there were still the pilots to contend with. Simon swooped aboard the basket, talons out. Though strong, the guards were unaccustomed to aerial combat, and every time they swiped at the raven, he zipped between their clumsy paws. "Sir Tode! It is time!" he cawed, flapping backward to avoid attack.

"Righto!" the knight hollered. "Just one moment!" He had gotten his rear hoof caught in the pile of netting and couldn't pull himself free—not that he was sure he wanted to. He watched in awe as Simon battled two bloodthirsty apes at once. Even without the benefit of a beak, the raven had managed to temporarily blind one and fell the other. But then, a third ape (who had been holding fast to his anchor rope all this time) hoisted himself over the edge of the basket.

"There's one behind you!" Sir Tode shouted, too late.

The ape snatched Simon and pinned his wings back to restrain him. "Don't know about you louts, but I'm feelin' *peckish,*" he said with a hungry laugh. The other two apes staggered to their feet and joined the fun.

"Sir Tode!" the bird gave a desperate squawk. "NOW!"

The knight was too scared to answer. He was too scared to think. He was too scared to breathe. He could only do one thing—*act!* He sprung from the nets and galloped across the basket at full speed. "Tally-hoooooooooo!" He leapt into the air, assaulting the apes with four hooves and all his heart. The beasts were caught so off guard that they stumbled backward, flipping right over the edge of the basket and into the abyss.

"Good riddance!" the knight shouted. It took him a moment to realize that one of the creatures still had Simon in his grip.

Without hesitating, Sir Tode grabbed a knife in his teeth and hurled it overboard. His aim was true, and the weapon's handle smacked squarely against the ape's head. "Who's there?!" the creature snarled, reaching up to check for blood. In doing so he let go of Simon, who immediately flapped to safety. The three apes spat and screamed and cursed until at last their voices were swallowed by the chasm forever.

"Did you see that, Simon?!" Sir Tode was trembling all over. "I did it! I slew a monster! Three of them!"

The old bird nodded. "You fought bravely. I owe you my life."

The knight looked down at the raven's talons, which had been seared by the embers. Smoke still wafted from the charred flesh. "Will you be all right?" he said.

"I will heal. Ravens are coal-born beasts. They do not burn as easily as most living things." Even now, his talons, though ravaged, were flexing with their usual strength. "Now, if you would take the helm, *Sir* Tode. It is time for me to see my brothers once more."

✦   ✦   ✦

When Peter and Peg reached the mines, they found the digging machine in high gear. Every slave in the kingdom had been reassigned to mining duty. The running-wheels that powered the machine were all stuffed to capacity, with more than ten children inside each one. With every step, the children pushed the massive drill deeper into the rocky wall. Peter strained to hear Lillian or the others amidst the noise, but it was impossible from this height.

"Faster, you maggots!" a guard shouted below, snapping his whip at the nearest batch of slaves. "I better see you running . . . 'less you want my pet here to catch up with you!" He slackened the leash in his hand and his sea serpent lunged toward the closest cage, snapping at the children's ankles. The terrified slaves raced to escape its deadly jaws, but of course went nowhere.

Peter listened to the scene with interest—it sounded like the sea serpents had somehow managed to widen the moat and could now almost reach the back wall of the cavern. The rest of the floor was covered in puddles, which he could hear splash every time the apes moved. "Do you see water flowing in from anywhere?" he whispered to Peg.

The girl stared through the darkness. Sure enough, there was a thin trickle of water running down either side of the drill. "It's coming from the clockwork beast," she said, astonished. "But how can water flow from rock?"

Peter listened to the sea serpents swimming back and forth along their ever-increasing shore, shrieking and hissing. The sound made his whole body tense up. Even if he *could* free all the slaves, those monsters were blocking the only exit. It was drown or be gobbled. *If only Peg's idea were possible,* he thought to himself. *If only we* could *call Frederick.* But no, the only path to the ocean was on the other side of that drill.

Or was it? Peter recalled something Sir Tode had said about the king finding cracks in the foundation—cracks big enough for sea monsters. "That's it!" he said with a sudden burst of excitement. The next moment he was on his feet, digging through his bag.

Peg stood with him. "*What's* it?"

"I think I have a plan to beat those serpents." He handed her his burgle-sack, which contained the goblet of slug lard. "You'll need to grease the locks alone for a while. But stay close—I might have to borrow your hands for something."

"You've already got hands! What are you doing?"

He opened his palm, revealing a pair of shiny, black eyes. "I'm going for a swim."

CHAPTER TWENTY-SIX

FISHING *for a* FRIEND

Peter knew that the moat would lead him to Frederick; the only question was whether he could find him in time. Reaching the water was simple enough—the apes were too busy whipping slaves (and the slaves were too busy *being* whipped) to notice much of anything. The sea serpents, however, detected him straightaway. As soon as Peter came close, they sensed his footsteps. Fast as a flicker, two creatures burst from the water, snapping and lunging for him.

Scared as he was, Peter remained still—he knew that any sudden movement might attract more serpents, which might in turn attract the attention of the guards. The boy hoped with everything in him that the iron leashes would hold fast; in order for his plan to work, he would have to touch one of the creatures . . . and survive. He reached out his hand and took a careful step closer. Then another. He could practically taste the rank, fishy breath steaming out from their mouths. He took another step. His hair flapped as a tongue lashed through the air. "Easy, girl," he whispered, extending his fingers. "I just want to pet you is all."

Three more serpents had been attracted by the commotion, and now five horrible heads strained against their leashes, trying to gobble the greatest thief who ever lived. Peter knew he had only moments before the apes noticed. He took another step. He thought his head would explode from the chorus of high-pitched shrieks. He reached his hand closer.

"Ow!" He jerked his hand back. A serpent's tooth had nicked the tip of his middle finger. "That wasn't so hard," he said with a weak smile. His nerves were starting to get the best of him, and he was trembling all over. Peter reached into his pocket with his uninjured hand and pulled out the black Fantastic Eyes. He took a deep breath and popped them into his sockets.

✦   ✦   ✦

Princess Peg was confused and frustrated. She had waited ten years to be reunited with her long-lost brother . . . only to be abandoned by him a few moments later. Peter had given no explanation beyond some nonsense about "going for a swim," and before she could respond, he had swung himself over the ledge and out of sight. Now Peg was alone with nothing but an old bag, a box of eyes, and a goblet of slug lard. She stared at these objects, caught between resentment and awe. Her brother made everything look so effortless. "Well, I told him I wanted to help free the kids," she said, slinging the burgle-sack over one shoulder. "Looks like I've got my chance."

Peg's first problem was in reaching the children. The moat water had by now cut her off from the clockwork beast, which meant she would have to wade across without the guards or sea serpents noticing. She looked down to the cavern floor and saw that Peter was already at the edge of the moat, doing something with one of the serpents—if only sneaking about was as easy for her.

The princess thought over all the things her brother had told her about the art of thieving. She recalled him talking about a thief in the Just Deserts whose "knack" allowed him to dress up like other people. Peg knew she couldn't make an ape costume, but perhaps she could make a costume that resembled something else in the cavern? She peered over the ledge, searching the shadows for anything that might provide a suitable disguise. By this time, the apes had all carried the boat parts aboveground for assembly, but Peg spotted a few supplies that had been left behind. She smiled to herself, realizing that these might provide just the cover she needed to reach the children.

Peg eyed the narrow stone path leading to the base of the mines. One of the advantages of never bathing was that Peg's skin was absolutely caked with dirt. Experience had taught her that if she kept her eyes and mouth closed, she could blend almost perfectly into her background. This ability to hide in plain sight had saved her more than once from passing guards . . . only this time she would have to employ the technique *while moving.*

What if she tripped and tumbled right over the edge? She took a deep breath and reminded herself that this was how her brother lived his entire life—and if he could do it, so could she. Placing one hand against the slick wall, she closed her eyes and took a first, terrifying step . . . rather, she took a terrifying *shuffle*. Afraid of tripping on a loose pebble, she slid her feet along the dirt, careful not to lose contact with the ground. She felt her way down one step and then another, until at last she was standing on level ground near the shore of the moat.

When Peg opened her eyes again, she saw at once why the stray planks and barrels had not made it aboveground: these unlucky pieces had been close enough for the sea serpents to reach—as a result, they all had giant, splintery bites taken out of them.

Peg checked the water and was relieved to see that the sea serpents were presently preoccupied with attacking each other. She tiptoed through the wreckage, looking for something that might serve her needs. She soon found an overturned powder cask whose lid had a hole smashed through it. She salvaged a lid from a nearby cask and made sure it would fit. Peg then crawled into the barrel and pulled the lid over the top. Inside the cask, she was again blind, even though her eyes were now open. "Let's just hope those sea serpents aren't hungry," she said and leaned her body against the curved wall, rolling the barrel toward the water.

✦ ✦ ✦

Peter almost instantly concluded that being a sea serpent was far more fun than being a beetle, sparrow, or for that matter, a little boy. There was the initial difficulty of rolling himself into the water, but after that, things felt right as reason. Though he was still blind, Peter's scales afforded him a new kind of "sight" underwater. Vibrations tickled his whole body—it was as though his entire length were a single finger, sensing the currents all around him. He could hear wonderfully, and he was able to direct himself by listening to echoes off the moat walls.

There was, of course, the complication of having a dozen other sea serpents trying to eat him. They were clearly territorial monsters and did not take kindly to Peter's appearance in their moat. When he finally managed to flop himself into the water, every one of the serpents lunged straight for him. Luckily, the underground moat was so narrow that they created a bit of a logjam. Peter also had the advantage of not being leashed to an ape; this allowed him to wriggle his way past the knot of creatures without serious harm.

Sir Tode's instinct about the fissure had been correct. Peter soon found a saltwater current flowing from a crevice in the rock floor. He wriggled through the crack and into open waters.

✦   ✦   ✦

After some bobbing and much bruising, Peg had managed to float her cask across the moat. The sea serpents—which she had feared might attack her—had been too distracted by something else in the water to pay her any mind. When the princess finally rolled onto shore and extracted herself from the barrel, she was met by a chorus of familiar voices.

"Your Majesty!" Scrape, Giggle, Marbles, and Timothy exclaimed as one. They were together in a single wheel, huddled around Lillian, who looked haggard but happy. Peg ran to meet her friends, taking care to keep out of view of the apes standing guard.

"You gotta break us out of here," Scrape said. "The apes got us working without naps or anything."

Peg knew that naps were the least of their worries. In a few short hours the ocean would be coming to drown them all. "Don't worry," she reassured them. "Peter's going to help you escape."

"I can't wait to see him," Marbles said with a sigh.

"Me neither," Giggle said with her own sigh. The two girls both had faraway looks and had slowed their pace considerably.

Scrape rolled his eyes. "If he's such a big hero, why'd he send the princess to do all the hard work for him?" The boy began walking more quickly, which forced the others in the wheel to keep up with him.

"He's got a plan," Peg said, wishing that she knew more herself. She thought of the last time she saw her brother; he was standing near the edge of the water reaching out to touch a sea serpent. "It has something to do with the moat . . . and the sea serpents."

"You mean those underwater monsters?" Scrape stopped, causing a pileup behind him. "Did the plan involve being *eaten whole?*"

At this suggestion, Giggle's face turned crimson. "Take that back," she said. "Say he's alive!"

"Oh, boo-hoo!" he taunted, singing, "*Giggle and Peter, sitting in a—*"

"Scrape," Lillian cut him off. "You know I won't abide slander in my cage. If you're going to talk like that, then you can march your shackles *and* your attitude right out of this slave wheel."

As much as Scrape enjoyed the *idea* of having a mother, he was starting to find the reality a little less fun. "Fine!" he grumbled, pulling up his chain. "I didn't want a stupid mother anyway."

"Hey!" Timothy grabbed his collar. "Don't you call my mum stupid!"

"Get your hands off me." Scrape shoved him backward. "And she is too stupid! All the grown-ups are dumb as doorknobs!"

Within seconds, the two of them were in an all-out brawl, rolling across the wheel, turning the contraption with alarming speed. The other children inside had to run just to keep from tumbling over. Lillian tried her best to pry them apart while Giggle simply trotted alongside them, bawling, "Say he's alive!"

Peg looked anxiously around her. The apes were going to hear them, and if that happened, they might see that one of the children had no chains . . . and was a fugitive princess. "Please?" she begged her friends. "The guards will hear you!"

"Ugly booger-sniffer!"

"Big dumb dummy-head!"

"Say he's alive *right now!*"

Peg tried slowing the cage from the outside, but she only got her hands knocked away. She tried issuing a Royal Decree for them to stop, but they only got louder. She had to find a way to draw their attention. Without thinking, she reached into the burgle-sack and removed the box of Fantastic Eyes. "Hey, look! A *magic* box!" She opened the lid and thrust it between them.

The children stopped quarreling, and the wheel ground to a halt.

"Are those . . . eyeballs?" Timothy said, looking a little ill.

Peg knew she was supposed to keep the Fantastic Eyes a secret, but this had been an emergency. "These eyes are the royal birthright of my twin brother, Prince NoName." She closed the lid and put the box away. "They belong to Peter Nimble."

The group looked at her, dumbstruck. It seemed impossible. She went on. "Now, you can either bicker and die or listen to me and get saved. There is a lot more at risk than just our lives. I would explain everything to you, but I honestly don't fully understand it myself." The princess stared at each one of them with her dazzling emerald-green eyes. "I just need you all to trust me."

There was a long silence. The girls were the first to speak. "We'll do anything for Prince Peter," they said with embarrassing synchronicity. "For *both* of you!" they quickly added.

"Peter rescued my mum," Timothy said, clutching Lillian's hand. "Count me in."

Peg looked to Scrape. The boy sighed, hands thrust in his pockets. "I don't know about Peter, but I'll do whatever the princess wants. Especially if it means getting out of these chains."

Peg smiled. "Thank you all." She took the goblet from the bag. "I'm going to be passing around a cup of slug lard. I need each of you to take a bit in your fingers and rub it inside the lock on your shackles. I know it smells bad, but it's the only way we can get all the locks open before . . ." She didn't know whether it was smart to tell them about the danger of drowning. "Before breakfast."

"Hey!" an ape shouted from the far wall. "Why's that wheel stopped?! Start movin' before I crack your noggins wide open!"

The children resumed marching, Peg with them. She watched as they passed the goblet amongst themselves and rubbed the substance onto their rusted shackles. She looked at the hundreds of other slaves around her who would need to do the same. The job for which she had summoned a hero was now in the hands of children. She glanced behind her at the waterline, which was creeping ever closer. "Wherever you are, Peter," she whispered. "Hurry up."

✦   ✦   ✦

Were it not for the fact that he was already *in* the deep end, Peter was at risk of going off it. None of the other fish would talk to him on account of his being a ferocious sea monster—eels, sharks, and even giant squids swam the other way when they saw him coming. Peter tried to make his voice sound tame and innocent, but every word he uttered—no matter how polite—came out as a bloodcurdling shriek. He was so desperate for help that he resorted to cornering fish against the reef just so he could talk to them. He didn't like bullying harmless creatures, but had no other way to get them to listen.

"DO YOU KNOW GOOD OL' FREDERICK?!" he would shriek.

"P-p-please, M-m-mister Serpent! Don't eat me up!" the flounder, or shark, or narwhal would beg. "I have a wife and guppies!"

"I DON'T WANT TO EAT YOU!" Peter would bellow, somehow unable to *not* yell. "I'M JUST LOOKING FOR GOOD OL' FREDERICK! HE'S A *DOGFISH!*" By this point, the other creature would usually have passed out from fear, forcing the serpent to continue his search elsewhere.

After several hours, Peter finally gave up. His fins were strained from swimming, his throat was sore from screaming, and his stomach was sick from drinking. Even worse, he had no idea where he was anymore. "I DON'T EVEN KNOW HOW TO GET BACK," he hissed, collapsing onto a bed of kelp. "THIS IS TOTALLY HOPELESS!"

It was in that moment of total hopelessness that Peter heard a faint voice echo through the water. "Hey, mate!" the voice hollered. "Heard you was lookin' for a dogfish?"

CHAPTER TWENTY-SEVEN
THE WINDS *of* WAR

Steering the flying machine was proving more difficult than Sir Tode had originally anticipated. In all honesty, he had sort of hoped the thing would run on its own, like all the king's other contraptions. This vessel, however, demanded a bit more input from its operator. It took several minutes of experimentation with the damper before he was able to keep the craft at a level altitude. The rest was straightforward enough; two pedals were linked to a small propeller that generated just enough wind to push the machine forward. Having no hands made working the rudder a bit tricky, but after some practice, Sir Tode was able to use his forehooves to control the levers and keep the vessel on course.

For Simon, the difficulty came in discovering that he was rather prone to *airsickness*. When flying with his own wings, all was fine, but perched aboard a rocking basket, he was poor-footed and bilious. After one particularly nasty bout of purging, the bird decided he would glide alongside the basket, landing only when his wings got tired.

In the meantime, Simon busied himself with throwing all the weapons in the basket overboard in the hope that it might speed their journey. He took up pikes, shields, nets, and knives in his charred talons and tossed them all into the great chasm below. As the flying machine became lighter, it did begin to move faster. Soon, flying alongside the craft became impossible, and Simon was forced to give up and ride in the basket the rest of the way, suffering through the occasional wave of nausea.

The palace soon disappeared behind them, blending into the dim horizon. They flew for many miles like this, with only a vast darkness surrounding them on all sides. Simon spent much of the time staring into the abyss, no doubt steeling himself for the battle to come.

Sir Tode was the first one to spot land on the other side. "Enchanted desert ho!" he exclaimed, squinting into the horizon. "Wait, scratch that. It's just some big, dusty cloud."

Simon hopped to the edge of the basket. "Those are the Winds of War," he said. "The ravens' wings are beating with such fury that they summon a phantom in the air, which draws the very stones from the earth, stinging the enemy's eyes."

"That means the Royal Guard is alive and flapping!" Sir Tode said.

"It means they are desperate," Simon corrected.

The knight took a lever between his teeth. "Then we haven't a moment to spare!" He tipped the rudder, piloting their vessel into the storm.

The winds became stronger, and Sir Tode had to raise the booms on either side to prevent the ship from capsizing. They reached the desert border and found what remained of the Nest, now a mountain of splinters. They could make out the shapes of bodies scattered among the wreckage—casualties from both sides. A trail of corpses led away from the border and disappeared behind a bank. "Looks like the battle's moved inland," the knight said, steering them on.

As they approached, a hundred violent sounds swirled through the air below—metal striking claw, beak tearing flesh, stones crushing bone. Unable to see through the sandy gusts, the pair let their imaginations fill in the grim details. Individual voices were becoming clear now. Sir Tode could hear the thief named Twiddlesticks shouting orders above the din: "Clip away, chums! Tear up your skivvies if you have to! Just keep them pigeons down!" It sounded like the thieves had used up all their nets and were resorting to making sacks from whatever scraps of cloth they could find.

There were smaller voices moving more quickly through the cloud. "Ravens deploy!" one of them squawked.

Simon's talons gripped the edge of the basket. It had been many years since he had heard that caw. "Captain Amos," he whispered.

Another familiar voice rang out. "Slash those canvases! We must free our brothers!"

"And Titus?" Simon was now beside himself. "Make haste, Sir Tode!"

"I'm trying, but these blasted winds keep knocking us back!" Sir Tode bit down on some rigging and pulled with his full weight. "Can you make out who's winning?"

Simon blinked, trying to listen. "Our numbers sound depleted. Ravens rely on a single leader to guide them in battle, but thieves are disorganized and unpredictable—I fear this chaos is working to the traitors' advantage." He loosed an anxious breath. "Still, Captain Amos is a great warrior. As long as he is on the wing, Justice will prevail."

The knight was not so confident. It sounded to his ear like the thieves were having significantly more fun than the birds. There was a giddy edge to their shouts of "Revenge!" and "Get 'em!" that made him nervous.

The flying machine broke through the eye of the storm, at last revealing the battle. Feathers and flesh covered the dunes. Directly below, they saw a great pit filled with canvas sacks. The ravens inside the bags were thrashing madly, trying to claw their way free. "They're taking the birds prisoner?" Sir Tode was confused.

"It is more efficient for the thieves to capture the ravens first and kill them later," Simon explained. "When our numbers fall low enough, they will start the executions." From the looks of things, that moment was fast approaching. Captain Amos and his troops tried to free their captive brothers, but every attempt just resulted in more losses. The pit of bags was fast turning into a pile.

The birds circled around for another attack, but the thieves were ready. A dozen men leapt out from hiding spots, bags in hand. "Got one!" Twiddlesticks was rolling on the ground, trying to stuff a bird into his sack.

It was Captain Amos.

"Leave me!" he called to his troops. "You must free your brothers!" He twisted his body around, trying to break loose. But no sooner had he looked up than he went still. "It cannot be," he whispered. Through the haze, he saw the outline of a magic barge . . . and perched on the edge of the bow was a face he had not seen for many years.

With a surge of new strength, Captain Amos tore himself from Twiddlesticks's grip. "Look to the sky, brothers!" he cried. "It is Simon, returned to us! Justice has—!" But his sentence was never completed. A small thief named Skip threw a knife clean through his heart. The bird gave a bloody cough, stopped midflap, and fell to the ground.

In the same moment, the other ravens tumbled to the sand as though their hearts, too, had been pierced. They stared at the fallen body of their brave leader—dead as a rag doll. Simon watched from above, the same horrified look on his face. The great Captain Amos had been slain.

With the ravens stricken, the thieves wasted no time in starting their executions. Twiddlesticks and the others waded through the pit, giddily stabbing the canvas bags. The few uncaptured ravens did nothing to stop them. They only watched—paralyzed with grief.

"Why aren't they fighting?" Sir Tode demanded from his seat. "They have to *do* something!"

"Do what?" Simon squawked hoarsely. "Without a leader, we can do nothing."

The knight rolled his eyes. "Then you bloody give them a leader!"

Simon was incredulous. "Me? I haven't even a beak to snap with. What do you expect me to do?"

Sir Tode hopped down from his controls. "I really don't have time to throw your own speech back at you. Suffice to say, 'Justice' compels you!" He snatched Simon by the tail feathers and flung him overboard.

The raven flapped in place, gripped with fear. How could he succeed where Captain Amos had failed? He shut his eyes, unable to watch the slaughter below. With each scream, he clenched his talons tighter, until the points cut through his charred flesh. The pain made him recall the words spoken to Sir Tode on the tower: *There are moments when Justice demands from us more than we would give.* The bird took a sharp breath, and when he opened his eyes again, they were full of determination. "Stoke the fire!" he cawed.

Sir Tode's chest swelled. "That's more like it, *Captain* Simon!" He clopped across the deck and pumped the billows with all his might.

Simon flew into the open furnace, scooping up two clawfuls of red-hot coals. He dove toward the sand and released them on the thieves below. The men screamed and cursed. Smoke, then flame quickly spread across the canvas bags—and within seconds the entire pit was consumed by a roaring blaze.

The birds surrounding the pit watched in awe. "Long live the True King!" Simon cried as he unleashed another fiery volley.

A thousand ravens burst free from their restraints, exploding into the sky. "AND LONG LIVE HIS LINE!!!"

CHAPTER TWENTY-EIGHT

PEG'S BREAKTHROUGH

nce she had been able to recruit her friends, Princess Peg found that the lock-greasing operation went surprisingly well. Word spread from one slave to another, and in a matter of minutes, every child there knew that the princess had come to rescue them and needed their help. The goblet of slug lard moved quickly among them. Each child applied the glop to the keyhole of their shackles, while taking care never to stop marching so the apes wouldn't get suspicious.

Just before daybreak, the goblet came back to Peg, empty as a yawn. Every lock had been greased up good and proper and was now ready for the ravens' arrival. *I hope Sir Tode and Simon get here soon,* she thought as she watched the clockwork beast chew away at the cavern wall. Huge salty streams of water were now gushing out from both sides of the rumbling drill, drenching the slaves below. The water level was steadily rising, allowing the sea serpents access to the whole cavern—were it not for the iron leashes holding them fast, they probably would have gobbled up half the slaves by now.

To avoid getting wet themselves, the apes had relocated to the raised stairway in back of the cavern. They passed the hours with a game in which they took turns pretending to momentarily lose hold of one of the monsters' leashes. Each time, the loosed sea serpent would instantly bolt for the children, only to be jerked backward at the very last moment. "Don't you tots worry!" the apes would howl, jingling their chains. "You'll all get a chance to pet these beasties soon enough!"

Peg couldn't help but worry about what was taking Peter so long. What if Scrape had been right? What if her brother, the long lost prince, *had* been gobbled up by sea serpents? She felt the precious box of Fantastic Eyes knock against her side with each step—she would have traded them in a second to see her brother's face once more.

By now the children were suffering from severe exhaustion. A few of them had even passed out and were rolling along the bottom of the cages, tripping up their fellow slaves. "What're you doing?!" one of the apes snarled when he noticed the disruption. "None of you sleeps till you've finished diggin'!" He let his serpent take a few good nips at the cages. The children pulled their sleeping neighbors to their feet and continued marching. "Aw, don't you worry," the guard said with mock concern. "When the drill breaks through, you can sleep as much as you want." This joke sent the other apes into fits of snorting laughter.

"Listen up!" one of the guards roared. "This here's your *official* slave-master speakin'!" The voice belonged to the ape named Maul. He had recently been put in charge of the mines, and he was enjoying his new position immensely. "From now on, all you maggots keep lookin' straight at the wall ahead of you. First one of you who turns 'round will be fish food. Got it?"

Peg and the others did as they were told. They marched forward, eyes fixed on the rumbling drill. "YEAH, JUST LIKE THAT!" Maul said. "KEEP IT UP!" Peg noticed that his voice had grown distant and slightly metallic.

"KEEP THEM HEADS FORWARD!" another voice snickered, also metallic. "NOTHING TO SEE BACK HERE!" Several of the others chuckled with him.

Peg listened to the tinny laughter echoing behind her. The sound reminded her of the brass horn the king had used to summon LongClaw. Deciding to take a chance, she disobeyed Maul's orders and glanced toward the back tunnel. Sure enough, the apes were gone. They had tethered the twelve sea serpents to a stalagmite near the base of the stairs.

"But why would they *leave*?" she muttered to herself. As she turned to resume her pace, a spurt of water burst from the wall and struck her in the face. She sputtered, glaring up at the clockwork drill—

And in that moment, she finally understood what was happening.

Peg realized that this magic beast was like a *giant shovel*. And the wall of the cavern was not endless rock, but a *thin layer*. On the other side was the "ocean" that Sir Tode had shown her on the map . . . and when that ocean broke through, each and every one of them would be drowned in the flood!

"It's a trap!" she screamed. "Everyone stop!" But the noise of the digging machine was so great that none of the slaves could hear her. She would have to *make* them listen.

Peg jumped out of her wheel and into the murky water. The sea serpents sensed her immediately and strained violently against their leashes. The girl kept a safe distance between herself and the monsters as she swam to a spot of dry rock. This had at one time been the island of rock where the children slept—now only the middle remained. Bolted to the center was an enormous iron ring, and from that ring ran a single chain that snaked across the cavern and through the shackles of every single slave. Peg took the chain in both hands and braced her feet against the floor.

There are some times when a person is in such dire straits that they are able to achieve the impossible—less by their own strength than by a strength that moves through them. For example, consider the old story of the long-haired judge who toppled a palace with his bare hands. For Peg, gripping the rusted chain in her thin fingers, this was just such a moment. With a mighty cry, she heaved against the chain, yanking it with all her might. Because it was attached to their ankles, when the chain moved, the children moved with it. The boy nearest to Peg was whipped right off his feet. He fell, knocking over the girl next to him and so on in a sort of "chain reaction." Soon there were hundreds upon hundreds of children sputtering and bickering in the knee-deep water, trying to figure out who had just tripped them.

The wheels of the digging machine stopped moving not a moment too soon. Peg could almost hear the ocean straining against the cavern wall. She dropped the chain and cupped her hands around her mouth. "Attention, subjects! I need you all to listen very carefully!" This time the children heard her and rose to their feet awaiting instructions. "Right now, we are all in grave danger," she called out. "On the other side of this wall is something that could kill us all at any moment!"

As it happened, Peg had much to learn about speech making. Her words, while accurate, were indelicate at best. No sooner had she uttered "something that could kill us all" than hundreds of children were seized with panic. Without even knowing what they were doing, they started running frantically away from the horrible "something" that was hiding just behind the rock. The drill jolted back to life, this time rotating in the opposite direction. Water gushed out as the drill slowly extracted itself from the wall.

Peg knew that the drill was acting as a giant cork, and if it became dislodged, they would be sunk. "Stop running! You're making it worse!" she shouted. But it was no use; the children simply wouldn't listen.

"CHILDREN!" a woman's voice boomed over the confusion. All of the slaves instantly stopped. They looked up to see Lillian standing atop a horizontal gear—drenched and furious. She waited, hands on her hips, until she had the full attention of every slave in the cavern. "The princess was in the middle of saying something, when *you* so rudely interrupted." She said "you" in such a way that made every child bow their head in shame.

Lillian curtsied to the princess. "We *apologize,* Your Majesty. *Please* continue."

"We *apologize,* Your Majesty," the children murmured. "*Please* continue."

Peg cleared her throat. "As you know, I'm working on a plan to get us all out of here. But you all have to do exactly as I say. An army of ravens will be coming soon to break open all of your locks—that's what the slug lard was for. When they arrive, you must not be afraid. Simply stick your shackled legs out of the water, and they will free you."

"What about the snake monsters?" a girl named Brag called out. "They'll gobble us up if we try to escape!"

"No they won't, dummy!" another voice said. "Peter Nimble, the true prince, has a plan to stop them!" Peg looked through the crowd to see who had spoken up for her brother. It was Scrape.

"He's right," she said, her cheeks flushing. "For now we just have to stay calm. I promise help is on the—"

"Hoy!" a voice snarled behind her. "What's all this then?!" It was Maul, who had come to see why the machine had stopped turning. He cracked his whip, and a dozen more apes appeared beside him. "I warned you maggots what'd happen if you quit workin'!"

Despite being all the way on the other side of the cavern, the children were still frightened; as they crowded backward, each step turned their cages—and the drill—a bit more.

"Don't move!" Peg said. "Stand your ground! You must be brave!"

Maul saw her and grinned. "Well, if it ain't the 'princess.' " As you may know, apes are great branch-swingers, used to covering tremendous distances without ever setting foot on the ground—a skill Maul demonstrated as he sprung from the top of the stairs, grabbed hold of one stalactite, then another, and dropped with a *crash* to Peg's side. Before the girl could react, he had snatched her by the neck. "King'll have me promoted for sure if I bring him your filthy hide." He licked his dripping tusk, grinning at the thought of delivering her still-warm head to Incarnadine. "Come to think of it, if I bring you in *dead,* he'll thank me even more."

Peg struggled to pry his claws from her windpipe, but he only squeezed tighter, crushing the life from her. She felt a thunderous pounding in her skull, and it seemed as if the torches were all being snuffed out one by one. Shadows swirled and darted around her— she was losing consciousness. The princess dropped her head, and everything went black.

✦　✦　✦

The next thing Peg knew, she was up to her neck in salty water, gasping for breath. Pandemonium swirled around her. Apes were splashing and shouting, swatting at the air. Tiny black clouds were swooping high and low. Maul was staggering blindly through the darkness, clutching his face. Peg shook her throbbing head, trying to follow what was happening. Those shadows. They somehow looked *familiar*. Suddenly, she realized what they were. "Simon!" she shouted, scrambling to her feet.

"Children first!" the raven commanded his brothers. "Titus! Keep the apes away from the machine!" Birds swarmed around the drill, diving into the cages. The slaves were ready and waiting with their shackled feet high in the air. The locks had been well oiled, and the birds' beaks popped them open with little trouble.

"Bravo, Captain!" another voice cried. Peg looked up to see Sir Tode perched atop the drill, cheering the troops on. "Now, let's show those apes what we're made of!"

"Agreed, friend!" Simon circled around to rally his flock. "Brothers, attack!" Ravens swept through the air, talons flashing. The primates were ridiculously outnumbered. Within seconds, the Royal Guard were driving them aboveground.

"Grunts, retreat!" Maul commanded, lumbering for the tunnels. The apes barreled up the steps behind him, snapping their whips and clutching their bleeding humps. When the last one disappeared, the birds let out a raucous cry of victory. The children cheered with them, throwing their open shackles into the air.

This joyous revelry, however, was soon replaced with another mood—one of mortal terror. At first no one noticed that Maul had unleashed the sea serpents before escaping. But when the first shriek-ing monster leapt from the water, complete mayhem broke loose.

The vicious creatures were finally free . . . and they were *hungry*. They still had on their iron masks, which prevented them from seeing exactly where the children were, but they could smell fresh meat close by. The children scrambled up the side of the digging machine, trying desperately to keep clear of the twelve sets of glassy-toothed jaws.

The creatures thrashed through the water, swatting birds out of their way with their tails as they lunged for the children's bare feet. Peg and her subjects scrambled atop the tallest gears of the machine, safe from the snapping jaws. "Hold tight," she commanded. "So long as we're up here, the serpents can't reach us."

One of the monsters jerked its head back, sniffing the air. It turned to the other serpents and shrieked in some devilish tongue. All at once, the twelve creatures clamped their mighty jaws around whatever clockwork they could reach and flailed wildly. Metal groaned as pistons were ripped from the machinery. One or two smaller children slipped from their perches, nearly falling into the water.

The princess clung to her trembling cog. "They'll tear the machine right out of the wall!" she called to Simon. The ravens attacked again, but their talons were useless against the scaly hides. Peg watched in horror as the serpents snatched up whole mouthfuls of ravens and spit them into the water.

As she desperately tried to conceive of a plan, out of nowhere a *new* serpent burst from the water, knocking the others aside. The twelve monsters shrieked with fury and went after this new aggressor. They smashed through stalagmites and boulders trying to get him.

Peg watched, confused, as the thin creature wriggled this way and that, drawing his attackers away from the children. Could one of the creatures actually be *protecting* them? In the dim light, she caught a glimpse of what she thought was a pair of shiny, black eyes. "Peter?" she whispered.

A deep voice shook the cavern. "Slow down, mate! Don't poach all the fun!" With that, an even bigger fish—one with floppy ears and a wagging tail—broke to the surface. "Leave some for Good Ol' Frederick!"

Children and ravens alike watched in awe as the enormous dogfish swished into action. The serpents flailed and snapped and spit as Frederick took their leashes in his mouth and throttled them against the walls. His teeth were not sharp, but his strength was immense, and the slithery creatures found themselves completely powerless against the broadside of his tail.

"Heads up, mates!" He snagged one of the wriggling serpents in his jaw and flung it clean across the cavern. The shrieking monster smashed into what was left of the digging machine, shattering it into a hundred pieces.

A deep rumbling shook the mines.

"The ocean's coming," Peg screamed. "Everybody, hold your breath and—!" This was all she could manage before the drill fell away from the wall and water exploded into the cavern, sweeping up every child, bird, and fish in its wake.

In a matter of minutes, every fountain, faucet, and bath in the kingdom was overflowing with saltwater. Smaller fish from the sea were floating into homes and hallways, flopping about the stone floors, madly gasping for breath. Water flooded down every stairwell and gushed like a mighty waterfall over every palace wall, filling the great chasm and sweeping over the Just Deserts. The desert kingdom had been transformed back into an island surrounded by glittering blue oceans.

Incarnadine watched the transformation from the comfort of his dressing room balcony. He smiled with great relish. At last he had put an end to his sniveling little brother's enchantment. His fleet of battleships—which only moments before had been suspended over an empty chasm—was now floating on the water, ready for war. A few hours earlier, he had spotted his airship touching down in the deserts. Any minute now, the vessel would return with a legion of thankful thieves, and his army would be complete. He wound the key in his armor, and the gears lining his body tightened, ready to spring. Beneath his breastplate was a cunning science that had felled a kingdom. The first of many. "Soon every corner of the map will learn to fear my name," he said, gazing out at the water.

Two doors burst open on either side of him.

"Your Highness!" LongClaw said, running in from the east.

"Your Highness!" Maul said, running in from the west.

Incarnadine swung around, glaring at them both. He had a rule about being interrupted before breakfast. "Out with it," he snapped.

LongClaw was the first to speak. "Sire, the airship, which I sent off without a hitch, failed to return this morning. I fear the thieves may have drowned in the great flood you so brilliantly wrought." The ape had spent much of the night debating whether it was wise to inform his ruler of what had really happened to the vessel . . . and had decided it was not.

"Spilled milk, LongClaw." The king waved his hand. "The flood *was* brilliant, though, wasn't it?" He turned to Maul. "And you?"

"The ravens are attacking!" the second ape said. "They freed the slaves from the mines and are makin' their way upground as we speak. P-p-please forgive me, Master!" He gave a feeble smile, hoping the king might extend to him the same grace he had shown LongClaw.

"Forgive you? Of course I forgive you." Incarnadine raised his gauntlet as if to let the ape kiss it. "But just this once." He flexed his pinkie, and a spring–loaded blade shot out from his wrist, slicing right through Maul's neck. The beast's head landed on the floor with a *thump*. His body slumped beside it.

LongClaw congratulated himself for making the right decision. "What is your command, Sire?"

The king flicked the sticky ape-remains from his still–singing blade and jammed it back into the scabbard on his forearm. "What else? We assemble for war!" He threw his cape back, marching for the hallway. "Sound the alarm! Rally your horde! Bring all citizens to the Eating Hall at once! If it's blood that brat wants, then blood she shall have!"

✦   ✦   ✦

Ravens poured from every faucet in the palace. The gushing seawater had carried them up through the plumbing and into kitchens and washrooms. LongClaw stormed down the main corridor, a spear in each paw. "Storm the houses, don't let any of 'em escape!" Behind him marched the rest of his horde, armed with nets and catapults.

Simon and his troops were fighting for their lives once more. Feathers and fur scattered in all directions as the battle spilled into the main palace. From the stairwell LongClaw bellowed orders to fire and reload the catapults. "Stay by the walls, grunts!" he roared. "Don't let 'em catch you in the open!" Ravens swooped and dove, pecking at the beasts with desperate fury. But these apes were far stronger than the thieves of the desert—one swipe of their mighty claws could slice a bird clean in half.

The water in the streets turned red with the blood of battle. Bodies from both sides lay strewn throughout the palace. The ravens were exhausted; they had been fighting for days at the Nest, then battling sea serpents, then swept up in a great flood, and now were warring against savage apes. The apes, on the other hand, were rested and well armed, having not only shields for close combat but also clockwork weapons that could take the skies. Crossbows shot arrows clean though the birds' wings. Giant catapults launched nets around them. Simon and his troops were trapped between hurtling weapons and slashing claws. What had once been an army of thousands was now only hundreds strong. And they were losing brothers every minute.

✦   ✦   ✦

As you might imagine, monstrous sea creatures from the deep are far too large to fit through conventional plumbing. Thus, when the ocean broke through the wall, Peter, Frederick, and the twelve angry sea serpents were all swept straight into what used to be the great chasm, which had since transformed into a vast ocean. In these open waters, the sea serpents proved much better fighters. Suddenly, Peter and Good Ol' Frederick no longer enjoyed the advantage that the shallow moat had afforded them. The shrieking creatures whipped through the currents, creating enormous waves that sent Peter crashing against the palace walls. They snapped at Frederick, ripping hunks of flesh from his side and tail. To make matters worse, the king's warships joined the fight, firing cannonballs and harpoons into the foaming sea.

"I'm no jellyfish, but this is gettin' pretty scaly, mate!" Frederick hollered to Peter as he fought off a pair of gnashing serpents. "I know a couple of shellbacks 'round these waters. This sort of thing's right up their gully. Mind if I give 'em a shout?"

"BE MY GUEST!" Peter shrieked, twisting free from a barbed fishnet.

Good Ol' Frederick dove deep into the ocean and loosed a mighty fish call. The entire sea trembled at the power of his voice. He returned a moment later. "That oughtta even things up a bit! Now, if we can just keep alive till they get here!"

Peter and Frederick decided to change their tactic from head-on combat to swimming-for-dear-life. At last they heard a deep rumble from the depths below. "That's them now, mate!" Frederick said. "We best keep to the shore!" The ocean erupted as six giant sea turtles burst to the surface, sending water churning for miles in every direction. Each was big as an island and twice as old. Their craggy flippers were lined on both sides with black tusks. Their shielded backs were covered in battle paint and primordial moss. The bale loosed a mighty war cry and attacked without mercy. They swung their limbs, shattering the warships. They tore at the serpents with their beaks.

"Careful you don't nip this little guy, mates!" Frederick placed a protective fin over Peter. "He's on our side!"

The sea battle had a rather swift conclusion, which ended in the twelve sea serpents being reduced to a few dozen wriggling pieces, drifting down to the sea floor. "They'll be back someday," Frederick said, watching the last flailing serpent tail disappear below the surface. "But no worries. It won't be in your lifetime."

✦　✦　✦

While ravens and apes were busy battling in the halls, the children found themselves awash in the palace sewer system. The exhausted, newly freed slaves tumbled up through channels and shafts, finally spilling out of the gargoyles' open mouths. They landed in a huge pile in the middle of the Eating Hall, dazed and drenched.

Peg and Sir Tode were among the last to emerge. They slid down the sputtering mound of children and then splashed to the floor. Peter's burgle-sack came bouncing after them and knocked the princess in the back of her head. As she stumbled to her feet, rubbing her head and draining her ears, she heard shouts from the hallway.

"Citizens! Follow me!" It was the king. And he was not alone.

Peg turned and began calling to the children. "Everyone, listen! There's something I must tell you about the grown-ups. The king has drugged—!"

Her words were drowned out as hundreds of adults stampeded into the Eating Hall, spears high in the air. Incarnadine led the charge, his spurs clanking against the wet floor. "Kill the monsters!" he shouted, racing toward his niece.

"KILL THE MONSTERS!" the adults echoed, racing toward their children.

The children struggled to extricate themselves from the pile before the grown-ups could trample them. Lillian pulled Timothy and a few others close, trying to shield them from the onslaught of crazed parents.

"Ignore their cries!" the king said over the din. "Kill them all!" He continued toward Peg, shoving aside anyone in his way. The princess tried to run in the opposite direction, but her uncle was too fast. "Get back here, brat!" He seized her by the arm.

The girl twisted against his iron grip, grabbing hold of the burgle-sack with her free hand. "Sir Tode!" she cried. "Get the eyes to sea!" She lobbed the bag over her head—it soared in a high arc and landed with a splash at his hooves.

"Grab that bag!" the king ordered. He had no idea what it was, but judging from the princess's desperation, it probably contained a secret weapon. A dozen adults obediently lunged for it, very nearly crushing Sir Tode beneath their shields.

The knight wriggled free with the fishhook in his teeth. "*En garde!*" he cried and swiped with all his might. Adults around him howled and collapsed, clutching their nicked shins. Sir Tode looped the burgle-sack around his neck. "I shall return, Your Majesty!" He galloped past his attackers and disappeared down the main corridor.

✦ ✦ ✦

When Sir Tode promised the princess that he would return, it was with some vague idea that he might be able to find reinforcements. As soon as he reached the outer palace, however, he realized how impossible that would be. In the minutes since he had parted ways with the ravens, their predicament had turned dire.

It seemed that no matter where the birds flew there was a javelin or mace waiting to meet them. Unlike the thieves, the apes did not waste time with clipping. Instead, they gorged themselves, ripping the ravens to pieces with their greedy mouths. Though Simon and his troops fought bravely, they were no match for the vicious Night Patrol.

Sir Tode raced through the carnage in search of Peter . . . but he was nowhere to be found. In fact, he couldn't recall having seen the boy since parting ways the night before. He assumed Peg knew her brother's whereabouts. She had shouted something to him about getting the eyes "to see." *But what on earth did that mean?*

His thoughts were interrupted by a hungry snarl. "Dibs on the cat!" Sir Tode clambered backward as an ape broke from the pack and chased after him. "Here, kitty, kitty!" it said, already drooling at the prospect of *knight tartare.*

A dozen ravens seized the opportunity and swooped down on the beast, pecking and scratching at its exposed hump with terrific fury. The ape crashed to the ground with such force that Sir Tode flew backward, tripping over himself and spilling the contents of the burgle-sack everywhere.

"Sir Tode!" a voice squawked. "You are not safe here!" The

knight looked up to see Simon—bloody, but very much alive. "We cannot fight like this much longer! Where is Her Majesty's army?"

"I'm afraid they're . . . busy," Sir Tode said, remembering the terrified screams of the slave children as they ran from their crazed parents. "It would appear that both sets of reinforcements are in need of reinforcements." He jumped to his hooves and set to collecting Peter's things, which were scattered across the floor.

Arrows whizzed past them on all sides. "Down the hall! That one's the leader!" LongClaw said, pointing toward Simon. "We kill him, and the others'll fall like finches!" A half-dozen apes followed his charge.

Sir Tode ignored the burgle-tools and went straight for the box of Fantastic Eyes. He snapped the lid tight and stuffed it into the bag.

"My brothers and I shall keep the apes occupied as long as possible!" Simon cawed, lifting Sir Tode off the ground. "You must protect the Line!" With that, he flung the knight through an open window into the chasm below.

Sir Tode, who had not expected to be *flung* anywhere, clenched his eyes shut and screamed with the full force of his lungs as he sailed toward the bottomless crag. But instead of hitting rock, his body plunged into foamy water. He bobbed to the surface a moment later, coughing and kicking. Before he could even cry for help, a great, lazy wave shoved him toward the castle and deposited him on the stone shore. Sir Tode wobbled to his hooves and looked at the sea before him. The Just Deserts—which had stretched from horizon to horizon—were now completely washed away. The palace behind him was all that remained of the Vanished Kingdom. "Not so vanished anymore," he said, shaking himself dry.

As if in reply, a hideous sea serpent broke from the waves and loosed a chilling shriek.

The poor knight nearly died from the fright. He leapt back and pressed himself against the wall. "D-d-don't eat me!"

The serpent remained still, glaring straight at him. It shrieked again, but this time in a *slightly less* murderous tone.

Sir Tode stared into the monster's shiny black eyes, which somehow looked familiar to him. All at once, he understood what the princess had been trying to tell him. *Get the eyes to sea.* "P-P-Peter?" he said, inching closer. "Is it really you?"

The animal shrieked back at him, gnashing its glassy teeth.

"Bloody gill, mate!" Frederick appeared from below. "How many times you gonna make him ask? He needs you to pluck his peepers out so he can change back into a little boy . . . though I can't see why he'd want to. Fragile as flounders, those humans are."

Sir Tode swallowed and took another timid step toward the serpent. "All right," he said weakly. "Let's get it over with."

It was a bit of a chore removing a pair of eyes with just hooves, but after some difficulty, Sir Tode was able to manage. The next thing he knew, his friend Peter Nimble was splashing in the water below him. "My goodness," he exclaimed. "It's really you!"

"More or less," Peter said, shivering. He was a bit disoriented, having been an enormous sea serpent only seconds before. He pulled himself ashore and flopped onto his back, taking a moment to remember how all his little boy senses worked. "Is it over? Did we defeat the king?"

"I'm afraid not." Sir Tode cast a glance toward the palace. "The apes have nearly extinguished Simon's troops, and the children are being attacked by their own parents."

Peter listened to the screams ringing out from the Eating Hall. He knew the effects of the previous day's Devil's Dram would wear off soon—but from the sound of things, "soon" was not fast enough. "We have to stop the grown-ups before they hurt the children," he exclaimed. "We have to make them *see*."

"I agree completely." Sir Tode took the burgle-sack, which had washed to shore beside him, and he brought it to the boy's feet. "I think it's time, Peter."

The emerald eyes.

Everything within Peter confirmed that the moment had finally come. At last he would try the third pair of Fantastic Eyes. His heart raced at the thought of what marvelous power they might wield. He knelt down and removed the wooden box from the bag. He took a breath, raised the lid, and reached inside.

But something was wrong.

"No time for cold feet," Sir Tode said. "Let's see them in action."

Peter's face had gone completely pale. "The eyes . . . they're *gone*."

CHAPTER THIRTY

THE BACK-STABBER'S BLIGHT

At first Sir Tode refused to believe it. But when he looked for himself, he found only an empty place in the box where the emerald eyes had been. "Good heavens," he said, recalling his skirmish with the ape in the corridor. "This is all my fault. I dropped the box . . . they must have fallen out . . ." His voice quavered. "Peter, I am so sorry."

Despite his uncanny ears, the boy could not hear his friend. Nor could he hear Frederick bobbing in the water beside him, or the clash of battle, or the children screaming. Peter could hear nothing but the hollow sough of his own despair. He had sailed over seas, trekked across sands, survived thieves, apes, and even dragons—all with the confidence that when the moment was right, the Fantastic Eyes would be just what he needed. He had even let himself half believe that this final pair was proof that he was some kind of prince.

But no more.

Without the emerald eyes, Peter was forced to acknowledge the truth: they were doomed. Incarnadine would execute the children, rebuild his fleet, and sail out to conquer the world . . . and it was all Peter's fault. His cheeks grew hot when he considered how it was he who had led Peg and the others into this war. A war they couldn't win. "The eyes are gone . . . along with any hope we had of victory," he said. "We have to surrender."

Up to this point, Sir Tode had been sympathetic. But no more. "Surrender?" He planted himself in Peter's path. "Surrender?! We shall do no such thing! We made a promise to the professor, to Peg, to Simon, to *ourselves* that we would see this quest through. Our friends are depending on us. You may never have to peer into a looking glass, Peter, but I will. And I don't want to see a coward staring back at me. I'm fighting, and if that means death, so be it. I'd rather die a martyr than live a milksop."

The knight spoke with such passion that Peter had no opportunity to interrupt. Instead, he was forced to *listen*. With every word, he felt more ashamed. Here was his best friend, unable to even hold a weapon, declaring that he was ready to fight to the death. In the silence that followed, Peter again heard voices behind the palace walls, but this time he truly *listened*. He heard Simon and Titus squawking, "Long live the Line!" He heard Scrape and Lillian shouting, "Protect

Her Majesty!" And above them all, he heard Peg telling the children to not be scared because "Prince NoName is coming!"

Peter knew that to give up was to turn his back on destiny. *His* destiny. Fantastic Eyes or not, he was committed. The boy reached inside his bag and wrapped his fingers around the cold metal of his fishhook. He removed the weapon, feeling its perfect weight in his hand.

Frederick sloshed closer to shore. "Not to pry, mate." He gave a nervous chuckle. "But you ain't plannin' to *fish* with that, are you?"

"No." He turned toward the palace, his face grave. "I'm planning to *fight*."

✦　✦　✦

Peter and Sir Tode ran as fast as they could. Streams of blood and seawater soaked the floor. Ravens and apes were squawking and snarling all around them. The battle was so loud and confusing that it was all Peter could do not to trip over himself. Even through the chaos, he could tell that his friend's report had been accurate: the ravens were losing.

They reached the apex of an open bridge, from which Sir Tode could study the movements below. "The apes are at the mouth of a broad corridor that connects to the long courtyard," he relayed to Peter. "If they reach the far end, it's over."

"Then we had better cut them off," Peter said. He ran through every possible barricade he could think of—but treacle and bear traps were in short supply. Shorter still was their supply of time. He could feel the morning sun prickling against his neck and knew that the Breakfast Bell would soon go off, as if to welcome the approaching horde. It was in thinking of the bell that Peter recalled his first night in the palace. After the chimes struck, all the doors had automatically locked. "We don't need to build a barrier," he said suddenly. "The king's got one ready-made for us!"

This time it was Peter who led the way through the battlefield. He kept his body crouched low, running his long fingers along the wall. He was looking for the secret passage that Peg's friends had used when they kidnapped him. If he could just get through in time, there might be a chance. The boy soon found a space in the mortar. "This is the spot!" he said, pulling back a stone. He helped Sir Tode into the passage and wriggled in after him.

Within the walls, the cries of battle lessened to a low roar. The space was too narrow for Peter to carry Sir Tode, and the knight was forced to follow, blindly tripping over sharp metal cogs with nearly every step. "On my first night here," the boy explained, "I came across a gate that blocked off the Eating Hall from the rest of the palace. I think we might be able to use it to stop the apes!" He decided not to mention that if they were still inside the walls when the Breakfast Bell rang, they would both be crushed flat by the gears.

Peter soon found the iron gate, which hung suspended from

motionless clockwork. He could hear battle sounds echoing through a broad slot at his feet. In one direction, apes were hunting ravens; in the other direction, grown-ups were hunting children. "Sounds like we're just in time," he said, taking hold of Sir Tode and dropping through the gap.

The two of them landed in the middle of the corridor, just ahead of the approaching apes. Peter ran to the wall and began searching with his hands. "I see a switch just to your left," Sir Tode said. The boy took hold of the lever and pulled with all his strength. There came a heavy wrenching sound, and the gate *clank-clank-clanked* down from the ceiling.

"The lock-pick's cuttin' us off from the chiddlers!" LongClaw said, tossing a dead raven aside. "Stop him!" He and his grunts charged ahead, hurling whatever weapons they had. Peter and Sir Tode ducked as spears, shields, pikes, and helmets clattered against the descending gate. The assault crescendoed with an ugly screeching sound.

The gate had stopped moving.

"Oh, drat," Sir Tode said. "There's a poleaxe wedged in the track along the wall." He looked up to see the apes racing for them at full bore. "Never fear! I think I can work it loose." Before Peter could object, Sir Tode ran to the other side and took the handle in his teeth. He pulled the axe free, and the gate crashed down between them.

"Sir Tode!" Peter pulled against the iron barrier.

"Go, Your Majesty," he called from the other side. The knight arched his back and faced the approaching horde. "I'll fight with the ravens!"

Peter nodded, and without another word, the two friends parted, each diving headlong into battle.

✦   ✦   ✦

The situation in the Eating Hall was looking truly hopeless. The adults had gotten the hang of their spears and could now poke and jab like a proper mob. Children ran frantic circles around their parents, trying to wear them out without getting skewered. Scrape had wrestled a weapon from one of the adults and rushed to get Peg away from the king. He and a few others formed a tight circle around her, keeping as much distance as possible between Peg and her uncle.

King Incarnadine stalked them through the chaos. He wielded not one but *two* swords, which he used to hack down anyone in his path. His face bore a delighted grin—he had dreamed of this moment for ten years and wanted to savor every minute.

The Breakfast Bell began to ring high above them, momentarily drowning out the battle. With each stroke, the water covering the ground trembled. By the time the bell finally stopped, Incarnadine had cornered them. He smirked down at Peg. "Time's up, *Your Majesty*," he said.

"You stay away from her!" Scrape warned, sounding braver than he felt. Marbles and Timothy stood with him, each clutching their own spear.

"Or what? You'll stick me?" The king walked forward, letting the points knock uselessly against his armor. A sweep of his arm sent all three children sprawling. Peg crouched in the water, defenseless and alone. "Looks like you're all out of heroes," he said with mock sympathy.

The princess tried to flee, but her uncle was ready. "Enough running!" He gave her a sharp cut across the Achilles tendon that hobbled her instantly. Peg collapsed, screaming as her wound filled with salty water. "Stop bawling. If I'd known you would grow up to be such a nuisance, I would have murdered you in your crib."

He took hold of her collar and raised her above the crowd. "Attention, citizens!" he called. The adults all immediately ceased their spearplay. "Do not kill the childr—I mean, *monsters* just yet. I want them to witness something first. This is what comes of all who defy your Great Ruler!"

"Hurrah for our Great Ruler!" the people shouted back.

Incarnadine carried a flailing Peg to a low stone step in back of the hall. He forced the girl to her knees and placed her head against the step. The princess winced as the rough surface scraped her cheek. She desperately scanned the faces of her shivering subjects— what a fool she had been to think that these children could topple a kingdom. Soon they would be dead, and it was all her fault. "You've won," she said, her throat stinging at the words. "Now kill me."

"If you insist." The man carefully positioned his blade above her throat. "Hold still, if you know what's good for you. As they say: Measure twice, cut onc—"

"LET HER GO, IMPOSTOR!"

A hush fell over the crowd as every adult turned to see who would dare insult their king. Standing in the corridor was a dirty boy of ten, clutching a long silver fishhook.

The vision sent a chill through the king's armored body. He could see that it was the lock-pick who had stolen his maps—but something about the boy had changed. He now looked less like some filthy urchin and more like Incarnadine's own brother, whom the king had murdered in this very hall. "What trick is this?" he breathed.

"My name is Peter Nimble," the boy replied. He walked steadily through the mob, keeping his every sense trained on the king. "*True* heir to the throne of HazelPort. Ten years ago you murdered my father and stole his crown. I have come to take it back."

The king knew at once Peter was speaking the truth. He looked to his subjects, who were watching the boy with uncertainty. "I command you not to listen to him!" he blurted. "His voice will turn the whole lot of you into *stone!*"

The grown-ups jammed fingers into each ear so as not to hear. A few among them also closed their eyes on the off chance that *looking at* the stranger might prove similarly dangerous. The children, however, defied the command. A murmur filled the Eating Hall as Peter walked past. "It's really him! It's Prince NoName!"

"Lies!" Incarnadine bellowed, unconsciously gripping the diadem upon his head. "He's a saboteur sent to destroy my kingdom!" He had spent ten long years brainwashing these people and wasn't about to let some prodigal brat ruin it for him. He dug his spurred heel into Peg's cheek, causing her to scream. "Silence those children this instant—or I'll cut the girl's head off!"

"They can't be silenced," Peter said calmly. He raised his fishhook, pointing it straight at the king. "If you release her, you can fight me for your precious throne."

Incarnadine sneered at the quaint proposition. "Risking your life for your sister? How very noble of you." He lifted Peg from the step and hurled her into the crowd. "Hold her fast," he ordered the two nearest adults, who set to wrestling her down. "After I finish the boy, I'll come back for her."

The thief and the king slowly approached each other. Though Peter could not see it, he bore a striking resemblance to the man before him. They both had the same dark hair, the same sharp jaw, and the same lean frame—though Incarnadine's was hidden beneath a hundred pounds of polished steel. Peter listened to the sound of clockwork *whirrrring* beneath the gleaming plate metal: springs tightening, pistons churning, gears grinding. Who knew what terrible powers that suit possessed?

The two were now pacing around each other in a slow circle. "Come along, *nephew*," Incarnadine taunted, daring the boy to strike first. "Don't be shy." Peter was more than shy—he was terrified. But to look at him, you would never have thought so. Sir Tode's lessons had at least taught the boy proper form, and the king's clockwork suit afforded him the luxury of hearing his opponent's slightest movement. He matched his uncle's every step like a shadow, ever mindful of the blades on each forearm.

At last Peter heard an opening. He lunged forward, sweeping his hook through the air.

The king was caught off guard, but not for long. He raised his armored palms just in time to grab the hook. He flexed his fists around the metal, bending it like taffy. "You're not much of a swordsman, boy." He ripped the weapon from Peter's hands and flung it to the ground. "That's all right. Neither was your father!"

Now Incarnadine struck back. He swung his swords in constant succession—one high, one low. Peter could barely jump to avoid losing his feet before the second blade came for his head. The boy somersaulted backward across the hall, dodging swipe after swipe. With each attack, the grown-ups cheered louder for their heroic leader—some even unplugged their ears to applaud.

Peter rolled between his uncle's legs and sprinted back across the hall to retrieve his fishhook. Incarnadine was right behind him, swords still swinging. Silver clashed against stone as the man pursued his prey. Peter tried to block the assault with his crumpled fishhook, but the weapon was useless otherwise. So long as the king wore his armor, it would be impossible to kill him.

"Some warrior you are!" Peter mocked his opponent. "Only a coward would hide behind plate mail to fight someone half his size!"

The king—who did not like being maligned in front of his

subjects—stopped to consider this. "Very well," he said, taking a step back. "Off it comes." His subjects cheered at this show of valor. He unhinged a clasp around his neck and the breastplate fell to the ground with a hollow clang. The *ticking* of clockwork grew louder, and Peter could now pick out individual cogs, pistons, and springs as they moved along Incarnadine's newly exposed torso. "But I should warn you, boy. The armor wasn't for *my* protection . . . it was for yours." He pushed a small lever at his side and the entire suit came to life. A hundred knives, spurs, and barbs sprang out from the clockwork, all spinning and slicing in a frenzied blur!

Peter listened to the dancing blades, barely able to conceive of what was before him. "I assure you, it's something to behold," the man said, reading his nephew's expression. "I fashioned it myself. Every inch, deadly." He flexed his gauntlet, admiring the blades *whirring* and *slicing* all along his arm.

Peter had been a fool to think he could taunt this murderer into a fair fight. He scrambled under the eating table to put some distance between himself and the king's armor. Incarnadine followed after him, walking straight into the table. The moment his suit touched the wood, the gears grabbed hold, chewing and slicing and crushing it into a million splinters. Adults and children shielded themselves as wooden shrapnel exploded in all directions.

Peter ignored the sounds and kept running until he came against the clock tower wall. He rattled the maintenance door but found it had been sealed shut with some kind of mortar. His only other option was a staircase jutting out from the facade—he had no idea where it might lead, but at least it would buy him some time. He clambered up the stone steps, zigzagging higher and higher above the hall.

The king watched him, somewhat amused. "A dead end," he called. "Too perfect!"

Peter discovered too late what his uncle meant: the stairs ended at a platform fifty feet above the courtyard floor. He searched in vain for a hatch or ladder but could find nothing that would help him escape.

Now that Peter was so thoroughly trapped, Incarnadine took his time moving up the steps. He gloated as he climbed. "Before me, no man in this kingdom had ever guessed at the clockwork wonders that lie beyond our seas. I alone sailed out to learn these dark magics . . . only to discover that they were not magic at all. They were figments, little nothings—a mere string of letters and numerals. And unlike magic, this 'science' could be mastered and *harnessed*." He let his arm graze the wall. Sparks shot out as the spinning blades whetted against the stone. People below cheered this dazzling display.

"Listen to them," he said to Peter. "They're powerless in the face of such tricks. I have transformed unthinking beasts into servants, and servants into unthinking beasts." His voice was thick with disdain.

Peter remained still, listening not to the man's words but to the sound of his approaching blades. Incarnadine stepped closer, lowering his voice to a venomous whisper. "But even better, dear nephew, was how this 'magic' helped me fly back to the palace, slip undetected into this very hall, and cut the still-beating heart from my brother's noble chest."

"Monster!" Peter hurled the fishhook like a lance. The point grazed Incarnadine's face, and the man staggered backward, nearly losing his balance. There was a murmur of horror when citizens saw blood flowing from their Great Ruler's cheek. Peter listened as his weapon clattered down the steps and splashed onto the ground below—so much for destiny.

Incarnadine erupted with rage. "You little worm!" He charged up the remaining steps. "Thought you'd avenge your precious parents? Thought you could steal the throne from *me?!*" He swiped his arm, catching Peter's shoulder with a dozen tiny blades. The boy collapsed, crippled with pain. "Stand up!" Incarnadine snatched him by the neck and lifted him clear off the ledge. Peter's feet kicked wildly in the air.

"You were never a prince." The king tightened his grip. "You're nothing but a pathetic! wretched! THIEF!"

As Peter fought to breathe, that one word rang in his head:

"THIEF!"

The insult echoed louder and louder until it was all he could hear.

"THIEF!"

It was true. Even if he had by some miracle won the fight, what did he know about ruling? He was a criminal. *He* was the impostor.

But then the boy recalled another, steadier voice—the professor giving his final benediction. *Remember your nature above all things.* All through the journey, Peter had assumed he had meant that somewhere inside him lived a noble warrior. But maybe he was saying the opposite? That Peter wasn't a warrior, but a dirty, sneaky thief . . . *the greatest thief who ever lived.* And why couldn't a thief be a hero? He suddenly understood how all the trials of his life—abandonment, Mr. Seamus, the Just Deserts—had prepared him for this moment. He gasped for breath, and his heart swelled with a new desire to fight. This time, though, he would fight the way he knew best.

He started with the Rascal's Questions.

Where was he?

Dangling fifty feet above ground, choking to death.

Were there friends nearby?

He could hear his sister struggling by the stairs, but she was too far away to help.

Were there weapons nearby?

His fishhook was lying useless on the ground below, leaving him only his hands.

But his were no ordinary hands.

Peter knew that the king's mechanical suit was no different from any of the locks he had spent his life mastering. All he had to do was find a way in. He focused his every sense on the *ticktock* of clockwork before him. He could hear every gear and piston running together toward a narrow gap just below the king's heart: that was his keyhole.

This realization, of course, happened in an instant. From

Incarnadine's perspective, there was no difference between the boy he had raised above the platform and the boy he was staring at now—no difference but the faintest trace of a smile. "Farewell, dear nephew," the king said as he drew back his sword. "Say hello to my brother for m—!"

Peter plunged his hand straight into the armor. He screamed as clockwork chewed through skin and fingernail and bone and the pain of a thousand hot pokers ripped through him. He slipped from the king's grip and collapsed at the edge of the platform.

With all Peter's screaming, it took Incarnadine a moment to realize that he hadn't succeeded in running his nephew through. In fact, his arm was still raised over his head, just as it had been. The gears had stopped whirring, and within seconds every joint of his terrible armor was locked in place, rendering him completely immobile. "What manner of curse is this?" He strained against the frozen suit. "What have you done to me?"

Peter was hunched at his feet, overcome with pain, but still alive. "What I was born to do," he said with a triumphant gasp. He raised his trembling, bloody hand to reveal a tiny brass pin—no bigger than a bodkin.

"Impossible!" The king jerked his head about. "You're just a child!"

"There's no such thing as *just* a child," a voice spoke from behind. The king craned his neck and saw Peg limping up the steps. She placed a hand on his body and gave a mighty shove.

Incarnadine tumbled off the ledge and crashed onto the ground below, piercing his throat on the silver fishhook. There he lay broken and bleeding, unable to wriggle free from the armor he had constructed. With a final gurgle, he went limp. And thus, King Incarnadine died just as the Back-Stabber's Blight had predicted: like a miserable worm.

A silence came over the Eating Hall. The adults were terrified beyond words. Never in their wildest imaginings did they think that their mighty ruler could be killed.

"Those monsters murdered our king!" one woman cried, covering her mouth. Panic swelled through the crowd as people started for the exits.

Peg helped her brother to his feet and stood beside him. She took a deep breath and shouted with all her might, "ORDER, SUBJECTS!!!"

For once, Peg's words got through; every man, woman, and child instantly stopped what they were doing and stared up at her. The princess composed herself and went on. "The man you worshipped as king was an impostor. Ten years ago, he seized this land from its true ruler, King Hazelgood." She took Peter's good hand in her own. "Today, we, his heirs, have returned to avenge his death and claim what is rightfully ours."

The adults' faces were flushed with confusion.

Peter squeezed his sister's hand, urging her to go on.

The girl took a breath. "Everything the king told you was a lie.

Your homes were prisons. Your feasts, poison. The 'monsters' he commanded you to kill were not monsters but your own children." There were a few shocked gasps as people struggled with this horrifying idea. Peg pointed to where Lillian stood with protective arms around her son. "That woman is one of you. Her real name is Lillian. The boy standing beside her is her child. Her very own." Lillian drew her precious Timothy closer, and the two hugged as if they might crush the world between them.

"Somewhere in this room is *your own* child." Peg said, voice trembling. "It's time you met each other."

Many a historian will tell you that a great performance is just as much a matter of timing as it is material. After missing their supper and breakfast doses of Devil's Dram, the grown-ups were no longer affected by the king's drug. When the princess spoke the truth to them, they studied the dirty-faced slaves standing before them and—as if waking from slumber—staggered backward, overcome by the truth about their "perfect" lives. Spears clattered to the ground as the adults remembered how they had been made to forget the Cursed Birthday. How they had lived as prisoners for all these years. And how they had very nearly just murdered their own children.

At that very moment, LongClaw and his horde charged into the Eating Hall, weapons high. They had been expecting to join forces with the king's army, gobble whatever children remained, and then crush the ravens once and for all. But upon entering, they were greeted by a different sight altogether. The adults' weapons were

PETER NIMBLE *and his* FANTASTIC EYES

strewn across the floor. Still more alarming, King Incarnadine was nowhere to be found. LongClaw scanned the scene with some confusion. "Where is he?" he snarled at the frightened people. "Where's your ruler?!"

"Up here," a small voice called out. LongClaw looked to see two children, almost identical, standing at the top of the clock tower stairs. The one with the bandage across his eyes stepped forward. "My sister and I have reclaimed what was rightfully ours. Your king is no more."

"You two?" The ape was now grinning. For years he had fantasized about seizing the palace for his own—stopped short only by his fear of the king's deadly armor. But now it seemed his moment had arrived. Even with ravens perched against the walls, the apes enjoyed a distinct advantage. "Well, Your Majesties," he said, stepping closer. "Way I count it, you're outnumbered."

"Not quite!" The girl stepped to her brother's side. "Subjects," she called out, turning her brilliant gaze once more upon them. "These are the jailers who kept your children as slaves. They tormented us for ten long years. And now they threaten us once more. How will you answer them?"

As one, every man, woman, and child seized a weapon from the ground and turned to face the horde.

The princess raised a spear above her head. "Then let us put an end to this cursed battle at last!"

The Night Patrol was polished off in a matter of minutes. Their cannons and catapults were trampled to bits by the massive wave of human soldiers, leaving the beasts defenseless against the ravens. Captain Simon and his troops finished off the apes with swift justice. Every toenail and tuft of hair was collected and dumped into the sea.

With the battle finally over, the adults rushed to find their long-lost children. The reunion that followed was perhaps the happiest moment in the history of the world; tears of joy ran so freely that the bloody streets were soon washed completely clean. Peter wandered among the restored families, searching for his own lost companion. The knight, however, was nowhere to be found. It wasn't until the afternoon that Peter's ears caught the familiar *clip-clop* of miniature hooves. "Sir Tode!" he exclaimed, rushing to meet his friend. He would have swept him up in a hug were it not for his right arm being bound in a sling. "I was beginning to think you were avoiding me."

"I was, in a manner," Sir Tode said sheepishly. "I didn't want to see you until I made things right." He pushed something across the stones to Peter's feet.

The boy reached down to find the Haberdasher's mysterious box. He opened the lid. Inside sat three pairs of eyes—one gold, one black, and one bright emerald-green.

"It's a miracle they weren't destroyed in the battle," Sir Tode said. "By my third pass around the palace, I had begun to lose hope. I finally spotted them tucked in a gutter, safe as could be. Don't worry, I rinsed them off."

Peter took the green eyes in his hand. Every atom within him confirmed that the moment had come: at last he would wear the eyes of Hazelgood. He imagined what sort of incredible powers they might convey, powers fit for a prince. He pulled the bandage from his head, slipped the eyes into his sockets, and blinked—

All at once the boy was struck down by a bolt of brilliant light. He screamed out as he fell to the ground.

"Peter!" Sir Tode ran closer. "What's wrong?!"

The pain was unlike anything Peter had ever felt in his life. He didn't care what these Fantastic Eyes were supposed to do—he just wanted it to stop. The blaze sliced through his pupils and went straight into his brain. He could hear it. Taste it. Feel it. Smell it.

Thrusting a hand into his uncle's armor was nothing compared to the agony he was now experiencing. He had expected the Fantastic Eyes to change his body in some amazing way—make him stronger or able to fly—but all they did was hurt.

His cries had attracted the attention of Simon, Peg, and a few others. They crowded around him, watching as the boy moaned in agony. The princess knelt beside him, terrified. "What's happening to you?"

Peter tried to speak, but could only manage a whimper. "I can't . . . stop it . . ." He curled into a ball and clenched his eyelids tight. Only then did the torture slowly subside, dulling to a faint throb. After a moment, he took a deep breath and cracked his lids once more. The light came back, shocking him from ear to ankle. This time, however, he forced himself to endure it. His heart was racing out of control. His legs were weak. His skin was pale.

And that's when it hit him.

"My skin," he said, gasping. "It's . . . *pale*."

"Good heavens, you're not turning invisible?" Sir Tode said.

"N–n–no . . ." Peter brought his hand closer to his face. "I can *see* it." The light was still excruciating, but now he could discern the shape of a palm and five long fingers. *His* fingers. Slowly, things were becoming clearer. He could see stones on the ground. He could see the crowd around him. "They're just normal eyes." He blinked, welling up with tears. "My very own pair of eyes."

Of course, there was nothing the least bit ordinary about these eyes, for they shone with a brilliance that would have shamed the sun. The people nearby saw his transformed face and bowed in reverence. Peter was more awed than any of them. He studied his elbows, his legs, the bottoms of his bare feet. Everything was beautiful and wondrous. He saw Sir Tode, understanding for the first time just how ridiculous the cat-man-horse creature was. He saw the sky, marveling at how it melted from blue to red to gold. "Is the sky always like that?" he said. "That dark part is my favorite color," then, "*I have a favorite color!*"

Peter had spent his entire life trapped in darkness—and now he was finally free. He rose to his feet, somewhat unsteadily, and looked straight into Peg's emerald eyes. "It's good to see you," he said.

She smiled back and took his hand. "It's good to see you, too." The people who witnessed this moment swore that, like Peter, the kingdom itself took a truer form. The ten years of captivity and oppression seemed to vanish all at once, leaving only a powerful hope in the world to come.

✦ ✦ ✦

At long last, the royal birthday that had been cut short so many years ago was concluded. There was celebration and dancing throughout the whole palace. Peter and Peg were crowned the king and queen of HazelPort. Captain Simon and his ravens were reinstated as the Royal Guard, and each bird was given a pair of golden spurs to commemorate their valor. To Good Ol' Frederick and his friends, the young rulers offered safe harbor for as long as they should like it. The ancient turtles—who had searched many years for a quiet home—gratefully accepted. They floated in a circle around the shores, creating six island moons, which protected the kingdom for the rest of its days.

Sir Tode was appointed to the position of Royal Storyteller. As you know, there is no nobler profession in the world, and the old knight enjoyed his post immensely. He regaled children and their parents with tales of derring-do. Among his favorites was the story of how he and Captain Simon single-handedly freed the Royal Guard from the army of thieves.

Peter's right hand, which had been damaged beyond repair in his fight against the king, had to be severed from his wrist. At his insistence, the surgeons and blacksmith replaced it with the barb of the giant's fishhook that had served him so well in battle. Peter Nimble's silver hand would prove a loyal companion for many adventures to come.

After a few months, HazelPort received its first visitor from the outside world. King Peter and Queen Peg were practicing their alphabets in Mrs. Lillian's grammar class when they heard a voice cry, "Ahoy, there!" from the harbor. The voice was a familiar one, and the moment Peter heard it he jumped from his desk and sprinted across the palace as fast as his royal feet would carry him.

"Mr. Pound!" he shouted, attacking the man in a great hug.

"Hello, Your Majesty." Mr. Pound clapped the boy on the shoulders, looking him over. "Why, I think you've grown a foot since I last saw you!" He led the boy toward the boat behind them. Its deck was piled high with stacks upon stacks of newly bound books. "The professor thought HazelPort could do with a good library. And he brought something else." He ran aboard and returned a moment later with a pair of winged zebras in tow. He carefully led them down the narrow gangplank. One of the creatures nickered, gently pressing its nose into Peter's cupped hand. The boy recognized it as the beast he had saved in the alley so long ago. "Hello again," he said softly.

Queen Peg, who had since caught up with her brother, stared at the creatures in awe. "Are those . . . *flying ponies*?" she said.

"You like them?" Mr. Pound patted their shining flanks. "The professor put the wings on only last week. They are a belated birthday present for the new rulers of HazelPort."

"You mean we can *keep* them?!" She gave a squeal of delight, throwing her arms around a zebra's striped neck. "Oh, thank you! Thank you! Thank you!"

"They aren't the only new arrival. The professor has granted me leave so that I might stay on a while here as royal adviser." He gave a bow. "If it pleases Your Majesties."

Peter's eyes glanced toward the empty horizon and then down to his feet. "Tell the professor it pleases us very much," he said softly.

Mr. Pound—who was not without his own extraordinary gifts—took the boy's shoulders. "I hear your disappointment, lad.

Professor Cake would have liked to come in person, but as you know, he's very busy with things back on the island."

Peter nodded. "Rescuing more strangers, no doubt," he said with a trace of a smile. The boy looked searchingly at the owly browed, red-nosed man. "He knew, didn't he? The message . . . the eyes . . . this kingdom . . . Professor Cake knew all along he was sending me home."

Mr. Pound gave an evasive shrug. "Ah, the old man is full of surprises." The next moment, he burst into a wide smile. "And speaking of surprises—who is this I see?"

"Make way! Step aside! Royal Storyteller coming through!"

"Royal Storyteller?" Mr. Pound could not hide his amusement. "An impressive title!"

Sir Tode clopped through the gates to join them. "Yes, well, I've retired from all that knight-errant nonsense," he said, polishing a hoof. "It was beneath my dignity, really."

Mr. Pound rubbed his chin, feigning disappointment. "It's a pity to hear that." He rifled through his pack and took out a black decanter with a waxen cork. "You see, the professor recently came across this *bottled message* from a rather distressed hag."

Sir Tode's whiskers twitched with apprehension. "G-g-good heavens . . . that's not a *curse* in there, it is?"

"Far from it. It's a cry for help. It seems the poor girl's gotten herself stranded on an island infested with *rats*." He raised an eyebrow. "You ask me, I'd think she'd be *pretty grateful* to whoever rescued her."

Sir Tode caught his breath, hardly daring to speak. "She might even . . . *undo* a certain enchantment?"

"There's one way to learn." Mr. Pound offered the bottle to Sir Tode. "I could have a boat ready within the week."

"A *week?* Why, that's . . . so little time." Sir Tode looked back at his newfound home, at Simon, Peg, and finally Peter. "Your Majesty," he said timidly. "I wondered whether . . . if you were willing, that is . . . perhaps you would join me?"

Peter squinted at the wide open waters, stretching into forever. There was a song in the waves that he had known his whole life. He smiled. "Maybe a short trip wouldn't hurt," he said.

The knight loosed a cheer, clopping about with joy. "Splendid! We must begin our preparations at once!" He snatched the bottle in his teeth and galloped into the palace. "Open the larder! Fetch me a map!" His voice rang throughout the halls. "Come along, Peter! Adventure ho!"

+ + +

The rescue of the stranded hag was but one of many legendary journeys Peter shared with Sir Tode. Though HazelPort would always be his true home, the boy knew he was not born to rule like his sister. He could never remain ashore too long without feeling the itch to sail out once more. Sir Tode always insisted on joining him—believing rightly that one should never leave a good friend to adventure alone.

With the help of Mr. Pound, Queen Peg was able to rebuild the palace into what a palace should be. The walls and floors were gutted of their clockwork. The mines underground were cleared of their chains, and from that day forward, chores of any kind were strictly outlawed.

Professor Cake never did manage a visit, but his floating library was a popular addition to the landscape; the people were able to learn all about important subjects like history and alchemy and poetics. Gradually, HazelPort drew itself onto the maps of the world—if only as a tiny speck. It was known among sailors as a small, hard-to-find place, filled with kind people and impossible wonders. It was by no means a paradise. There were squabbles and arguments, crimes were occasionally committed and feelings sometimes hurt. But on the whole, the kingdom was a happy one, where all the children obeyed their parents and all the parents doted on their children.

And so it went in HazelPort. As time passed, the children of the kingdom grew to have children of their own, and those children had more children, and so on. The story of Peter Nimble and his Fantastic Eyes was handed down to each generation—the tale of the prince who became a thief to become a king.

❧ Acknowledgments ❧

This is a book about thievery, and in writing it I committed a great deal of theft myself. I swiped my dedication from G. K. Chesterton; I snatched inspiration from countless other worlds, characters, and books; even more, I stole time— minutes, hours, days—from beloved colleagues and friends. The following is a partial list of victims . . .

My family, which consists of a storyteller, an artist, a listener, and a looking glass. Whatever home Peter Nimble longed for, it probably looked something like mine.

Marshall and Betty Burke, who supported and adopted me as one of their own.

My early readers, including Laura Fern, Kirby Fields, Chandra Howard, Margaret Robertson, Kevin Snipes, and Mary Unser.

Jon Huddle and Howie Sanders, who took me on before anyone else.

Chad W. Beckerman and Gilbert Ford, who made this book an object worth holding.

Susan Van Metre and Jason Wells, who sent it out into the world.

My wonderful editor, Tamar Brazis, who saw *Peter Nimble* for what it could be and doggedly insisted I make it so. She is as brave as she is brilliant.

And finally my friend, mentor, and advocate, Joseph Regal, who sits atop his own island and sifts through thousands of glass bottles, each holding a story; I am so grateful that from all the bottles, he chose mine.

Please accept my most sincere thanks. I hope you all consider the hours well spent.

CHAPTER ONE

THE PYRE *of* PROGRESS

It has often been said that one should never judge a book by its cover. As any *serious* reader can tell you, this is terrible advice. *Serious* readers know the singular pleasure of handling a well-made book—the heft and texture of the case, the rasp of the spine as you lift the cover, the sweet, dusty aroma of yellowed pages as they pass between your fingers. A book is more than a vessel for ideas: It is a living thing in need of love, warmth, and protection.

Few people have ever understood this fact so well as Sophie Quire—a twelve-year-old girl with chewed fingernails, pigeon-toes, and a disturbingly intelligent gaze. Sophie loved books beyond reason. Indeed, she loved them more than she loved the world around her. It was the very thing that made her unique, until it made her *dangerous*. But we are getting ahead of ourselves, which is also dangerous. So light a lamp and find a comfortable chair, and I will tell you her story.

+ + +

It was a crisp, windy morning in Bustleburgh—perfect weather for burning books. Thin trails of smoke rose up from chimneys all across the city, raining down flecks of burned paper. A small bell rang above the door as Sophie Quire stepped out from her father's bookshop and into the cold street. She shivered, breathing in the sweet, ashen air. People had taken to burning their old storybooks in their fireplaces to ward off the autumn chill. The smell would have been lovely if it weren't so disheartening. She watched as embers drifted past her and wondered: Were any of those books hers?

Her gaze moved to the door of the shop. Tacked to the lintel was a handbill someone had posted in the night:

NO NONSENSE!
All citizens are compelled to attend the
annual Pyre Day ceremony on the twenty-seventh
of this month, storybooks in hand.
Join your fellow Bustleburghers
as we cast off the shackles of childish superstition and
boldly march toward a modern, sensible tomorrow!

Sophie tore the poster down before her father could see it. As if either of them needed reminding about Pyre Day.

She wondered what this latest celebration would mean for her father's bookshop, which specialized in the very sort of "nonsense" that the city seemed determined to destroy. Her father tried to follow the newer fashions, stock only certain types of more improving literature, but what if that wasn't enough? Where would the two of them go if the shop closed altogether? She threw the poster to the ground and pulled her hood over her tangle of black hair. She couldn't waste her time wondering *What if*—she had work to do.

Sophie ran through the city, keeping to the smaller streets whenever possible. It was just after dawn, and Bustleburgh was quiet but for a few dockworkers and beggars and sentries finishing their night rounds. She kept her head down as she ran, her hood pulled low over her eyes so as not to attract notice. Most people in Bustleburgh were pale—so pale, you could almost trace the blue veins beneath their skin. Sophie, on the other hand, had dark skin and darker hair, which made her feel like an outsider. These features she had inherited from her mother, who had been born on an island far beyond the continent. Sophie had asked her father the name of the island many times, but her father—as with all questions regarding Sophie's mother—remained maddeningly silent. She sometimes wondered if he even knew the answer.

Sophie passed the inner canal, the academies, the counting-houses, the courts, and even the entrance to the crypts, where her mother had been laid to rest twelve years before. Sometimes, when Sophie felt particularly alone, she would sneak down and visit those forgotten depths.

She continued moving in the direction of the Pyre grounds, which lay just beyond the river. At several points in her journey, she had the sensation of being followed. She even once thought she heard footsteps echoing somewhere behind her, but when she paused to listen, she heard nothing. "You're just being a worry-weevil," she muttered to herself as she ran down a narrow staircase that led to the eastern shore.

Sophie, however, was not being a worry-weevil, for at that very moment someone *was* following her every step—stopping when she stopped, running when she ran. The reason she did not see this someone was because she did not think to expand her view above the streets. If she had, she might have glanced toward the rooflines. And in doing so, she might have noticed the slender figure of a boy crouched behind a chimney, attending her with keen interest. The boy wore a threadbare riding coat and a salt-stained tricorn hat. He clasped in one hand the strap of a canvas satchel, and in the other what appeared to be a very sharp harpoon, its silver point flashing in the early-morning light.

Where Sophie went, the boy followed, hopping silently from roof to roof as easy as you please. And if Sophie had managed to spy this acrobatic pursuer, she would have been struck by one thing above all else:

The boy was wearing a *blindfold*.

✦ ✦ ✦

Sophie cut a wide path around the docks until she reached the ancient stone bridge that connected Bustleburgh to the rest of the hinterland empire beyond. She ran past the Wolves of Dawn—a pair of massive lupine gargoyles that towered over the Wassail River. It was said that these stone beasts had defended the city from invading armies in ages past. She was half surprised not to see NO NONSENSE! signs looped around their necks. She petted the rightmost wolf paw as she passed, for luck.

Rows of modern gas-burning lamps lined the sides of the bridge, their flames creating an eerie, flickerless glow that reflected off the river far below. On the opposite shore was a clearing encircled by a high stone wall that had been constructed to cut off travel to and from the Grimmwald, a dangerous forest that loomed just beyond the city. Two guards stood at attention at the iron gates, muskets propped against their shoulders. Rising up behind them was the Pyre of Progress—an enormous mountain composed not of rubble but of *books*.

Bustleburgh, you see, was a city in the midst of a great transformation. For centuries, she had been home to myriad wonders and oddities—creatures and artifacts one might expect to find in fairy tales or nursery rhymes or any number of ballads. In recent years, however, the common folk had become leery of this heritage, and they began to suspect that these stranger elements were in some way holding them back from progressing into the modern world. And thus the No Nonsense movement was born.

For as long as Sophie could remember, every autumn brought a new vote about what type of "nonsense" to burn next. First it was fairy fruit. Then it was any object forged by dwarfs. Then it was any object that talked. Then it was alternative medicines and certain baked goods. Then it was (puzzlingly) windup toys. Then it was clothes that were too bright or flamboyant. Then it was any good imported from a foreign land. Then it was anything deemed too old—tapestries and paintings and spindles. Now, at last, it was storybooks.

For months, guards had been raiding libraries and school-houses, gathering up storybooks of all kinds for the annual Pyre Day ceremony. When that day came, Sophie's bookshop would also be purged. Of course, sensible things such as reference books and scientific periodicals would continue to be sold, but anything silly or frightening or fantastical or the least bit entertaining was to be summarily burned. Many people in Bustleburgh giddily predicted that this would be the largest Pyre to date. As if that were a thing to celebrate.

Perhaps you have heard the famous bit of wisdom about how the making of an omelet requires the breaking of eggs? This philosophy, while technically true, does not account for the fact that omelets are universally disappointing to all who eat them—equal parts water and rubber and slime. Who among us would not prefer a good cobbler or spiced pudding? Sophie often thought that Bustleburgh was not unlike the omelet maker who, having grown obsessed with his task, had decided that all eggs everywhere must be broken at any cost. While she acknowledged the convenience of living in a modern city, she wasn't sure it was worth the destruction of so many wondrous things . . . especially if those things included books.

Keeping her head down, she snuck off the bridge and approached the edge of the wall. She found a place where the stone had crumbled away to create a hole big enough for a twelve-year-old girl. She wriggled through the gap and pulled herself to her feet.

Sophie dusted off her frock and gazed at the pile of discarded storybooks. Through the early-morning mist, she could see a row of guards unloading wagons of more books near the front gates. A few more guards were distributing stacks of Pyre Day announcements.

Sophie crept toward the nearest wagon and crouched behind its back wheels. She then stood on tiptoe and peered into the bed. She was always surprised to see what sorts of books had been thrown out—often she found stories she remembered selling in her father's shop. She removed a heavy old book and inspected the cover: It was a tattered collection of tales about Saint Martin the Bruin King. At one time not so long ago, every child in Bustleburgh would have known these stories by heart; now they were consigned to the Pyre. A few pages were torn, and the spine was a bit frayed, but the damage was nothing that couldn't be repaired.

She reached back into the wagon and found two more interesting books: a slim volume of hinterland nursery rhymes and an annotated treatise on temperaments of the constellations. "Hello," Sophie whispered. "I'm taking you home." She gingerly wrapped the books in her cloak.

"You there!" a voice cried from the gates.

Sophie looked up to see a guard pointing straight at her. He was fumbling with a whistle on a chain around his neck. Clutching the books, she raced back toward the wall as fast as her feet would carry her. A sharp whistle split the air as guards stormed after her, shouting, "Stop, thief!"

Sophie wriggled back through the narrow hole, tearing her cloak on the edge of a rock. She ran onto the bridge, the books tight against her chest. She kept her eyes fixed on the crumbling stone buildings at the far end of the opposite shore: If she could just reach Olde Town, she could easily lose her pursuers in its alleys. She was nearly to the other side when she saw two uniformed men appear at the foot of the bridge—night sentries returning from their rounds.

"Stop her!" the guards from the Pyre cried.

The sentries heard the cry and rushed to block her path. "Halt!" they called, lowering their muskets like spears.

Sophie very nearly ran straight into the points of their sharp bayonets. She collapsed to the ground, gasping for air. The two guards from the Pyre joined their compatriots, and now Sophie found herself surrounded. "On your feet," the one who had first spotted her said, jabbing his bayonet to show he meant business. "Drop the nonsense."

Sophie stood, but she did not let go of the books. She cast an irritated glance at the giant wolf statues towering over the bridge. *So much for good luck.* She edged toward the stone railing, briefly wondering if she might be able to swim to safety. She was a strong swimmer, but the stone walls along the river were too high to climb— between the current and the temperature, she would probably freeze before getting to the docks. And even if she did survive, the books would not.

A fifth man approached from the direction of the Pyre. "At ease," he said in a sinewy voice. Sophie peered out from her hood to see a rail-thin man wearing an immaculately tailored blue coat and wielding a polished ebony walking stick that clicked against the cobblestones.

The soldiers stepped back and saluted the man. "I–I–Inquisitor Prigg," said the first guard, clearly nervous. "I didn't know you were up and about this early."

"Progress never sleeps," he said coolly. "And neither do I." Inquisitor Prigg was known far and wide as the architect of the No

Nonsense efforts. He undertook this task with a zeal that seemed almost superhuman, documenting every single object that went onto the Pyre. The man stepped in front of Sophie, who kept her head down. "Let's have a look at our thief." He lifted Sophie's hood with the tip of his cane.

The guards, seeing Sophie's dark skin, all stepped back. "A foreign spy!" one of them cried, drawing back the flintlock of his musket.

Prigg's lip curled in a look of pure disgust. "Your imagination is outstripped only by your stupidity. What spy would waste her time with storybooks?" He grabbed Sophie by one wrist and peered at her hand. "Note the calluses on the inside of her thumb and forefinger, indicating needlework. Observe the dried ink in the beds of her fingernails. And in the tips of her hair . . ." He leaned close, sniffing some clumpy strands that had fallen loose from Sophie's braid. "Wheat paste." He let go of her hand and stood back. "She works for the bookseller in Olde Town. Quire, I believe."

Sophie was shocked to learn that this important figure knew about her father's shop, but then, Inquisitor Prigg seemed to know everything about everyone.

"The bookseller probably put her up to it!" one of the guards said. "You—girl!" He poked his bayonet at Sophie. "Does your master know what you're doing here?"

This was a common mistake: Sophie so little resembled her father that few people knew they were related. "You can't charge me with anything," she said. "The ban against storybooks doesn't begin until Pyre Day."

"And what a glorious day that will be," Prigg said in a tone of genuine relish. "But the books were stolen from *our* Pyre, which *is* a crime." He removed a small notepad from his breast pocket and began writing. "You are hereby charged with trespassing and destruction of city property."

"*Destruction?*" Sophie said. "You're planning to burn them."

"The fine is five dulcets—"

"Five dulcets?"

"*Per book.*" Prigg gave a prickly smile and continued writing. "If you cannot pay that fine—"

"You know I can't," Sophie said. "That's more than the shop makes in a month." She could feel a flush of hot anger spreading across her face, and she briefly considered what the fine might be for shoving Inquisitor Prigg over the side of the bridge.

"Very well." He put his book away. "To ensure you pay this sum, you shall be confined to the High Dudgeon until the debt is discharged." He nodded to the guards, who marched toward her.

Before Sophie could respond, two of them had seized her by the arms and lifted her off her feet. The stolen books fell from her hands and onto the ground.

"Stop it!" she cried, pulling against their grips. "Help!"

Sophie did not know why she called for help at that moment,

for there was certainly no one nearby who could hear her plea, but words, as you know, sometimes have a way of slipping out. And to her profound surprise, no sooner had she called *Help* than an answer came—

"LET HER GO!"

⌘ About the Author ⌘

JONATHAN AUXIER lives outside Pittsburgh with his wife and their adorable pet umbrella (which doesn't get nearly enough exercise). This is his first novel.

You can learn more about him and Peter Nimble by visiting www.TheScop.com.

This book was designed by Chad W. Beckerman.
The text is set in 12.5-point FF Atma Serif, a
modern typeface that incorporates transitional
elements similar to those found in Baskerville.
FF Atma Serif was designed by Alan Dague-
Greene in 2001 for the FontFont type foundry.

The interior chapter illustrations were
drawn in pen and ink by Jonathan Auxier.
The title page illustrations were drawn by
Gilbert Ford. The display type was designed
by Maria T. Middleton.